PENANCE

SWALLOWS AND PSYCHOS BOOK 2

K.L. TAYLOR-LANE

Lizzie

K.L Taylor-Lane

ISBN eBook - 978-1-7399897-2-9
ISBN paperback - 978-1-7399897-3-6
Written by - K. L. Taylor-Lane
Cover design by — Cat at TRC Designs

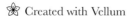 Created with Vellum

DESCRIPTION

Regret, remorse, repent.

With the ghost of my past unexpectedly crashing back into my life, his presence threatening to tear through everything I've built, I'm quickly losing grip on my sanity.

Voices start to whisper, infecting me with their poison as I struggle to battle against them. Mentally forced down into the deepest pits of hell, phantom hands trying to bury me in the fiery decay. Removed from my throne, my kingdom crumbling at my feet, my tarnished soul fractured and bleeding. I can't see a way out of the darkness alone.

But with the help of my fearless onyx-eyed demon and protective golden-eyed beast, I don't have to anymore.

My bones waging war with my flesh, my insides churning with uncertainty.

I face my fears.

Stalking my way through the shadows, twisting the descending fog into a weapon I can wield, I ready myself to stand-off against those that threaten to hurt me.

Wait.

You can see them too... right?

For Mark, my soulmate,
for always finding me in the dark.

NOTE FROM THE AUTHOR

This is a reverse harem, meaning the female main character will have three or more love interests and will not have to choose. The harem grows throughout the series, meaning there is not an established harem in book 1. It is a medium/fast burn romance.

Please be aware this book contains **many** dark themes and subjects that may be uncomfortable/unsuitable for some readers. This book contains **very** heavy themes throughout so please heed the warning and go into this with your eyes wide open.
For more detailed information, please see pinned posts on the author's socials.

The characters in this story all deal with trauma and problems differently, the resolutions and methods they use are not always traditional and therefore may not be for everyone.

This is book 2 of a planned trilogy and DOES end on a cliffhanger.

This book is written in British English. Therefore, some spellings, words, grammar and punctuation may be used differently to what you are used to. If you find anything you think is a genuine error, please do not report, instead contact the author or one of her team to correct it. Thank you!

This book and its contents are entirely a work of fiction. Any resemblance or similarities to names, characters, organisations, places, events, incidents, or real people is entirely coincidental or used fictitiously.

PROLOGUE

Max

I think today is the worst one of my life.

The woman who provided for me, who cleaned my cuts and scrapes, baked me rainbow cookies when I was down. The one woman I could always rely on, who would always be there to give me warm smiles or yell at me when I deserved it. Protected me, taught me, saved me. Gave me the very best of everything she could.

My grandma is being buried today and I fucking hate it.

I'm hunched over on the end of the bed, forearms resting atop my spread knees. I glance up at my reflection in the floor length mirror before me. My jet-black hair sticking up in all directions, turquoise eyes bloodshot from too much weed and whiskey. My shirt wrinkled and untucked, hickeys from blurry, *unknown faces covering my neck -from everyone but the one girl I actually want to touch me.*

I'm a fucking mess.

The mid-morning sky is dark. Rain hammering down in sheets, the wind howling wildly, battering the bare tree branches so they scrape and squeak against the single pane glass windows. It's fucking freezing in here. The wood around the windows rotten and split, allowing the arctic wind to whistle through the gaps. The house is falling apart, yet it's the only place I've ever really felt at home. Now the council want it back to move some other poor fucker in, that, or it'll be condemned like a bunch of other council owned properties on this street.

My grandma's things are all boxed up; her entire life dismantled, wrapped up in newspaper and tossed into card-board. My mother ransacked the place first, obviously, the cold-hearted bitch. God, I fucking hate her. Getting her slimy mitts on anything that was worth more than a tenner, fucking scumbag. Once she'd pinched everything she could pawn, Kyla-Rose helped me pack up the trinkets and photographs, all the things that actually meant anything anyway. My grandma never had expensive things, just a few little bits and bobs that were precious to her.

"Maxi?"

Her gentle, delicate voice wraps around me like silk, softly drawing me back into the room.

"Yeah?" I rasp, my throat dry from all the smoking and heavy drinking I've done the last few days.

Her tall, skinny frame stands awkwardly in the doorway, her long white hair tucked behind both ears. A knee-length black dress with long sleeves tight on her body. Her milky white legs bare, feet in her usual scuffed, black Doc Martens. She knots her bony fingers together before her, subconsciously chipping away at her black nail polish as she stares at her feet.

Kyla-Rose is the light in my life, an angel in a pit full of black hearted demons. She's strong, determined and so perfect; everything about her is it for me. She's been it for me since I was five years old.

"Can I-" she swallows nervously, shifting her feet on the worn beige carpet. "Can I help you with anything?" she almost whispers.

Her beautiful eyes finally drawing up to meet mine making my heart stutter to a stop in my chest.

God, she's fucking spectacular.

Heartbroken grey-green orbs stare back at me, a little too big for her heart shaped face. Doe-eyed, innocent, striking. She sucks her bottom lip into her mouth, nibbling on the already torn skin. She has a habit of doing that, I'm constantly plucking it free from between her teeth. She's been anxious more lately, quiet, subdued. I wondered if her dad had mentioned anything to her about what I'd done but I think she would have brought it up by now if she did. She's fiery below that timid surface. It's one of the things I love most about her.

"Come here," I order.

Without hesitation she steps fully into my room, stopping just before me, her eyes never leaving mine, I reach my hand out to her. She doesn't think about it. Just drops her cold hand in mine, her cool fingers sliding up the inside of my wrist.

"It's okay to be sad, Lala," I tell her, looking up at her, her bottom lip trembles, unshed tears glistening in her eyes.

"I'm supposed to say that to you," she whisper-laughs,

swallowing down her emotion, making me love her even more for it.

"It's okay, we can both be sad together, Princess," I slide my thumb under her eye, catching the tears from her bottom lashes. "We both lost her," I offer her a tight smile, it's the best I've got right now, everything's gone to shit.

"I'm so sorry, Max," she blinks rapidly, her eyes rolling up to the ceiling, the long column of her ivory throat stretching deliciously as she tilts her head back.

Such an innocent, vulnerable thing to do, little does she know it makes the rabid wolf inside me want to plunge his fangs into her. Mark her up, bleed the wound, make it scar. A little piece of me on her for eternity. I hold down the chesty growl that wants to release. I'm rapidly losing control of hiding my feelings for her.

Don't go there, Maddox.

Taking in a deep shuddery breath, she looks back down at me, a soft smile on her chewed lips. She reaches up, running the fingers of her free hand through my unruly mop of hair. I let my eyes slip closed as her fingers dance lightly over my scalp, it could send me off to sleep, she's so gentle. I inhale deeply allowing her creamy, citrus scent to soothe me.

"Stand up," she coaxes quietly, and I do, as if I could ever deny her anything.

She slips her hand from mine, her fingers ghosting over my chest, goosebumps erupt over my skin at the barely there contact. Her fingers begin unbuttoning my shirt, my eyes snap open, my fist latching around her thin wrist.

"What are you doing?" I ask harshly, shaking her in my grip, her brow crinkling as she stares up at me.

"Your shirt buttons are in the wrong holes," she whispers innocently, dropping her gaze to the tight grip I have on her wrist.

I release her quickly, turning my back on her. Taking over undoing and redoing my shirt buttons, avoiding eye contact with her while I pretend to concentrate. I see her behind me in the mirror reflection, her eyes boring holes in the old carpet. Her shoulders slumped, thick curtains of hair hiding her angelic face from view and my chest aches.

I'm a fucking arsehole.

"Rosie, I'm sor-"

"No, it's okay, I shouldn't have. I'm sorry, I didn't mean anything by it, I was just trying to help."

"Lala," I implore, turning back to face her.

Her watery eyes look back up at me as I cup her cheek, taking her wrist in my other hand, massaging the reddened skin. She looks at me like I'm her whole fucking world and something inside me just breaks. A single tear rolls down my unshaven cheek as I drop my forehead to hers, my breath shuddering as I wrestle to contain the sobs that so desperately want to rip free.

"You can cry if you want to, Maxi. You'll still be the bravest man I know, I won't tell anyone," she whispers and that shit hits me straight in the fucking soul.

God, I love this girl.

"Let's go, Princess," I whisper.

Dropping a chaste kiss to her forehead, pulling back and getting myself together. I tuck my shirt into faded black jeans, buckle my belt, and turn down my shirt collar. I grab my leather jacket. Kick my unlaced boots on and grab a large black umbrella on my way down the stairs. Kyla-Rose waits for me at the bottom, peering out the open door at the dreary day. I poke the umbrella out first, popping it up and holding it for her to step under. I drop my jacket over her narrow shoulders, watching as she burrows into it. I slam the front door shut behind us.

The cold church is almost empty. The Vicar stands in his pulpit, a small choir off to the side and a few people I don't recognise sit in the pews. Grey stone floors, high vaulted ceilings and heavy rain battering the stained-glass windows, all add to the sombre mood.

I prop the wet umbrella beside the door, Kyla-Rose clutching my warm hand in her cool one. She looks up at me, offering me a kind smile that doesn't reach her eyes. She's devastated just as much as I am. We both loved my grandma, almost as much as we love each other, as selfish as that sounds, it's the truth.

Sometimes another person enraptures you so much, nobody else really matters.

Lala's skinny fingers squeeze my thick ones. Tugging me forward, we traipse down the aisle, taking a seat at the very front of the church. The Vicar approaches, offering us his condolences. Saying a short prayer over my head and telling me he'll pray for me. It's a nice gesture, church just isn't for me, I'm not religious. I only turn up when someone needs burying.

Tragic really, I suppose. I wonder if I'd be happier if I did believe in something, had a group of people who prayed for me and shit. I guess that's out of the question now, knowing that the devil's claws are already hooked in me deep, there's no way out of hell when you only purchased a one-way ticket.

The Vicar's voice carries through the vast building but I'm not really paying attention. All I can think about is not having my grandma waiting to greet me when I get home every day. Lala nudges me with her shoulder, my head snapping in her direction, she gestures with her head towards the Vicar.

His dark eyes hold nothing but pity.

"Would you like to say a few words, son?" he asks me gently and I look back at Lala in a panic.

Fuck, I'm no good at this, I didn't know I'd have to speak…

"I can, if that's okay, Maxi?"

"You don't have to," I shake my head, running my sweat slicked hands down my thighs.

"I'd like to," she murmurs just loud enough for me to hear.

I give her a relieved nod, knowing I'd fuck it all up.

Lala steps up, the Vicar taking her hand and giving it a gentle squeeze, she takes her place behind the wooden podium. She flutters her lashes, knotting her fingers together. It's her nervous tell. She licks her cracked lips, looking up, her eyes finding mine, she takes a deep breath.

You can do this, baby.

"Ruth Sharpe was the most beautiful, caring soul I ever had the pleasure of connecting with," she smiles softly, her big eyes crinkling ever so slightly at the corners. "She was always waiting for us when we got home from school…"

I don't focus on the rest of her words; I just watch Lala's face. Her big grey-green eyes focus on mine throughout everything she says. She smiles, laughs, occasionally glancing down shyly, her eyes always reconnecting with mine when she looks back up. Her eyes betraying her every emotion, she's baring her soul,

7

showing me just how much my grandma meant to her, to us. I feel a small smile tilt my lips as she slides back into her space beside me, her thigh pressing up against mine. I drop my palm to her knee and squeeze.

"Thank you," I whisper.

She smiles, lacing her fingers atop mine as the choir start to sing.

Holding the black umbrella above us, the rain continuing to pelt down. We're standing in three inches of mud at this point, but Lala doesn't seem to care. We watch the coffin as it's lowered into the ground, the Vicar flicks holy water, saying more words and prayers until it's just the two of us left standing.

"I'm so sorry, Max."

"Me too."

"She loved you so much, more than anything," she whispers to me.

Her malnourished body tucked safely into my side, I rest my chin atop her head, breathing her in, I sigh.

"I know, we were both her world, Lala. Don't you forget that, she loved you too."

"I know she did," she shifts from beneath me.

Looking up at me with a soft smile, stretching up on tiptoes, she presses a delicate kiss to my stubbled jaw. Electricity rolls through me as she sighs, dropping back down onto flat feet. I draw her into me tighter, needing to feel her against me. We stand like that a while, the sky getting darker, rain getting heavier until she speaks, shocking the fuck out of me.

"I love you, Maddox Sharpe," she whispers the confession without looking at me.

My mouth drops open, suddenly very fucking dry, my breath stuttering in my chest.

Loves me?

I grip her chin between my thumb and finger, the sudden pressure making her wince slightly as she cranes her neck back to look up at me. Despite her six-feet of height, I still tower over her at six-four.

"Look at me, Lala," I order, my voice slightly shaky, her eyes still downcast, I grip her tighter, forcing her gaze to meet mine.

"I'm so-"

"Don't you dare say you're sorry," I growl. "Do you regret saying that?" I ask nervously, words clipped.

She swallows, licking her chapped lips, "no," she whispers, "I don't regret it," her voice hoarse.

My heart gallops, my ribs struggling to contain the out-of-control organ inside my chest. I take a breath, still forcing her to look at me.

"We're endgame, Lala, you and me. Soulmates of the darkest kind, you'll always be mine."

She sucks in a sharp breath as I drop my hand to her throat, my thumb caressing her pulse point as it hammers beneath her pale skin.

"I love you, Kyla-Rose, you were born to be mine," I lean into her still frozen body, my face nuzzling into her neck, I smile against her silky porcelain skin. "And one day you will be," I promise with everything I have, dropping a forbidden kiss to her temple.

I turn us around, still shielding her with the umbrella, I retake her hand as we put our backs to my grandma's grave and walk away.

Unknowingly leading her, hand in hand, to our own fucking funeral.

CHAPTER 1

KYLA-ROSE

"Max?" I blanch.

Haunting turquoise-blue eyes burn into me, heat razes across my flesh, the devil's tongue lashing at my overheated skin.

This is a dream. It's not real.

I squeeze my eyes shut so tightly I see stars beneath my hot eyelids, sweat beading along my hairline as I rapidly count to ten in my head.

Breathe.

My whole body trembles, my nails digging into the wooden banister as I try to keep myself on my feet. I slowly crack my eyes open, the demon inside me hissing at what she sees.

Maddox *fucking* Sharpe.

In the flesh, the devil himself stands before me. Icy white skin, raven black hair and ocean-coloured eyes, his square jaw dusted in light stubble. God, he's so fucking beautiful.

I hate him.

All the air whooshes from my lungs, my chest deflating. My eyes unnaturally wide, a brick drops into my stomach. My fleeting moment of happiness going up in a thick cloud of toxic smoke, leaving me empty and gasping.

Am I going to be sick?

The world spins, my legs waver, my grip on the banister so hard I could splinter the wood. I can't see, can't hear, can't fucking breathe. My lungs scream at me but all I can do is stare and try to stay upright as the room warps around me. I can't take my eyes from his, those dark pools of inky turquoise, like a haunting, a ghost, no, *the* ghost from my past. I think I might be dying.

Am I already dead?

Did I die during a threesome?

What a way to fucking go…

"What the *fuck* are *you* doing here?" he growls, spitting venomous words at me, his tone alone sharp enough to cut.

My heart shatters like fragile glass, tiny dagger-like shards piercing me from the inside out, now I really can't breathe. I don't even remember how to. What the fuck is happening?

"Nox!" Kacey hollers from behind me.

His deep voice piercing the air, the sound penetrating my ears, forcing the rest of the room to quickly come back into focus. The heavy bass of the music, laughing and chattering from the partiers fills my head. Kacey hurdles his hulking frame down the stairs, rushing past me, smashing through my grip on the banister, he dives on the ghost from my past. Max's face lights up as they hug and then Huxley is rushing past me on my other side. Jumping the bottom stairs and diving in on the bro-huddle happening in the opening of the front door.

I can feel myself shaking as I watch the three of them, all smiling, happy to see each other. Three men I love or *loved* at one stage or another in some sort of fucking reunion. My hands tremble so much I can't get a grip on anything, my fingers ache as I try to cling to the banister. My eyes refusing to blink in case I miss something. What is happening? How can this be? Why the fuck is this happening to me?

Then suddenly as though a bucket of ice-cold water is dumped on me, I catch my breath. I inhale lungful after painful lungful of air, gulping it down like a dying goldfish. Swiping a quivering hand over my head, tearing at my roots.

Breathe, breathe, don't lose your shit.

Do not lose your shit.

Be calm.

Don't panic.

Control your fucking self you psychotic bitch.

And that does it. I boil over. Frothing and foaming as my insides scream and tear each other apart. My chest heaves and heaves, my breathing more and more erratic as my heart thunders like the feet of a thousand racehorses against the track.

I am going to murder him.

"EVERYONE GET THE FUCK OUT!" I roar and I feel a hundred pairs of eyes slowly turn in my direction, caution and awareness in their stares making my skin prickle.

I'm shaking so hard I'm definitely gunna throw up or pass out, maybe both.

Huxley turns to look at me, my eyes meet his horrified ones for a split second. Dark eyebrows knitted together, his jaw tense, I look away. Kacey says my name, that dominant, low, possessive growl of his that has my insides dragging me towards him, begging me to obey. An underlying rasp of concern on his tongue.

He knows.

They both know.

My boys know me so well, they know I'm unravelling, they can taste it in the air. The distress rolling off me in thick, cloying waves. I can't look at them right now, I feel too sick, my bottom lip wobbles and I squeeze my eyes shut as a wave of nausea crashes over me.

"NOW!" I scream at the top of my lungs, using the last of my energy to ensure everyone hears the threat in my tone, no voice breaks and no wobbles.

I'm quickly coming apart at the seams, and I don't know what'll happen if I do.

Then another familiar face is appearing in front of me, tearing through the red mist that's engulfing my vision.

Gremlin.

"Boss, what can I do?" he asks me with a serious frown, taking in my almost catatonic state.

I don't think I've ever been this bad; I'm losing my control rapidly.

"I need Charlie, *get* Charlie, I need Charlie," I repeat mumbling through my shivering.

He nods, instantly tapping away on his phone as he bellows out another command.

"YOU HEARD THE LADY, EVERYONE OUT, MOVE IT PEOPLE!" Gremlin shouts.

Circling his hand in the air to gesture wrapping it up, I take another step back up. If I don't, I'll most definitely do something I may or may not regret.

I use both hands to hold myself up, digging my nails into the banister on either side of me, nails splitting the wood. My entire body trembling so hard my teeth are chattering, my ears buzzing with static, my breathing so out of control I'm not sure how to get any air in. A sharp pain ricochets up my spine as my coccyx hits the solid wood of the stairs, my hands dropping from the banisters like they weigh a hundred pounds. I squeeze my eyes shut, touching my forehead to my shaking knees.

I can't breathe.

'We're endgame, Lala, you and me. Soulmates of the darkest kind, you'll always be mine.'

CHAPTER 2
MAX

L ala.
        Is here.
        In my house.
What in the fuck is going on?

My eyes scan the room as the last of the guests file out, walking around us as we're still stuck standing in the doorway. They murmur their awkward thanks, Merry Christmases and goodbyes as they pass but I don't really hear them at all. My ears are ringing, my heart thundering in my chest, why is she here, in my house? And looking like *that*?

Holy mother of god.

She is astounding, breath-taking, beautifully fucking *damaged*. Her heart shape face and razor-sharp cheekbones are fiercely feminine, her hair's longer than it's ever been and a shimmering silver in colour, she's so fucking beautiful. She's a woman now, full breasts, slim waist and curvy hips. And all that ink. *Fuck.*

My cock thickens in my jeans at the mere sight of her but it's those grey-green eyes I've been dreaming about for the last ten years that really capture my attention. They've haunted not only my dreams, but my nightmares. But they don't look the same. Not as I remember them, not as I've pictured them over and over. They're haunted, shadowed, shrouded in darkness, frightened and sad, *so* fucking sad.

Why you so sad, Lala?

My heart is cracked in two, bleeding. I'm *always* fucking bleeding. I've been bleeding without her for the last ten years and now here she is, in my fucking house.

The way she's looking at me right now cuts me to the bone, she *hates* me and worse than that I think she's scared. Of me?

It takes everything in me not to run my hands through my hair. Sink a cigarette between my teeth and walk out, but looking at this broken girl, I can sense the danger. It wafts off of her in thrashing waves, threatening to drown everything and everyone in its swirling storm.

Kace and Hux both look at me with confusion in their expressions, but I can't speak, I can't even breathe, let alone explain to them what's happening right now. I'm not sure in this moment I even know how. So fucking damaged, my warrior, *where are you?* My knees wobble so hard I'm sure they're about to buckle beneath me and I'll hit the deck. If getting on my knees in front of her will help, in any way, any way at all, I'll fucking do it. Anything to get her to stop looking at me like that, like I did that to her, put that look in her eyes, I didn't.

Did I?

Kacey looks to Huxley, some silent communication passing between them. How the fuck do they know my Lala?

Kacey turns around and takes a few steps up, slowly, cautiously, silently. The big brute barely makes a creak on the wood as he approaches, like he's closing in on a wild animal. He reaches out slowly, ever so gently laying his hand on her knee.

Lala flies to her feet, backing herself up on too-high heels, her palms raised out in front of her.

"Don't touch me," she shakily whispers.

Her voice breaking, Kacey drops a step back trying to show he's not a threat.

"Darlin'?" Huxley calls stepping closer to the base of the stairs.

Darlin'?

Why the fuck's he calling her Darlin'?

"Please, I don't want to hurt anyone, just… just back up," she chokes out between stuttered breaths.

Raising her palms higher in the air, her arms are shaking so hard, her fingers vibrating like the wings of a hummingbird.

"Charlie's coming," Tommy says calmly as he steps in front of me, "what else can I do, boss?"

Boss?

Tommy's our mate from the army. He took leave and never came back; told us he got a better paying job. I see why now.

"Charlie's coming," she murmurs. Fisting her hands in her hair, yanking at the glossy strands. "Charlie's coming," she repeats, lost to herself.

"Sweetheart, *please*," Kacey begs, and she slams her hands over her ears like she did when we were children, her head swinging side to side.

Tommy's phone rings and he steps out the front door.

"No, no, no, no, no," her chest is heaving up and down so rapidly I'm worried she's going to pass out.

"Kacey, get her off the stairs," I manage to say but it comes out as a bark, aggressive and demanding.

Huxley narrows his eyes on me before returning his attention to my girl, she wobbles on her heels and Hux rushes forward. Passing Kacey, he drops to his knees before her, his hands raised out in front of him, palms out, fingers splayed in submission.

"Come down from the stairs, Darlin', please, you're going to hurt yourself," he pleads, his voice breaking like he really truly cares.

What the hell is going on here?

"I need you all to back away, I ne- I need to get to the kitchen," Lala says, suddenly very calmly.

Like a switch has been flipped, she removes her hands from her ears, tucking her long silver hair behind them. Her gold hoops glinting in the yellow light.

A different monster inside her emerging now.

"Okay, whatever you need," Huxley agrees.

He doesn't turn his back to her. Instead, he stands, walking backwards as she moves forwards cautiously, both taking their time, descending slowly.

Kacey grabs my shirt in his fist, his eyes still tearing into hers. He hauls me into the dining room to the right of the stairs, essentially giving Lala a clear path to get to the living room and kitchen. He doesn't release his grip on my t-shirt, like he's using it to anchor himself. I've never seen him look so worried about anything before, not even in the field when we were walking through fucking landmines.

The whole first floor of our house is open plan, the stairs sit centrally opposite the front door, the dining room and bathroom to the right, the living room and kitchen to the left.

Huxley's retreating form hits the landing, he backs up until he's flush against the wall, sliding along it towards us.

Lala stops just before she hits the bottom step, her gaze locking with Kacey's, a shiver runs up my spine at the cold, vacant look in her eyes.

"I'm going to need a sturdy chair, with arms," she tells him without further explanation.

Despite her trembling, she turns sharply, gliding as gracefully as a ballerina through the living room. Her silver sheet of hair fanning out behind her like glittering streamers in the wind. Huxley follows behind, stopping in the middle of the living room. Lala steps around the kitchen island, dropping to the floor behind the counter. Huxley glances back at Kacey who shakes his head. Looking between the two of them, I'd say they're really fucking concerned. I don't understand the dynamics here, who even *is* she to them?

All anyone needs to know is she's *mine*, it's been written in the stars since the very moment she was born.

Lala stands back up, something in her hand, her eyes gliding over me like I'm not even here. It hurts like a sucker punch to the gut to be dismissed so easily by her. The dangerously sharp splinters of my heart puncture my chest. And I find myself stumbling towards her.

"Lala," I say with a frown of confusion, I *need* her to look at me, acknowledge me properly.

"DO NOT CALL ME THAT!" she screams, my feet stopping dead in their tracks, her entire body shaking with rage.

The glint of metal in her hand catches my eye, a knife.

Noticing the same thing as me, Hux and Kace both step between us, shielding me from her or her from me?

"Kacey, get me a chair, I need it *now*," she says shakily.

Her words barely above a whisper. He rushes to

the other side of the room, returning instantaneously with a wooden dining chair.

"Do we have rope?" she questions as Kacey places the chair between us.

Less than twenty feet stands between us, and even after all these years separated, I've never felt further away than I do right now.

"Rope?" Kacey asks and she shakes her head.

"Never mind. We don't have time," Lala says quietly, almost to herself.

Her body still trembling, her chest heaving for breath, she drags the chair back, sitting herself in it. She still looks so beautiful, even through her desperate despair. She's so fucking beautiful. I need to touch her. I need to run my fingers over her pale skin, trace every swirl of ink with my tongue. I need to be reacquainted with the girl I so desperately love. Every fucking part of me was made for her.

Planting her left hand over the arm of the chair, she flips the knife open with her right, a long, fine switchblade. She studies the steel blade for a moment, looking between Huxley and Kacey, she smiles. It fucking cuts me that she looks at them like that. But her lip curls, her dimples deepen, and her smile becomes something else. Something wild and manic, desperate. And then she's thrusting the blade into the air, slamming it down through the back of her hand with all her strength. The blade daggering all the way through her hand and the wooden arm of the chair. Essentially stabbing her in place, she grits her teeth through the pain and the most awful sound I've ever heard -with an injury like that- fills the room.

Silence.

Pure fucking silence.

She makes no sound, the fact that she's just daggered herself to a chair should have anyone screaming with pain. I should know, I've tortured people using similar tactics, but I have never once witnessed anything so unsettling in my life.

It's the actions of a true psychopath.

What the fuck happened to you?

Like a wave of calm has suddenly washed over her, her breathing starts to slow as she watches her hand drip thick crimson onto the old carpet. She leans back in the chair, dropping her head back, her chest expanding as she takes slow even breaths, regulating her breathing.

"What the fuck did you do?" Huxley snarls at me.

I frown at the accusation.

"You're not serious? I didn't fucking do *anything*! I just came home!"

I back away from him, running my hands through my hair. Pacing in a tight circle, I breathe deeply through my nose.

"Sweetheart, talk to me," Kacey placates. dropping to his knees in the floor space between us. "Can you tell me what's happening right now? What's going on inside that pretty head of yours, beautiful?" he asks Lala gently.

His shoulders sagged, oversized body trying to look small, less intimidating, submissive.

I grit my teeth, hearing him call her beautiful, not that it's not true, obviously, anyone with eyes can see just how fucking perfect she is. But hearing it fall from his lips in a way that only familiars would speak makes my jaw pop as I clench my teeth so hard, I could snap a tooth. I swear to god they better not be fucking. Kacey can get anyone he fucking wants but he can't fucking have her, she's *mine*. I just need to reclaim her. I never lost her, not really, we were just separated for a time. But fate is a cruel mistress and she kept us apart a *long* time. Too long.

"I can't do this, this isn't fair," she brings her face forward.

Tucking her chin, looking at him with sad eyes, this girl is fucking hurting and I can't do anything for her because she doesn't *want* me. I remember a time when I was *all* she ever wanted.

"Can I come nearer? I promise I won't try to move you. I just want to comfort you, can you let me do that?" Kacey asks her and her bottom lip trembles.

Her gorgeous eyes glazing over with unshed tears. With that being enough of an answer, he shuffles on his knees along the worn carpet until he's before her, she looks down at him and shuts her eyes tightly.

"This isn't working," she exhales.

"What isn't working?" Kacey asks her gently, like he's trying to tame a beast.

Approach with caution to avoid a venom-filled bite in the process.

"This fucking knife isn't gunna hold me, Kace, I need more," she says through gritted teeth, her gaze darting over his head, locking with mine. "I'm going to kill him unless you can keep me in this chair," she says robotically.

A shiver works its way up my spine and Huxley turns to face me head on, blocking my view of her.

"What did you do?" he seethes, his dark eyes flaming with rage, my mouth opens but no words come out.

I'm overwhelmed, drowning in despair, I'm angry, I'm sad, I'm so fucking confused.

The front door slams open, ricocheting off the wall sending it flying back into the person entering. I snap my head to the right and internally groan. Even though I knew he was coming, Lala asked for him, of course he'd get here. Even so, why has this had to happen today? I've been travelling for fucking hours and all I wanted to do was have a drink with my boys then fuck off to bed. Instead, I'm dealing with this.

Charlie *fucking* Swallow.

Brilliant.

His tall, chiselled frame glides into the room, sweeping through like the grim fucking reaper. Shirt-less as is usual for him, I don't know if I've ever seen the guy in a shirt, *it's fucking December*. Like a silent assassin he assesses his surroundings. His eyes flying between the other two men in the room, neither of them seems to care he's here, Kacey actually looks *grateful*. Do they know Charlie Swallow? Because even the most feared men on the planet would be wise to cower under his emerald glare, not be fucking happy about his arrival, regardless of the situation.

Charlie's gaze bypasses me before doing a double take, stopping him in his pursuit to his younger cousin. He tilts his head to one side, narrowing his eyes on me, watching the pulse point in my neck like the apex predator I know him to be. Without shifting his position, as though he's made of stone. He rolls his eyes over to Lala, taking in the scene before him. Tucking away every detail and drawing his own conclusion. There is no hesitation when he lunges forward, striking like a viper, his iron fist smashing into my stomach. It happens so fast, I never saw it coming; all of the air in my lungs whooshes out of me as I double over, clutching my stomach.

I deserved that.

"You're fucking lucky that's all you're getting," Charlie whispers gruffly to me as he gives me a harsh tap to the face. "Be very fucking careful," he warns me lowly, the hairs on the back of my neck standing on end at his unmistakable threat.

Charlie Swallow is not someone to fuck with.

I'll be honest. I'm not *scared* of him, but I am cautious. He is a *very* dangerous man and anyone that says otherwise is a fucking moron. He's a cold, ruthless, calculated killer and if you upset him, you'll know about it, Charlie does *not* hold back, especially when it comes to Lala.

I remember him turning up at our school once. Lala was about thirteen at the time, I was in my last year, smoking by the front gate. He breezed through the gates, straight past me, his sights set very clearly on someone in particular. He stormed through that school building, walking straight into the middle of a religious education lesson, grabbed some little prick by his throat and made him piss himself in front of the whole class. Apparently, he'd said something rather crude about Lala and Charlie wasn't gunna sit by and let anyone talk about his baby cousin in that way.

That's the type of man Charlie Swallow is. It only got worse when he was stolen away from his family, subjected to god knows what and returned in an even more twisted way than he left. A man that survives half a year of torture, giving out no information *and* doesn't wind up dead as a result, should get a world of fucking respect in my opinion. Even if I don't particularly like him, I respect him.

"Ky," Charlie greets his cousin in that gruff, damaged voice he has.

Without being instructed to, Kacey automatically slides out of the way, allowing Charlie access.

I carefully straighten to standing, but fuck me, I think he broke a rib, my breaths come in short rasps, but I ignore the pain. I've had worse.

"Charl," Lala grits out. "Everything fucking hurts," she almost whines.

Her legs jumping, her free hand tapping her thigh, all tics of someone struggling to keep it together.

"Tie me to the chair," she breathes out.

Charlie swipes his tattooed hand over her hair, cupping her face as she looks up at him. Whatever he sees in her eyes spurs him into action and he silently nods his head. He turns back to face us. Kacey moving back into the space he occupied only moments ago, murmuring pretty words to the broken girl in the chair.

Charlie crosses back towards us. Pointing at me, "you, don't fucking look at her or I'll remove your eyeballs from their fucking sockets and gift them to her as earrings. You got it?" he growls, I exhale sharply sending pain hurtling through my side.

"Charlie-" I start but he instantly cuts me off.

"We are not friends. You do not fucking look at her. If she didn't have some sort of fucked up feelings for you, you'd be a dead man. Regardless of what she says, I still know her better than she knows herself. So, you fuck her up, *anymore*, any more damage, from *you*, I'll end you, am I quite fucking clear?" he rasps out. The strength of his voice rapidly declining with every threatening word, the strain on his damaged vocal cords more than obvious.

I pale, I stop breathing, I stop moving. The useless organ in my chest hammers blood through my lifeless body as I grit my teeth and nod my head. The only part of his threat that has any effect on me is the part where he said she has feelings for me. *Fucked up feelings,* but still, any feeling is better than no feelings at all, right? Well, whatever they might be, I'll take them. Even if she wants to chain me up and torture me, I'll fucking take it. Anything to get even a second's worth of attention from her. I need her to see me.

"Grem, rope," Charlie orders Tommy.

The nickname new but their relationship clearly not. I'm trying to piece all these things together. Tommy is Gremlin. Kyla-Rose was referred to as boss. Charlie ordering Tommy around. It appears the baby Swallows are moving up in the ranks.

Seconds later Tommy moves back through the still open front door, handing a thick loop of black rope over to Charlie. Gracefully moving back through the living room, Kacey once again shifting to one side, his eyes never leaving Lala. She looks up at Charlie, giving silent permission. Within a couple of minutes, Charlie successfully ties her trembling body to the chair, her arms free, the knife still protruding out of her hand.

The silence in the room is deafening.

"What do you want me to do?" Charlie asks her softly and she shakes her head.

"I don't know, Charl. All I know is if I get out of this chair, I swear, I'm gunna kill someone. Don't let me do it, Charlie," she rushes out, her chest containing a sob.

He smooths his large hand over her hair. She

closes her eyes, like a pet to his master, she leans heavily into his touch. Although looking between the two of them, it appears Charlie's the pet and Lala's *his* master.

"Can you tell me what's going on, Darlin'? I'm worried sick about you over here. I don't want to pry, but you're scaring the shit out of me," Huxley says suddenly, breaking the tense silence.

The way he looks at her with such despair, I can *feel* there's something going on there, the air crackles and ripples between them.

"I-" she starts, swallowing the sob caught in her throat, her eyes glistening with unshed tears.

She looks up at Kacey, who cups her face with a lover's touch, tracing his thumb over the apple of her cheek in comfort.

Please don't let this be happening to me.

He can't have her.

She was always meant to be mine.

There will never be anyone else for me.

"No," I choke out.

The wind knocked out of me without the need of physical contact this time. No, the realisation that my best friend is interested in the love of my life has my heart faltering in my chest.

"No, what?" Huxley frowns at me, his dark brows pulling together as he looks at me. "You wanna explain to me what the fuck's going on, Nox? Because *you* sure as shit have some fucking explaining to do," Huxley growls and I fist my hands in my hair.

Charlie releases his hold on her, entering the small kitchen, he starts pulling open drawers, carelessly riffling through them.

"This is *my* Max," Lala confesses quietly.

The way she says *my* with such disappointment guts me to my core. Both men snap their attention onto me.

"I think this is the universe's way of saying fuck you," Lala laughs bitterly with a grimace, finally wincing at the pain from her hand.

"Lala," I breathe, and she slams her eyes shut at the sound.

"Please don't call me that," she whispers, her words a little slurred and my face drops.

Charlie starts wrapping tea-towels around her impaled hand, the white and blue checked fabric quickly turning red, and I just stand there as everyone works around me. Tommy on the phone explaining her injury. Kacey kneeling at Lala's feet. Charlie keeping her wound bound, trying to stem the blood flow and I'm just standing like a useless statue. Everything moving around me and I'm not able to do anything about it.

I don't know what to do or say, she can't even *look* at me. I'm destroying her without even trying. My beautiful brave girl, *where did you go?* Three pairs of angry male eyes continuously flicker to me, waiting for me to say something, *do* something and I've never felt more weak or useless in my entire existence.

Because that's all it's ever been without Lala, a

pitiful existence, not living. I could never truly live without her. When I was deployed, I was reckless, unruly, I didn't watch myself, I didn't care. I tried to contact Lala before I left, but she refused all my contact attempts at that juvie. I sent her a letter every chance I got when I was deployed, for years I wrote to her and she never wrote back.

When I went back for her that night it was already all over, the warehouse was nothing but steel bones and ash and she was long gone. I never should have left her, but if I hadn't, we wouldn't have lived to see another day anyway. I thought she would have never survived without me, everything I've ever done has been for her, until we were separated, and I regret everything about that night every day. But she left me too. I'm not the only one guilty here, she left *me*, and I needed *her*.

Rage suddenly fills me, dragging up the past and slamming it into the present. Why is Kacey looking at her like that? Why is she looking at him like that? What's Huxley so goddamn protective over? Unless they've both fucked her, oh god, I'm gunna be sick. White hot rage prickles over my skin like flames licking at my flesh. As though I'm only just now realising the severity of the situation. My hands fist at my sides, my teeth grinding each other into dust. My carefully disguised temper just can't stay hidden anymore and I do the only thing I can.

I explode.

"This is fucking ridiculous!" I roar, spit flying from

my mouth. "Get out of that fucking chair, Lala! What the fuck is going on here anyway? Hmm? You better not be fucking her Kace or so fucking help me I will *end* you," I snarl, throwing my hands in the air.

Kaccy narrows his eyes on me, seemingly growing in size with temper. He flies to his feet, stepping up to me in less than a second. His forehead pressing against my own, trying to force me back a step.

"You'll what?" he hums, a mocking laugh escaping him. "What you gunna do, you fucking arse-hole. Fight me?" he laughs again as I shove at his chest.

"Are you fucking him, Lala?" I shout over his shoulder. "You are *mine*. You're fucking mine! You can't fucking do this to me!" I yell. Fisting my hands in my hair as I'm overcome with fury, "you were always supposed to be mine! Don't you remember? Please, *Lala*, don't fucking do this, I can't lose you, I *won't*," I snarl, pacing like a caged lion, the heat of my skin is too intense, I strip my leather jacket off, tossing it away from me.

"Untie me, Charlie," Lala says so calmly, quietly, blankly, her face pale, eyes glazed.

Using her free hand, she wraps delicate fingers around the shiny black handle of the knife, ripping it free effortlessly on a sharp exhale. Tugging it harshly from the cloth wrappings, much to everyone else's protests. Blood bubbles from the wound, rushing over her fingers and down the arm of the chair, dripping a heavy, dark puddle onto the carpet.

"Charlie," she whispers when he hesitates, "now, please," she requests almost silently.

At her softly spoken command Charlie moves towards her and in a few swift movements the rope pools at her feet. He reaches out a hand to help her to her feet, but she ignores it. Her grey-green gaze laser focused on me, holding my eyes so fiercely I'm afraid to move. Enthralled by her piercing stare as the green slowly overtakes the grey, her pupils dilating.

"I am not yours. Not anymore," she states without emotion, conviction ringing true in her words, and I die a little more.

"I don't understand any of this!" I finally manage to choke out. "I didn't do anything!"

A caustic laugh bubbles from her throat. Her fingers tightening around the handle of the blade. Blood pouring from the open wound in her other hand, but she doesn't even look at it.

"You didn't *do* anything?" she whispers, disbelief in her tone.

Brushing her sodden hand over her face and through her hair, leaving a thick trail of crimson in its wake. Half of her face covered in it as she drags it over her long silver strands. Her shaky grip tightening on the knife before she throws it away. She laughs louder, shaking her head, her body trembling violently. This amount of blood loss can't be good for anybody, I don't know how she's even still standing. Her hands slide up into her hair and she pulls hard at the roots, blood pouring freely from the jagged wound, soaking her long silken hair. She mumbles incoherently under her breath as her body starts to sway.

"Lala?" I whisper after a moment, turning my head to the side to try and see her beneath her curtain of silver hair.

Charlie stands sentry behind her, his eyes locked on me fiercely.

"THEY RAPED ME, MAX!" she screams, the shattered words exploding out of her quivering body.

Finally lifting her lost eyes to mine. I blanch, the sadness in them, the anger, the *hate*. I can't fucking stand it, her words nearly knock me to my knees. I look at Kacey and Huxley but they're both watching her with the same expression of shock as mine. My stomach bottoms out, my knees waiver and I have to brace a hand against the wall for support.

I'm going to be sick.

I rush past them blindly, straight to the kitchen sink, throwing up the contents of my stomach. I can't fucking deal with it and it hasn't even happened to me.

Who touched my precious girl without her fucking permission?

I'll *kill* them.

I throw up until I've got nothing left to expel. I run the tap, washing my mouth out with water, but nothing will ever cleanse the bitter taste of ash from my tongue. Not from that, not ever, her words are going to be forever branded on my soul, seared there with guilt, just like the look in her haunted eyes at her admission.

"I should leave," Lala whispers, sounding exhausted.

I don't turn to face her, I'm too ashamed, if I had been there, no one would have ever had a chance to hurt her because she would have always been right by my side.

"No, Darlin', please don't go," Huxley pleads with her. "I'll do anything to keep you."

I hear the distinct sound of someone hitting the worn carpet and I know he's dropped to his fucking knees.

"You still want me?" she whispers and what's left of my black, bleeding heart cracks inside my chest.

I don't turn around. I feel like a fucking intruder in my own house, encroaching on a private moment between lovers.

"What the fuck, of course we fucking do, we fucking *love* you!" Kacey cries, "of course we want you, my god, Kyla-Rose, Sweetheart, we just want to be with you, that's all either of us wants."

And there I have my answer. I shouldn't even be surprised. She's too easy to love. Of course they both want her. I'd be lying if I said it doesn't bother me. It fucking kills me. But if she won't have me, they're the only people in the world I'd ever trust with her. They'll protect her fiercely. They'll protect her long after I'm gone, because let's face it, I can't stay. I shouldn't. I can't be around her and have her look at me like that, I'd sooner die.

"You don't care that I'm *dirty*?" she stutters.

And tears I can't hold onto any longer break free, silently streaking down my face, burning across my skin like acid.

I haven't cried a single meaningful tear my entire life that wasn't over this girl, the only person to ever be worthy of them.

My hands placed either side of the sink, I bend my elbows and lean forward. I just want to stride through the room and grab hold of her, fold her into my arms and promise her that everything's going to be okay, but I can't. She doesn't need me anymore. From the sounds of it she needs my two best friends instead. I don't think I even feel jealous, just numb. Desperate sadness and shame claws at my insides, choking me. How can we ever move on from this? Whatever happened to her, she blames me for it and I fucking hate myself.

I hate myself for getting angry.

I hate myself for being aggressive.

I hate myself for loving her when all I do is bring her pain.

I know the story of how she got arrested. I know she did it through her temper. I told her to wait for me and she did, only she waited so long, when I still didn't return, she destroyed the building where I destroyed her innocence. And for that I will never forgive myself.

"You're not dirty!" Kacey growls, his anger so palpable I can taste it, "I never want to hear you say that ever again, do you hear me?" he orders, and she whimpers, I spin around so fast, how fucking dare he upset her?

Only he hasn't, *I* have, *me*.

Let it go, Maddox.

"Kyla-Rose, answer me. Use your words," Kacey demands as she looks up at him through tear filled eyes like he's her entire world.

"I hear you," she confirms on a shaky exhale.

"Good girl," Kacey praises.

Stroking his thick hand through her bloodied hair, cupping the back of her head. He exhales sharply, and I swear the relief in his voice boots a hole through my aching chest.

"First aid kit?" Charlie asks the boy, both of them looking to me.

I'm already getting it from the cupboard under the sink. Gripping it in shaky hands I steel my breath and grit my teeth, I walk it over to Charlie, allowing him to take it from me. I get clean tea towels and a packet of antiseptic wipes, placing them next to where Charlie now kneels on the floor before moving back into the kitchen to keep my distance. Not because I want to but because I have to. For her sake, Lala needs me to stay away. And if that's what she needs then that's what I'll do because I've never been able to deny her. I'll do whatever it is she needs from me, even if it threatens to destroy me in the process.

"Ky, sit in the chair for me, I need to do something with this until Jacob gets here," Charlie instructs, and she drops like a dead weight into the bloodied chair.

Charlie runs through questions, probing how she feels, his thick raspy voice soothing as he holds her wrapped hand up in the air between his fists.

She stabbed herself because of you, Maddox.

She stabbed herself for you, Maddox.

Why are we always fucking bleeding?

I suck in a sharp breath, instantly groaning at the spearing pain in my side. Huxley looks up, his brow creasing as he gets to his feet, he crosses over to me, he's pissed off but he's still my brother.

"Let me see," he says to me with the inclination of his head, motioning for me to lift my shirt.

I do as he says and wince. I look down at the same time Huxley's brow creases deeper. Huxley's fingers prod over my rib cage like he's drumming a fucking xylophone, but years of practise tells us both what we need to know.

"It's bruised but it's not broken," he tells me, and I nod, pulling my shirt back down.

"Hux-" I start but he shakes his head.

"Not tonight, we'll talk about this tomorrow," he tells me, eyes moving back to Lala.

He releases a deep sigh, massaging his chest where his heart lies. It must ache at seeing someone he clearly cares about like this, but I bet it still doesn't hurt like mine does.

"Okay," I say, my eyes falling away from her like I'm not worthy to look at such a precious thing.

"I missed you, brother," Huxley tells me.

His dark gaze moving back to me, he gives me a tight smile. Dropping his hand to my shoulder, he squeezes it.

"I'm glad you're home, even if things are kind of fucked up right now. You know we love you," he says sincerely, and I nod.

I know they love me. They're all I've had for the last ten years, my best friends, my brothers, my family. I never could have survived without them. They ground me.

All I can do is nod. Words seem to evade me as I find my gaze drawn back to the centre of the living room, to the centre of my universe. Kacey and Charlie sit on their knees, each of them holding onto one of Lala's hands. Her face and neck smeared with her own blood, her heavy-lidded eyes glued to Kacey as he speaks softly to her. She smiles at him lazily and leans forward, he moves in, kissing her lips and my heart shatters.

She's supposed to be mine.

"Maybe I should go. I'll get a hotel room, I don't want to make this worse," I mumble quietly to Huxley.

His eyes pinch together painfully, but surely, he can see my being here isn't going to work. I feel like an intruder in my own house, but Lala doesn't need me around her right now and it's obvious my boys want to care for her. I'm so fucking ashamed of myself. I'm so confused, I need to know what's happening here to understand but at the same time I'm so goddamn afraid. Kacey and Huxley, both, are better men than I am. She deserves someone who will love her the way she deserves to be loved.

"No," Lala says softly. My eyes find hers as she looks over her shoulder at me, clicking together like a magnet.

"Stay, this is your home."

"Honestly, it's fine. I'll be fine," I say, although I so want to stay here and be near her, just being near her is enough.

For now.

"No," Lala says more firmly this time, but a tired sigh slips out anyway. "Stay," she murmurs, and Huxley elbows me in the arm as he jerks his head towards her. "Stay here, Max," she says barely above a whisper.

I nod, keeping my gaze averted, I can't bear to look into those big, sad eyes. The pain I see in them just fucking kills me.

CHAPTER 3
KYLA-ROSE

I wake up sandwiched between Huxley and Kacey, sweat pouring down my back and chest from their combined heat. I don't even have enough room to flip onto my back, the bed is just too small, but I desperately need to get out of it, I feel like I'm on fire. Sliding down to the end of the mattress, the silky sheets beneath me helping my sticky body glide out from between them. My legs dangle from the end until I manage to drop to my knees. As soon as I'm out from between them I instantly find it easier to breathe.

God, I'm so hot, the two of them are like bloody furnaces.

The room is dark, curtains cracked, it must be early morning because outside those curtains the world is trapped in darkness. It doesn't get light until around eight-am during December, sometimes even later, depending on the weather.

I pad lightly over to the bathroom, my sweaty feet hitting the cool tiles, my shoulders relaxing with the frosty change in temperature. I sit down on the toilet, a shiver working its way up my spine as the cool air hits my naked flesh. When I'm done, I stand, leaning over the sink, I wash my good hand, wincing at the pain in the stitched one. I regret doing it *now*, but I had to. In the moment it was my only logical option. Instead of lashing out at someone else, I hurt myself to get some sense of control. I was so enraged and uncontrolled, if I hadn't physically attached myself to that chair, I know I would have committed murder.

Thoughts of killing don't affect me. Not ever. I'm blinded to the motions of it now. But killing Max? My soul cries at the very thought. My demon inside hisses, thrashes, threatens, because as much as I blame Max for everything that happened to me, deep down I know that isn't fair. Yes, he left me that night and didn't come back. That, that I can blame him for. Being raped in juvie? Not even remotely his fault.

Cause and effect.

Action and reaction.

That's all this life is.

I'm so exhausted that all this feels like it happened months ago rather than hours, and yet, here I stand in the dark, staring at my shadowed reflection in the mirror. My eyes looking far too much like my mother's.

I thought I knew *exactly* who I was, I've spent the last four years being queen of the fucking underworld, that's who I know how to be. This Kyla-Rose, Lala, I don't know how to be either of those people anymore.

Do they even exist?

Spending time with Huxley and Kacey started to show me a different life, in the last five weeks I've changed so much. I've just declared my fucking *love* for these men, that's a word I haven't uttered to a man since Max. Sure, I tell my family I love them, I tell them all the time because I never know if that day will be my last. I could be taken out at any second of *every* day, so I need to keep reminding them just how much I love them, so they'll never have to wonder.

And I'm going to have to do that now for Kacey and Huxley too, because I realised tonight that I do love them, truly. Even imagining my life without them strips me to the core and my heart hurts. They've both shown me nothing but kindness and love and *warmth*, maybe a little too much of that if my body temperature is anything to go by right now.

But I need them.

My *soul* needs them, calls out to them, screaming to be tethered to them.

Then Max turns up.

I've spent so long trying to hate him that I was certain if I ever saw him again, I'd kill him then and there. A thought as frequent and as sure as the sun rising and setting every day. And that is what I wanted to do last night, but not for the reasons I thought I would.

I didn't want to kill him because he abandoned

me and I hate him. I wanted to kill him because I don't feel *either* of those things when I look at him, *at all*. That's what hurts me most. It's that no matter what's happened to me, I have never stopped loving the little boy with the stern face and turquoise eyes. And that guts me. I can take any physical pain, I've been trained to withstand the obscenest types of torture. I've taught myself how to disconnect my brain from my body and crawl into that dark little space inside my head. Mental pain I've been suffering with my whole life in various forms and seeing Max last night brought all of that and more bubbling to the surface, gasping for air and refusing to drown.

I don't think I've ever truly healed from *anything*. I'm always fucking bleeding because deep down I'm still so madly in love with him and everything we could have been, that I hate myself for it. I tried to cut him out of my very existence and when that didn't work, I tried to cut *myself* out from this existence.

Pushing myself up from the sink, I tip-toe back into the bedroom. Stooping down to grab one of the boys' t-shirts -whose it is, I'm not quite sure- and pull it over my head. My hand now pulsing with pain, I pull my hair free from beneath the collar, letting it flow down my back.

When Charlie and Jacob left, reluctantly that is, after fixing me up and shooting me full of blood, my body sucking it up like a dehydrated vampire. I showered, my wounded hand wrapped in a plastic bag, Huxley silently cleaning the blood from my hair, massaging my scalp with deft fingers. I watched it swirl down the drain as he washed me, staring until the water ran clear, the soapy bubbles disappearing from view as he held me close. It felt like I was purging a piece of my soul.

Then the boys cuddled me up in bed. The three of us together, just the way I had hoped for earlier on in the evening and I felt a little better. But nothing will feel truly better until everything is right between me and Max, and I'm not sure it ever will be.

Ever can be.

This was all supposed to be easy, it *was* easy, with me, with them, with *us*. I opened myself up to the possibility of being happy without Max. I thought I'd be alone forever. I didn't *want* anybody around me. I imagined Charlie and I would just stay together as we are, wreaking havoc and spilling blood. Forever the infamous *Chaos Twins*. I didn't *need* anybody else. Just me and Charlie.

But then I met my two boys, and everything moved so fast. I've never been one to do things in a *normal* way, follow etiquette and protocols and do things the *right* way. I've just done what feels right. So, I sucked those boys into my whirlwind of a life, attached my soul to theirs and stitched myself into their hearts. I can't imagine not having them around me. Knights protecting their queen. They could never leave me now. I would just drag them back. Be it kicking and screaming, I would make them stay. I would chain them up and keep them forever.

But now everything in my head feels fuzzy and complicated. I'm sane enough to admit that I'm too *in*sane to deal well with complicated. I don't cope well under that kind of emotional pressure anymore, not since everything that happened. I'm triggered by a lot of things, I'm not perfect, I'm actually pretty imperfect, but that's how I find I'm most happy, I don't want to be *fixed*.

Squinting my eyes to peer through the darkness, I find both my boys still sleeping soundly. Turning away from them, I twist the door handle gently. Pulling it slightly towards me to avoid the creak, just as I've been doing the last ten days when I've snuck downstairs in the middle of the night. I'm nocturnal in my normal life and so sleeping during the night is not my forte. I'm always so busy working I only usually get four or five hours at most and it's usually during the day due to the nature of my work, but I've adapted my habits while I've been here to suit the boys'.

I let myself out into the hallway, clicking the door shut almost silently behind me. I take the stairs soundlessly and pad through the living room in the dark. All the furniture is back in place, the puddle of my blood cleaned away. You'd never know a party had ever taken place in here just a few hours ago, let alone the chaos that followed. It's pitch dark, but I don't need the light. I can easily find my way around this house under the cover of darkness now.

I move into the kitchen, opening the fridge. Smiling at the little pots of vanilla yogurt that Huxley bought in this week's shop, the same one's I had at my first breakfast here. If only I knew that first night I visited this house, that Max lived here too.

Fate is a cruel, cruel mistress, I'll give her that.

Fucking bitch.

Shaking my head, I bypass all of Kacey's protein shit and search out Huxley's secret stash of chocolate milk. He hides them inside the salad drawer because he thinks I never open it.

I leave the fridge door open a smidge for the sliver of light it offers me and hop up onto the counter. The cold marble making me hiss through my teeth as it connects with my bare arse. The heating went off before we even got into bed, so the downstairs is overly cool now. Holding the bottle between my bare thighs to aid in my one handedness. I twist the cap on my stolen milk, swallowing some down, swinging my legs back and forth, I breathe deeply. Just needing a minute to really breathe.

I'm a lot calmer now than I was earlier. I've had time to think, clear my manic thoughts and pick through them one at a time. Seeing Charlie leave hurt a little, I've missed him so much, but it's best I'm not around him while he's still working, or I'd find it too difficult not to involve myself.

I wonder who he's playing with tonight.

On the other hand, I couldn't wait for Jacob to finally go. Jacob was shocked to see Max. I don't know if I've seen Jacob have a non-aggressive reaction to anything in years. What shocked me even more was that he didn't say a word. Not a single fucking word left his mouth as he took it all in. I thought he'd at least *say* something, but nope, not a peep. I'm not even really sure what to make of that, other than he's probably thinking up an overly long speech to thoroughly bore us all with. Something that'll include words like *furthermore* and *abhorrence.* Ya know, shit that'll send everyone off to sleep.

On the plus side there's only a few days until Christmas and we're going to Dee's like usual. The whole family and extended attends, by extended I mean Frank and Carol, Gremlin and Rubble. I'm guessing Jen will attend with Gremlin this year, but I could be wrong. She'll only have been invited if Grem's serious about her.

My boys are coming with me. Apparently, they don't do Christmas with their families and choose to spend it together instead. So of course, Dee extended the invitation to them as well. I swallow another mouthful of milk, instantly souring as it hits my stomach.

Max.

He'll be here all alone on Christmas day. I rub my knuckles over my chest at the prickle inside, what do I do? I can't let him stay here all by himself.

Can I?

My hand starts to throb, making me wince. Needing something stronger, I hop down from the counter. Abandoning the stolen milk to reach up on top of the cabinets; I have a bag of weed up here somewhere. I stretch up on tippy-toes, my borrowed t-shirt riding up, exposing my warm flesh to the cold as I skirt along the counters until my fingers rustle plastic.

Yes.

I scissor the fingers of my good hand at the tiny piece of plastic managing to tug it forward. Pulling it down, I hop back up onto the island and start the process of rolling a joint.

I grind the bud until I feel little resistance, easier said than done when you only have one usable hand, so I have to clamp the grinder between my legs. It takes me a minute to get there, but I do. Still using the sliver of light from the cracked fridge door, I put a few accordion folds into my filter and then dump as much weed into the paper as I can. Making sure to add those precious little THC crystals on top and then roll, lick and twist.

Practice makes fucking perfect, that's all I'm gunna say. I pop it behind my ear and roll a second. The ritual of it soothing me, keeping my mind busy as I grind and roll the perfect joint. I leave it all out on the counter and then clamber around in the dark for a lighter. I swear to god I had about ten of the fucking things a few hours ago and do you think I can locate one?

I huff in frustration and take a breath. I dig around in the cupboard under the sink for matches. A tiny noise on the other side of the island has me pulling free my gun -that I thankfully thought to stash beneath the sink. I spin around on my heel, removing the safety, aiming for a body shot at the wide, tall silhouette in the dark. 'Cause you know, headshots in the dark are more or less sure to miss their target. But a body shot or *ten,* that's when you know you're on the money.

"Whoa! Easy, it's just me," a deep voice, smooth as silk, whispers into the darkness.

I heave a deep sigh, flicking on the safety, placing the gun down beside the remnants of my joint rolling. Without saying a word, I continue my search under the sink. *What the fuck am I even looking for?* I pull up short for a minute, that voice having completely rattled my brain. Of all the men in this house, why does it have to be him who found me down here in the dark? And I've hardly got any bloody clothes on.

I should see him and rage. Cry. Scream. Have any fucking reaction other than the one I'm currently having. All I feel in his presence is *us.* He kick-starts something inside me. Everything in me feels drawn in his direction, his never-ending pull. Sucking me into his vortex just like it did when we were young and stupid, and I was oh so infatuated with him. I loved him more than the sun loves the moon, he was my everything. I needed him more than the air in my lungs from the very first day I opened my eyes.

Matches.

That's what I'm looking for.

I continue shuffling through the plastic tubs of crap when I touch a small cardboard box, I give it a quick shake to check its contents, *bingo*. Straightening up, I close the cupboard doors. When I turn back to the island, Max is still frozen on the opposite side of it. I can't see his features in the dark, but his head is bowed in submission and my heart lunges in my chest.

Swallowing down my confusing feelings, scratching their way down my throat like sandpaper, I squeeze my eyes shut tightly for a second.

Do I, or don't I?

"Smoke?" I whisper tensely, offering him an olive branch I probably should have burnt instead.

I will never learn. I'm not even sure I want to learn my lesson when it comes to the demon before me. He was carved from a piece of the Devil himself. Born of hellfire and sinister intentions.

Perfectly created to spit fire and raise hell, designed for the Queen of the Underworld.

His body flinches as if I slapped him, his head snapping up like he didn't expect me to *actually* speak to him.

"What?" he mumbles back, his lips barely parting with the question.

I take a joint from behind my ear, popping it between my teeth.

"Dope, Max, do you wanna smoke with me?" I whisper again and I hear him suck in a sharp breath. Being brave I spit out the words before I can think too much on them, "if you change your mind," I shrug nonchalantly, leaving my statement open as I thumb the air in the direction of the back door.

Before I can change my mind and run back up to the safety of my lovers' arms like a coward, I turn my back on him. I slide the top bolt free, then the bottom one and then finally twist the key in the lock. When it twists and clicks twice, I grab my leather jacket off the hook and pull the door open, the winter wind instantly pricking at my skin.

I lay my jacket out on the concrete step, softly closing the door behind me and sit down. The icy air sending goosebumps skittering all over my exposed skin. Pulling my knees up I tuck my t-shirt over them. My arse is still fucking freezing, why didn't I put any damn knickers on? All my favourite bits are gunna fucking freeze at this rate and I've only just started using them again. Lesson learnt I suppose.

I take the little box of matches, struggling to strike one alight with only one hand, the flame dances wildly as I finally light the end of my spliff. Inhaling deeply, holding the thick, sweet smoke in my lungs, I tilt my head back with my eyes closed before finally releasing a sticky cloud. The wind whipping it away as quickly as I release it, like it never really existed to begin with. After the second toke, the pain in my hand is already lessening, my brain fog clearing.

The moon casts a beautiful shimmer of light down around me. I take a moment to just appreciate it, the hundreds of stars glittering high above me, it's peaceful. Free.

All I've ever wanted to be is free.

Like my surname would suggest, I'd love to sprout

wings and fly, but I continuously find myself caged, metaphorically speaking of course. Charlie only ever locked me in an actual cage once and it was boring as fuck. I stabbed him in the thigh and bit a teeny, tiny piece of his ear off. That part was fun. *Obviously*. Every time I notice it now, I smirk, and he scowls knowing what has my attention. All part of our routine.

In all seriousness, he was trying to show me what it was like to be trapped in a cage, but it didn't have the desired effect. After only a few hours I was losing the will to live, knowing I could get out at any second.

Charlie didn't get that luxury the time he was locked up by our enemies. I was in juvie then; I didn't even imagine someone I loved could be suffering like I was. Charlie was supposed to be going to MIT, not stolen away, and tortured for almost six months. Poked and prodded with sharp objects through the steel bars of his cage, chained by the ankle with not enough space or slack in the shackle to move inside his tiny prison. Men pissing on him while laughing around their cigars. Dragging him out and beating him over and over. Yet, he still didn't talk. Wouldn't. Even when they brutalised his throat so badly, they ruined his voice forever, leaving in its place a deep, shadowy growl. Not that I don't enjoy hearing that rasp he has now, it's a beautiful sound that curls around you, demanding your attention. Devastating you with whispered promises of violence and death.

Charlie has more courage and loyalty than anyone

I have ever known and everyone I haven't met yet, there is no one superior. Not in my eyes. Charlie is the most angelic, pure demon to ever exist. His blood is black, but his soul is divine. A sparkling clear white that shines brighter than the sun. My revere for him is greater than anything else I have in me.

I take a long drag on my blunt and the pain in my hand all but disappears, leaving nothing but a dull ache in its place. Also, it's kinda itchy, but I dunno if that's in my head or not. This is *really* good weed.

The door clicks open behind me and Max bravely steps out, shutting it softly behind him, he fidgets awkwardly next to me for a moment, I sigh.

"Sit down, *Maddox*," I instruct.

He grunts in response, pretending he didn't want instructions but we both know he needed them. He shuffles about, then climbs down, placing his feet onto the second step, perching on my jacket beside me. Without looking at him, I offer him the joint. He pinches it from between my finger and thumb, very careful not to touch my skin with his.

As much as I want him not to touch me –because I'm pretty sure that will trigger shit I'd rather not deal with right now- I also wonder what it would be like if he did. Would we still have that undeniable spark? Are the palms of his hands still rough and calloused but the back of them smooth as silk, his fingernails cut short and neat. The black titanium ring he always wore, still on his right ring finger. I shake my head, clearing those dangerous thoughts. There's too much history here. Enough emotional baggage to sink a ship.

Max and I pass the joint back and forth until it's finished, he pinches the end, dropping it into a cracked flowerpot. It's already filled with the butts of my other joints and cigarettes. Kacey hates cigarettes, like *really* hates them, almost as much as Jacob does, so I sneak out here in the middle of the night to spark up without ridicule. I know it comes from the best place in his heart, but I could die today, so really, what's a cigarette? I'm pretty sure being the resident psycho of a crime syndicate will kill me long before weed and cigarettes ever could. Or maybe I just don't care about extending my life, maybe I'm trying to cut it short. Ensure that I'm only here for the shortest time I can manage. I don't know.

"I don't know what to say, La- *Kyla*," Max stutters with a heavy sigh and I can *feel* his eyes on me.

They burn a hole in the side of my face like a laser beam the longer he stares but I just can't force myself to look at him. I hate hearing my name fall from his lips like that. I was *never* Kyla to Maddox Sharpe, just like he's never been Maddox to me. He was always Maxi. My Maxi. The same Maxi who taught me to play *twinkle, twinkle little star* on the piano. Maxi who pushed a kid off the jungle gym for pulling my hair. Maxi who kissed my scraped knee when he taught me to ride his bike.

Then it was Max who punched a guy at a party when I was thirteen for pressuring me to drink, even though I'd said no four times already. It was Max who held my hand at his grandma's funeral and whispered promises of soulmates and never-ending love into my ear. And it was Max who took my virginity and said everything he had to do was for me. '*Everything I've ever done has been for you, Lala*', that's what he told me. And I believed him then. Do I believe him even now?

A small part of me wants to believe everything he ever told me was true. That it was all for me and that he loved me and that he'd die and kill for me. Maddox Sharpe is one of the most intense people I've ever met. Yet, tonight, he faltered, a crack in his impenetrable veneer. He was vulnerable, he was angry, he was *jealous*, he was scared, he was *sick*.

Was he sick because of what I said happened to me or was he sick because he thinks I'm tainted now?

"You can still call me, Lala," I whisper into the dark, the vulnerability almost choking me. "Or Rosie," I swallow and from the corner of my eye I see his shoulders drop a fraction.

"I don't suppose saying sorry to you will help me *or* you any," he breathes heavily and my gut twists.

"I don't want you to say sorry," I tell him gently.

A frown on my lips as I process yet another truth I inadvertently blurt out. I thought for the last ten years that's exactly what I wanted, but sitting here now, I realise it's not good to dwell on the past, not with Max.

I see his fingers dance restlessly against his thighs, so I take the other joint from behind my ear, popping it between my teeth. Max takes the matchbox from beside my thigh, his fingers barely grazing my skin. He strikes a match, I lean into his cupped hand, lighting the tip, I inhale, and we begin the soothing cycle that is weed culture. *Take a drag, pass it around.*

"Would it make *you* feel better to say you're sorry?" I ask him quietly as he takes the lit joint from between my fingers.

Sometimes it's not about receiving an apology from the person who has wronged *you*, sometimes it's about letting them make amends for *them*. To soothe their own soul a little, even if it hurts. And I'm okay with that if that's what he needs.

My eyes roll to the left to look at him a little higher. He's got a white t-shirt on, the thin fabric stretching across his muscular chest and broad shoulders, with his tight black joggers. His arms still covered in ink just like I remember, one of his hands decorated with pieces of *me*. I don't look any higher, I can't bear to look at those eyes.

Those turquoise eyes, a deep ocean blue but sometimes a clear seafoam green. The eyes that turn midnight blue in the dark, and a light jade in the daylight. They strip me bare, plunging deep for secrets. I can't let myself be any more vulnerable than I've already been lately. I've been slipping, so those ice bricks I once used to barricade my heart are currently going back up, in order to keep Maddox *fucking* Sharpe out of my heart and my head. But sitting this close to him, the heat from his skin rolling off of him in waves, warming mine even in the icy wind. His scent; the smell of tobacco, musk and his own brand of sweetness. Something pleasant like icing sugar is already invading my senses, making me lightheaded and confused. Max has always been able to break through any walls I erected to keep him out. He smashed through them with a single look, a sledge-hammer crashing through everything I ever built.

"No, I don't think anything will ever make me feel better if I'm honest," he mumbles back, vulnerability dripping from every confessional word.

This man is such a fucking contradiction. He's so confusing. He was angry at me earlier, then he was disgusted by me and now he's sorry. What am I to make of all this? Honestly, I don't have the mental capacity to even try and work this shit out, especially not after inhaling all that beautiful marijuana. Which has strangely given me some clarity on all this. His apology is *so* not required, it really won't help me heal in any way whatsoever and I'm also not ready to start listening to excuses about why he didn't come back for me that night, or even attempt to contact me after.

It's because he didn't care.

"So, don't say it, let's just smoke this and then we'll go to bed," I say sincerely as he passes me back the blunt.

His whole body going rigid, both of us pinching the last of the joint.

"What?" I ask my voice barely above a whisper as my eyes are automatically pulled to his.

As I meet his midnight blues my whole body goes as rigid as his, my heart thundering in my chest, my breath hitching and knees weakening. If I wasn't already sitting on this damn concrete step, I think I would have hit the floor.

"Nothing," he almost shouts, growling out his words, his eyebrows drawing tightly together.

Releasing his hold on the joint like it singed him.

"I'm going to bed," he suddenly announces.

Throwing himself up from the step and rushing back through the door, slamming it shut behind him. I jump at the sound, the vibrations from it running over my skin, leaving me cold, alone, and really fucking confused.

CHAPTER 4
KYLA-ROSE

"Huxley Harrington-Griffin put me down this instant!" I huff as he heaves me up from the back step, my lit cigarette flying from my hand into the wet grass. "I'm not playing, put me down!" I squeal on a bout of laughter, his long fingers grasping at my hips as he holds me high above his head. "I mean it! *Huxley!*" I scream as he spins me.

Suddenly dropping me low, my body falling through the cool air before he snatches me around the waist, dragging me in against his hard body.

"Stop screaming, you'll upset the damn neighbours!" he chastises with a smirk as he places my feet down, the morning dew seeping through my thick socks.

"You don't have any neighbours, you idiot," I roll my eyes.

Slapping my uninjured hand against the hard planes of his chest. I wriggle against his hold, but he doesn't release me. His arms tightening around my waist in the most delicious pinch.

"Anyway," I say, finally giving up on trying to break free. "You love it when I scream for you," I wink with a sexy smirk, flipping my loose hair over my shoulder as he drops his lips to the newly exposed crook of my neck.

"Urgh," he groans, his warm breath feathering against my cool skin. "You're so goddamn sexy I can't even deal," he complains, and I feel the hard evidence of his words in his jogging bottoms pressing against my lower belly.

"We're home alone, right?" I whisper mischievously.

My teeth nipping against the shell of his pierced ear. I watch as the hair on the back of his neck stands, a wicked smile curving my lips. He draws back to look at me and when he sees the wanton expression marring my face he grabs hold of my hips. My legs automatically climbing up his body, wrapping around his waist. His lips find mine, desperate and hungry as he carries me back inside the house. I kick the back door shut behind us before he slams me down on the kitchen island.

Huxley leans into me, his thick cock instantly lined up, already knowing where it wants to be. I can feel the bar of metal through his tip pressing against the heat of my molten core, ready and wanting. His lips leave mine for a fraction of a second as I coax him out of his shirt, he helps me pull it up and over his head, so I don't overstretch my injured hand. Dropping the fabric to the floor, revealing his hard chest and rippling abs. He tugs mine off too, adding it to the pile at his feet. Hux hisses through his teeth as my bare breasts press up against his naked torso, my already hard nipples brushing over his firm chest, the metal of my piercings cooling his skin.

Huxley kisses me, his tongue seeking mine like he needs me to breathe, to *live* and I *know* now that I do, in fact, need him to keep living. I'm not sure I was even really alive before these two men came into my life. I was just going through the motions. I destined myself to live a life alone, that's why I volunteered to take over the family business so easily. I fell into the position that Uncle Dee's boys didn't want because I needed something to give me purpose. I thought I was ruined for all men.

Maybe now they know the truth I am.

I draw back as that dark thought enters my head, sending my mind swimming. My hands spring up trying to cover my bare breasts, the back of my injured hand accidently hitting Huxley in the jaw as I shove his mouth from my chest.

"No, no, no, stop!" I shriek, pushing Huxley in the chest with my free hand.

He stumbles backwards away from me as I scoot myself further back on the counter. Drawing my legs up to my chest to cover myself, dropping my head to my knees.

"Darlin', what's wrong? I'm sorry! Did I hurt

you?" panic rings clear in his tone, but I can't focus on him enough to bring me back.

Untethered from my anchor, my mind freefalls, memories springing to the forefront of my mind.

"Look at me, you little bitch," my personal officer -the man responsible for looking after my wellbeing while I'm confined to this prison- orders as he backhands me across the face for the third time.

Black stars dance in my vision, my jaw going slack as I try to stay conscious.

"If I tell you to fucking do something I expect you to fucking do it," he spits through gritted teeth.

Hot spittle hits my cheek as his fingers dig into the soft flesh of my bare hips.

"I want you to be fucking present," he growls. "You'll learn to enjoy these moments between us, even if it takes rigorous hours of training," he snarls. "You can lie to yourself all you want but I know you want this just as much as I do. Even your body knows what it wants, it's so responsive. It's not like anyone else is ever gunna touch ya now, is it?" he purrs.

His poisonous breath turns my stomach and I heave, earning me another slap across the face, this time re-splitting my already busted lip. Hot crimson trickles down my chin, flooding my mouth with its copper taste.

I struggle to keep my eyes open, my head lolling to the side. His harsh thrusts into me making my battered body jar against the metal table. His colleague restraining my arms high above my head. Stretching my body at an uncomfortable angle, his grip leaving more bruises on my already beaten wrists. I try not to breathe, not to move, not to think, because it's no fun for them if I play dead. And I have to try and find even the smallest amount of control, somewhere, even if it is just my reactions.

His rough hand grips my chin, forcing my face back to his. Using his rough fingers, he smears my own blood across my face. I avert my eyes, retreating into that dark little cavern inside my head.

"FUCKING LOOK AT ME!" he roars in my face.

His spit hitting my skin, his other hand groping my bruised breasts as he squeezes them too roughly. I don't really feel the pain anymore, I don't think I really feel anything.

"Your nipples taste like the sweetest berries, little love. Do you know that?"

He's trying to make me speak, react, roll my eyeballs in his general direction but I don't.

I'm mute, silent, broken.

I wonder if I'm dead.

I feel dead, and I think of my cousin Charlie, and what it is he's doing right at this moment. He told me once he felt like he was a figment of his own imagination, maybe a reflection stuck on the wrong side of the mirror. He said sometimes he didn't understand why he was here, and he thought of ways to get out. To just get. The. Fuck. Out. And I've never once related to that as intensely as I do right now.

My heart constricts inside my black and blue chest, the mottled flesh taut over my useless organs and cracked ribs. Stretched tight, my insides aching desperately with every breath. And I suddenly regret begging my social worker to let me stay with my mum. How I pleaded to stay with her, in that damp little hovel with no heating and mould on the ceiling, a toilet that never flushed properly and needles.

So many fucking needles.

How I would have to be careful where I trod when I woke up in the mornings after one of her benders. How I'd clean up her vomit from the cracked linoleum floor in the kitchen; pale blue and white checks turned yellow with age. Pick up the threadbare sofa cushions and generally put the house back together. All while dodging grabby hands from strange men I didn't know and locking myself inside the bathroom whilst I cried, refusing to use the cold shower in case one of them picked the lock.

I think of my uncle, his weekly visits. How he would look so disappointed every time I said I wouldn't move in with him and the boys, 'cause I needed to look after Mum. How he'd crease his brow and frown, but not argue with me. I realise now he was trying to protect me. I thought he was trying to rip a crying babe from her mother's bosom. But it's only now I see what he was really trying to do.

Save me from fucking drowning.

Be the father I needed, one living outside of fifty-foot prison walls. Treat me better, buy me shoes that fit and wouldn't give me blisters. Provide me with a warm, safe bed to sleep in, not a rotting mattress with a pillow as old as me and mismatched kid sheets. I never took his offered 'pocket money', I didn't want Mum getting her hands on it and buying more smack. She'd scream at me during her come downs. Hiss and spit and cry. Hit me over and over and over until she passed out from exhaustion. But she's dead now, so it doesn't really matter anyway.

My insides battered and bruised as much as my outsides.

Cuts, bruises, and scars mottle my pale skin. I only ever had one scar before I came here, on the back of my thigh. I got stuck on a bit of barbed wire fencing when me and Max were up to no good, we were always up to no fucking good. I needed fifteen stitches and half a bottle of vodka to get me through the pain. Turquoise-blue eyes flash in my mind then, but I banish them away, sending them into a dark untouched corner of my mind, shrouded in shadows and painted with blood.

Some of my new scars are white, some pink. Others, the fresher ones, raw and red, angry and fiery. Sometimes they cut me with a knife. They tell me I bleed for them because I refuse to cry but I don't cry for them or *bleed for* them. *I would do those things only for me.*

If I'm not dead yet I wish I were.

This is hell.

"Darlin', please, come back to me," Huxley pleads as I blink at him.

My whole body trembles, my teeth chattering, my mind dark.

"I need to get clean," I say frantically.

Huxley blinks back at me, his eyes wide as I scramble to get off the counter. I fling myself to the floor, half crawling as I hurry to stand, pushing myself up on my split hand.

Everything about you is disgusting.

You're nothing.

Worthless.

"I need the noise to stop," I plead to myself, whispering, as my feet stumble to carry me into the downstairs bathroom.

Just like your junkie mother.
Nobody will ever love you.
Just like she didn't.
She couldn't *love you.*
You're unlovable.
Dirty.

Turning the shower taps with shaky hands, I twist the temperature dial to as high as it will go. Slamming the door shut behind me, twisting the lock with quaking fingers. I'm vaguely aware of Huxley banging against the door but I can't hear his words, my ears are buzzing too loudly. My heart pumping blood through my useless veins, the dull thunk of it torturing me. The thudding hammering its way through my hand, my stitches pulling and tearing the skin. My already destroyed tendons screaming as fire bolts through them like lightning, my fingers numb and useless.

I need it all to stop.

I strip off my leggings and socks, my top still lost on the kitchen floor. Smearing myself with scarlet before launching myself beneath the scalding spray. Dropping to my knees, I sit beneath the boiling water, willing it to clean me.

Cleanse me.

Phantom hands brush over my skin making me grit my teeth, I squeeze my eyes shut tight. Rocking myself back and forth, I hum, comforting my fractured thoughts. What can I do to make it better? What cleans things?

My eyes snap open frantically, searching for something.

Anything.

Soap's not strong enough, I need to strip this pain away, the feelings. Get rid of it all. Make me fresh. Clean. New.

I crawl across the small shower base, thick steam billowing around me as I reach out. My working fingers latching around the neck of a yellow bleach bottle sitting beside the toilet. Unscrewing the cap with my teeth, I spit it away from me, tipping the almost full bottle, up-ending it down my chest. Covering myself with as much of it as I can before tossing the empty bottle away from me. I scrub at my skin frantically with every ounce of energy I have, my skin angry and raw as I work my one good hand over myself.

I want my boys to want me, and I can't be like this for them. I feel like my past is rushing back, haunting me, unnerving me, *ruining* me. Destroying me and everything I've built. Like the sea swallowing a sand-castle. It looks impenetrable, built sturdy and strong but at the end of the day, it's just sand, singular and fragile pieces.

I'm coming undone. Poisoned stuffing finally bursting through the delicate stitching that once held me together.

The smell of bleach fills the windowless room,

burning my eyes. The extractor fan not engaging because I didn't turn the light on, keeping me submerged in the darkness.

I just need all the voices to stop.

I crawl on my bare knees to the cabinet under the sink, the cold tile floor bruising my knees as I scramble over them, water puddling around me. One hand hanging limply at my side, my other fumbling to find the gun I have hidden in here. I've stashed weapons all over this house; there are enough guns and knives tucked around this place to stock a small armoury. I feel safer that way, knowing I have access to something deadly, the thought makes me smile. My fingers find the grip and I rip it free, taking it back into the shower with me, a flood of water trailing across the floor. I need to make everything stop. Just for a minute. I need to feel the silence.

The scalding water pounds down heavily against my hot skin. Singeing my flesh like acid, dripping from my bones and washing down the drain but I'm still *dirty*.

"Always, always dirty," I cry, fisting my sodden hair.

Tapping the muzzle of the gun against the side of my head, the heavy metal of it feeling feather light in my grip. I suddenly hear muffled voices somewhere close by but I'm so far away now. I *want* to be far away. I'm too damaged. I was stupid to think I could have a relationship with someone, *someones*. There must be some ulterior motive for them, there has to be, why are they doing this?

They're liars.

It's all lies, Kyla-Rose, they don't want you, they want to ruin you, destroy you, finally end you once and for all. You could end it now, before they take all the control away from you, take the power and silence it.

"Shut the fuck up!" I scream, my trembling hand hammering the muzzle into my temple over and over. "I can't do this if you don't shut up, stop fucking talking, stop the fucking whispers!"

My breath all but leaves my body, I can't get any air in. The hot steam fills the room with clouds, the bleach smell suddenly overwhelming, the gun still gripped firmly in my uninjured hand. A river of blood flowing from the other, coating me in crimson, the water turning red.

Breathe.

Fucking breathe.

The bathroom door flies open. Kacey's huge body barrelling through it, the solid wood splitting against its gold hinges. The hall light illuminating just enough of his sunshine-coloured eyes, widening obscenely large as he looks at me. Huxley and Max crowd in behind him, filling up the space, their presence eating up all the air, casting me, once again, in shadow.

"I need the noise to stop," I plead with him, my voice barely a whisper. "I need the quiet, stay back," I say shakily.

Putting the palm of my wounded hand out in

front of me, gesturing him back, warning him away. The ruined stitches snagging harder at my torn skin, my fingers almost useless as my entire arm screams in protest. Blood running down my arm at the stretch, dripping from the crook of my elbow.

"Sweetheart, put the gun down. Slide it over to me, please," Kaccy requests calmly, his amber-yellow eyes still bright and beautiful even in the dark of this room.

Kacey; my protector.

The water pounds down on my back and a smile ghosts my lips as I look at him. He truly is an angel, devastatingly handsome, but his jaw is set, his teeth clenching, and his forehead creased. I frown at what I see on his pretty face.

"Why you so sad, Big Man?" I ask him quietly, my words mumbling, tilting my head to one side as I consider him.

My eyes flick to Huxley next. His eyes so black in the darkness of this windowless room that it frightens me a little, his usual laughter and light all but gone from them. I screw my face up as I look at him. He's supposed to be my safety.

Why are they looking at me like that?

Because they know you're broken.

I ram the gun into my temple as I squeeze my eyes shut, breathing harshly through my nose.

"I'm sad because I'm scared, Sweetheart."

Kacey's deep voice rumbles through me,

comforting the darkest parts of my soul. My chest tightens and pulls but I keep my eyes shut tightly.

"I make you sad," I suddenly realise, a crystal-clear moment of clarity illuminating the darkness. "I don't want you to be sad, Kace," I whisper over the drumming sound of the water, pounding into me like the fists of demons.

"You don't make me sad, you're frightening us, Sweetheart, all of us. We just want you to put the gun down, we don't want you to hurt yourself," he tells me, but his words aren't connecting with my brain.

What are we even doing in here?

The side of my head pulses with pain as the water scalds my skin. The scorching inferno in my hand unbearable as it throbs in time with my erratic heart-beat. A thrum of heat runs through my fingers as I squeeze the gun tighter in my good fist, watching as the water carries the thick flow of blood down the drain from my other.

Always fucking bleeding.

A sob tears from my raw throat, dry and stinging from inhaling bleach. The gun clattering to the shower pan, the sound of it echoing heavily in the small space. Then the heat hits me, and I feel the pain tearing its way through my body as I cry out. In one long stride, Kacey climbs into the shower. His towering body reaching over me, fully clothed, he turns the water to freezing. The immediate change in temperature forces tears from my stinging eyes. Huxley takes the gun from the shower, dropping it into the sink. Kacey crashes to the floor behind me, holding my raw skin in his huge arms. The cold water drowning us both, my teeth chatter as heaving sobs rack my trembling body.

"It's okay, I'm here," Kacey murmurs against my hair.

Opening his legs, dragging me back into him. Holding my naked body under the freezing spray, he clamps his legs over me as I try to get away from the water.

"It fucking hurts, Kace, let me out," I tremble through chattering teeth, but he doesn't let up, trying to soothe my burnt skin.

I can't bear to look at him, at any of them, seeing me break down, yet again, is embarrassing as hell and overly fucking exhausting for everyone.

"I'm sorry," I whisper, my shoulders deflating as I start to relax into him.

I need to apologise to Huxley. My eyes try to search him out, finding him through the open door, sitting on the bottom stair, his head in his hands.

"Do-does h-he hat-hate me?" I whisper, my voice breaking more through my chattering teeth as I look at the defeated man.

"Who?" Kacey asks me, his grip tightening around me, my bare breasts squeezed harshly beneath his corded forearm.

"Huxley," I choke out, emotional tears pricking the back of my eyes as I watch his shoulders heave.

"No, he doesn't hate you, he's upset with himself,

he'll be okay. He's not upset with you, Sweetheart," Kacey reassures me, but I know I did that to him, my beautiful caramel skinned, dark eyed boy.

I broke the man who isn't afraid of being broken because he isn't afraid of *anything*.

As I stare at him, his position doesn't change, he doesn't move. He just sits like that for as long as I'm in the shower with Kacey before a dark figure blocks my view. Without looking at me, Max drops a pile of fluffy white towels onto the floor in the open doorway and moves over to his friend. Max grips Huxley's shoulder, giving it a squeeze before sitting beside him. Speaking quietly, he drops his arm around his friend's shoulder, pulling him in for a sideways hug.

"I wa-want to get o-out, Kacey," I say, my body feeling fucking hypothermic.

Without a word he turns off the water and scoops me up into his arms.

Hissing through my teeth at the burning sensation across my abused skin. He places a small towel on the closed toilet lid, sitting me on it before wrapping my shivering body in two more oversized bath sheets. When he's stripped off his wet clothes, slinging them into the shower with a splat, he wraps a towel around his waist. Towel dries my hair and scoops me back up. Clutching me close to his chest like I'm something precious to him, walking me past my other boys. *Boy.* I internally scold myself; Max isn't mine anymore. I don't think he ever really was. Something inside me hisses and growls at that but I ignore my demon, now is most definitely not the time for that.

Kacey sits down on one of the navy couches with me in his lap. Wrapping my bleeding hand tightly in another small towel, dragging me in against his chest, gently running his big hand up and down my stinging back. Resting my chin on his broad shoulder, I peer over at Huxley and Max.

"I keep hurting everyone," I say on a soft exhale. "This won't work, Kace," I breathe in defeat.

Finally realising that this is exactly the type of life we would always have. We'll have a few good days and then something someone does or says will trigger me or I'll have a manic episode where I hurt everyone around me. Until one day, I just wind up killing someone and that is something I cannot live with. I'd never forgive myself if I hurt one of my boys.

"Stop it, I don't wanna fucking hear that shit," Kacey bellows at me.

Gripping my upper arms painfully, shaking my towel covered body, my chattering teeth rattling inside my skull. I lean back to see his face, he's angry, really angry, because I've hurt his friend which means I've hurt him too. I try to shuffle myself from his lap, but he grips me even tighter, making me wince.

"I'm not fucking doing this with you anymore. We fucking told you we were all in, that includes *all* the parts, not just the good. I swear to god, you're killing me. Stop trying to fucking run away from us. We're gunna work through this together," he growls but it's not even anger in his voice anymore, it's *pain*.

"I-"

Stopping myself, I swallow the lump in my throat, nuzzling my face into his neck, pressing my lips to his pulse I kiss it softly.

"I'm sorry. I just don't want to hurt anyone, I love you all," I say sadly, trying to explain.

Kaccy doesn't speak, he just clutches me tighter to him. His grip hurts but I know he needs this, so I don't say anything. I just sit quietly while he keeps me close because I need it too. I'm pretty sure he already knows what I have to do next but neither one of us says anything, and although I fucking hate myself for it, that's once again *my* issue, not theirs.

It's only as I close my eyes, I realise I said *all*.

CHAPTER 5
HUXLEY

"Morning, Hux," Nox grumbles. Slinking into the kitchen from the back garden, the door slamming shut in the cold wind behind him. His feet bare; wet with dew from the frosty grass, loose, black joggers, cuffed at the ankles. Another cigarette already tucked behind his ear, dark bags beneath his bright blue eyes. Nox yawns, scratching at the day-old stubble shadowing his jaw. He ruffles fingers through his jet-black hair, the length a lot longer than when we were away fighting. Pushing it away from his forehead, he sits on a bar stool.

I shove a mug of coffee across the counter, black, no sugar, extra hot. The way he's been drinking it for the last ten years that I've known him. He puts the steaming mug to his lips, immediately swallowing down the scalding liquid and I cringe. The boy can't have any fucking taste buds, he must have burnt them all away by now, surely.

"Mornin'," I rasp, tiredness thick in my throat.

"Huxley," Nox sighs, pushing his thick, straight hair back from his face again.

Another habit. We're all full of strange tics in this house it seems.

"What?" I reply curtly.

"It's not your fault," he tells me coolly.

Fingers laced together, clasped around his mug, he leans forward on his forearms, his eyes seeking mine.

"I should have been more…" I pause, finding the right words, sighing in frustration.

My hands planted on the marble island, I drop my head forward between my shoulders.

"*Sensitive.*"

"Huxley," Nox's well practised Lieutenant voice cracks like a whip, my eyes automatically snapping up to meet his.

Old habits die hard.

We needed Nox out in the field, he kept everyone in fucking check, never steered our platoon wrong. We only nearly lost one of our trio once and that was only Nox's fault because he put his trust in me. *I* steered us wrong.

"It's *not* your fault."

Those words feel familiar too. Nox said those exact words to me when we nearly lost Kace. I felt responsible then, too. It was me who said it was clear, I was wrong. I barely survived being at war as it was, let alone having to do it after watching my brother die. It makes me sick just thinking about it. Every time that thick scar across Kacey's throat catches the light I clench my jaw.

I nod, slowly, agreeing to a certain degree. Deep down, I know it's not entirely my fault, but I still feel somewhat responsible. She hasn't freaked out like that with Kace. I must have done *something*.

"She's scarred," Nox says nonchalantly.

Emotionless, like he really couldn't give a fuck either way. Just tossing out a piece of information like it means nothing when we both know that's not true. He spoke about the white-haired love of his life every night when we were deployed.

"You understand that, Hux, you probably better than anyone. I know you feel bad, that's your girl," he says that last part roughly, losing his carefully polished mask for a moment.

Pushing his coffee cup back to his lips, "she loves you, she wouldn't be here otherwise."

I nod again, swallowing the dry lump that's been lodged in my throat since yesterday.

I had my family's doctor come look at her hand, it needs surgery, he said. Tendon damage, maybe a nerve issue. Kyla-Rose wasn't listening, didn't hear a single word the Doc said, staring off into space. Those too large eyes swirling with darkness as she remained bundled in Kacey's huge arms. Refusing to be pulled from him, her nails clawing into his forearm, ensuring she stayed put. An ache I didn't know

I could feel, ripping my insides open as I watched her disappear inside herself. I listened to the Doc though, guilt eating away at me with every word he said. After all, it's my fault she ripped the wound open in the first place. She slept with Kacey last night, he took her upstairs once she'd fallen asleep with him on the sofa and we didn't see either of them again.

Nox and I sat up together, down here with the TV on, neither of us watching it. Him talking and trying to comfort me all night, distract me. Neither of us slept. It took everything in me not to ask him about their history. I need to know, to understand, to *fix* things. But I didn't. We just went silent after a few hours. Both lost inside our own heads. I've seen some shit in my life, but never something quite like that. I don't know if I'll ever be able to unsee it, un*feel* it.

I rub the back of my neck, anxiety and tension building up in the muscles there as I heave a deep sigh. I need to get my game face back on. I'm not a worrier usually, but this morning just feels *wrong*. I'm the one who's usually cracking the jokes, making light of whatever shit we find ourselves knee deep in. But I just *can't* today.

"Maddox," I finally utter, his full name falling from my traitorous lips like a prayer. A *plead*. "I need to know," I swallow.

Placing my green mug down on the island between us. Me standing, him sitting. He eyes me warily, ever the closed book.

"Why'd you leave her?" I ask even though it's really not my business.

I'm the fixer. I'll make it my business so I can understand. See it from all sides. Mend it, stitch all the shredded pieces back together again.

Nox's face scrunches, his usual bitter scowl momentarily disappearing as he rubs a hand over his face, his other hand clasping his coffee mug so tightly his knuckles blanch.

"It's not really right to tell you," he sighs softly, unusually gentle, his words just an echo of his usual heavy tone. "Before *her*."

I nod once, resigning myself to my fate of not knowing, possibly ever. Because the likelihood of those two stubborn arses having a conversation where neither one interrupts the other and no one ends up with a slashed throat, is slim to none. I wonder if they'd let me mediate. Well, probably not. It's definitely worthy of a private conversation. That's what worries me actually, *Christ*, look at me! Still worrying!

"But I will," Nox rasps.

That gets my attention, my internal bullshit ramblings coming to an abrupt halt as my dark eyes snap up to meet his bright ones.

"You know I told you about the Southbrook gang?" he asks, his eye twitching at the mere mention of them.

I nod silently in response, knowing any interruptions could cut him off. He's like the plug stopper in a bath that is suctioned so fucking tight it's impossible to drain the water out. That's what Nox is like with all his fucking secrets.

"Well then, you'll remember that when I was fifteen, I joined up, just dealing weed in the hallways at my high school. It wasn't anything heavy, no blood spilt, no fighting, no *jobs*. I just got my weekly weight, got told what to sell it for and that was it. Then when I left school, I moved up. Went to the streets, pills, powders. You name it, I could sling it. It was easy money as far as I was concerned. Then I got the odd muscle job, beat someone just enough to teach them a lesson. Every week my tasks got a little more violent, a little extra threat in the requests, things to make me prove my loyalty. I panicked, thinking of Gran and Lala. I didn't want their names tossed around as a way to get to me, so I cut Lala off completely. Told her I wasn't interested in hanging out with little girls anymore."

"To protect her," I murmur in understanding.

He nods, "anyway, by the time I hit eighteen, that apparently wasn't going to cut it anymore." Nox swallows another sip of his coffee, his turquoise blue eyes shining. "For my *initiation* I had to take someone out. I put it off for as long as possible, always coming up with excuses. I was scared fucking shitless. I didn't wanna kill someone, I just wanted to make money for my future. Get my girl out of her toxic fucking household, it's not like every-fucking-one hadn't tried already. So stubborn, so fucking *loyal*," he growls as though that's an insult, but there's appreciation in his tone.

There's nothing Nox finds more attractive in a person than their unwavering loyalty.

"So, one day I get given an ultimatum, I have to hit my target tonight or *she'll* be the target. I didn't give a shit about threats against *me*, but not against her, so I had to do it. Even if she thought I hated her, I watched her everywhere she went, everyone she spoke to, saw every boy she *kissed*," he hisses, and I can't help the light chuckle that escapes.

Nox's eyes narrow on me. I pull my pinched finger and thumb across my lips, pretending to zip and lock them up, tossing the imaginary key over my shoulder. I waggle my eyebrows at him, he shakes his head, but he smiles.

It's what I'm good at, relaxing a situation, making people smile. I haven't got any *real* talents, but I can do this.

"That's the night it all happened, one of my boys told me he saw Lala walking in the dark, thought I'd wanna know. I instantly panicked in case someone grabbed her to get to me anyway; I thought I'd hidden my affection towards her so well," he scoffs, like he should have known better. "So, I went to look for her. Then, well, you know the rest I'm sure," he looks up at me in question.

"The short version," I confirm, and he winces.

"My time was running out, I had to leave her, I

shoulda took her with me, taken her home. I don't know, I thought leaving her there, she'd be safe," he sighs heavily, running a hand through his thick hair. "I think about it all the fucking time, what I coulda done different, what I shoulda said, where I shoulda taken her. I should have gone back sooner. It's the only thing in my entire life that I regret. I don't know how to fix any of this, Hux," Nox's voice cracks with his confession.

I reach across the counter. Cupping the back of his head I draw him forward, pressing my forehead against his. His eyes closed, his breath shuddery as he tries to keep his emotions locked down tight, like if he lets one slip it'll completely ruin him.

"I'll help you," I promise, "you can fix this."

He nods against me, and I release him to stand back up.

"You've gotta stop being an arsehole," I tell him. "I know that'll be difficult for you since you currently sit on the throne and all. But you need to fucking try. Because if she decides to come down those stairs this morning and strangle you, I'll let her," I tell him.

"I know."

"You've gotta make it up to her. You cannot *have* her. She is not *yours*. Currently she's mine and Kacey's, she could be *ours*. But you have to learn to fucking share, Maddox, because Kacey and I, we're not giving her up. You know what Kacey's obsessions get like and even I can see this is different. He'll gut you over her, he fucking *loves* her. *I* love her. You don't get to be all jealous and possessive. And then *if* she forgives you,

you don't get to come in and steam roll everything to rebuild it to *your* liking. Everything is to *her* liking or not at all. Am I clear?"

Nox stares me down for what feels like forever. Waiting for me to yield, roll over like a puppy, show my belly and submit to the snarling wolf. But I don't, I *won't*. Finally, his gaze drops, and he nods, a defeated sigh leaving him in a rushing exhale.

"Also, you're lucky she didn't stab you, she's really not shy, dude," I warn with a raised brow.

"Yeah, I know, she wasn't like that before," he blows out an exaggerated breath, his eyes locking onto mine once again. "I liked it," the fucker smirks and I snort.

I feel myself needing to adjust my dick at the thought of her holding a knife to my own throat, but I manage to resist.

Jesus Christ, I'm turning into Kacey.

I look up at the sound of heavy footfalls on the stairs. Kacey's huge body rounding the banister, his sleep filled eyes hardly open as he mumbles under his breath to himself. A hand shoved down his joggers, the other running through his forward flop of blonde hair. He drops onto the stool beside Nox, drumming his fingers on the countertop before snaking them across the counter, snatching Nox's coffee straight from his hands.

"What the fuck?" Nox frowns.

My eyebrows jump into my hairline. Kacey doesn't drink caffeine.

"Care to explain what *that*," I flap my hand in his general direction, "is all about?"

He mumbles, sliding the coffee back to its rightful owner, rubbing the heel of his large hand into a tired eye.

"In English, dickhead." Nox grunts.

Elbowing the big, inked beast, scowling into his now mostly empty coffee cup.

"It's just disorientating waking up without Kyla-Rose," Kacey grumbles, yawning.

His giant mouth wide enough to steal all the room's air like some sort of black hole vortex, I can practically see his tonsils.

"Disorientating," I repeat, shaking my head, "what the fuck are you talking about?"

"Well, when you go to bed with someone and then wake up without them, it's a little fucking disorientating," he growls.

That possessive monster rearing its ugly head, he's still surprisingly good at sharing, regardless.

"Yes, I understood that fucking part," I snap back, "but if you didn't wake up with her, then where the hell is she, you big lummox!" I slam my hand down on the counter as his yellow eyes lock on mine.

"Ain't she down here with you?" he blanches, rapidly looking between Nox and I. "Outside?" he questions, already moving to check, sliding the stool back and heading for the garden.

"She's gone," I state knowingly, rubbing a hand down my face, I catch the piercing in my eyebrow and sigh. "It's my fault. I fucked it. Yesterday, I scared her."

I squeeze my eyes shut as Kaccy slams the back-door, the window above the sink rattling in its frame.

"You did no such thing!" he booms, "she was worried about *you!* Kept saying *she* felt bad for scaring *you.*"

I crack my neck, tilting my head from one side to the other.

"You can get her back," Nox says quietly, staring into his coffee, his brow drawn, he swallows. "She doesn't ever do what's best for *her;* she'll think this is her saving you a problem-"

"She's not a fucking problem!" Kaccy shouts, his teeth barred like a wild beast.

"*I* know that, just sit the fuck down, you twat," Nox barks.

Kaccy growls back like a fucking dog, foaming at the mouth, but follows the order all the same, parking his arse back onto the stool.

"Huxley, call Elijah, *don't* call Jacob, that's the last person we need a lecture from," he sighs, pinching the bridge of his nose. "Kaccy, get a fucking grip, we'll sort it out, all right? Lock down your animalistic bull-shit and take a breath. Yesterday was a fucking shit show. Today's a new day. Let's just go get your girl back, okay?"

Nox looks between the two of us, his pitch-black eyebrows high on his head, awaiting our agreement. We both nod, and then I'm dialling Eli. Kaccy moving back to the stairs and Nox knocking back his leftover coffee before disappearing after him.

Driving into the familiar underground carpark of the Swallow family's tower block is intimidating to say the least. When you're treated like the enemy that is. Kacey and I lived here for two weeks with Kyla-Rose, coming and going as we pleased, never encountered one issue in or out. Today, however, we've been stopped and searched at both security stations before we even hit the down ramp. The car was checked, we were checked, not that they took our weaponry… just logged it. So there must be some sort of trust there. Well, that, or they're all just super confident in their skills that three, armed, ex-military men don't even hit their radar.

Now, we're slowly crawling down the winding tarmac. Nox driving our blacked-out Range Rover cautiously into the basement as though we're descending into the fiery pits of Hell. It feels ominous. The whole twenty-minute journey did. Silence the entire way, none of us knowing what the fuck to say.

This all feels like the end to something that hasn't even really started yet. Didn't have a chance to be watered and nurtured, grow into something fucking beautiful. It could be beautiful, I think. Whether that be as a threesome or a foursome. I don't mind shar- ing, we're all a little bit fucked up in our ways. We can each bear a portion of the weight, hold each other up when one of us is knocked down. Four broken people, each with their own trauma, every single one of us bathed and decorated in blood.

I've never been careful with a woman before. Not until I met Kyla-Rose. I never wanted to be soft. My dad's soft, mum's a hard arse, she treats him like shit, and he worships the ground she walks on. Not sure why, she's a fucking arsehole most of the time. Corrupt and knee deep in political filth. Dad's old money, Mum's new money, what a fucking joke. My whole family is a fucking mess. That's why I wanted to create my own.

I couldn't wait to escape that toxic house and I did just that at eighteen. The army called to me as my escape, I met my two brothers, and the rest is history. I'm just a fake doting son now. I strive for a quiet life with that woman, so I just do the shit I really can't refuse. Politics is all about appearances, after all.

Nox parks the car, backing into a space as I look out, seeing Eli already waiting for us. Dressed head to toe in black, from his boots and baggy cargo pants to his t-shirt and jacket. His arms folded across his chest, one leg kicked up against the wall beside the lift. The only thing that has him standing out in this dimly lit basement is his stark white hair. Otherwise, he'd have blended perfectly into the shadows, regardless of his six-foot-six height.

Everyone in this family dresses in black.

Kacey and I are out of the car before it's even

fully stopped moving, making our way over to Eli as quickly as we can. Desperate to see our girl. I need to hold her, press my face into her long, silky hair, inhale that beautiful coconut, citrus scent and never let her fucking go. I'm probably the most relaxed when it comes to my relationship with her, I'm chilled, never pushy, there's things I'd like us to do, just, when she's ready. I can wait. But the thought of never getting to cuddle her again has me fucking catatonic.

"Where is she?" I boom, my chest shaking with simmering panic.

Fuck.

Eli lazily raises a brow at my outburst, not moving from his casual position against the wall. He smacks his gum, blowing a lime green bubble before it snaps against his lips. He scrapes it off his bottom lip with his teeth, watching me as he does it again. I close my eyes and inhale a deep breath. Nox claps a hand over my shoulder from behind and squeezes.

Relax. You're the only rational one in the entire group.

"Let us up," Kacey says calmly.

Trying to keep himself from making demands, he motions with his head to the lift doors beside Eli. Eli swings his gaze to Kacey, running his eyes up his body, feet, torso, head. He glances at Nox, eyes narrowing just the tiniest fraction before schooling his reaction. He finally nods at me, pushing off the wall.

"You're packing," he states, turning his back on us as he hits the call button. "Good. I hear it's a fucking mess up there. Two rules," he snaps his gum again before continuing. "No one gets out, lads, and what-ever she says goes," he swings his gaze back over his shoulder, idly eyeing each of us individually. "What the queen demands, the queen receives. I wouldn't deny her if you value any particular parts of your-selves," he deadpans with a slight smirk as the lift bell dings and the doors open.

What in the fuck are we about to walk into?

The four of us crowd into the lift, Kacey and Nox stand sentry behind Eli and I as we ascend. Eli continues snapping his gum, the nervous energy of the unknown prompting Kacey to start humming a song under his breath. My dark brows pinch together as I glance at the reflection of him in the polished black doors.

"Are you humming the '*muffin man*'?" I ask in disbelief, that irritating tune implanting itself inside my brain, a seed taking root for at least the next week.

"Yup," he shrugs, his beast sized hands shoved into his overly tight jean pockets.

I pinch the bridge of my nose in exasperation.

"You seem awfully calm all of a sudden," Nox observes warily, "almost, *excited*," he accuses as a large grin splits Kacey's face.

"I am excited," he states blandly, clearing his face of his wicked smirk. "I hope there's something I can cut up."

Eli snorts, "of course you do," he chuckles dryly, "match made in fucking Hell," he shakes his head as the elevator comes to a stop. "Get ready, lads," he warns, stepping out of the doors into the pitch-black entryway.

I glance back at Nox who shrugs as Kacey barges past me out into the hall.

The entire apartment is in darkness, every window we pass as we follow behind Eli has its blinds, drapes or curtains closed. There's no light coming from anywhere and if I hadn't been here before I'd have no fucking clue where I was going. As it stands, I have been here before, lived here for a short while, so whilst everything around me is painted black and shrouded in shadows, I already know we're headed in the direction of the dining room.

Stopping outside its large, arched, doublewide doors, Eli places both of his hands on the handles I know to be gold.

"Just be," he pauses.

Rolling his eyes up to the ceiling before he continues, like he was trying to pluck the right words from somewhere.

"Circumspect," he smirks, pushing both doors open at the same time and stepping in, immediately moving off to one side.

I can't see shit, but I know my girl's in here.

I can feel her.

The room is darker than I've ever seen. The large, floor to ceiling, heavy black drapes are tugged tightly shut, blocking the glass wall entirely. A large, glass, oval dining table sits dead centre, it could easily seat eighteen people, high back velvet chairs lining both sides. A thick white rug beneath it, the kind that your bare toes can't help but push themselves into.

The hiss of a match draws our attention to the far end of the table. The small flame lighting Kyla-Rose just enough to see her. The lit stick pinched delicately between her finger and thumb, she cocks her head. The matchbox tucked beneath her chin, watching the flame dance closer and closer to her fingers. She drops it down, the flame dying as she strikes another. This time she reaches slightly forward, lighting tall candles perched in a candelabra. More light illuminating her perfect features, the light dancing in her large eyes and revealing her two companions.

One sat either side of her. Brute on her right, his raven-black body sitting up in the chair, tucked into the table. His big pink tongue lopping out one side of his mouth. A gold crown perched on top of his flat head, his usual heavy gold chain collar proudly around his neck. Thick globules of dribble dropping onto the glass tabletop. And then there's Angel on her left. The white she-devil mirroring Brute's stance, her muscled Pitbull body angled slightly towards Kyla-Rose. No crown sitting on her head but a large gold curb chain dripping with blood red rubies adorns her neck. Both dressed exactly as Kyla-Rose treats them. Like royalty.

"What are you doing, baby girl?" I ask her confidently as I notice the black china dressing the table, dainty teacups with gold handles and matching saucers.

"We're having tea," she rasps, her quiet, husky words scratching themselves into my soul.

"Tea?" I repeat, a little unsure.

She doesn't respond, doesn't look up. Nox and Kacey silent behind me, allowing me to take the lead. I can be gentle when I need to be, I can talk people down.

Usually.

"In that case, we'd love some tea! May we join you, Darlin'?" I ask her in my usual cheery tone.

I take a step further into the room, more confidently than my last. This is my fucking girl, I can run with this shit. Silently, Kyla-Rose drags three cup and saucer sets towards her. Which is when I notice her injured hand tucked up tightly against her chest, cradled against her breastbone. My chest prickles, a shudder rolling through me. I can't stand seeing her hurt.

I wrinkle my nose, taking another step into the dark room. She lifts the large teapot and begins pouring into each cup, before filling a cup in front of both Angel and Brute. The latter of which immediately dives into his dainty teacup, snorting and lapping at the obviously cooled tea. I smile at that, I fucking love these dogs. I spent hours trying to get them to like me without having Angel rip one of my hands off.

I roll my shoulders back and stroll down the long length of the table. Kyla-Rose placing the teapot down, her eyes rolling up to watch me approach from beneath her heavenly thick lashes. I take the black velvet chair directly beside Brute, patting him on the chest as I settle in my seat. Kyla-Rose straightens her head before tilting it to the other side. Without taking those beautiful storm cloud eyes from mine, she pushes a cup and saucer towards me. I reach across Brute, purposefully brushing my long fingertips over hers. She freezes, looking down where our fingers barely graze and shudders, her shoulders shaking. She shuts her eyes tightly, sliding her fingers back towards herself before opening them and staring down her other two boys.

And I say *two* because let's face it. Nox is here to stay. I'm already on board, not to say there wouldn't be teething problems, but still. I'm just waiting for the other three fuckheads in this potential relationship to realise it.

"Are you having tea?" she slowly blinks up at them, once, twice, her large, pretty grey orbs staring hard, face blank of all emotion, lost inside her own head.

Don't worry, baby girl, I'm gunna find ya.

Kacey moves first, bravely taking the seat beside Angel. She snaps at him as he slumps into his seat, a manic grin on his face as he says, "down, girl. Bloodthirsty just like your mama, huh?" he chuckles, the sound deep as he bravely pats Angel's shoulder, scratching the place beneath her collar.

Nox silently moves into the seat beside mine, stiff and unsure as he slides his chair beneath the table. He briefly flicks his gaze to mine, and I subtly nod letting him know I've got this.

"So, Darlin', anyone else joinin' this soirée, or will it just be us?" I ask with a smile, plastering on fake confidence, *fuck*, I wanna hold her so bad.

"Mmm," she hums, bringing a teacup to her gnawed lips, even in only candlelight I can see they're bitten raw. "Charlie is coming," she says after taking a sip, her husky voice dripping the words like thick honey.

"How long will he be, Sweetheart?" Kaccy asks casually, stroking Angel's back.

"Shouldn't be long now," she almost sings, and I freeze at her new tone.

This one dark and sinister, the new smile accompanying her words makes my heart stutter in my chest.

"He had to make a stop along the way."

CHAPTER 6
KYLA-ROSE

My heart pounds erratically inside my chest, slamming against my ribcage, adrenaline coursing through my veins as I chew on my bottom lip. The anticipation of what's to come sends heat shooting up my spine in excitement. Huxley, Kacey, and Max being here only adds to the thrill, and the best part? The best part is they have no fucking idea what's in store. They haven't seen me play yet, and I have a feeling this show's going to be my best one yet.

I won't need to question this lowlife specimen bottom feeder; I just need to cleanse my soul and he's a part of the reaping.

A baptism in blood, an unholy eucharist, a divine exorcism, a blood oath and soul splitting ritual. I was born of crimson and hellfire, birthed in ash and reborn of the Devil himself. I just need to remember how to use that to my advantage.

I've gone *soft.*

I know, I can hardly believe it either, but don't worry, 'cause that's all about to change.

"Eli, if you could please take the dogs down to Charlie's," I call gently, my voice uncharacteristically sweet and smooth, carrying through the air effortlessly.

Without further comment, Eli whistles sharply, instantly gaining their attention, both my babies hopping off their velvet thrones. Brute's crown flung from his big head as his heavy gait carries him from the room. The door clicks softly behind them as they exit, I lick my cracked lips.

"Not long now," I murmur to myself.

Checking my good wrist for a watch that isn't there, my other hand uselessly pulled to my chest. I don't ignore the pain; I use it to fuel me. Pulling on it, letting it rock through my demon, she snarls and snaps and hisses as I ready her. I glance up from my teacup, looking to my left. Kacey sits, his eyes on mine, those glittering, golden orbs trap me, my breath stops, heat spreads through me, instantly flooding my core.

God, he is fucking beautiful.

"What are you up to, Darlin'?" Huxley asks cheekily.

Drawing my attention, his soft, teasing rasp cutting through the fire inside me, but instead of extinguishing it, he only ignites it further. Adding to the flames and heat rampaging through my veins.

I offer him up a coy smile, my head tilting to the right. I let my eyes rove over his trim body, knowing that beneath that too-tight white t-shirt is the finest set of abs I've ever had the pleasure of running my tongue over. I look back up at him, his caramel brown skin, luscious peach lips and those soul penetrating, coal-coloured eyes. My smile turns almost shy as he smirks at me, that cocky, arrogant, but oh so delicious, confident attitude. Fearless. That's what he is, absolutely fucking fearless. Huxley is everything I want to be.

Looking past him to the ghost of my past, Maddox fucking Sharpe, his ice white skin, raven-black hair and bright turquoise-blue eyes. He's everything familiar and distant to me. My past and possible future smashing together in a head-on crash. Like Titanic meeting its iceberg, Romeo and Juliet loving each other even though they shouldn't, like fire and earth, water and wind. A colossal collision of all of those things and more as I look at him. He's everything I always wanted and everything I should never have.

But let's be real for a sec, we all want what we shouldn't. Even if it kills us in the end.

I wonder how far they'll let this thing go. How long a leash will they let me have, do they know I can never be kept? Never be trained, never roll over and play the sub in this relationship. They can't muzzle me, they never could, and frankly, if they tried, I'd have to consider keeping them in the dungeon like Charlie does with Dillon.

They can never leave me, just as I could never really leave them. When I walked out of their house this morning, I felt the most fucked up and messed up mix of emotions I ever have. I left thinking I was protecting them. Saving them from all the heartache and trauma I'll inevitably cause them.

Saving them from me.

But I quickly realised they don't need saving; they're just as broken as I am, and they thrive. I will *never* find anyone else as perfect for me as them. We can either heal together or burn in hellfire and honestly, I couldn't give a fuck which, as long as we're together.

And Max?

If he can sit through this round and learn to take instruction, not raze this whole thing to the fucking ground. Then maybe, just *maybe*, I'll hear him out. Can we ever be Maxi and Lala again? Does he want me to be Lala, or Kyla-Rose?

Who the fuck do *I* want to be?

Both.

Distantly I hear the lift bell ding, pulling me from my thoughts. I twist my teacup around on its saucer so its handle sits at a ninety-degree angle. I look up at the closed doors, adrenaline spiking, I cock my head. An earth-shattering scream rips through the blanket of quiet, all three sets of eyes snapping to mine, and I giggle. A girly, deranged, twisted sound that rings loud in the room. My head angled slightly down, chin almost tucked, I peek up through my thick lashes, silver falls of hair curtaining my face. My good hand slips beneath the table, stroking up my thigh. I palm my butcher's cleaver and grin.

The double doors explode open. The wood cracking with the force as Charlie kicks through, dragging a very unwilling participant in his wake. Charlie's hand clasped tightly around his mangled ankle, the body being dragged across my floor on his front. Writhing in pain, a terse scream tearing from his throat, the sound almost raspy. I shiver, a tremor racking through my body as I huff a laugh under my breath. Charlie locks eyes with me, his glistening emeralds just visible in the dim light, staring inside me. Inviting my demon out to play.

I place my good hand atop the table, clutching my meat cleaver. My fingers curled around the handle, the thick steel blade catching the candlelight. I stand, cocking my head to the left.

"You broke his ankle?" I enquire, Charlie tilting his head, mirroring my own stance.

"It was an accident," he grunts. "He tried to dive out of the sunroof," he shrugs, his voice croaking.

"Get him up," I instruct gently, my tone cool and calculated.

Charlie and I always in perfect sync, knowing that between the two of us, the situation is always in our control.

Charlie drops his ankle, his leg thunking to the

floor. The man screams out, the shrill sound piercing through the blanket of quiet. Charlie immediately swoops low, one fist gripping the back of his jeans, the other fisting his hair. He heaves the screaming body up, slamming him face down on my dining table and forcibly shoving him towards me. The wind knocked out of him, he doesn't struggle when he stops sliding, trying to catch his breath, he groans.

I grip my cleaver tighter, my fingers flexing slightly as I adjust my hold. I step up onto my chair, using it as a hop up onto the glass tabletop. My heavy, black Doc Martens thump along the sturdy glass, bringing me closer to my prey. I stop just before him, the groaning man's face a mere inch from my boot, I drop into a crouch. My injured hand still clutched tightly to my chest, my other slowly lowering the cleaver tip to the glass between my feet, I rest my hand on it.

"Did you miss me, Sidney?" I rasp, the question acrid on my tongue.

"Pl-please, I didn't know, I di-didn't know," Sidney snivels, choking on his own snot and saliva.

I curl my lip in disgust at his blithering.

"Didn't know what, Sidney?"

"That it was, th-that yo-you, you, it was you, I didn't know, please," he cries.

I look up at Charlie, standing sentry at the end of the table, the doors thrown wide open behind him revealing nothing but more darkness.

"You've been watching me, Sidney." I say coldly, my eyes still locked on my cousin. "And I don't like that. I don't like that at all," I tut, dropping my gaze back to him.

"Pl-please," he begs.

Great sobs racking his body, shockwaves of his suffering running through the glass tabletop, the vibration working its way through the soles of my boots.

"Do you know what that sounds like to me, Sidney?" I ask.

Lifting my cleaver from the table, I run the tip down the crown of his scalp, not pressing in, not drawing blood, nothing more than the ominous feeling of steel against skin.

"*Begging*," I state viciously, my blade finally breaking skin at the nape of his neck, just a nick in my anger but I pull back.

Control is important.

"Do you remember when *I* would beg, *Sidney*? When I would cry, kick and scream?"

I stand up, his head craning back to look up at me, his eyes red and pupils blown, tears and snot streaking down his shadowed face in equal parts.

"I'm sorry!" he wails, "I'm fucking sorry!" he spits in anger, hatred marring his words even in his faux apology.

I laugh, my head thrown back, my eyes shut tight, my blade wielding hand pressed against my concave belly. I laugh so hard tears stream down my face.

"Oh, Sidney," I chuckle darkly, "you don't have to say sorry. I don't need your fake fucking apologies, you piece of fucking shit. I really only need one thing from you."

I grin, my lips spreading wide like I carved a Chelsea fucking smile into my own cheeks. I quickly drop back down into a crouch. Running my blade beneath his jaw, I press, forcing him to twist his head up to face me at an almost unnatural angle. Dropping my lips so they ghost across his, our gazes' level.

"I just need to make you bleed," I whisper, carrying my last word, my breath fanning across his face.

He cries out as I stand abruptly, biting into my lip so hard I taste blood. I smash my booted foot down into his face. Something cracks, an unnatural wail falling from his lips as I kick his face again, this time I'm not disappointed. There's blood, his jaw sitting at an odd angle making me smile. I take a few steps back, kicking, smashing and stomping the china as I go, as if it were never there to begin with, until I'm stood over Max. I grin down at him, still seated in his chair, his hands balled into fists atop his thick thighs, encased in tight, black denim.

"Light some more candles if you would, Maxi," I beam, before twisting away and stepping down onto a chair, hopping from that to the floor.

Max moves, stealing the matchbox. Moving around the room, he starts by lighting the mirrored sconces. That'll give me enough light to really be able to enjoy myself.

"So, on a scale of one to ten, how much does your

foot hurt, *Sid?*" I ask as I walk along the length of the table.

Bypassing Charlie at the end, I step in front of him, sliding my hand still holding onto my knife, across his bare chest. His body rippling beneath my touch, I wink conspiratorially as I pass him. Rounding the table, I drop the tip of the cleaver to the glass, pressing down just hard enough to elicit that uncomfortable screeching scream of metal on glass. I groan in satisfaction at the sound as Sidney flails around on the tabletop like a fish out of water.

"Let's play a game, little Sidney. You ever played *Would You Rather?*" I ask innocently.

Genuine intrigue piquing my appetite, I cock my head. Surveying his squirming body as he claws his way to the edge of the table. Like an earthworm dried out by the scorching sun, trying to squirm his way back into the moist soil, desperately clinging to life.

His fingers curl around the edge, readying to heave himself over, just as Kacey appears. Grabbing a hold of him, flipping him over in one violent flash of movement. Sidney's body slamming back down onto the table, this time facing up, the air whooshing out of his lungs at the impact.

"Answer the fucking question," I order, my voice turning sinister.

I slam my hand down onto the table, the steel of my cleaver clattering against the smooth glass.

"Ye-yes, yes, I have," he whimpers, his words

slurred, his mouth slack, the desperate sound slowly soothing my soul.

"Good!" I beam.

Dropping my chin to the back of my hand resting on the tabletop, my knees bent in an almost crouch. I stare into his beady little eyes as he watches me warily.

"So, I'm going to ask you a *Would You Rather* question and you're going to answer! You're not supposed to think too hard on these answers, you're just supposed to go off instinct. So, if you don't respond quick enough, there'll be consequences." I raise a brow at him, still smiling my Cheshire grin, "you got it?" I ask excitedly.

He nods silently, sniffing hard. He blinks, trying to pull himself together, as much as is possible when you know you're at the mercy of expert predators.

"Relax! It's just a game!" I say flippantly as I stand back up.

Nodding at Charlie who moves opposite me. Sidney's eyes flick nervously between us.

"Okay! Here goes!" I tap the flat of the blade against my chin, my eyes rolling up to the ceiling as I think. "*Would you rather,* lose your fingers or your toes?" I hiss, Sidney whimpering at my words. "Quickly, Sidney! You're running out of time!" I pressure with a dark chuckle, my body trembling as I watch him squirm.

"Fingers!" he screams as much as is possible with his damaged face. "NO! NO! I meant TOES! *Fuck*! I want to keep my fingers!"

He lifts his head up in a panic. Just about to move his hand as my cleaver comes sailing down over his knuckles, cleanly severing his filthy fingers from his body. Blood splatters my face, hot, thick droplets against my cheek. Sidney's screams filling the air around me, my body thrums with excitement.

"Okay," I say casually, ignoring him clutching his fingerless hand to his chest. "*Would you rather* scream or cry?"

"What?" he blubs, his tear-streaked face paling irrefutably at my question.

"Come on, Sidney, you know the rules! Tick, tock!" I sing, clucking my tongue.

Sidney sobs deeply, the fear bubbling from his chest, his entire body erupting in full blown shivers. Blood pouring from his cleaved knuckles, a river of it running down his hand, trickling over the side of his throat, dripping onto the table beneath his head. I watch the steady drip start to pool, momentarily distracted. I zone out watching it until another scream tears from Sidney's throat, this time it's choked. My gaze snaps up, Charlie's fists wrapped around his arm, snapping his elbow back sharply. Bone crunching and cartilage popping, Charlie twists his arm even further, tugging on it sharply as he pops his shoulder free of its socket. Sidney screams in protest, his legs thrash-ing, his booted feet drumming against the table in a rather *irritating* fashion.

My vision tunnels in on his flailing legs, my hearing dying a death as I grip my knife tighter. Too loud, too *fucking* loud. Feet planted firmly, I twist my entire body back, raising my arm high above my head before bringing it down full force over his knee. I hear nothing as I twist my cleaver, nudging it free before I bring it down again. Ruthlessly slamming the steel into him, over and over. Lost to the sensation of brutal vengeance until a hand is suddenly gripping my shoulder. I rear back, twisting around, bloodied cleaver in hand as my eyes lock on rich verdant orbs.

I heave in a breath, my lungs burning as oxygen floods them. I blink, the room coming back into focus. Charlie's hand runs down my bare arm, his fingers dancing over the inside of my elbow before latching around my slim wrist. His rough fingers curling over mine, he lowers my arm. His eyes never leaving mine, he takes the crimson steel from me, placing it carefully down on the tabletop. His hold on me strong, grounding. My hearing returns, my rapid breaths the only noise in the darkened room. My shoulders drop, muscles relaxing as I exhale, slow and deep.

I glance over my left shoulder, a bloodied, carved corpse lies sprawled in the centre of my dining table. His face caved in, jagged lacerations slicing through every visible inch of skin. I inhale slowly, the stench of copper heavy in the air. I blink up at Charlie as he releases my good hand, blood saturating every part of me. Soaking through my string vest top, blood seeping into every crease of skin as it rolls down me.

I shiver as Charlie steps back, a rush of cool air separating us, a sardonic smile on his perfect pout.

Blood flecked skin and crimson soaked hair, he winks. Skirting around me and exiting through the double doors, the candlelight flickering as he slams them shut behind him. I turn fully to the other end of the room. Tilting my head to one side, I suck on my bottom lip, pulling it between my teeth as I eye my three monsters.

One with a demon so close to my own, dark, and depraved and *hungry*. His twisted insides a stark contrast to his golden god exterior. Hair the colour of the honey and eyes made of spun gold. His chin tipped down, those ravenous amber eyes drag up my body, inching up from my booted feet to my blood-streaked face. Kacey's nostrils flare as his eyes lock with my own. A million silent words passing between us. The corner of my mouth tilts up as I pop my lip free, and he groans. His thick fingers sliding over the bulge in his jeans, he squeezes, knuckles blanching white in the shadows, my thighs instinctively clenching.

Movement catches my eye, pulling my attention to the fearless predator in the room. His playful expression illuminating his coal-black eyes with fire. He shifts in his stance, his feet planted firmly, tight, lean thighs encased in black denim. A white t-shirt stretched across his muscled chest, the fabric pulling as his shoulders flex. I swallow as he smirks, that cocky, boyish grin, that melts me. My entire body thrumming with fire as he flicks up a pierced eyebrow, a silent question, a *dare*.

Do you want to play, baby girl?

I moisten my lips, my tongue sliding over my bottom lip then my top. I massage them together before switching my gaze to the devil inside the room. This one with bright narrowed eyes, dark brows furrowed together, fists clenched. Muscles in his thick forearms straining against tattooed skin. So much history, hurt and love.

Danger.

I swallow down all the things I want to say. My treacherous tongue momentarily choking me as I keep schtum, now's not the time to be unpacking that baggage. My demon instead deciding on a different approach.

"I want you to sit down, Maddox. I want you to keep your eyes on me, and I want you to be silent. Or you can leave now," I offer, my insides knotting at my statement.

Max stares at me for a long moment, already knowing he can't walk out now, or he'll never be welcomed back. Breaking our stare down, he slides a velvet chair back, leaving ample space between him and the table, before smoothly dropping into it. His legs spread wide, his posture relaxed, his open hands resting atop his thighs.

"Eyes on mine, Max," I instruct lowly.

And although I can see him spewing venom at me inside his head. Predictably some nonsense about not taking orders and how he hates being told what to do, *blah, blah, blah.* I smile as he keeps it in.

Closing the distance between us, I confidently step up to my two men. They stand shoulder to shoulder, Huxley only an inch or so shorter than Kacey. Their entire focus on me and me alone, I practically preen under such rapt attention.

"Take off your shirts," I purr.

My husky voice raspy with desire as they both effortlessly tear their contrasting t-shirts over their heads, the fabric falling to the floor.

I eye Kacey as I step into Huxley. One useless hand still clasped against my bosom, I rest the other against his bare chest. My fingers stroking crimson across his rich caramel skin, his pec twitching beneath my feather light touch. Kacey's demonic gold orbs watching my every movement. I dance my hand down Huxley's abs, my fingers just barely brushing skin, unpressured, unhurried. My fingers snag on his waistband, the rough denim harsh against my hot fingers, I pop his button free. Kacey bites down on his bottom lip, his nostrils flaring as he watches me slide down Huxley's zipper. The kiss of metal teeth on metal teeth the only thing occupying anyone's attention.

Huxley's breathing kicks up as I guide my delicate hand down the front of his tented boxers. Slipping my bloodied fingers between firm muscle and tight cotton. Circling my fingers around him, using the blood of my enemy as slick, I squeeze hard, pulling at his painfully erect cock. Huxley's hips buck forward, him hissing through his teeth makes my lips kick up as

Kacey's eyes narrow on my hand's hidden movements.

I tilt my head slightly, my hand still working Huxley over, neither man touching me.

But this is all about me.

My wants.

My needs.

My pain.

"What you think, Big Man?" I lick my lips, running my tongue seductively over my teeth. "Should we let his monster cock out to breathe a little?" I tease, my fingers closing as tightly as they can around Hux's dick, still hidden beneath the cotton of his black boxers.

Huxley rocks forward with my jerky movements. Kacey's eyes locked on mine, I slide my gaze over to the frustrated devil in the chair.

"What d'you think, Max?" I question, my gaze looking up through the shadows of my lashes.

My lips curving into a sadistic grin as he clenches his jaw.

"Nothing to say?" I taunt, secretly appreciating his rule following so far.

How far can I push him?

Kacey growls low in his throat, the sound making my thighs quiver. I release Huxley, slipping my hand up to the elastic band around his hips, curling my fingers over the fabric as I shove it down. Working him free, using my booted foot to pull his jeans and boxers the rest of the way down. Huxley kicks his boots off instinctively, kicking them and his clothes away, standing before me in all his naked glory.

And fuck me, *is he glorious.*

I turn my gaze to Huxley now, my full attention on my dark eyed demon. I flutter my lashes as my nipples brush against his chest. Tilting my head back, my lips against his clean-shaven chin.

"Kiss me," I murmur, my whispered demand being carried out instantly.

Huxley's teeth crash into mine, biting my tongue as he sucks it into his mouth. Luscious teasing licks and pulls as his pierced tongue devours my mouth. His long fingers curl into my waist, a dangerous pinch of pain as my hips slant against him, his erection grinding against me. He pulls away from my mouth, his lips latching onto my jawbone. Sucking a trail down to my chin, the tip of his tongue sliding across my bloody skin, the cool metal of his tongue bar making me shiver. Teeth nipping savagely at my clavicle, I arch into him, my good hand aimlessly reaching out to seek another piece of my soul.

Thick fingers grip mine; Kacey's firm hold tugging me free from Huxley. We both move with the motion, Huxley naturally curling into my back. His hands snaking around my front, his thumbs tucking themselves into the high waistband of my leggings. Kacey grunts as he presses in close, his hips undulating as he moves himself against me and I groan. My head drops back against Huxley's shoulder as he viciously marks my throat with his biting, claiming me for the world to see.

I'll wear his marks proudly.

Kacey takes my lips with his brash movements, he tears into my top lip, teeth splitting the skin, I cry out. The sound muffled by his mouth as he sucks and pulls my essence into his mouth. I let my eyes roll onto Max as I shove Kacey's jeans down with my good hand, his mouth never leaving mine as he gets the rest of his clothes off.

Max's eyes glint with rage. His fists clenched so tight; I can practically hear his knuckles cracking. But he doesn't waver, his eyes having not left mine once. A fire lights inside me, a blazing inferno as Huxley edges my leggings off.

Kacey drops to his knees, his thick hands tugging my boots off. He throws them away, dragging my leggings and knickers all the way down. I rest my good hand on his head as he lifts one foot then the other, freeing me of my bottoms. Huxley stands back a few inches, his hands working their way beneath my blood-soaked vest top. He fists the stringy straps, ripping them away from the rest of the cotton so I don't have to raise my injured hand. Huxley rolls the stretchy fabric down my flat belly, Kacey's thick fingers brushing his as he takes over. Rolling the stretchy fabric down the rest of my body, helping me step free of it and then his face is thrust between my thighs, his tongue running up the length of me.

Huxley twists my head to the other side of his

chest, ravaging the opposite side of my neck. His tongue bar rolling down my throat as Kacey's mouth latches onto my clit making me purr. The vibration of the sound sweeping through my tight body as they devour me. Huxley's hands, one on my hip, the other sliding up and under my chin, his fingers flexing on my throat, I groan. Kacey's tongue lashes my clit, my thighs quaking as he carelessly tosses my leg over his shoulder, widening me for him, his fingers digging painfully into my tattooed flesh as he eats me.

Slurping at my entrance, sucking and swallowing as I cry out. Huxley grips my throat tighter, cutting off the sound as Kacey's tongue delves inside me, his thumb working my clit as his tongue consumes me. A rogue orgasm rips through me like a tornado, only encouraging him to work harder. My overheated body slumped back against Huxley, the steel length of his huge dick digging into the base of my spine.

I want to feel him inside me.

On the cusp of my second orgasm, I forcibly kick my leg free from Kacey's shoulder. Shoving him back with my foot to his shoulder, he sprawls backwards with the surprise contact. Huxley stops attacking my neck, looking over my shoulder at his friend. Kacey looks up at me, his eyes rapidly searching mine, his chin shining with my arousal in the flickering candle-light. My body aches for more of their touch but this is about *my* control.

I walk down one side of the table, my good hand gripping Sidney's calf as I pass, dragging his butchered corpse with me until his body hits the floor with a thunk.

I hop up onto one of the chairs, using it as a step up onto the table. My bare feet padding through Sidney's blood and chunks of entrails. Kicking aside pieces of broken china as I walk the glass top like a catwalk. My hips sway, the dancing light casting shadows across me as I move, dainty light footsteps carrying me to the end. I stand tall, looking down at my two hell beasts, both gazing up at me like a goddess bathed in sin. Cocks standing to attention, eyes firmly on mine, I glance over to Max. Leant forward in his seat now, wrists atop his spread knees, his clothed torso hunched forward, hiding anything below his belt. I lick my lips, quickly returning my attention to my two faithful hounds.

I slowly drop to my knees at the edge of the table, the blood beneath them helping me slide my thighs wide as I stare between my two men. Arching back, my bare breasts pushed forward, my good hand reaching back for the cleaver. Sitting forward, I bring the tip to Kacey's chest, his breathing even. I press the blade in, breaking skin, forcing blood from the incision. I drag it through his flesh, a small, bloodied line dug into his skin. Placing the knife back down, settling it on the table between my thighs. My fingers curling over the lip of the table for balance, never taking my eyes from the gold ones staring back. I open my mouth, flattening my tongue, I run it up the valley of his abs. His sharp inhale making me hum in response as I fill my mouth with copper. I lap at the incision, sucking gently, my teeth nipping at the torn skin, all the while my eyes remain glued to his.

Kacey groans deep, his large hand cupping the back of my head. Encouraging me to go harder as he drags me tighter against him, filling my nostrils with his mint and earth scent. I swallow him down as he loosens his hold on me. Huxley massaging my thigh, his fingers kneading the muscle, his teeth grazing my shoulder, eliciting a low groan from deep in my chest.

My skin is on fire, my blood electric, body pulsing with need.

"Get up on the table, Huxley," I command, my gaze swinging to his as I recollect my blade.

Huxley moves up behind me, his legs coming around either side of mine, dangling over the edge. Not caring about the blood in the slightest. I'm his sole focus, nothing exists beyond this room.

It's just us.

Just *this.*

His palm splayed over my chest, he draws me back into him, I shift my hips. Backing up until his hot shaft is nestled firmly between my cheeks. His short exhale blowing across the side of my face.

"You're fucking beautiful, baby girl," he breathes into me making me shudder.

"Lay down, Huxley," I rasp, my husky voice just audible as I lock eyes on Max.

Demonic blue orbs stare at me hard, his eyes don't leave mine. He doesn't stare at my naked, sweat slicked body streaked in crimson, just my eyes. And he eats me alive with that fucking gaze.

Everything inside me thrums as Huxley flattens himself behind me, his knees over the table's edge, me sill nestled between his dangling legs. He grips my hips, lifting me up above him, helping me slide down his hot length. We groan in unison, Huxley shifting beneath me, my back to his front, his huge cock filling my cunt effortlessly. My hand clasping his knee, the new angle making me see stars, I start to ride him. His hand on my hip, the other threaded in the bottom length of my hair. He stays painfully still as I circle my hips, lifting up and dropping back down, earning a symphony of pleasure in response, I hum with delight. All of those sounds are for me, *because* of me.

I smile, sitting up as I ride Huxley. Beckoning Kacey forward with the curl of my finger, he obliges like I tugged on his leash. The look he throws my way makes me pant as I wrap my fingers over his shoulder. He leans in, his lips smashing into mine, my bleeding lip, his blood on my tongue. We wrestle, his tongue trying to stroke mine into obedience all while I continue to show the dominance. I bite down on his tongue, sucking it into my mouth, Kacey growling in response. My hand moves to his, our fingers linking together. I bring our joint hands to the table, pressing his palm into the sticky puddle of blood. Swirling our linked hands around in the mess. When his hand is fully saturated, I curl our joint fingers around his pulsating length. His cock hot and heavy beneath our hands, we groan as I slide our slick hands down his throbbing length.

This is what we've been waiting for. This union, something unholy and filthy and very fucking *right*.

Kacey's eyes roll into the back of his head as we work him over together. My thumb brushing over his pierced tip, swirling his pre-cum with the blood, I continue to fuck my other lover. I bounce up and down Huxley's thick cock, nipping and sucking at the cut on Kacey's chest. The one *I* put there.

I want to own him.

Releasing his fingers, encouraging him to continue to stroke himself, I retake my knife. Still grinding myself down on Huxley, heat a blazing inferno between my thighs. I bring my blade back up to Kacey's chest. Working the tip of the heavy blade into the top of his right pec, just beneath his collarbone. His eyes lazily opening so he can watch me work, I start to carve into him. Wielding my oversized blade with a steady hand, slowing the roll of my hips to accommodate my task. Clenching my pussy around Huxley, I carve one line and then another and another. Three deep lines sliced together in Kacey's chest. I lap at the wound, long, leisurely licks with the flat of my tongue. Proud of my artwork, I lean back, admiring the weeping 'K' carved into one of my soulmates.

"I fucking love you," Kacey rasps, his voice thick with arousal as his fist corkscrews over his cock.

My eyes lock on hit, nothing but adoration staring

back at me. It makes my tummy clench and my heart soar like a hundred birds suddenly taking flight. Tears prick the backs of my eyes as I gaze into his. Those golden orbs tear me down, building me back up with such strength I feel as though I can defeat anything.

In a snap movement, I grip his thick neck. Wrapping my fingers around his scarred throat I squeeze. He grunts, his head dropping forward, resting against my own, I cut off his breath. I can feel his throat trying to work beneath my palm, his pulse hammering against my slim fingers in protest as I thrust myself down on Huxley's thick shaft. My pussy tightening as he pushes me forward, his palm splayed on the bottom of my back. He slams up into me, ruthlessly pounding himself inside of me. The piercing in his tip hitting my cervix has me crying out. Kacey's face reddening without oxygen, he continues to fist his thick length, his hand working overtime, knuckles blanching as I start to come around his friend's cock. My fingers still clawing into his throat, I hold tight, the heel of my hand pressing into his windpipe.

Huxley roars beneath me, his hips slamming into me mercilessly, my knees knocking into the glass table beneath us. His grip on my hair arching me sharply backwards. The swift change of movements painful, the tips of my hair grazing his sweat slicked chest. My grip on Kacey intensifies as I try to keep myself stable one-handedly. My core tightening, Huxley's cum floods me, painting my insides, my pussy walls fluttering around him. I scream out my release, the guttural moan tearing from my raw throat. Quickly searching out my third demon, my eyes lock on Max's intense blue glare as I ride the wave of my orgasm at the same time Kacey erupts, his cum splashing over my cunt. I drop my hand from his throat, my breathing erratic.

Kacey cups my cheek, still gasping for breath he brings his lips to mine in a kiss so passionate it almost kills me. He steals my breath, his lungs sucking life from me, I give it willingly. Wanting him to have everything he needs from me, even my life.

Huxley's hand reaches between us, his palm on my belly as he slides himself up to sitting. His cock still seated inside me. He secures me between their protective bodies, our legs dangling over the edge of the table, Kacey standing between our knees. Their chests expanding rapidly as they seal me between them. Kacey pinches my face between his thumb and finger, tearing away from our kiss. He turns my head over my shoulder, my lips instantly meeting Huxley's. Hux grips the nape of my neck, his tongue pillaging my mouth with rapt violence. His piercing clanging against my teeth as his tongue strokes mine with long sultry licks. I shiver as their hands smooth over my blood slicked skin. Huxley smiles against my lips just as Kacey's teeth sink into my right shoulder.

I grit my teeth, my eyes pinging open. Heat rushing to the intense pain emanating from my shoulder as Kacey's jaw locks on my flesh. I squirm in their hold, Kacey not letting up, Huxley circling his arms around my waist. Banding me to him as Kacey bites into me so hard I see stars. This is who he is, animalistic, wild and raw. My golden eyed beast finally making me his. No one needs flowers, jewellery and proposals when you can have your lover's teeth scarred into you forever.

My attention wavering as I move past the pain. I feel myself sway. Coolness rushing through my veins as the pain becomes so unbearable, I bite my own tongue until I taste blood, but I don't tell them to stop because I want this.

I want *them*.

Their claiming.

When Kacey finally releases me, his tongue lapping at the hot trickle of blood running down my chest. I reach blindly for the cleaver, dragging it forward, the steel screeching over the glass. I shakily place it in Huxley's hand, knowing that biting is only for my primal mate.

"You too," I breathe, my eyes closed, head slumped back against his chest.

He hisses as I turn my head, my teeth teasing his nipple before he gently slips out of me. Spinning me in their hold, my back against Kacey's front, his arms automatically coming around me. I feel high, blissfully in control and sated. Content, happy, grounded.

Finally safe.

My monsters will always keep me safe.

Huxley tucks a knuckle beneath my chin, tilting my face up to his. His coal-coloured eyes locking onto my own, searching for consent. I smile. Reassuring him, I trace my fingers down his chest, pressing the pads of my fingers against his heart, I nod.

"Nox, toss my knife," Huxley rasps, his voice low.

He stretches out his hand, effortlessly catching what's thrown his way without looking. I look down through my barely open eyes just as Huxley flicks a pretty little blade free.

"Give me your lips," he orders and too tired to object, I lean in.

His lips press against mine urgently but delicately, like I'm made of glass, something special he wants to keep safe.

He tilts my head, arching my neck back into Kacey's chest, he brings the blade to my chest. I hiss through my teeth as he carves three little lines just below my left clavicle. He goes over them, and then again and then a third time before his thumb presses into his mark. Smearing the blood around, making my eyes snap open, I peer down at the dainty 'H' carved into me, the horizontal line at an angle.

"My turn," he whispers, placing his little knife into my palm.

I hum my approval, "lie back," I hush as he does as I say.

Leaning forward, Kacey's arms releasing me, I trail kisses down his abdomen, my tongue flicking out over his right hip bone. I lap at the spot I want to make my mark before working the blade into his deep caramel skin. Carving a two-inch cursive 'K' into him forever.

I collapse over his chest, his hand smoothing over the back of my head, his fingers working through my tangled silver mane.

"Shh," Huxley soothes, "close those beautiful eyes, Darlin', you're safe, we've got you," he whispers.

His orange, woody scent soothing me even further, his other hand stroking down my spine.

"Always, baby girl," he promises as I succumb to the darkness, letting my heavy lids finally close.

CHAPTER 7
KACEY

I step into the billowing steam, head tilted back, hot water hitting my face. My hands instantly pushing back through my blonde hair as the harsh spray soaks me. I run my hands down my chest, my fingers picking at the slightly scabbing 'K' carved into me. It's slashed through a large patch of shaded black ink, so it'll scar up nicely.

It's two-am. We all crashed for the rest of the day after our fuck session. Well, fuck session doesn't really do what we did justice, that makes it seem *less* when it was most definitely *more*. A bonding ritual, mating in blood, claiming with marks, cementing our triad of souls. Three fractured pieces, carving themselves into each other, joining together to make something fucking beautiful.

A macabre declaration of love.

My appreciation of our woman only skyrocketed that much more as I witnessed her butcher someone that hurt her. She ruthlessly took back a piece of herself. I don't think she realises all the things she screamed as she chopped him up into pieces. Blood coating her inked skin, her wounded hand tucked tightly into her chest, her grey-green eyes swirling like storm clouds. She was gone, disconnected, laser focused on her task. Every time the cleaver came down with a crunch-splat I smiled just a little broader. Watching my other half through the eyes of my demon was fucking spectacular.

I'm enthralled by her, completely and utterly in awe.

Every single part of me wanted to kill him myself, one of her *abusers*. Tag team with Nox on a little torture adventure weekend, we haven't done that in a while. But this wasn't my kill, wasn't my revenge, it wasn't me who was wronged and demanded penance.

It feels as though I've known her my entire existence. I'm pulled so rapturously into her orbit, I don't know how to do anything else but follow her. Let her lead, be her faithful disciple. Worship her, protect her, sit at her feet as her most servient hellhound. I want to submit, obey and watch her flourish with us. Because I'm confident we can do that, allow her to thrive spectacularly with us.

I want nothing more than to free this world of her tormentors, sink my teeth into their throats and tear them out. Carve through their chests, rip open their insides and procure their hearts. Present them to her on my knees, wait for her to pet my head and reward me with one of those coy, closed mouth, sex goddess smiles, her dimples carving up her cheeks. Tell me I've done a good job and then let me plunge my tongue into her cunt. Obviously, I'd have easy access, in my head Kyla-Rose is always naked. So am I. Always together and fucking. Sometimes I imagine her letting me make love to her. Where she lets me top her for once, be in control, push her and push her until she sobs my name, her nails clawing into my back. Her fingers sliding through my blood and painting it across her. Decorating her body in my essence, coating herself with my protection.

Kyla-Rose looks beautiful in blood. I thought I liked her in white. I think I prefer her in red.

I helped dispose of the corpse once she was carried off safely in Huxley's arms. Charlie, Nox, and I worked together in silence. Charlie only growled at Nox once during the process, which I'd call progress. Thing is, Nox just ignores it, expecting to be treated as the wrongdoer by this family, rightfully so, he fucked up. However, I found myself doing something I didn't expect. I growled back... louder, *angrier*, protectively. I bared my teeth and held his scowling green gaze.

Up until now I've been careful around Charlie Swallow, knowing he's the one I need to appease. He and Kyla-Rose have a *very* special relationship, one I'm sure lots of people don't understand. There aren't many lines drawn between them, there is nothing that is too far. They do, say and act together in a way that just fits them. They mirror each other in a million entangled ways, and I will never do anything to interfere in that.

Nevertheless, Nox is still my boy, my brother. He always will be. In our fucked up little family, we protect our own. And even if my demon snaps and hisses every time I catch those glassy eyes lost in memories, locked on our woman, I still love him. Despite what my green-eyed monster thinks. So, regardless of what happened in the past, he's here, he's present and he's not going anywhere.

Charlie held my eye as I growled back, him at the head of a rapist, me at the feet. We stood and squared off, it was a very long minute, but he backed off. Yeah, the infamous Charlie Swallow let it go, and I swear I saw the ghost of a smile on his lips as we hauled the corpse into the lift. Nox didn't say a word, but I definitely sensed shock, he thinks I'm pissed at him.

I'm not.

Okay, a *little* pissed.

But mostly I'm *jealous*.

Even thinking the word makes my stomach swirl with acid. I've never been jealous. Of anyone. I don't think I even really knew what it felt like until I thought about Nox's hands on my girl at sixteen. Having her for the first time and then leaving her. I wouldn't have left her; I would have wrapped her up in me and suffocated her with everything I was. She never would have taken another breath again without having to inhale my scent along with it. I would never have steered more than three feet from her for the rest of her life. I might not now. I wonder if it's possible to stich our hands together, so I never have to let her go.

She can't leave me.

My dick grows hard at the thought of always having her so close. Constantly in my eyeline, her creamy coconut scent taking up permanent residence inside my nose, her inked skin permanently touching mine.

My fingers curl around my cock, my hot shaft throbbing in my palm as I squeeze. My eyes close, thumb rolling over the head, massaging a drop of precum into the pierced tip as I tease back the foreskin. I bite my lip, back pressing into the cool tiles as I work myself. Imagining Kyla-Rose's silver hair wrapped around my split knuckles, her large eyes peering up at me, watering and innocent beneath those thick lashes. Her delicate neck arched back, my teeth marks raw in the space between neck and shoulder as I guide my steel cock between her swollen lips. My fist twists in a rapid motion, tugging my dick aggressively.

Thinking of fat tears leaking from the corners of her stormy eyes, my thumb wiping them free of her flushed skin as she hollows her cheeks and sucks me deep. Slipping my thumb into my mouth, sucking them down. I hum at the thought as I move my fist faster, squeezing tighter and tighter. My balls drawing up as I imagine her swallowing me down, her throat working tightly around my length.

I fist my cock, tugging my balls with the other hand, making me explode. I groan, cum hitting my belly, the hot water instantly washing it away as I release the iron grip on my dick. I slump against the tiles, a thin sheen of sweat at my temples. I step back under the spray, fully saturating myself in the heat, scrubbing the rest of my body with Kyla-Rose's girly citrus soap. I rinse off and hop out. Drying off, I scrub a towel down my body and pull on some loose grey joggers.

Leaving the bathroom, I peer through the darkness at the large bed. A huge dog either side like furry, muscled bed bars, and one big lump in the centre. Silver hair fanned out across the pillow, Huxley's arm thrown above his head. Kyla-Rose sprawled over his chest, the thin silk sheet barely covering them. His skin dark to her light. A beautiful fucking sight that immediately has my dick stirring again. I never thought I'd get turned on knowing my girl was also fucking my best friend, but here we are. Before I bounce into the bed and wake sleeping beauty, I head out into the darkened hallway, clicking the door closed behind me.

I wander into the kitchen, helping myself to some water, grabbing an apple as I exit. I make my way through the penthouse towards the large living room in the back. It has an entire wall made of glass and when we stayed here before I loved sitting by the windows and watching the world go by at night. Turning down the hall, the floor cold beneath my damp feet, I find light spilling out from the open archway of my destination. Twisting the cap off my bottle of water, I swig some back, condensation running down my fingers, the plastic creaking beneath my grip.

Nox sits on the piano stool, his bare back to me, gaze on the windows. The tall lamp in the corner is on, illuminating the room enough to see, but not too invasive for the middle of the night. I slump down in the far corner of the white sofa, it's a U shape, positioned so it focuses your view on the world outside. Nox looks at me without turning his head, his bright turquoise eyes flicking in my direction.

Neither one of us speaks. A slightly uncomfortable silence. My demon claws at me, my skin prickling. I think back to earlier, he watched me mark Kyla-Rose as mine, but she wanted him there, in the room while she was vulnerable, that screams trust. Her eyes locked on his multiple times while Hux and I gave her pleasure, let her wrap us around her taloned fingers and take charge. She needed it, retaking control.

She looks at Huxley sometimes, and I can practically hear her silent questions. She wants to know how he does it, finds no fear in anything, dives into shit headfirst without an ounce of hesitation. Never phased by anything, it's not that he's unafraid, it's that he'll fight tooth and nail to protect what's his and doesn't let fear hinder him. It's admirable, it's one of the reasons I love him.

Even when I was tangled in razor wire after the

explosion. The hot desert sand burning beneath my back, sharpness in my neck making my breathing stutter, he wasn't afraid. He knew, he fucking *knew* he was getting me out of it. His determination is unlike anything I've ever known. It's how I know he'll be able to help our girl through this, he'll pull her through the nightmare, show her how to trample out her fear and use it as a weapon. Control it, twist it into something she can wield.

"She needs to go to the hospital," Nox's deep rumble cuts through the silence.

His body turned towards me, one hand resting on the ivory keys, the other atop his thigh. Anger spikes sharply in my chest, hitting me out of nowhere as I dig my canines into my apple. Juice sluicing down my chin, I slurp the syrupy liquid from my fingers. Wiping the back of my hand over my face, I slowly crunch the fruit.

"*You* don't tell me what to do," I tell him slowly, the husk in my voice cutting. "She's not your concern."

"Bollocks, that's fucking bullshit and you know it," Nox growls, his finger pointed at me from across the room, his abs rolling as he grinds his teeth. "I'm just as concerned for her as you are."

A smirk on my lips, I roll my eyes.

"Oh really?" I scoff, a light laugh slipping through. "That why you left her, you piece of fucking shit."

I raise a brow as I tear another piece of flesh from

my apple, the sweetness filling my mouth as my mood sours.

"You *fucked* her, you *left* her, you didn't go back. You let her get taken away from you, because you're such a safe place, aren't you, *Maddox*. So reliable and protective, you tossed her to the fucking dogs, you're supposed to be the goddamn wolf," I sniff.

My nostrils flaring, I lean forward. Forearms resting across my knees, apple in one hand, the other clenched into a fist. I glance up from my tattooed feet, a hammerhead shark on one, a scorpion on the other. My eyes narrowing in on him beneath my brow, he stares back.

"It wasn't fucking like that, and you know it. You know I'm not like that."

"Never leave a man behind, that's what you instilled in us. What about young, damaged, *vulnerable* little girls, Maddox? Those are free game, are they? Let them be torn up and destroyed, picked apart by vultures, but you've always got your boys' backs, is that it?"

"What the fuck is wrong with you, Kace? I was fucking eighteen, I made a mistake! I never did that to fucking hurt her!" he throws himself up from his seat.

I force myself to relax back.

"Why are you goading me? You've got her, I haven't, what is your fucking problem?"

He slams his hands against his thighs in frustration. A vein throbbing in his temple as he pushes his hand through his thick, dark hair.

There he is.

"You," I state calmly, swallowing another chunk of apple. "*You're* my fucking problem, Nox."

He blinks, slowly, pushing his hand back through his hair, the black strands sticking up all over the place as he stares at me. I mask myself, refusing to let him see everything I feel. But I must not do a great job, for one second he's staring at me like he wants to knock my teeth out and the next he's smirking. A tiny tic at the corner of his mouth, his top lip curling before a full-on cocky smirk takes over.

"You're jealous," he huffs a laugh.

The words prickle me, like poison burying beneath my skin, irritation cold and icy working through my veins.

"Kacey, you're jealous and you've actually *got* the girl, you're so fucking dumb, man," he chuckles, the sound so dismissive, I feel the growl starting in my chest.

Squeezing the apple in my hand so hard it bursts into pieces, fruit and juice scattering across the floor as I fly up from my seat. A snarl escapes my bared teeth, my chest rising and falling rapidly as I work to keep myself calm. It's one thing to admit to myself that I'm jealous, it's quite another for him to say the words out loud, manifesting them into reality.

I don't like feeling vulnerable, this isn't me at all, but I've also never felt competition with one of my brothers before either, especially not over a woman. But then, Kyla-Rose, she's so much more than that.

She's the other half of me, completes me, holds me together and calms my demon, petting him into submission. I've never felt so protective of someone before. I feel this innate need to curl my thick arms around her, pull her in so tightly to my chest that we merge together. Keep her barred inside a prison made of bones, my life the only thing she needs. There would be no safer place for her than with me. I can keep her safe, I *will* keep her safe, even if it's from herself.

Nox squares off, legs spread, shoulders raised, his fingers flexing, curling and uncurling into fists by his sides. His square jaw ticking, teeth grinding.

Just two lions fighting over the top female, both needing to rut into her after tearing the other's throat out.

I take a step closer, my demon demanding I prowl, we circle each other like we do when we spar in the ring. His practised stance matching mine as we face off in the living room, a single light on, the city at my back. The deep indigo sky casting shadows, clouds hiding the bright glow of the moon.

"You know what, you should be jealous, Kace," Nox taunts.

His full lips twisted into that ugly smirk, the one he uses when he knows he's already bested his enemy.

"I will take her from you," he shrugs, "from you *both*, and she'll come willingly. She was born for me, built for me, we slot together perfectly, everything about her sings to me. Her soul is the other half of mine. Always has been, always will be. She may be *fucking* you, she may even lie and say she *loves* you, she may even believe it," he snorts a laugh and I flex my fists. "But it's always been me, *will* always be *me.* You're just a big body to warm her bed and satisfy her cunt. You know that when it finally comes down to it, because it will, she'll choose me. I'm branded in her very essence. Her and I are the fucking finish line, we're everything you'll never have together, because *you're. Not. Me.*"

And then I lunge.

My body springs from the floor, leaping at him, my fist sailing into his smug face. His head snaps to one side as I smash my fist into his jaw, once, twice, three times. And then he flies right back at me, his knuckles pounding into my face, my top lip splitting, blood filling my mouth. I lick it off, swallow it down, it only adds fuel to the fire. Hooking my foot behind his leg, I tug him forward, but he doesn't falter. He grips my bicep with one hand, smashing his forehead into my nose. As he pulls away, I slam my fist into his ribs and headbutt him right the fuck back. Blood pours from our faces as I shove him, he goes willingly, separating himself from me, we continue to circle one another.

"How's it feel, Kace? Always being second best? Never quite good enough, are ya, man? Kyla-Rose wouldn't even take you this time without throwing your fucking wingman in the mix," he laughs, the sound accompanied by a slight gurgle at the back of his nose.

I could cause him more damage than he ever could me. I held back, but he's riling me up and I feel my control slowly snapping. I breathe through my mouth, blood trailing down the back of my throat.

"I'm her fucking beginning, middle and end. *You?* You're a temporary bus ride, like she wanted to get the train, but the service was interrupted so she had to *settle*," he hisses the final word and I snap.

I rush him. My shoulder slams into his stomach, knocking the wind from him. He grunts, his hands fisting my shoulders as I lift him up and slam him down. My body crushes his, his head smacking the floor as we drop down. My thighs either side of his, I straddle him, pummelling my fists into everywhere I can. He blocks me more than retaliates but I'm that much bigger than him, broader, taller, stronger. I see red, beating every inch of him I have access to until his whispered words cut through my rage.

"She doesn't love me, man. She's just not that goddamn stupid, Kace."

I rear back, breathing hard, my knuckles and face bleeding, my chest heaving as the red mist evaporates. I look down at my brother, his face busted, blood smeared across his chest. I climb off him, rolling onto my back beside him.

"You didn't mean any of that, did you?" I ask, already knowing the truth.

He chuckles, groaning at the pain in his side from the action.

"You know I didn't," he tells me honestly. "You feel better for that, man?" he asks me, and I snort.

"No, I'm gunna get my arse beat tomorrow for busting up your pretty face, you arsehole."

I roll my eyes, turning my face to look at Nox.

"Why'd you do that?"

"'Cause you needed it," he shrugs casually, turning his head to face me. "You're my brother and you're hurting. I *know* you. Plus, I deserve it," my former platoon leader tells me earnestly.

I slump against the floor heavily, my body going limp, melting into the wood.

"Don't take her away from me," I hush, vulnerability dripping from every word.

Because he could, if he wanted to, I know it.

Kyla-Rose Swallow and Maddox Sharpe's story is not finished.

Not by a long shot.

"I would never," he growls back. "I couldn't if I wanted to," he states sharply, giving me his full attention. "You actually think her love for you is that fickle? She's got her claws in you so deep, she's practically a piece of you. She's not going anywhere you're not."

I think on that for a moment, staring at the white ceiling, both of us breathing hard.

"You think she really feels that way?" I ask softly.

I've only ever had these sorts of talks with my brothers, never felt at ease with anyone else. Feels weird to be talking about someone, who has at some point in her life, been in love with us both.

"I know she does," he rasps almost sadly. "That girl loves with her whole being, she doesn't do anything by halves, that's why my gran loved her so hard. It's why I- why I *did*. She's easy to love, easily loves others, the world isn't kind. I never wanted it to hurt her the way it did, the way it *does*."

"We'll find the rest of 'em, hunt 'em down, and catch whatever other cunt is harassing her," I promise, my voice a growl.

"What other?" he queries, his brow drawn, blood seeping from his eyebrow.

"She got a *note*. She also said she saw someone watching her, two someones actually," I tell him about the warehouse, and Sidney being the guy in the car park when she was out with Frank. "I don't know, Hux and I have been keeping an eye on things with the boys. She's had two other notes sent, a bunch of beheaded roses," I confess, swiping my hand over my face, twitching my nose as I touch the split bridge of it.

"I take it she doesn't know about the rest," he asks with a raised brow, I shake my head in answer. "She's not gunna like you keeping shit from her, man," he groans, shifting up onto his elbow, he pinches the bridge of his nose.

"I know, I was gunna tell her, but, well, it was Charlie's idea. Apparently, he wanted to try and deal with it, so that Jacob didn't witness any more of her *moments*. He was pushing to have her committed last week. Don't wanna give him anymore ammo. Jacob's quite good at strongarming his dad apparently, although I can't see Dee agreeing to that."

"Unless he thinks it's in her best interests, to keep her safe," Nox adds.

His eyes staring off, lost in thought as I sit up, my leg bent so I can rest my arm atop my knee.

"We need to keep her safe, Nox, she won't survive in a place like that. I'm not putting her there. I don't want her drugged up and out of it," I snarl possessively, my top lip curling at the thought of being separated from my mate.

"Too easy for an enemy to attack. She'd be unprotected, vulnerable to a hit, anyone could take her out in the blink of an eye. Patient records are not really the *closed* things everyone says they are, we know that, look at the work we do. How long does it take Hux to hack a hospital record? Five, maybe ten minutes?" Nox sighs. "But we do need her hand fixed, Kace, *she* needs it fixed."

I nod in agreement, "I think Huxley's going to work on it, he's good at talking to her about shit that scares her."

"She worships him," Nox comments, his eyes rolling to meet mine. "She used to be afraid of everything when we were younger. Huxley's afraid of nothing, I see the appeal."

"He has a certain way with her, he worships her right back."

"Mmm, as I said, easy to love," Nox shoulders me with a smirk and I snort.

"How do you think Hux is gunna be tomorrow? Think this has dragged shit up for him?" Nox asks after a few quiet minutes. "I get worried about him when stuff like this is brought up," he says thoughtfully.

I contemplate his question for a moment, we both know our brother, and how he processes.

"Maybe, but he's been fine all the other times. He knew right off the bat someone had put his hands on her though, that first night at the house. Huxley just *knew*," I roll my eyes over to Nox. "He told me to be careful with her, they didn't speak for more than five minutes, but he felt something."

Nox looks over at me, his movements slow and cautious. I let him ponder for a moment, there's a lot of trauma here. Things we'll need to pick through carefully if we want a future together without secrets. But then, we've always been good at working our way through minefields.

"He'll tell her," Nox comments quietly, "she'll understand better than anyone else ever could, he needs that. He's got that in Kyla-Rose, he just needs to be honest."

"He's not going to add to her stress, he's too self-less. He'll tell her when the time's right." I nod. "We mustn't rush him, let him find his own way."

Silent agreement between us, both bruised,

153

bleeding and lost in thought. We watch the low winter sun steadily make its first dull appearance.

We all have shit to work through, but I truly believe Kyla-Rose could help heal us all. And by heal, I mean understand. She can't fix us, just like we can't fix her. I don't want to *fix* her, just like I don't want to be fixed. But slotting our four fragments together, no matter how broken and abused the shards are, could push us all further towards happiness. Whatever that may be for us, whatever it means, I think it starts with her.

CHAPTER 8
KYLA-ROSE

I groan, flipping onto my back. Brute's throaty snoring in my ear, his heavy paw pressed into my side. I elbow his belly, trying to shuffle him over so I can get a little breathing space. When he doesn't shift, I grunt, cracking an eyelid to find his dark brown eyes already on mine.

"You're a lazy lump," I grumble even as I nuzzle myself further into his giant furry body.

This is why I'll always have big dogs; you can't cuddle something the size of a gerbil this way. Brute snorts over the top of my head, grunting in that sleepy, *'I've just been disturbed and now I'm uncomfortable,'* kind of way and I smile against his warm chest. Flinging my good arm over his back, slipping my fingers beneath his gold chain, I scratch my nails into his neck.

"You're such a good boy, Brute," I tell him. "Even

if you do take up too much space," pressing a kiss to his nose, I shuffle and sit myself up.

I stifle a yawn as I continue to scratch him, his long legs stretching out as the sheets pool around my waist. He nudges my other elbow with his big head, knocking my injured hand up into my chin. I've been clutching it to my chest for a few days now, nursing it like a wild animal would a sore foot. I know that's not healthy, but I just don't like people touching me. I've never had good experiences with doctors.

I climb out of the bed. A black t-shirt I wasn't wearing when I went to bed last night, hitting the tops of my thighs. I pull the fabric out with my fist, bringing the soft, well-worn cotton up to my nose and suck in a deep lungful of oranges.

Huxley.

After brushing my teeth, and properly washing last night's make up off, yeah, yeah, I *know*. But don't lie and say you've never done it; we both know that you have. I head straight for the kitchen, knowing that's exactly where I'll find at least one of my boys. I make my way through the sunlit apartment, the heavy blinds, curtains and drapes pulled open wide, the hazy morning sun flooding my darkened halls with natural light.

The wood warmed beneath my bare feet feels nice, but it doesn't feel like it's Christmas in a couple of days. It's Christmas Eve tomorrow and my house feels like it's never even heard of the damn word. There's no stubby little tree with personalised ornaments and mint, striped candy canes on every other branch. No coloured lights tacked up around the ceiling. It feels like it could be any other day. It makes me miss the boys' home and I've only been back here a single night. That's probably the real difference. The boys' house is a *home*, my house is just, well, a house. It isn't cosy, it's like a gothic prison tower block and I suddenly think I actually kinda hate it. The dogs would love a garden, even a small one like Kacey, Huxley, and Max's.

"Jesus H Christ, you look like you had a fight with an octopus," Jacob's very unwelcome voice chastises as soon as I enter *my* kitchen.

I'm assuming he's referring to my hickey covered jaw and neck. I am absolutely peppered with bruises and teeth marks, but I'm struggling to find a fuck to give.

I like it.

Jacob's completely taken over the marble top peninsula, his large, obnoxious newspaper, *'The Independent'* laid open before him. Half-drained cup of tea to his left, a plate scattered with toast crumbs to his right, a bakery box opposite his paper. His thick forearms folded over one another where he's sitting on a stool.

"You knowww," I hum, dragging out my last word. "You don't *have* to stay here. You could move in, sayyy, four floors down and claim your own space. It's been vacant for you for like three years," I comment casually.

Silently wondering where he stayed last night because it certainly wasn't here.

He's always been reluctant to *move in*. Wants to be so far removed from the family business, he couldn't possibly slum it here with the likes of us. You know, the people who love him, regardless of job titles.

Pulling the fridge open, my hip propping the door from closing on me. I search the shelves for a little pot of vanilla yogurt that I quickly realise I won't find, because Huxley isn't the one who stocks this house. I frown, sighing as I come away empty handed, letting the door swing shut behind me. I was falling into a dangerous routine, sleeping at night, eating yogurt in the mornings. *Scary shit*. Domesticated life is so far removed from my idea of what I want that I can't believe how easily I seem to have slipped into it.

I used to love having Jacob stay here whenever he was back from his travels. He used to fill my head with exciting stories. I for sure think Jacob's a hero, but lately all he does is reprimand me for behaviour I'm not willing to change.

Behaviour I *won't* change.

Not for Jacob, not for anyone.

Regardless of what he thinks.

"I need to be here to keep an eye on you," he murmurs casually, like I need parenting.

I lean back against the fridge doors as he finally looks up from his paper.

"What is that supposed to mean?"

I frown, my brow dipped low, my lips pursed. I do not feel very happy with that comment, like, *at all*.

"You're not my father, Jacob," I inform him flippantly.

He's my oldest cousin. Although, our relationship paints him as more like my big brother. He's always made sure I'm all right, but he's never actively treated me quite like *this* before. Like a naughty child, one who won't follow instruction or a wild horse that can't be broken. I'll never be one to wear a saddle, my spirit cracked and tamed, allow a harness to be tightened around my snout and tied off to a post.

I'm a Swallow through and through, wings spread wide, wind in my feathers, the sun on my back, soaring through endless blue skies.

Wild and free.

But most importantly *free*.

"It means you cannot follow a simple instruction; you were told no working."

My mouth opens to interrupt, to tell him that *Sidney* was not a *job*. That Sidney was all about personal gain for me. Hacking up one of my rapists felt like the most enrapturing experience I could have ever hoped for. I don't know why I waited so long to do it. Sidney stalked me in the shadows at a coffee shop, made everyone think I summoned him from the deepest recesses of my mind. Made me start to think I'd imagined his presence. I didn't, he was there, watching me, I didn't ask him why. I didn't care why at the time. I definitely should have gotten that out of him first, still, where there is one rat there is always another. It wasn't a wasted experience. I feel *light* this morning. Despite the throbbing pain in my hand.

Plus, the event that followed afterwards was nothing short of legendary. I will never forget that for as long as I live. Couldn't if I wanted to.

I'm branded.

Not just my skin with fresh scars, my soul is singed too. Steeped in blood, carnage and wicked declarations of the darkest kind of love.

But Jacob holds a single finger in the air between us, hushing my rebuttal before it even begins.

"You were told," he begins, his bright emerald eyes locking onto mine as he starts to count out points on his hand.

His eyes are slightly different to his brothers', they've all got emerald green, pure and thick and solid in colour. Whereas Jacob's have a heavenly hint of glacial blue in them, a ring right at the very centre, circling his pupil. Albeit beautiful, it makes him feel *cold* sometimes.

"No jobs, no stakeouts, no enforcing, no plotting, no kidnapping." His eyes narrow on me at that one.

His strong jaw clenching as he holds his hand up in the air, his comments currently tallying five on his thick fingers and thumb.

"And certainly, no *killing*," he hisses the word like it burns him to force it through his teeth, like he's so far beyond that.

Never one to get his hands dirty, is he, our Jacob.

"And so, you will be punished for not following orders. You know how these things work, Kyla-Rose, you should have followed instructions. But then, we both know that's why you find yourself in these situations so often."

He pauses, tutting as he drops his gaze back down to his paper, essentially dismissing me. I half turn away, my back mostly to him, ready to storm out of the kitchen to cool down. I don't want to always argue with him, despite what he thinks, when he mutters beneath his breath.

"Like mother, like daughter."

I spin around sharply, gaping at him for a long second, my mind completely reeling, is this some sort of *joke*. What the fuck is happening here? Who even *is* this man?

"Um, excuse you, arsehole, firstly, *punished?* What the fuck is this shit?!" I shout, slamming my good hand down on the counter between us. My fingers splayed wide as I stare him down.

"'*Like mother, like daughter*', huh?" I mock.

Steam practically billowing out of my ears, my temperature skyrocketing as he frowns up at me.

"Who the fuck do you think you are? You don't even work for Dee! Now you're here, sitting in *my* fucking house, eating *my* fucking food, like *you* own the goddamn place! I don't know what sort of fucking authority you suddenly think you have over me, but you have *none*, Jacob. *Fucking none*. No one fucking controls me, not anymore. So don't you dare come in here, reading *me* the rules, telling *me*, what I can and cannot do. That's not your fucking job!" I scream, my rage flaring so hot, I see red.

"Why are you losing your temper over something so trivial, just take your punishment, whatever that may be, learn your lesson, do better next time. It's really not that hard, *is it?* Stop being so sensitive," he tilts his head, looking at me like I'm some sort of idiot. "As for the mother-daughter comment, where the hell did that come from?" he scoffs dismissively, once again returning his attention to his fucking paper.

I turn in temper back to the fridge, pushing down the intense need to wrap my fingers around his throat. I grasp the door handle instead, pulling it open and slamming the door closed, over and over and over. The suction on the door makes me rip it open harder and harder with every tug. My breath panting through my lungs, I finally fling it shut and turn back to him. My finger pointing in his face as Nox and Kacey appear in the open space behind Jacob, but we both ignore them, this is between us.

"You fucking *what? Sensitive?*" I hiss. "You throwing my *dead* mother in my face is me being *sensitive? 'Like mother, like daughter'* you said! I fucking heard you."

I blink at him, suddenly at a complete loss for words as he stares at me with confusion. My vision blurs as I heave in short, shallow breaths.

"I think this is a slight overreaction," Jacob sighs, like *I'm* the one testing *his* patience. "Do you need something to calm you down, Kyla-Rose? I'm sure you must be in a lot of pain with that injury."

A blonde brow slowly tracking up his forehead, ignoring my comments on his hushed bullshit. He folds his hands together, elbows resting on the counter, chin sitting on his knuckles.

"I can prescribe you some pain killers. Have you been smoking weed? You'll knock yourself out with too much of a mixture," he offers, like his words hold any weight, as if they mean *any-fucking-thing* to me at all.

I stand back, shaking my head, my fingers raking through my long hair.

"Who even are you?" I ask, my face pulled into a mask of confusion. "You cannot just pretend like I didn't hear you! MY MOTHER, JACOB!" I scream, pulling on my hair so hard, strands snap and curl around my sweat slicked fingers. "You sit here, so high and mighty, like a fucking *king*. You won't get your hands dirty, but you'll comment on my fucking *mother*?"

"Kyla-Rose, I didn't say anything about your mother," he says quietly, calmly, squinting at me slightly, a different expression, a different face.

No snarl in his lip, no malice in his tone, no fucking guilt on his face.

What the hell is happening.

"Don't lie," I scoff, shaking my hand out to untangle the hair from around my fingers. "You can't just say something like that and then pretend you didn't when I call you out on it."

"Kyla-Rose," Jacob says softly, in that caring brotherly love way he has when he pacifies me. "I swear to you, I didn't say that," he blinks at me slowly, allowing me to see his truth.

And it is, the truth, he opens himself up to me, letting me see.

He didn't say that.

I frown harder, my lips parting slightly as I attempt to regulate my breathing.

I heard it, I heard him.

"You- that's wha- but you said that. When I turned to leave, that's what you said, J," I stutter.

My gaze flicking over his head to my loyal golden-eyed hellhound and the blue-eyed devil of my past, standing sentry like they're just waiting for my word. Whatever it may be, they'll action it, such loyalty, even though Max couldn't do that for me before, him standing here now means something.

"You did say that," I whisper, my gaze dropping to my feet.

I sense Jacob shift, his stool feet sliding back, a shadow slowly approaching as I stare at my toes. Thorns and wilted roses twisting over the tops of my feet. Winding their way up my ankles where they start to meet small swallow birds, all of it intertwining together. My black nail polish chipped on my big toe, just the top corner but enough for me to notice.

A big hand slowly appears in my vision before

dropping onto my shoulder, it's warm and large and comforting. It covers my whole shoulder, making me feel even fucking smaller than I already do inside my head right now.

"Have you taken anything this morning?" Jacob asks me gently.

Referring to his ridiculous cocktail of painkillers that I'm most definitely not touching. His other hand cupping my check, a firm but comforting pressure on my jaw. His thumb smoothing a circle beneath my eye.

"Look at me," Jacob requests and I swallow.

Lifting my face to meet his gaze. He tries hard not to frown. I try hard to keep my walls up.

"Let me give you something," he murmurs. "Just something to let you get some proper rest, yeah?"

I find myself nodding absently. Even as he releases my face and disappears down the hall, I can still feel the heat from his hand. I'm not hearing voices. They never sound like Jacob, they usually sound like, well, *me*. And I don't hear them *out loud*, even when I freak out, I know it's in my head. The words almost mock me, the whispered uttering that sounds so familiar and real, I don't know how I'll stop thinking it.

Like mother, like daughter.

"You okay, Sweetheart?" Kacey coos from across the room.

Like I'm his most fragile possession, not like I'm his blood slicked queen, crushing skulls with my boots and chopping up rapists with cleavers. Like I'm that dainty, crystal glass, swallow bird bauble on our Christmas tree.

I get that needling in my chest again, that prickle of pain and if I hadn't already got a hand clutched to my chest, I'd want to rub my knuckles over the sharpness there. Every time I do something to help me take back a little power, retrieve a tiny piece of myself that was lost to the wind, something else happens leaving me feeling even more deflated. Dejected, depleted. I sigh out a deep breath, just as Huxley enters the room like a whirlwind.

"Darlin', we need to talk," he spits out.

Like he's built up the courage to say this part but dreads the next, wants to get the words out as quickly as he can so it's over quicker too. Huxley's fearless, he never needs to find courage, he has it in endless amounts. It oozes from his pores, glints in his coal-black eyes, seeps through with his flirtatious words and cheeky winks. Which is why my spine instantly straightens, everything in me flips into high alert.

I ignore Kacey's questioning. Max looks at Huxley like he could strangle him. Kacey drops his head back, muttering something like *give me strength*. Which is when I suddenly realise just how fucked up Max and Kacey's faces are. Before I can even open my mouth to question them, Hux is moving toward me. grasping my hand in his warm one, long fingers wrapping around my own.

"Come with me," he says, already leading me out of the kitchen.

He drags me down the hall into the rear living room that we seem to use for everything. It's one hundred percent the view I'm telling you.

Huxley sits me down on the sofa, squatting before me, crouching down low so I have to look down at him. His big hands resting on my bare knees, his eyes studying my face for a moment. His gaze surveying the bruising, the teeth marks, and my crumpled hair. I saw it in the mirror when I brushed my teeth, it looks like a haystack that's been sucked through a tornado, but I just didn't care. Huxley reaches up, his long fingers running through the tangled strands, carefully picking through some of the knots.

"I want to take you to the doctor," he starts and my breath hitches.

"I don't want to go to the doctor," I say flatly, instantly.

My response coming automatically, it doesn't matter if I need to or not, I just can't go.

"Jacob can fix me," I add quietly.

"Jacob isn't a specialist hand surgeon, we've been through this, Darlin'. Don't you wanna be able to stab people with both hands again?" he smiles teasingly.

One of those slow sexy winks I like so much gets thrown my way and the bats that reside in my tummy take flight. Yeah, bats, not butterflies. I'm too dark in my core for anything requiring light to survive.

"Huxley," I say quietly.

Swallowing past the clog of emotion in my throat, trying to be as honest as I can be.

"I really don't want to go to the doctor. I don't want to be alone with strange people and I really, really *can't* be put under," I almost whisper, my eyes hurting with the searing heat at the back of them.

Huxley stares at me for too long. His endless dark pits, the colour of the night sky, boring into me, he doesn't even blink as he looks up at me. Like he's diving far deeper than anyone is safe to. My soul draws in, curling in on itself like a tiny, grey wood-louse trying to protect itself as Huxley's impenetrable gaze devours our every secret.

"How about," he starts gently, licking his luscious peach-coloured lips, his tongue piercing glinting with the action. The click of it against his teeth as he flicks it in thought. "I take you to my family's doctor, just you and me. I'll stay with you the whole time, I'll be in the surgery with you, if that's what you need. I'll even fuck up my afro with one of those fucking shower cap hairnet things," his eyebrows dance like wiggly cater-pillars, the smirk building slowly as the corners of my lips curl up slightly. "There's my girl," he hushes, leaning in, pressing his soft lips to mine.

Our kiss is a soft, delicate thing, such a contrast to the way he attacked my face last night. I mean, I'm wearing the evidence of said devourment like a shiny purple collar this morning.

"When?" I ask once he's broken our kiss, leaving me wanting more, I always want more of Huxley.

Already knowing he's booked it all in, that's why he could tell me he'd stay with me throughout the whole thing with such confidence, because it's already fucking scheduled. You have to pick and choose your battles in this life; this is one I'm waving a white flag at. I'm not arguing with him when I know it *is* what's best for me. I really need my fucking hand.

"Thought we'd get Christmas out the way first, so, twenty-seventh. They'll do the scans, x-rays, the whole assessment, give you your options or talk you through whatever and then surgery, *if* it's needed. If you prep the day before they'll do it all then and there. You've got a private room, I can stay with you, we'll station people you trust on the doors, entrances, exits, fire escapes. Whatever you need. And I won't leave your side. At all, the entire time. You pee, I pee," he beams, and I snort, knowing he's absolutely serious.

"You got this all figured out then, huh? Thought this was just a friendly chat," I cock a brow, trying and failing to hide my smile.

"Shut it, you," he chuckles, rising out of his crouch and locking his long, lean arms around me.

His face in my hair, he inhales, sucking in a deep lungful of me and him, because I really only smell like his t-shirt. I press a kiss to the side of his neck, my good arm looped around his lower back. I relax into him, settling into his strong embrace.

"I love you, Hux," I whisper almost breathlessly, because fuck, I really do love him.

"And I love you, Darlin', so fucking much."

CHAPTER 9
KYLA-ROSE

Christmas Eve

"**W**hat in the fuck are you doing?" Max bellows the following afternoon as he steps into *my* living room.

He's staying here with us, and I'm not really sure why, but I haven't asked him to leave, and he hasn't told us he's going to. I guess until I decide how I feel about it, he's staying. So…

He stops in the open archway, his black booted feet at my eye level, black, skin-tight, ripped jeans clinging to his muscular calves. I swallow down my mouthful of vanilla milkshake, letting the paper straw pop free from between my lips. I lick over my bottom lip, slowly raising my book up towards the ceiling, my thumb pinched between the pages, so I don't lose my place. Tilting my head farther to look up at him. My neck twisting uncomfortably as I take in his crisp white t-shirt and scuffed, black leather jacket. His knuckles blanching as he clenches and unclenches his inked fingers, his left hand branded with *me*.

The place where his thumb and index finger meet, an old-school style swallow is tattooed, the rest of his hand a large, shaded rose. Thorns wrapping themselves around the rest of his pale skin, down his fingers, up his wrist, disappearing from my perusal inside his leather sleeve.

"Oh! Welcome home, darling! You sound like you've had a wonderful day!" I mock, my lips morphing into a petty, sarcastic smile as I blink slowly at him.

"Why the fuck are you sitting like that?" he growls, the sound low and toxic.

Goosebumps smatter across my bare arms, the little blonde hairs standing to attention.

"I'm reading, *obviously*," I scoff, like *he's* the idiot he tries so hard to make *me* out to be.

I cross and re-cross my ankles, wriggling my toes inside my fishnet socks. I repainted my chipped toenails, black to red. As scarlet as blood, the rich colour makes me think of oozing insides and bloodied knives and all things gruesome and nice. It was an obvious choice.

"You're upside down," he states solemnly, as though I, myself, am unaware of my current position.

My back flat on the seat, thighs pressed against

the back of the white couch, the top of the seat supporting the backs of my knees, feet upright in the air. My head hangs off the edge of the cushion, long silver hair trailing over the floor. I honestly don't see the issue if I'm comfortable, I'm not hurting anybody.

"Thank you, Captain Obvious," I mock in my best sergeant major voice.

Slapping my book down on the floor beside my head, saluting him stiffly with two fingers, my brow drawn, eyes hard. His sea-blue eyes narrow on me, wrinkling at the corners. I try not to look directly at them, although I could paint you a picture of their colour just from memory. I'm intimately familiar with everything about this man. Instead, I focus on his nose or his eyebrows, sometimes his lips, I can't look at those for long either, they're too perfect.

God, I hate him.

I continue with my book, sipping on my shake. Kacey says I fill my body with too much crap. He's been trying to get me to drink his weird puke-looking protein shakes.

I told him they taste like grass.

He laughed.

I wasn't joking.

Anyway, whilst Kacey's at the garage, being a sexy, grease covered mechanic, I'm consuming as many full fat vanilla shakes as I can cram in. You know, to balance out all the *healthy* shit he'll make me eat later. Poor Hazel will start to think she's out of a job, not that I ever eat much of what she cooks anyway. Huxley just likes food. He's currently out getting me little vanilla yogurts. I'm certain they wouldn't taste the same if anyone else were to buy them.

"You're so fucking weird, divvy bitch," Max grunts, finally stepping fully into the room, his heavy boots carrying him over to the wet bar in the corner.

"Ooo, I haven't heard that one before," I sass back with a dismissive shake to my head, although, any insult from Maddox Sharpe cuts me a little.

I secretly follow him with my eyes. Cataloguing the way his shoulders tense as he passes by my place on the couch, relaxing again when he's a safe distance away. He shrugs his leather jacket off, hooking it over the back of a bar stool. Leaning over the sink he washes his hands, he dips low, splashing his face. Running wet hands through his flop of thick black hair, pushing it back off his face. The taps going off, standing, he dries his hands on the bottom of his t-shirt. The rough action revealing a sliver of tattooed skin, giving me a peak at those delicious dimples in his lower back.

"Why are you so grumpy, Maddox? What's up your arse?" I ponder loudly, "or is it the lack of something up there? Which is it? I can certainly help with the latter," I sing-song my offer, batting my lashes as he turns sharply to scowl at me.

His bulbs of turquoise narrowing, his lip curling into a snarl.

"Oh! Not into arse play, Maddox? Whoops! Sorry!

My mistake!" I fake giggle, once again turning my attention back to my book.

Not that the book is very interesting, it's one of Jacob's. One of the only ones I could find on the top of some of Jacob's unpacked boxes currently residing in one of my spare rooms. I would have dug a bit deeper, but it was kind of exhausting riffling through all his stuff with only one hand. I wish he'd just fucking move in downstairs already and take all his crap with him. Why he feels the need to take up an entire room with boxes full of old paperwork and shitty books is beyond me.

Anyway, the book's about boats, I'm sure it's great if you like boats. Not that I have anything against them, obviously, I mean, they get people places and stuff. So that's, urr, helpful? God, I need something else to fucking read.

"Don't you have anything better to do?" he spits.

I tuck my lips between my teeth to stop myself grinning at him like the maniac we both know I am.

"I doooooo," I hum, lazily rolling my eyes back over to his. Hiding the fact that my breathe catches every time I look at him, even upside down he's fucking beautiful. "But I'm not allowed to do them, soooo," I shrug my shoulders gently, going back to my book.

"*Sooo*," he mocks in a high-pitched tone that sounds nothing like my own. "You're just gunna sulk and hang upside down on the sofa?"

"I'm not sulking," I inform him. "And there's

nothing wrong with the way I'm sitting," smooth voice remaining calm even as my irritation spikes.

"Oh, you're not?" he chuckles, the piss-taking sound making me grit my teeth. "Sure seems like you've got your knickers in a twist, Princess," he hisses from behind the bar.

I slam my book down onto the couch beside my thigh, huffing out an exhausted breath, hating the fact he can get to me so easily.

"Okay, what do you want, Maddox? Hmm? You've got my unwavering attention, what do you want?"

"Me? *Want*? Nothing," he chimes innocently, making my eyes pinch tightly.

"*Nothing*?" I mimic back to him. My glare finally making its way up to his face, -his chin to be exact- "you've worked this hard to get my attention. You've got it, and now you want *nothing*?"

"Oh, no, I already got what I wanted," he says quietly, his all too familiar deep timbre wrapping me up so tightly in heat, I want to scream.

"And what did you get, Max?" I grit out, my teeth grinding together so hard my jaw aches.

"I got on your nerves," he shrugs off casually, so casually in fact that it makes me want to commit fucking murder.

He pushes up on his elbows, straightening up from leaning to standing, as though readying himself to leave the room.

"Well, actually, now that we're in conversation.

There's something I'd like to say to you, *Maddox*," I start, my eyes finally locking onto his heavenly aqua-marine ones.

My breath just stops in my chest, time slows, my heart kicks into high gear and I bite my tongue so fucking hard I taste blood. The haunting look in his eyes sucks the life right out of me. His soul locked up tight, his demon playing dead. My heart aches so hard it's like I've plunged a knife so deep inside my chest, it's imbedded in, never to be removed again. Even if it were, a piece of the blade would remain behind, just to keep twisting and twisting and *twisting*.

Carnage and destruction.

That's all we'd be.

Everything between us is ruined.

We are so far beyond repair that nothing could ever fix us.

We're nothing more than dense shadows and wistful memories.

Something inside me just cracks, a chasm of long-ing, of wishing, regrets. Everything just stings for a minute. A *long* minute. I stare at him, he stares at me, but it's not in the same way. When Max looks at me, all I feel is this uncomfortable itch, something so deeply rooted that I'll never be able to soothe it. Max will forever be a piece of me, a tiny, splintered frag-ment stitched into the very fabric of my soul. Some-thing I could never remove, even if I tore myself apart looking, he'd still always be there. He's in my very essence, such a strong-willed pain in my side that I'd almost ache more without it.

I suddenly suck in a sharp breath, my eyes blinking, refocusing my attention. He's sneering at me now, that violent hatred roaring like a fire behind his cyan eyes. His bottom lip split, nose bruised and cheekbone a pale shade of violet.

"Oh, yeah?" he chuckles, the sound venomous and deadly as he rolls his eyes dramatically.

"Yeah, actually," I tell him, throwing myself into sitting.

The quick motion making me momentarily dizzy as the room flips, but I don't care. I get to my feet, extra sway in my step as I close the large distance between us. Bypassing that fucking piano, my fingers running across the ivory keys as I pass, not hard enough to play, just enough to draw his eye. We both know why that piano's there, why I couldn't not have one in my house. Even though all I can play is fucking '*twinkle, twinkle*,' it's because of him. Because I'm so self-destructive that I just had to have the hideous monstrosity to ground me. To make me think of a simpler time, one where I wasn't a murderer, where I wasn't a victim left bleeding at the hands of perverted men. Where I was just a teenage girl irrevocably in love with a boy who had her whole heart. Every fucking damaged piece of it was for Maddox fucking Sharpe.

"If you ever, and I mean *ever*," I hiss, "lay your hands on my fucking boyfriend again. I will *end* you.

He is *mine*. I am the only one allowed to fuck that man up, do you understand me, Maddox? Do not make an enemy out of me. I'm not the same little girl you fucked over and left behind," I hold his gaze for a second, making sure my promise sinks in.

Eyes unblinking, I sling my hair over one shoulder. Twisting in place, I start to march across the room. My socked feet whispering against the floor when a large hand clamps around my upper arm, violently tearing me back. I grunt as my back hits Max's front. The air knocks from my lungs as he spins me around so fast, I momentarily lose my sight. My back slams into the glass wall, my head ricocheting off the window with a thunk. Max's fist snaps out, his firm grip tightening as he flexes his fingers around my throat. Blue eyes ablaze, his thumb crushing my pulse. I smirk, my good arm hanging limply at my side. I'm not fighting him off, this is a game of whose dick's bigger. And. I. Will. *Win*.

I chuckle in his face, my head relaxing back into the cold glass even as his grip tightens further, erasing all space between his palm and my neck. His fist around my throat like a lava hot collar, his heat seeping into me, scorching my insides. Tobacco and sickly-sweet icing sugar surrounds me in a dense, cloying cloud, his scent overwhelming every inch of me. Something about it feels so fucking right, him pinning me down, me unafraid. I clearly don't have a normal person's response to asphyxiation.

I suppose I just enjoy violence. It is my first language, after all.

"You threatening me, Princess?" the devil hisses and I grin, licking my waxy lips, noisily smacking them together.

"I don't make threats, *Maxi*," I rasp. "I make fucking promises," I whisper.

Allowing my gaze to drop to his lips, before slowly drawing them back up to those haunting turquoise eyes.

"Do you want to play?" I ask teasingly, my head tilting to the right as much as is possible in his hold.

He allows the movement, but I think it's subconscious.

Max's breathing is heavy, his hard face pulled into anger, his nostrils flaring, jaw clenched. His rapid breath fanning across my face, if I were to push forward the slightest amount our lips would touch. But I don't. That'll only lead to a fucking catastrophe. Max's chest rumbles with a low growl, his eyes narrowed firmly on mine. I blink up at him slowly, letting him see the new me, not the quiet little school-girl he once knew.

"Don't fucking test me, Kyla-Rose," he warns, his deep voice sending goosebumps across my flesh.

It's like the room just dropped twenty degrees, everything about Maddox is cold. Threatening, haunting and ice. Fucking. Cold.

Movement over his shoulder captures my attention. Rubble moves into the room, just a single step inside the archway.

"Get the fuck out," Max snarls, snapping his gaze over his shoulder.

Rubble doesn't move, not a flinch in sight, approaching a step closer instead.

I laugh then, like really laugh. Tears gather in my eyes as I wheeze through my crushed windpipe.

"He works for *me*. He doesn't take orders from *you*, you fucking idiot," I force the words through my teeth, feeling bruises starting to form, blood gathering beneath the skin.

Max turns back to me, a look of disgust on his face, I only grin harder, my dimples practically splitting my cheeks open.

"We're good in here, Rubble, thank you," I tell my silent guard roughly.

He nods once, turning away, footsteps silent. He could be tucked away in the shadows just outside the archway for all I know, he likely is, he's very good at guarding from the shadows.

"Do you have a point to prove, Max?"

His grip tightens until I can't breathe at all, his fingers compressing my airway. Oxygen screaming inside my lungs to be set free, let alone heave any in. Yet, my smile doesn't falter, all toothy and white, my lips stained red. My eyes glassy as they fill with moisture, but I refuse to give in. Even as my head spins, my mind whirling with memories of a sombre little boy with magical smiles and a comforting voice. I don't bring my arm up, I let it hang there, not fighting. My other still tucked up tight to my chest. My vision splatters with white, the edges blurring, my vision tunnelling. Angry blue-green eyes plead with me to struggle and although every inch of me wants to give in and do just that, I don't.

I will win this, even if it ends with me passing out.

As petty as that sounds, this is all about making a point.

I'm the fucking alpha, not this dickhead.

Just as my eyelids start to flutter and my mind wanders, my body drifting along in the waves, weightless and free. My throat is freed, my lungs automatically sucking in lungful's of sweet air, choking on the feeling as it burns my insides. I double over as Max steps back, distancing himself from me. My good hand splayed over my thigh, still coughing and spluttering but grinning from ear to ear like the Cheshire fucking cat.

"I feel like we're in a stalemate, Maxi," I wheeze out.

Choking on my laughter as I start to straighten, groaning as my head spins.

"You wanna fight for your boys? 'Cause I think I've already won," I shrug, his eyes narrowing on me so hard his eyes are nothing more than slits. "They'll follow me fucking *anywhere*, and I know how much you don't like to share," I gloat as I step into him.

I give him credit; he doesn't move away from me. I trace my index finger down the centre of his chest.

My clawed nail lightly scratching over his white t-shirt, snagging the thin fabric. Just as I hit his sternum, my eyes still locked firmly on his, he seizes my hand, his fingers tightly wrapping around my slim wrist. I smirk, swallowing down every old feeling I had for the disturbing little boy down the street. He leans in, his head beside mine.

"Wherever I go, *they* go," he spits, his lips brushing over the shell of my ear. "If I wanted to take them away from you I could," his bellicose words strike me like a knife to the chest, forcing me to suck in a sharp breath, angering my aching lungs.

I didn't want to let his words affect me, but that struck me out of nowhere. That's my biggest fear, isn't it? My *only* fear. What if they leave me, choose someone else, even Max, over me? What if he does take them away from me, they've been a trio for ten fucking years. Kaccy, Huxley and I have been fucking for all of five fucking minutes.

How can I get them to stay with me?

I feel the frown hit my face before I can help it. Max draws back, cocky smirk firmly in place as he thumbs my bottom lip. I swat him away but he just chuckles, tugging on it harder, his thumb grazing across my bottom teeth. I gnash my jaw as he withdraws his thumb, growling with my new rasp. My throat feels like I've swallowed razor blades.

"Aww, don't be like that, Princess," he mock pouts, that evil glint in his devil eyes as he swiftly runs his gaze up my body.

Sneering like he finds me severely lacking.

"When the novelty of shared pussy wears off, maybe they'll keep you on the backburner for week-ends or summink'."

He shrugs loosely, and I don't think, I just move.

My good hand comes up, the back of it connecting with his cheek so hard, the sound echoes in the silent room, his head whipping to his left. My breathing ragged, I stare at the side of his face, his jaw working as he turns back to face me. The imprint of my knuckles blooming cherry red on his cheekbone, every part of my hand slowly appearing brightly on his pale skin. Anger blossoms inside me, taking root, spreading through my veins like wildfire, unstoppable and unpredictable.

Danger flashes in his eyes just before he rushes me. Slamming me back into the windows, his nose touching my own, his gaze flickering between my eyes. His chest heaving, brushing against my nipples with every breath he pants. I hold his gaze, the demon in me desperate to be released, to face off against the devil in him.

His hands aggressively stroke up my sides. Squeezing too tight, my black vest top the only thing separating skin to skin contact. His heat sears through the flimsy fabric. His grip firm and unyielding, like he'll never let me go, lock and fucking key but we're two parts of the same lock. There is no key, the key would be our salvation and that's just not what we're about, we're pure chaotic destruction, me and Max. To the bitter motherfucking end.

We crash together, teeth colliding, lips melding as though they've never been apart. His tongue instantly sliding into my mouth, hands gliding effortlessly beneath my top. Max's knee locked between my thighs, hot, heavy hands running over my flesh, grabbing, and groping every inch he can access. Palms running up my stomach, his thumbs flick over my pierced nipples. A groan escaping me, he swallows the sound as though it were his own, my fingers sliding into his hair, tugging on the roots, hauling him closer.

I nip at his lips, bottom then top, mauling his mouth like a savage animal. He attacks my throat, suckling on the newly forming bruises made by his rough hands. My head drops back against the glass, his mouth working down my throat to my chest. My top sharply tugged down, the fabric snagging beneath my clutched hand, exposing my breasts. Nipples turning to granite as the cool air washes over them.

"Fuck, you have perfect tits," he purrs, his lips immediately latching onto one as if he just can't help himself.

His teeth tugging the metal bar through my nipple as he massages and plucks on the other. A hand planted on my lower back, he arches me away from the window, drawing me flush against his muscular body. My head still resting against the glass, I groan long and low. My fingers still tangled in his mess of raven hair, drawing his head closer as he feasts on my breasts. Minding the wounded hand still clutched to my chest, he moves from one to the other, heat rushing through me at his less than careful attention.

He uses his teeth, his lips, fingers, assaulting every part of me. Every nerve ending in my body is screaming, it aches, it burns, but it feels oh so fucking good. His hand leaves my breast, smoothing and dipping down over my stomach. His fingers finding my elastic waistband, smoothly working his deft digits beneath my lace underwear like a seasoned professional. His index finger slides through my wet folds, I jolt at the contact. He hisses as he removes his mouth from my nipple, nipping at it once more for good measure.

"Fuckin soaked for me, ain't ya, Princess," he smirks, flicking his eyes up to mine.

His tone cocky, lustful and too fucking familiar, he dips back down towards my tits.

"Max," I breathe, his gaze snapping back up to mine in an instant, his full attention hanging on my every breath.

"Princess," he growls, and it takes every fibre of my being to continue with my planned route.

"Let go of me," I tell him.

My breathing calming as I watch confusion coat his features.

"What?"

"I said, let go of me," I tell him, straightening up, finding my feet quickly as his hand slips out of my bottoms.

"I don't understand," he says softly and I almost break.

But I don't. I keep my goddamn composure because this isn't only about me and Max anymore.

"You need to learn, Maddox," I stand tall, shoulders back. I look him in those beautiful pools of blue, the confusion in his features has arousal practically coating my thighs. I get off on this sadistic shit, but I ignore it. Leaning into him, my lips brushing across his stubbled cheek. "Bad dogs don't get treats," I whisper in his ear with a breathy laugh, just as he shoves me away from him.

I don't struggle, I let him push me. My feet sliding me backwards in my fishnet socks, I tuck my boobs away. He fists his hair, knuckles blanched, dick hard. The sight of it pressing aggressively against his tight jeans has me biting my bottom lip to curb further laughter.

"You fucking bitch," he snarls at me, frothing at the mouth with rage.

He slaps his hands against his thighs in frustration. His fists curling so tight the bones look as though they're trying to tear free.

"No, Maddox. *You* fucking bitch. You thought you could just stroll up in here with your pretty eyes and miserable fucking demeanour and what? Take over? Have me to yourself? Stab your boys in the back, fuck them over and take me back? And when that didn't work, you thought you'd get in my fucking pants and then tell them I what? Cheated? You think you can put them off? Steal them away from me? What is your plan here?" I throw my head back with a raucous laugh, its brash and loud and dramatic, probably a little scary.

I shake my head with a raspy chuckle. My hand running through my hair, fingers gliding through the long strands. My right fist curling around the ends, tugging hard. The pinch of pain switching me up another gear.

"No. You misunderstand me; I *know* I can. And it's not fucking stealing if they're already *mine*," he hisses. His stern face boiling in rage, his lips red and swollen from our kissing. If you can even really call it that, it was more like an attacking. "I don't need to sabotage anything," he shrugs casually, folding his thick arms over his chest. "You'll do that all by yourself, you psychotic little bitch. Damaged goods, right *Lala*," he smirks as my breath catches.

Damaged goods.

I've heard that before.

Although, I now find I quite like damaged goods.

"Got anything else, Max?" I tilt my head, my eyes roving over his hard, inked frame. "Psychotic little bitch is almost a compliment," I smile, my hurt burrowing down deep.

My demon putting out that fire and kindling a new one.

"I've got one for *you*, actually," I smirk, tapping the tip of my index finger to my lip. "How about *coward*? How does that sound to you? I think it has a certain ring to it, myself," I shrug loosely. "It's accurate at the very least."

"Fuck off, Kyla-Rose, you know fucking nothing," he spits back.

His brow creased deeply, his entire posture screaming danger, but all I hear is *push me.*

Push me, push me, push me.

"I did *fuck off*," I mock, tossing my head from side to side. "TO PRISON! You piece of fucking shit!" I roar, my entire body trembling as I seethe, gritting my teeth and sucking in a harsh breath. "My mother *died*. You fucked me over, and I went to fucking juvie! YOU LEFT ME! You said you'd *never* leave. But you did! You left me not only once but *twice*! You distanced yourself from me after Gran's funeral, you kept me at arm's length for over a year! *Then* you have the audacity to hunt me down in the dark, boss me around, trying to sit there telling me how it is. Fill my head with bullshit and I *knew*. I just fucking knew that night it was the end, and I fucked you anyway, more fool me, Maddox. More fucking fool me, and to think I thought you were serious about coming back for me. Thought you were serious about us, how it was gunna go, the *future*," I snort in disbelief.

"I did come back," he tells me. "I came back. *You* were the one gone. The building was being hosed down by the fucking fire brigade and *you*. Left. Me." Max pushes both hands through his hair.

Sighing so heavily that his body visibly deflates, making mine react in a similar way. I feel my own lungs shrivel in response, my anger slowly melting with it.

"You left me first," I whisper back, but it holds no power.

There's no real weight to those words, it's just a thing we do, isn't it? We always want to be right when we feel we've been wronged. To counter back. When you hold hate for someone without their side of the story, you always have to have the last word. Everything's a competition. Everything feels like it's the end of the motherfucking world.

Max grunts, blowing out a breath. His shoulders dropping even further as he brings his gaze onto me. I'm not looking at him now, staring down at his feet. The back of my eyes burning as I think of that night, how awful and perfect and thrilling it was. It was everything I wanted and everything I knew I shouldn't. But I went there anyway, temptation and greed. That's how I feel now when I look back on that night. I was selfish for the first time in my life because I could be. Because the woman who hated me was dead and I was finally free. I think it's why I didn't tell him about it. I didn't want her evil, even in death, to taint our moment.

"You just had to wait, that's all, Lala. You just had to fucking wait for me. None of this shit would have happened if you'd just fucking waited," he lashes out the last part in frustration, but I don't think it's only for me, it sounds more like it's for him.

For us.

"I-" I hesitate, the words dying on my tongue as I swallow the lump in my raw throat.

Sucking in a shaky breath, I glance up.

"I thought you weren't coming back, I thought you'd left me. It's what you did, Maddox. You fucking left me when I needed you, numerous fucking times, and then you'd pop back up and interfere when it was something that bothered *you*. Why the fuck would I *ever* expect you to keep your word and come back to me? What did I have to go off other than your desertion? Why would I sit there in the dark for four fucking hours, and think, '*oh, yes, I'm sure he's still coming back, I'll just wait here until I die,*'. What part of any of this makes you think I would have had some sort of deluded fucking belief *in you*? When you were nothing but a fucking let down."

Max stares at me, his tongue rolling across his front teeth. He sniffs back his emotion, snuffing out any and all tells that could reveal how he actually feels.

"For what it's worth," he starts, swallowing hard, his Adam's apple bobbing violently in his throat. "I always intended to come for you. I just, I shouldn't have even left you there in the fucking first place." He sighs so hard, so defeated that my entire body shakes in response. "I got myself in too deep, into some real bad shit, Lala. I was so fucking stuck, I was drowning in quicksand. And I-" he pauses, his intense gaze so strong my knees almost buckle. "And I thought I was doing it for you, but I realise now that although I thought I was, it was probably more than that. I thought I was doing it for us, but I just, I steered myself wrong. And then it wasn't about *my* survival anymore, it was about yours and you didn't even know it. The Southbrook gang," he starts to say, and I tremble.

I tremble so hard that there's absolutely no hiding it now. The same gang that ruined my dad's life. Max knew that, he knew the shit they blamed my dad for. He got locked up because of them, and then Max went and worked for the same fucking gang.

I bring my good hand up to my chest, taking a step back as my breath gets caught in my throat. My skin so hot it itches, and I want nothing more than to claw it all off. I want to be momentarily deaf, just so I won't have to hear whatever it is he's going to say next. I don't know if I can handle it. The way his heavily lashed, turquoise eyes bore into mine. Setting me alight in every sense of the word as he flays me with his words.

"They were going to come after *you*, Lala. Because of me and instead of just telling you, I did what they wanted. I had to carry out a job for them, do as I was told, or it was you they were going to take. I was scared, so fucking scared because you are right, Princess. I am a fucking coward. I was and I am. I should have just admitted I was in over my head, but I thought I knew best. I should have asked your family for help sooner. I wanted to do it on my own, prove to them I could protect you, be independent. I wanted to

fucking save you in every sense of the fucking word.
But really the only person you needed saving from in
the end was *me*. And when I got back to you that night
you were gone. I thought you were fucking dead,
burned alive in that fucking warehouse, taken from
me forever. And in a way you were taken from me,
dead or alive you were gone, and it killed me. I died
too."

I drop my curtain of hair forward, letting it shield
me from the room. Keeping me safe behind the sheet
of silver as I process his words. This is not what I saw
happening today, it's Christmas Eve. We're going out
tonight, just my boys and me, well, and Maddox. I'm
supposed to be happy, not whatever it is I'm feeling
right now.

All I can picture now is a burning building.
Firemen rushing around, thick cloying smoke heading
towards the heavens, flashing blue and red lights and
Max. Max just standing there, his brow creased, panic
thudding through his chest. Tears in his eyes as he
wonders what happened to me. My heart cramps, my
shoulders hunch, I heave in a shuddery breath.

And all I say is, "you shouldn't have touched me,
Maddox. You shouldn't have come to find me, you
should have stayed gone, left me alone. You were
doing such a good fucking job of it, you should have
fucking let me be."

My thoughts spiral as I travel back in time.
Desperately trying to cling onto my anger from then
because if what he says is true and he did come back,

then what leg do I have to stand on? I don't. I have no one to blame for my actions but myself. But I knew that, didn't I. I knew everything that happened that night was my fault, at least partly. It wasn't only Max who was to blame. We both played a part. I should have told him about my mum. He should have told me about the Southbrook gang. Maybe if we'd communicated none of this would be happening right now. I grip the roots of my hair, my fingers fisting tightly against my scalp, nails scratching at my skin.

"Lala, you don't mean that."

"I do!" I yell, tugging at my hair so hard strands snap free, tangled around my fingers. "I do mean it. I regret all of it, it ruined my life. Look at me! Look at me now, Maddox! Do you fucking see this? Look at what it's all done to me!"

I throw my arm out by my side, gesturing to myself wildly. My thoughts start to morph together, the past and the present twisting viciously inside my head and I just need it to stop for a second. My breaths come out in short pants, my lungs desperately trying to fill.

"I can't do this, not today," I rasp.

My eyes squeezing shut, panic taking over me. Starting from my chest, radiating out, infecting my veins like fast acting poison.

"Lala."

I feel him move closer.

I step back. He exhales sharply, frustration, I know

it well. My lungs heave, nothing works. My eyelids hot, my throat scratchy.

"Lala," he tries again, but it sounds further away.

My legs wobble as I bring my hand to my face, covering myself, trying to take a deep breath.

"Darlin'?"

My eyes ping open. I spin around so fast I almost faceplant the floor, but I catch myself. Huxley's there, standing in the archway, arms full of shopping bags. He slowly lowers them to the floor. His coal eyes on mine, even as he bends low, untangling his fingers from the loops of fabric handles, his gaze never falters.

"Come to me, Darlin'. It's okay," his warm voice entices me, smooths over my anxiety, I take in a breath. "That's it, Darlin', come to me, I've got you."

My feet shuffle towards him, his tall, lean frame, my light in the dark. His deep caramel skin glowing, his thick arms open, tempting me closer. Another breath, less pain in my chest. Another, deeper this time, my head clearing. Then I'm in his arms, banded tightly around me, smothering me with oranges and sandalwood. I breathe him in deeply, my lungs burning in delight. His hand smoothing over the back of my skull, cupping my head, my face in his chest. The cotton fabric of his t-shirt cool from outside, comforting against my heated cheeks. I hum against him, the vibration rolling through his chest.

"That's it, baby girl, I got you."

CHAPTER 10

KYLA-ROSE

"We nearly ready to go, Darlin'?" Huxley grins at me as I wander into the kitchen.

After I got my panic attack under control, Huxley snuggled with me, Angel and Brute for the rest of the afternoon. Max popped his head around the door, saying he was sorry, I said sorry too. He walked away with a nod, my chest ached just a little less. I don't wanna keep fighting with him. It hasn't solved anything as of yet, we've got enough going on, why keep adding to it.

Hux's coal black eyes run down my body in appreciation.

"You. Look. Hot."

He whistles lowly, taking in my tight, black leather trousers, one of Kacey's huge, black t-shirts tucked in at the front, hanging out at the back. A cropped, red leather jacket draped over my shoulders, studs on the shoulders. Sleek, high ponytail that I forced Rubble to assist me with. He did it without complaint, and he was gentle. A full face of make-up, smoky black eyes, heavy winged liner and Christmas red lipstick.

"Thanks, I-" my words stopping suddenly.

My brain registering the fact that his lean arms are elbow deep in shopping bags. He was literally out buying yogurt…

"What in the fuck is all that?" I query, my face creasing as I assess just how much he's actually rifling through. "I thought you put the food away earlier?"

"I did."

He grins ever wider, his white, toothy smile splitting his cheeks as he shoots me a flirty wink.

"What's all that then?" I wave a hand at all the bags still full on the worktop.

"Well, I figured, after Christmas," he starts, walking around the peninsula.

Grunting as he heaves another stuffed, reusable bag onto the counter beside the fridge, glass clinking and plastic rustling.

"After your hospital visit," he says with a raised brow, and I roll my eyes. "We'll be holed up here for a while. I wanted to get all the stuff you actually *like*. Unless you wanna keep being force-fed kale salads by the *healthinator*," he smirks, referring to Kacey and his extreme healthy eating regime.

I gag at the thought of his half-dozen raw eggs being necked back every morning without so much as a flinch. I'm seriously impressed by Kacey's dedication. That man doesn't put any shit inside that beautiful body, and it shows. But I'm far too distracted by that delicious pull of Hux's peach lips, twisted up on one side, his dark eyes glinting with mischief, to do anything but screw my face up at the mention of kale. Let alone comment on his new nickname for my golden eyed beast. I'm sure Big Man's gunna absolutely *love* that one.

"Exactly!" he nods cheerily, turning back to his bags of *stuff,* pulling out item after item.

Mesmerised, I watch him place down socks, a DVD and a candle.

A candle?

"Huxley," I start, biting my bottom lip, chewing on the torn skin as he pulls out a forty-eight pack of batteries. "What the fuck are those for?" I question quickly, my eyes widening.

He whips back to face me, his hot hands clamping onto my flared hips. His fingers curling into my skin, thumbs running over the sharp curve of bone. He draws me into him, being careful not to trap my injured hand between us, pressing a kiss to the top of my head. Affectionately, lovingly, despite the tightening of his hands. Leaning into me, his face dropping slightly forward so he's level with my own.

"Things," he whispers.

His teeth latching onto my earlobe, biting down on the soft flesh. Sucking it into his wet, sinful mouth, his tongue bar flicking over me. I go lax in his hold, every tense muscle in my body turning to jelly as he softly blows his hot breath over my wet lobe. I shiver, he chuckles. Grabbing hold of me and spinning us around, lifting me into the air, he slams my arse down onto the island. His body effortlessly sliding between my automatically parting knees. He shucks me forward, my cunt pressed tightly against the hard length in his jeans. His zip snagging my leather clad pussy in just such a way, I gasp.

He draws his face back. His eyes flicking between my own as he grinds his hips forward, the metal zip snagging over the seam in my leather trousers. I gasp again only making him smirk harder.

"Are we in a rush?" he queries.

Pulling his bottom lip into his mouth, he pops it free with a smacking sound, tongue bar clacking against his teeth. His canine digging into his lip, denting the skin, blanching it white from the pressure. His obsidian orbs lazily hooded.

"I have some time," I whisper, my voice breathy.

"Oh? You do? You, *have some time*," he mocks, arching his pierced eyebrow with a cocky grin, one that has my thighs quivering.

"For you," I whisper against his lips, my gaze lifting to meet his hungry one.

My fingers sliding beneath the back of his tight jeans.

"*Always*," I growl, savagely biting down on his bottom lip, my palm squeezing a handful of his boxer covered arse cheek.

He jolts as I lick over his closed mouth, my

tongue delving between his lips, pushing its way inside to tangle with his. He sucks my tongue into his mouth, his teeth grazing it as I fuck his mouth with mine. He palms my lower back, thrusting himself against my core, tugging me forward. His long fingers wind my ponytail around his fist, tugging my head back so sharply my eyes water. He bites down my neck, his slick tongue laving the sting before he suddenly draws back. His fingers gripping my jaw and chin, pinching my face. He twists my head back, arching my neck, his eyes flicking over my pale skin.

"What the fuck is this?" he rumbles, the vibration working its way through his chest, like a rolling thunder cloud.

Twisting and turning my head in the opposite direction to get a good look at my new bruises. I'm so smothered in hickeys and bruises anyway; you'd wonder how anyone could pinpoint one from another. But my boys? My boys see everything.

"It's nothing." I curl my fingers around his wrist as he narrows his eyes on me.

No words passing between us. I hold his attention, he flares his nostrils, his grip on my face tightening another fraction making me wince. He releases me with a hushed sorry, his other hand coming up. Both hot, calloused hands cradling my face between them.

"I'll kill him," he breathes against me, his forehead dropping to mine as my hand moves from his arm to his face.

"It was my fault, we-" I swallow hard, but don't need to finish.

Huxley nods against me, his eyes sliding closed, he breathes out a long, slow breath.

"You're figuring shit out," he sighs softly. "I won't stand for him hurting you, Darlin'."

"I know, I'm okay," I soothe.

My thumb gently sweeping across his dark skin, his thick layer of lashes tickling the tip of it.

"Anything else?" Huxley asks quietly after a moment. My breath catches. "It's okay Whatever it is, you can tell me, baby girl," Huxley soothes me, his voice low and calm.

Fearless.

"We kissed," I answer vulnerably, self-hatred evident in every whispered syllable.

Please don't hate me.

"And?"

"He-" my breath rushes out of me. "He touched me, sort of, well, he did, but it wasn't- it was just," I frown at my own fucking spluttering. *Jesus, fuck, just spit it out.* "My boobs."

"Just that?" he questions.

"An-and he slid his finger over me, once, and then I told him to stop," I whisper, my voice cracking, eyelids burning.

Please, someone, somewhere, don't take them away from me.

"Show me," Huxley rushes out faintly.

"What?" I blink, drawing my face from his to look at him, *read him,* his hands still caressing my face.

"Show me where he touched you, *how*."

"I don't understand," I frown, my brows knitting together.

"Bottoms off, then scoot back," he instructs.

Stepping away from me, pulling my boots off with him. Tossing them over his shoulders, he rolls my socks down, tossing them too, in a similar direction.

My cheeks flame as I unfasten my button and zipper. My working hand pushing at the waistband. The left side then the right, back and forth between the two as I struggle to wriggle them down my legs. Huxley can see my struggle, but he doesn't aid me, just watches my movements with rapt attention. Silently patient as I finally use my feet to kick them the rest of the way off, leaving me in red French knickers, t-shirt and jacket.

I shiver as he steps forward, his eyes fixed on my inked body. Goosebumps erupt over my skin at his attention. And when those dark eyes finally lock onto mine, the fire behind them scorching, my breath catches in my throat and my ears ring.

"Face forward. Plant your feet flat on the counter. Bend your knees and spread your legs, Kyla-Rose," Huxley instructs, and my body climbs another degree hotter.

My cheeks ablaze at this point, they must be a startling shade of pillar box red.

"Huxley, I-"

"Stop talking," he barks at me and it's like my body suddenly knows its master.

Without conscious thought, any at all, I find myself in his requested position. I have to lay my palm out behind me, leaning myself back a little to hold my weight. Everything inside me is screaming not to take orders.

But this is Huxley.

And although, *this* is new.

He's ours, I remind my demon.

He's still mine, he will never hurt me.

So, I hold the position.

Huxley approaches me, slowly stalking around the counter. I don't try to follow him with my gaze, I'm too laser focused on doing exactly as I'm told. *And he didn't tell me to look.* I can play along. Even if I don't know all the rules yet, I'll follow his lead. I like games.

He stops directly behind me, his hand snapping out. Pulling my ponytail back so my neck cranes. My eyeballs rolling as far back as they can to try catch a glimpse of him.

"Show me how he touched you, Kyla-Rose," Huxley's voice devoid of emotion.

The order cracks like a whip and I find myself tensing slightly. It's not because I'm uncomfortable, I'm just- this is *new.*

Supporting my weight by fisting my ponytail, I wobble slightly as I bring my one hand forward. My fingers finding my throat and closing around it. I dig my thumb into my pulse point, trying to mimic Max's earlier touch as accurately as I can.

Offering me his free hand, Huxley reaches forward.

"Use me, place my hand where he touched you next."

I let go of my own throat, my breathing short, sharp pants. I place his big hand beneath my baggy shirt, sliding his palm up over my belly until it rests on my right breast. My chest heaves as he tightens his fingers around the heavy flesh as I return my hand to my throat.

"What else?" he grits out.

His voice dominating my every sense, making me lose the need to make my own decisions.

"He rubbed his thumb over my nipple," I gasp out as the pad of his thumb violently circles my nipple, his forefinger joining it to pluck at my hardened peak.

He flicks the metal bar through it, sending the vibration straight to my core. I groan, squirming atop the cold marble counter as he forces my head back with his grip on my ponytail.

"Stay still," he snaps.

"Yes, *sir*," I whisper, my throat arched painfully, I push the words through my trembling lips.

He growls in response, his hold on my breast so intense, my heart hammers against my ribcage. Evidence of my desire rushes from me, quickly coating my inner thighs, running down the length of me. My thighs tremble as his breath fans over the back of my neck.

"What *else?*" he grits out the repeated question as

he aggressively flicks my nipple. I cry out as he twists it between his fingers. "That's it, cry out for me. Let the whole fucking building know what I'm doing to you," he grunts, suddenly releasing my ponytail.

My good arm flails as I release my throat, trying to catch myself. The sudden disappearance of his body behind me has me gasping in panic, when a firm grip on my neck, replacing the one I had on myself, drags me forward. Huxley's finger and thumb lining my jaw, my chin cradled between the two digits.

"Good girl," he hushes, his words pushed out through gritted teeth.

His charcoal eyes as pitch as the night's sky, glinting with something akin to madness, he draws my face towards him.

"*What. Else?*"

I tremble then, a shiver vigorously rakes up my spine, my cunt clenching around nothing. Knees wobbling and feet burning as I try to hold my position. Huxley holds my entire weight with his grip on my face, his thumb smoothing along my jaw. His dark eyes swirling like black holes, dropping to my lips.

"Come on, Kyla-Rose. You know the rules now," he encourages menacingly, his luscious peach lips lifting into a cocky smirk.

I collect his other hand in mine. The weight of it feels like lead in my trembling fingers as I plant his hand on my knee, guiding his long fingers down my quivering thigh. My hand still atop his, I move his fingertips to the edge of my lace knickers. My eyes following the seductively slow movement, my pale, inked hand against his deep caramel one. The contrast makes my heart flutter. Huxley is so goddamn beautiful. I almost smile, when I suddenly realise, I feel nervous, like, I want so much to impress this man. I want to make him happy. I want to freely allow him to control me because it feels *good*.

"Look at me," he barks, and I jolt, my wide eyes snapping up to meet his obsidian gaze.

Empty, bottomless pits stare back at me, but I can feel the heat stirring in him. I want nothing more than to trace my fingers along -what I already know to be- the thick, hard length of him. Hot and silky and *so* hard. But I don't reach out, instead, keeping my eyes on his, I guide the tip on his middle finger beneath the lace of my knickers. He sucks in a sharp breath as his skin instantly becomes slippery with my wetness. I trace the tip of his finger up the length of my wet slit, his chest heaving with ragged breaths. I swallow hard as I circle his finger over my clit, quickly removing his hand from me and placing it down flat on the counter.

"That was all," I whisper almost silently, my breathing matching his.

"Good girl," Huxley breathes, making me tremble with the praise. Bringing me forward with his strong grip on my throat, his lips ghosting over mine. "What happens to good girls, Kyla-Rose?" he asks, his words imprinting themselves upon my parted lips.

I suck in a deep breath, trembling as I'm overwhelmed with the rich scent of oranges and sandalwood.

"I don't know," I rasp softly.

He cocks an eyebrow, that confident smirk flitting to his face.

"You *don't know?*" he mocks with a cocky chuckle. "You need me to remind you?" he asks, his head tilting to one side.

His eyes roving over my bare legs, before returning to my grey-green ones.

"You still *have some time?*" he laughs deeply, the sound genuinely humorous.

My warm, playful Huxley shining through.

All of this.

All of him.

It's all, just, *new…*

"Yes," I whisper nervously, still unsure exactly where this is going.

But for once, I don't feel afraid of the unknown. It's Huxley, this man would *never* steer me wrong. Strangely, I sort of feel *empowered*. Taking instruction isn't me being weak, it's kind of like I'm taking charge, more so than when I'm barking the orders. This is me *choosing* to let someone else take the wheel. And it feels like emancipation, only, I'm releasing my own shackles. Just, with a little help from my fearlessly, selfless lover.

I relax fully into his hold then, and he smiles, feeling the tenseness dissolving out of my bones, *for him*.

He releases my jaw slowly, giving me enough warning this time to balance and hold myself up. My good hand slapping down beside me as Huxley's long fingers drop to the button of his jeans. Never taking his eyes from mine he dramatically flicks the button free. Torturously slow at dragging down his zipper. I feel my thighs wanting to squeeze together but I refrain, concentrating on his every movement. I want my reward; I don't want to break his rules when I'm just about to get what I want. I'm desperate for his hands to be back on me. I swallow hard as Huxley reaches inside his boxers, shoving them down along with his jeans so they sit just below his arse. He palms his cock, its heavy, thick, monstrous length sitting in his hand, his long fingers teasing back the foreskin. The silver piercing catching the light, glinting under the bright, overhead LEDs.

"Come here," he demands.

Trying to maintain my position, I slide myself forward until my legs are pushed up so tightly to my chest that it almost hurts to breathe. My shins flush against his firm chest, he draws me into him with his other hand on my lower back. I rock in place, slightly unsteady as he forces my knickers to one side, pressing his tip against my clit. The metal cool against my overheated flesh has me sucking in a sharp breath.

"*Fuck*, you're so wet," he bites out. "Fucking drenched for me, Darlin'. You like being told what to do?" he teases, that warm smirk back on his face.

It lights me up inside like a fucking Christmas tree,

the way he looks at me. My pussy clenches, desperate to be filled as he teases my slit. Rubbing his pierced tip up and down, pressing forward the slightest amount, dipping his dick through my slick.

"Look at us, Kyla-Rose. Watch while I touch you," he tells me sternly, brooking no argument.

I drop my gaze to between my thighs, glistening with moisture. Huxley's fist wrapped around his huge cock has me sucking in a sharp breath. His hand at my back fists the material of Kacey's t-shirt, gathering and bunching it into his fist. Pulling it taut, revealing the shape of my nipples beneath, puckered peaks straining hard enough to cut glass.

"Don't take your eyes off of us, Darlin'. Not unless I tell you to," he orders.

"Yes, sir," I whisper, still watching as he moves his pulsating cock up and down through my heat, his piercing tapping against my clit.

I watch as he starts to enter me, his cock still in hand, circling the base of it with his forefinger and thumb. He pushes into me, slowly, *torturously* slowly. The contrast of my pale skin, his dark and my blood red lace knickers is so fucking erotic. My breath stills in my lungs as he finally bottoms out, his thick, hard length disappearing inside of me. My eyes flutter, struggling to stay open as we groan together. I pant, my head dropping forward, resting against his shoulder, I keep my eyes locked on where our bodies connect. Watching as he starts to slide out of me, his length wet with my juices. He drops his head to my shoulder, mimicking my position. I can feel his eyes boring into the side of my face as he slides almost completely out of me, nothing but his pierced tip remaining inside. I uselessly clench around him, trying to force him to stay, but he just chuckles darkly in my ear.

"I'm in control here, baby girl."

It's not even a question.

I gasp as he suddenly slams into me, brutally forcing the air from my lungs. My hand flies up, gripping onto the nape of his neck. My nails dragging across the metal bar pierced there, I flick it for good measure earning me a shudder. Settling, I curl my bony fingers around the back of his neck, my thumb twisting in his tight, brown curls. Huxley draws out of me again, my pussy not having enough time to adjust to him before he's mercilessly slamming back into me.

"*Fuck*, you feel good," he breathes against the side of my neck, his eyes still on me, my cheeks heat as I groan.

I watch his cock glide effortlessly in and out of me. Carnal desire floods through me as I work to keep my eyes focused. All I want to do is look at him, let those big, dark eyes eat me alive. But instead, I follow orders. Watching as his movements get faster, his hips slamming into my pelvis. My cramped thighs screaming as I writhe on his dick. Wetness sliding down me, dripping onto the counter. His grip increases on my neck, his thumb violently caressing my pulse point.

"Look how fucking wet you are, Darlin'. Look at me erasing *his* touch, you belong to me, you know. All of you is for me, to do whatever I want with," he tells me breathlessly.

His hips working overtime as he forces his huge length into me, over and over. My cunt clenching around him, trying to force him to stay deep inside me.

"*Yes*," I groan, my eyes still locked on his dark, glistening cock hammering away at me.

"Tell me," he bites out, his teeth scraping down my throat. "Fucking tell me, Kyla-Rose," he orders, his voice raspy with desire.

"Yes!" I cry out. "I'm yours," I breathe.

My eyes threatening to close as he lets me drop back slightly in his hold. Angling me in such a way I see stars.

"To do whatever you want with," I pant, the words clawing their way out.

"That's it," he encourages, his grip on my shirt making the cotton seams crack with the pressure.

My walls clamp around him. Wet slapping filling the room as I claw at his neck, my nails carving into his sweat slicked skin. His teeth bite down on my jaw, he sucks his way along, nipping at my chin. Releasing my throat, he grips my face, turning me to face him. My gaze still locked on where he thrusts into me.

"Look at me, baby girl. Eyes on me now," he orders breathlessly, his hips never faltering as he increases his pace.

The second my eyes lock on his, my orgasm hits me out of nowhere. My eyes never straying, he pounds into me harder and harder. The tip of his cock smashing into my cervix, his pulsing length ruthlessly rubbing against my front wall. My legs shake as he sinks his teeth into my bottom lip. I cry out as he groans into my mouth, my tongue massaging his. My swollen lips assaulting him as I work my teeth down his throat. His pace picks up even further and I'm lost to the sensation. Wave after wave of heat crashes through me as he squeezes me close, my chest plastered against his. His hold on my back crushing, he finally let's go. Shooting his cum into me, coating my insides, he slows his pace. His hot breath fanning across my sweaty neck, he finally slows to a stop.

Still keeping me close, he releases my face, dropping his hand to my ankles. One by one, he draws my legs out from between us, letting them gently hang over the edge of the counter. Pins and needles race like wildfire through my muscles, I stretch my feet out, wiggling my toes. Huxley still sitting snug inside my wet heat, I wrap my legs around his waist. The heels of my feet digging into his arse cheeks, drawing him closer. He places a soft kiss against his initial carved just below my exposed collarbone, my t-shirt having slipped off one side.

"I love you," I whisper against the side of his throat, his pulse hammering against my puffy lips.

"I love you," he murmurs back, his dark eyes flicking between my own, he captures my lips with his.

Passion burns through me as I think about what we just did. Erasing our last kitchen experience, just a few days earlier, replacing it with this. I feel lighter. Huxley kisses the breath from my lungs, breathing his own life force back into me. Filling me up with warmth before he draws back.

Delicately pulling out of me, tucking his cum soaked cock back inside his boxers, he catches me watching. Smirking, he hooks his finger through the crotch of my French knickers, about to tug the lace material back into place, when he drops his gaze, pausing his action.

"You're so fucking beautiful, my cum between your legs, my love bites on your neck," he pauses.

Running his other hand up my thigh, shoving up my baggy t-shirt down to reveal my collarbone further.

"My mark carved into your chest," he flicks his coal eyes up to mine, his calloused thumb running over the fresh scab. "I just want to be a part of you, always have a piece of me on you," he murmurs.

His gaze running back down to where his finger is still hooked into my knickers. Gliding his other hand lower, he runs his two forefingers over my sensitive flesh. Dancing his digits through our joint mess where it leaks out of me. I watch with rapt attention as he scoops up our release and suddenly shoves it back inside me. My back arches as I groan loudly. His fingers twisting inside my pulsing core, forcing his cum back inside me. My walls sucking on his fingers as he lazily pumps them in and out of me.

"That's it, Darlin', come for me again," he says, his tone light, teasing.

He curls his fingers inside of me, his thumb rolling firmly over my swollen clit. I slam my good hand down onto the counter beside me, my sweat slicked palm slipping backwards. I knock something onto the floor as I try to keep my balance. Huxley's long fingers fucking our combined release back into me, every time some escapes, he slides his fingers through it and slams it back in. I jolt as his rhythm picks up, one hand still holding onto my knickers, his thumb vigorously attacking my clit. I let myself drop back onto the counter, my back arching as he hits a deeper spot. My legs trembling, I thrash my head side to side.

"Huxley!" I almost scream as he coaxes another punishing orgasm from me.

I go lax, melting into the cold marble counter as he finally pulls his fingers free of my quivering walls. I open my eyes to slits when I hear him groan, my eyes rolling onto him sucking his fingers into his mouth. His tongue circling the digits soaked in us. He winks at me, releasing them with a pop. He reaches forward, my arm flapping around like I'm trying to make a snow angel, I reach for him. My arm touching something cold and wet as I raise it, he clasps my hand, pulling me to sitting. I frown down at my arm, Huxley's brow creasing as he twists it in his grip.

"Darlin', you're bleeding," he says, almost like a

question as I turn my arm, peering at the little red spot on my elbow.

"What is that?" I mumble aloud. "It's not mine," I inform him, confusion marring my tone.

In unison we both start to look around me, trying to find the source of the blood. Huxley steps around the counter. Coming around the right side, he bends low, lifting a white pastry box. I frown harder, seeing the small red stain on the bottom of it, the little bit that seeped through now smeared on my elbow. He steps up beside me, twisting to face him, he lays the box on the counter. His dark eyes flicker up to mine but I just shrug. I don't know what it is either.

Huxley places his thumbs beneath the lid, flipping it off quickly. My shoulders deflate as I peer inside the box at a small dead swallow bird in a tiny patch of blood. It's rich, inky blue feathers are clumpy and dry. The usual shine to its smooth body is long gone. I raise my hand to scoop the little feathered creature up when Huxley swats at me, slapping at my hand.

"Don't touch it. It could have something on it," he scolds me, leaving the box where it is and sliding me off the other side of the counter.

He places my bare feet on the floor, my t-shirt dropping to cover my thighs. I peer up at him, concern etched into his beautiful features. I frown harder, Huxley doesn't worry about anything.

"Like what?" I ask, wrinkling my nose, "anthrax or something?"

"Maybe," he answers coldly, glaring at the box like

it killed his puppy. "Does Charlie ever bring dead things home?" Huxley asks me gently, hope heavy in his voice.

I shake my head, "not *dead* things. And not animals, he loves birds," I say sadly, looking back over my shoulder to the ominous white pastry box. "This wasn't Charl," I state. "How'd that get in here?" I murmur, more a wonder than a question I expect an easy answer to.

"I don't know, Darlin', but I'll find out," he promises, dropping a kiss to the top of my head as I continue staring at the box.

"Someone's been in here then," I nod, "someone who isn't us."

Huxley grips my chin, gently turning me back to face him as my stomach clenches. His dark eyes instantly capturing mine.

"Put your trousers on, go get Nox," he instructs.

Tapping his hand to my bum to hasten my pace, I pull them on as he collects my boots. I walk through the hall, sending Rubble to the kitchen on my way to the living room. Familiar piano chords grow louder as I approach, my heart thundering in my throat. Max sits with his back to me, his large body curled into the piano. His shoulders and back muscles straining against his t-shirt as he expertly caresses the keys.

I stop in the archway, leaning my right shoulder against the wall, silently admiring his reflection in the glass window. His eyes squeezed tight, head dropped slightly forward as his thick arms work their way across the keys. A haunting melody flooding the large room.

"Max," I call, his hands stopping instantly, he spins to face me.

"You're finished fucking then?" he bites, "*erasing my touch from your body.*"

"There's a dead bird in the kitchen," I tell him.

My voice wobbling a little. Ignoring the words he spat, words that could have only been heard had he been there, *watching.*

"You fucked in the kitchen. Your fucking guard standing watch outside like some sort of perverted spectator and now you're just popping in here to tell me about a dead bird. What the fuck is wrong with you? I've been sitting here waiting on you like some sort of mug, listening to you come for *him.* For you to now decide you'll grace me with your presence. What the fuck, Lala?"

"You're an arsehole. He's my boyfriend, it's my kitchen. Fuck you," I try to sound vicious, annoyed, angry, bite back, but my voice trembles.

I swallow hard as he stands from the little stool, my eyes latching onto where it sits behind him. Memories of him perching me beside him on my 'big girl's stool' assault me. My skinny little hands always stabbing at the keys too hard. His larger ones covering mine, his fingers directing mine where to go. I swallow the dry lump in my throat, rapidly blinking my eyes as his shadow falls across me.

Surveying my face, "a bird?" he repeats with a frown.

I nod, "a swallow, a dead one," I exhale. "Someone left it in the kitchen," I tell him a little blankly.

Someone's been in my house.

Completely violating me and my privacy, getting through security numerous times. There're checkpoints, keycodes, handprint scanners, and more locks than I can count just to make it into the main lobby. Let alone get access to one of the elevators. My skin itches at the very thought, like a million insects dancing across my flesh. I wrap my good arm around myself, pressing hard into my side.

"Lala," Max breathes softly.

His big hand coming up slowly, he drops it down on my shoulder.

"What can I do?" he asks gently, squeezing me comfortingly.

I feel tears prick my eyes.

"Hux wants you."

Shrugging his hand off me, I turn away sharply, heading to the intercom. I press for Charlie, it beeps a few times without answer. Max wanders past me slowly. I can practically feel his eyes boring holes into the back of my head. I sigh heavily, pulling up my big girl pants and forcefully dissolve the emotion on my face. I'm not letting this deter me, we have plans tonight that we're already running late for.

I hit the call button for the basement.

"Boss, Rubble's filled me in on the situation. I'm just on my way up, I've contacted Eli and he-"

"Gremlin," I say sternly, cutting him off. Every ounce of my being wanting to crawl into bed and hide beneath the silk sheets. "I still want to leave in five minutes."

Silence greets me on the other end, and I crease my eyebrows as I wait.

"Yes, boss," he finally replies but I'm not happy with his tone.

"Problem, Grem?"

"No, boss," he immediately answers, only making me frown harder as I disconnect.

I wander back into the kitchen. Rubble, Huxley and Max all hunched over, examining my gift. Rubble's so fucking close he's practically got his face in it.

"No anthrax then?" I deadpan, the three of them snapping their gazes over to me.

Rubble shakes his head once before righting himself. I grab my jacket, tossing it back on. Threading my good arm into the sleeve, draping the other side over my shoulder.

"Are you ready?" I question, tapping my booted foot impatiently as Max blinks over at me.

"What?" he blanches.

"Christ, are you stupid? I said are you ready? *To go*?" I shake my head as he just stares at me, his mouth popped open. "Never mind, I'll go on my own," I tut, spinning on my heel.

"You seriously want to go now?" Max asks as though I'm mad for even thinking it.

"Err, yes, I want to go. I wanted to go half an hour ago too, why would I suddenly change my mind?" I query, shaking my head at him in irritation.

"Well," his black eyebrows draw together, shadowing his turquoise eyes, his lips thinning as he clenches his jaw.

"Well, nothing, it's a bird. There's nothing I can do about it now, it's already dead. What are you suggesting, Maddox? That I attempt to give it the kiss of life? If that's the case, I think you should book onto a first aid course asap, your skills need a serious update if you think there's any hope for a creature that's been dead for what looks like days."

Huxley looks between the two of us, moving in front of me, his heavenly dark eyes full of concern. He grips my hip, tugging me into him. I crane my neck back, looking up at him. His six-foot-four height feels like so much more when he surrounds me in every sense of the word.

"Do you think this is a good idea, to go now? We could call Kacey at the garage and tell him to come straight home instead of meeting us out. Shouldn't we deal with this," he circles his hand in the direction behind him. Gesturing to where Rubble is currently lifting the box from the counter, "first?"

A sensible suggestion.

"No, it's Christmas Eve, I want us to go out," I snap, instantly regretting using that tone with him.

His gaze softens, his grip tightening on my hip as he dips down, dropping a kiss to my lips.

"Let me grab my phone, then we'll all go, okay?"

I nod, my lips pressing against his for a second greedy kiss. This one lasting longer but nothing more than our lips searing their imprint into one another. He taps my bum, taking off down the opposite hall.

CHAPTER II
KYLA-ROSE

I sit behind Max in the rear passenger seat. Ending my call with Charlie, I tug my hair free from its restricting scrunchie. Resting my forehead against the cool glass of the window. Charlie says the bird's a barn swallow. Barn swallows, although mate for life, the females can have multiple life partners. Polyamorous apparently. Charlie knows his stuff, so I didn't question it. Although, he did voice his concern that this seems to be rather specific. More personal than business. Not that we thought any differently anyway, but this just helps confirm what we suspected.

Someone's after *me*, not my businesses.

Frank driving at speed through the typical English weather. The downpour of rain started just as we all climbed into our designated vehicles. London whips by in a blur, the sky, the roads, every single building, all fly by in varying miserable shades of dreary grey.

The sporadic flash of colour thrown in, a post-box or telephone box jumping out with its proud red paint. Bridges and shop shutters coated in tags of brightly coloured graffiti. I sigh as quietly as I can. My warm breath misting the window as raindrops continue to spatter the outside of it.

Never missing a trick, Huxley's fingers find my hand. His long digits winding through mine, resting them on the centre seat between us. He doesn't say anything, he doesn't have to, but I feel myself breathe a little easier at his warm touch. My soul sighing with his comfort.

Knowing someone coulda been in the house makes me feel all kinds of dirty. I'm getting a headache just thinking about it. Gremlin says there's no way, absolutely no fucking way, someone could have got inside there. It's more guarded than Fort Knox. My head pounds, my pulse thumping angrily in my temples. My hand pulsating with pain, Jacob shoved a handful of pills at me again this morning which I didn't take, again. I don't trust his back-alley prescriptions not to knock me on my arse. I'll take the pain over pills thanks, makes me feel a little more alive anyway so I won't complain. He'd love me out of it, shoved into an institution. He tried to sell it to me a couple years ago, '*rehab for the mind*' he called it. I snort at the memory, thinks 'cause he's a surgeon he knows fucking everything. I love him, but fuck, sometimes it's too fucking much.

I just need to get Christmas and my impending

possible surgery outta the way, then I can start my life back up. Hunt my weird arse stalker and gut him like the spineless snake he is. Or *her*, I 'spose. Although, I've never pissed off a woman other than my mother. So unless her rotting corpse has come back from the grave to haunt me, it's likely to be the other member of our species. The one with the meat swinging between their thighs.

Bloody Nora.

Why is that even a phrase? Like, what did Nora ever do to anyone, who the fuck even *is* Nora? All these stupid phrases are always named after women too, Jeez Louise, Debbie Downer. A man likely came up with them all.

I groan, my mind suddenly pulling me in a different direction. Thinking of all the shit I've missed out on over the last two weeks. All the shipments I wanted to monitor, the street deals and collections I enjoy keeping an eye on. All swept out from beneath me, like the rug's been permanently pulled out from under my feet. I've got my fingers in so many pies it'll be impossible to rein it all back in. I'll have a permanent headache until at least late March at this rate.

My mind whirls until the car eventually comes to a stop.

"We're 'ere, Darlin', open your eyes," Huxley murmurs.

Leaning across the seat, his voice rasping in my ear, teeth nipping at my lobe, he unclips my seatbelt.

I sit myself up, strapping knives to my thigh.

Shoving a gun, all removed from the seat pocket, down the back of my leather trousers. My too-big t-shirt tail untucked, hiding it from view. Frank comes around to open my door. Swinging my legs over the side of the seat. Huxley drapes my red leather jacket back over my shoulders from behind as I slip from the car. My hand in Franks, I drop my booted feet down into a murky puddle. Three cars filled with our men pull up behind Frank down the narrow side road. Tall, yellow brick buildings on either side of us, a line of cars on the left and two large shutters covered in bright graffiti on the right.

A few feet past those shutters awaits our destination. From the outside The Black Heart pub looks like any other simplistic building. Sitting in the heart of Camden, it could pass as a shop, a private gallery or even a fancy-pants estate agents. Dark grey painted panels, with dark tints on the doors and windows, no signage to mark it. You can't hear the music booming from inside, but you can feel it. The heavy vibrations pounding their way through the crumbling tarmac, shooting right through the soles of your feet. Plucking at your heart strings like a heavy metal rocker with an electric guitar. I take the lead, Frank staying with the car and the rest of the men as Max and Huxley flank me. I push the door open, heavy bass hitting me in the face like a slap to the cheek.

My boots thump in time with the music as I weave my way through the eight o'clock crowd. The walls painted matte black, smothered floor to ceiling in framed band posters and memorabilia. Lots of it from local metal bands and artists that have played here. Custom neon lights are placed haphazardly in between, a blood red inverted cross, the word 'Hell' in electric purple. Then there's the little alcoves slotted in the walls, like little church niches filled to the brim with skulls, candles and anti-Christ nick-nacks. A statue of Mother Mary in another, draped with rosary beads, splattered with what appears to be blood. A pig at her feet, a green mohawk stuck to his little piggy head, painted black combat boots on his trotters. The thick beams across the ceiling are coated with stickers, beer mats and signage. The large dark wood bar sits to one side, illuminated by the liquor shelf lighting and not much else. As is expected for Christmas Eve, the place is packed.

Squeezing myself between bodies to get to the bar. I huff in frustration as a huge guy blocks my path. I think about stabbing him in the back of the thigh just to get him out my way. It's a fleeting thought as an arm forces its way through the bodies before me. A large hand fisting my too large t-shirt in his hand and savagely pulling me through, his thick fingers grazing my tits. *That's* the motherfucker I'm gunna stab. As I'm practically suctioned through the tight gap, hissing as my wounded hand gets whacked with an elbow. I grip the knife at my thigh, drawing it the second I'm at the bar. My blade sweeping through the air, pressing against his thick, scarred, tattooed throat.

"I love it when you make me bleed, Sweetheart,"

Kacey booms a laugh as I narrow my eyes on him, my body sagging slightly in relief.

"The fuck?"

"Thought you were gunna sneak in here early without me, baby girl?" he chuckles.

He was supposed to meet us here after the late shift at the garage, it appears he got off early.

His thick fingers still fisting my -his- shirt, he drags me into his chest. My body sliding perfectly between his parted thighs, like two connecting puzzle pieces, where he perches on an old bar stool.

"Would I ever sneak away from you, Big Man?" I smirk against his lips.

My eyes flicking between his as he fists a hand in my hair, massaging the back of my skull with thick fingers. The pressure has my eyes closing, a soft moan slipping between my lips. His other hand at the small of my back, clutching me closer. His already hard cock pressing painfully into my lower belly. I flick my blade closed, slipping it back into the strap at my thigh, so I can dig my nails into his. His big hand runs down my back, over the hump of my arse. He groans at the feel of supple leather beneath his calloused palm. His fingers grabbing a handful of my arse. His hips thrusting forward on the bar stool as he draws my body closer, giving himself a teasing friction. I let him manipulate my body, using me how he wishes, it's good not to have to think sometimes. And I trust Kacey wholeheartedly. Dragging sloppy kisses across my jaw, I suck in a deep lungful of him, letting every-

thing about him overwhelm and excite me, raw earth,
bergamot and mint.

I groan, his teeth sinking into my bottom lip,
nibbling and sucking it into his mouth, releasing it
with a pop. He kisses me, his lips melding and
working with mine, kissing me like I'm the only thing
in this world that can keep him alive. I slide my
tongue into his mouth, wrestling for control, we attack
each other. My body humming with satisfaction as he
grips me so hard I stop breathing. My hand sliding up
to the hollow of his throat. My thumb caressing the
ragged scar there, he growls into my mouth. Taking
control and claiming me right here in the middle of
The Black fucking Heart.

Blood roars in my ears as a familiar body closes in
behind me. Oranges and sandalwood mingle with raw
earth and mint. It's like my body knows its favourite
cocktail and she's a *very* thirsty bitch. Every nerve
ending in me comes alive, my blood screaming as it
bolts through my veins, my core clenching as wet heat
floods down my thighs.

Huxley's hand curls around my right hip, his
fingers digging into me, his hot skin searing me
through the thin cotton t-shirt. He brings his head to
the other side of me, whispering loud enough for
Kacey and I to both hear.

"Could you maybe not try to mount our girl like a
wild beast in heat in the middle of a fucking pub?" he
growls, a shiver shooting up my spine at the dominance in his voice.

Kacey breaks our kiss with a chuckle.

"Let 'em look, man, they could learn summink," he laughs.

Dropping his gaze down to my face, his eyes flicking between my own.

"You okay, Sweetheart?"

I lick my lips, my hand moving up to his face, fingers cupping his cheek. My thumb wiping away the smear of red lipstick at the corner of his mouth. I gnaw on my bottom lip. Leaning back into Hux, tilting my head, watching Kacey's heated gaze strip me bare. His mind's eye bending me over the bar, rutting into me over and over until he forces me to come on his cock.

"I'm good," I smile breathlessly.

He beams in response, Huxley's grip on my hips tugs me into his chest, his arms banding around my front, crossing over my chest protectively as I settle back into him.

"Four pints of Camden Hells, when you're ready, Gina," Kacey calls flirtatiously over the bar.

The inked, blue-haired barmaid nodding in response.

A minute later four pints are slid before us. I lean across the bar, the thumping bass from below pounding through my bloodstream.

"Gina!" I yell over the music as she turns to walk away.

She glances back at me over her shoulder, I wave a fifty at her.

"Eight Zombie Brains, and a bottle of The Kraken too, please!"

Her lips tilt up at one corner, she nods, turning away and returning with eight tall shot glasses. A generous serving of peach schnapps goes in, a squirt of crème de menthe, the green mixing with the clear. Irish cream poured over the back of a teaspoon topping up the glass and then a quick splash of grenadine for the red colour and sweetness. I grin as I slide her the fifty, my eyes locked on the ugly drinks that look exactly like gross little brains.

"Urr, I thought we were having a quiet drink, Darlin'?" Huxley laughs, a nervous bite of energy in his tone.

"Don't remember saying that," I shrug truthfully. "Come on, let's find Mr Grumpy and make him neck these drinks back. Might put some sort of expression on that miserable fuckin' face."

I spin out of Huxley's hold. Grabbing a pint and leaving my men to work out the rest as I find my way to the booth Maddox is occupying. Placing the pint down on the cherry wood table, sliding my arse onto the bench seat opposite him. Placing two fingers on the cold glass, I slide it across the table, planting it before the despondent devil. His turquoise orbs flicker between me and the beer suspiciously, making me grin wide.

"D'you spit in it or somethin'?" he grunts, a scowl firmly set in place.

I fight my smile growing wider, savagely biting into my cheek, I cock my head.

"Peace offering," I shrug.

My jacket slipping off my good shoulder, tugging the huge t-shirt with it and exposing my skin. Max raises a brow at my honesty. His eyes tracking the raw bite mark Kacey gave me in my shoulder before his gaze snaps back up to meet mine. He picks up the pint, bringing the glass to his plump lips, condensation rolling over his fingers as his eyes stay on mine. He tips it back, parting his lips, his throat working down the chilled liquid. His Adam's apple bobbing in the pale column of his throat. His hand tattooed with *me* gripping the glass tightly as little drops of condensation drip to the warm red wood of the table. I imagine leaning forward, lapping the water from his thorn woven fingers. Twirling my tongue around his digits, sucking them into my mouth, but I don't. Instead, I smirk as he exhales, satisfied from his refreshing beer, placing it back down onto the table.

"Didn't say I didn't spit it in, though," I shrug again.

My jacket sliding off the other shoulder, dropping onto the bench seat with a soft thud.

"You're such a bitch," he growls lowly, meaning every word, his eyes scorching every inch of my visible skin, and I laugh.

"I know," I tease, a smirk threatening his lips at my agreement.

His blue eyes twinkle as they lock on mine,

creasing at the outer corners as he suppresses his real smile. His harsh, square jaw flexing. The historical pull between us is undeniable as heat soars through my veins. At the same time a cold shiver racks me, conflictingly sending goosebumps erupting out all over my flesh. I swallow, my breath hitching as he places his large hand down on the table. I watch him as his fingers flex, hesitation riding him hard as he over-thinks what he's doing.

"I'm sorry, Lala, for earlier," he says earnestly.

His deep, silk voice caressing my very bones. The sound stroking my insides into a frenzy, my attention drawn to his lips then his eyes.

"I forgive you," I say on instinct, the words whooshing from me without so much as a conscious thought.

My teeth chew away anxiously at my bottom lip as he watches me. He sighs, running his hand through his thick head of hair. The raven-black strands harsh against his pale skin. Blue and green veins just visible beneath the inked skin as his knuckles fist, tugging at the roots. His elbow dropping to the table, he reaches across, the movement smooth and confident. The rough pad of his thumb gently swipes across my mouth, tugging my gnawed lip free from between my nibbling teeth.

"Don't do that," he rasps, his gaze locked on where his thumb caresses my lip.

His inked fingers sliding over my jaw, encasing my face in his strong hold. My breath stills in my chest.

The tip of my tongue cautiously sliding through my teeth, lazily rolling over his thumb, tasting the salt of his skin. His grip strengthening on my face, I feel my core tighten, my lungs screaming to be released but I'm completely consumed by his touch. Fingers rough against my face, his turquoise gaze setting a fire alight inside of me, my demon preening and purring under her devil's unwavering attention.

"Lala," Max breathes, my body leaning fully into his touch like it just can't help itself. My eyelids fluttering as he cups my face like I belong to him, "I-"

"Fuck me, Darlin'. Was all this really necessary?" Huxley complains, suddenly appearing at the end of the booth, cutting Max off, my attention snapping up to him sharply.

Max's hand drops from my face like I burnt him. Our moment dashed, burning up and turning to ash, disintegrating before our very eyes.

Huxley balancing drinks, a pint in the crook of his elbow, one in his hand, a tray in the other. Placing the shot filled tray down first, he manoeuvres the two pints to the table without spilling a single drop.

Kacey slides the unopened bottle of spiced rum to the centre of the table as he climbs into the bench seat beside me. Pint in hand, his thick arm dropping over my slim shoulders. Tucking me protectively against his huge body so I'm not crushed to the wall. Max shuffles along giving Huxley enough space to climb in beside him, before reaching across and snatching up a shot. Doing the same, I grin smugly, knocking it straight back. Biting my lip at the look of disgust on Max's face. He hates Baileys.

Kacey's fingertips brush the outside of my arm, tracing circles into my skin. I look up at him as he swallows his pint down, his scarred, inked throat bobbing. I gaze up at him, unashamedly admiring his rough but pretty features. The tattooed ivy weaving its way up his neck, curving onto his skull, the blonde hair shaved bare to show off all its delicate lines.

"You're so fuckin' beautiful," my lips release the breathy words before I even have time to think them through.

Looking down at me from the corner of his eye, Kacey places his near empty glass onto the table. Turning back and grinning at me wide. He pinches my chin between his finger and thumb, drawing me towards him. Dipping his head low, his mouth brushing against mine.

"Thank you, Sweetheart. You're pretty fuckin' beautiful too," he murmurs a chuckle against my parted lips.

Every word feeding me as he crushes his lips to mine. His tongue slides between my parted lips, licking into my mouth like a savage. He nips at my lips, our teeth smashing together sharply, fisting a hand in my hair. He breathes into me, sighing so deeply it fills me up with such satisfaction I melt. My hand smoothing up his jean clad thigh where he's twisted towards me. My body practically cradled between his thick thighs. I graze the tip of my little finger over the hard bulge in his tight jeans. Kacey moans into my mouth, his other hand clasping my waist, squeezing hard, he heaves me into his lap. My knee knocking the table, a quiet *oh shit* murmured from Hux as I hear the splash of liquid hit the cherry wood. A small chuckle escapes me as Kacey draws back, his hungry citrine eyes flaying the flesh from my bones. He swipes the corner of my lips with his thick thumb, sucking the scarlet red lipstick from his skin in the next second. His tongue wrapping around it devilishly slow.

"I'm not sure how many times I'm gunna need to request this tonight, but I have a feeling it's going to be a few." Huxley sighs dramatically, making me raise a brow at him, a sly grin on my face. "Can you please not fuck our girl in the middle of a pub?"

I laugh then, a real chuckle bursting free from my chest. Kacey laughs with me, thumping his weight back in the seat. I slide from his lap, his head resting against the frosted glass partition separating our booth from the next.

"Maybe you just need another drink to warm you up to the idea, mate," Kacey beams. "Dunno what ya problem is, Hux," Kacey dances his eyebrows suggestively. Huxley's inky eyes narrowing on his friend. "We all know you're the exhibitionist out of our little trio," he tosses out, his huge shoulders shrugging.

"Shut the fuck up," Huxley hisses. My lips parting in surprise at the venom in his tone, he stares at Kacey like he just spewed a dark secret.

My head tilting in observation, I lick my lips, *intrigue*. My attention drifting to Max throwing his third shot down the hatch. Wincing in distaste as he swallows it, desperately trying to separate himself from the conversation.

But I want him to look.

I want him to *see* me, with *them*.

It kicks the fire inside me, like a hornets' nest, it's angry and it stings. Embers and ash exploding from the crackling heat when those beautiful sea-blue eyes are on me. His gaze scorching a trail across my flesh as my other two hellhounds lick a soothing trail across me in its wake. I know he watches. Skulking in the shadows, silent feet stopping outside my bedroom door, his ear pressed against the wood. It should feel invasive, weird, intrusive. But all I get from it is this feeling of comfort. Wrapping around my spine like silk bows, caressing my soul with his presence. Safety seeping from his pores, spilling into mine.

My gaze sliding back to Huxley, Kacey's firm grip on my shoulder, my breathing quickens. Those coal black eyes sweep up my body, his lip curling up at one corner. A dirty wink tossed haphazardly in my direction, I suck in a sharp breath, my entire body humming with pleasure. Kacey chuckles, nuzzling his chin on the top of my head. Breathing me in deeply as he scent marks what's his. His arm drops from my shoulders, smoothing down my spine, winding around my lower back. My gun pressing into his forearm, his thick fingers pinching my upper thigh, he drags me closer. Untucking my t-shirt from my leather trousers, the bulk of fabric covering me to my knees. Deft fingers work to free the button, he drags the zipper down in immediate succession. Working his hand into the tight fabric, slipping beneath the red lace, he growls lowly as his thick fingers find my aching centre.

Kacey's breath heavy in my ear, my eyes still locked on Huxley's. Kacey slides a thick digit between my wet folds. Every instinct in me is telling me to put a stop to this, but my knees widen automatically, brushing against Max's beneath the table.

"Tell them how wet you are, Sweetheart," Kacey growls and I shiver.

His finger sliding torturously slow up and down my slit, ignoring my clit and driving me wild.

"What?" I breathe the question, my voice cracking as desire pulses through me.

"Tell *them* how wet you are. *Both* of them," Kacey pants in my ear, his breath fanning hair across my face.

The taste of beer on my tongue lingering from our kiss. The thump of heavy bass vibrating through the soles of my feet from the floor below. The historical scent of cigarette smoke that's locked deep in the old walls overwhelms me. I lick my red-painted lips and for a second, I stop breathing. My eyes flick between Huxley and Max, both their gazes firmly locked on me. Searing me with equal looks of lust as Kacey finally plunges a finger inside my wet heat.

"I'm *so* wet," I groan.

Loud enough for someone else to hear had the place not been packed wall to wall, people's backs to us as they stand around in groups.

"For who?" Kacey growls, his sharp teeth nipping viciously at my throat as he continues to pump his finger in and out of me.

It's effortless the way he undoes me, and he knows it.

"For you," I breathe, squirming on his hand squeezed in the crutch of my too-tight trousers.

"And?" he rumbles, the animalistic grunt forcing liquid to gush from me, soaking his hand.

"And Hux," I whine, staring right into those obsidian eyes lit with a fire reminiscent of the one in my core.

"*And?*" he coos at me teasingly.

His thumb finally flicking my clit and making my thighs clench, attempting to squeeze together.

"*And?*" I echo in confusion, my head dropping back, knocking against the frosted glass panel.

"Yes," he hisses in my ear, "and?"

I glance at the devil. Those turquoise eyes stealing my breath away as Kacey sinks another thick, inked finger inside of me, stretching me with a delicious burn. My legs unable to widen further, the leather trousers restricting both our movements.

"*Max,*" I breathe, just loud enough for my voice to kiss Max's ear.

His body rolling as his hands fist on the table.

"Max," I repeat more confidently, making sure he can hear the truth, Kacey smiles against my skin.

"Good girl," he praises huskily, his nose running up the column of my throat, he breathes me in. "Do you want him to touch you, Sweetheart?" Kacey questions, his voice low enough for only me to hear as he nibbles on my lobe. "His hand on your hand, nothing more unless you want it, you can say no."

I swallow as Kacey picks up his pace, my pussy sucking on his fingers. Trying and failing to pull him deeper, demanding more, *needing* it. Praying to the devil himself to let me come. But Kacey is apparently the master of edging because every time his fingers brush against that super sensitive spot inside me he slows. Leaving my body trembling and aching for release.

"What do you say, Sweetheart. Shall we test his sharing capabilities?" he chuckles against my skin.

The vibration thrumming through his teeth, the sound working its way into my very bones. I nod, slowly removing my right hand from his thigh, nervously placing it on the edge of the table. Kacey kisses my cheek, the warmth of his lips against my goosebump covered skin has me shivering. Turning his head to face his boys. His free hand slides onto the back of mine, pressing my palm into the table, guiding us towards Max's clenched fist. I look up at him through my lashes, my heart hammering in my chest at the fear of his rejection. Kacey's fingers still pumping into me at an unwavering pace even as he focuses his attention elsewhere. Max looks down at our approaching hands with a frown, my eyes instantly diverting onto Huxley. Our gazes lock, giving me a comforting nod, he winks at me again and I feel the tension easing out of me. Huxley giving me the bravery to, once again look over at Max.

"Hold her hand for me, bro," Kacey instructs casually.

Kicking my feet further apart with his booted foot, making me gasp. My teeth slam down into my bottom lip as the vibration from his kick runs up my legs. Pulsing in my clit that is so very desperate for attention. Max drops his gaze down to our joint hands. Kacey's lifting from mine, returning to his pint, swallowing the last drops of amber liquid before he places it back on the wood. The movement so casual as though he's not knuckle deep inside my pussy beneath the table. Max looks up at me then and although tempted to avert my gaze, I don't. I hold steadfast. Kacey twirls his fingers inside of me, I pant, an unbidden whine clawing its way up my throat as Kacey's thumb ghosts across my clit. I stamp my foot in frustration. Huxley chuckles as a look of sheer exasperation takes over my face.

"*Please*," I breathlessly heave out the words, my tongue too dry as I try to wet my lips.

"Please what, Darlin'?" Huxley mocks, enjoying my pain far too much.

I'll remember that when he tries to ram his

monstrous dick down my throat later, I might just *accidently* catch him with my teeth.

"Please, for the love of fuck, someone make me *come*," I groan at being denied.

Toxicity in every syllable as Kacey's thumb *just* misses my clit again and his fingers draw almost all the way out of me.

A hand slides into mine atop the table, my head snapping up, gaze instantly colliding with Max's. His fingers finally locking between my own, gripping me like he can't believe he ever let go. I tremble at the intensity in his gaze. My throat closing as Kacey slams his fingers back inside me so ruthlessly that I come the second he rolls his slick thumb over my clit. My head snaps back, knocking into the glass partition with a thunk. I cry out, Kacey's free hand slapping over my mouth, my hot breath puffing against his hand. I bite into his palm, my chest heaving with breaths as I come around his fingers. He continues to glide his fingers in and out of me, his thumb lazily stroking my clit as I start to come down.

When I open my eyes, three ravenous beasts stare back at me as though I just put on the best damn show of their lives. Kacey pulls his fingers out of me, removing his hand from my trousers and doing them back up. He looks at Huxley as I look between the two of them, matching mischievous smirks on both their faces. Kacey rests his elbow on the tabletop, his hand glistening with me. My lips pop open, my grip tightening on Max, his thumb smoothing over the back of my hand. My breathing picking back up as I glance around at the other punters whose attention is thankfully *not* on us. Kacey leans into me, his lips skimming over mine, a smirk the devil would be proud of on his lickable lips. He leans back slightly, bringing his fingers closer.

"Suck," he commands.

Without hesitation my mouth opens wider, ready to take his thick fingers into my mouth. But instead, his arm moves across the table. His elbow firmly in place, he reaches across, offering his slick fingers up to the devil. I watch with rapt attention, my juices shimmering like diamonds under the low lights. Kacey's fingers scissoring in front of his face. Max never takes his eyes from me. My breath stuttered to a stop in my chest, heart thrashing wildly against its boned prison, screaming to tear free. I wait, *we* wait, seconds feel like hours and my insides churn as I see anger flair in his clear turquoise eyes. Just when I think this is over, he leans forward. Taking Kacey's thick fingers into his mouth, his cheeks hollowing as he sucks. He twirls his tongue over them, sucking them hard into the back of his throat and I'm still not breathing. I'm hanging over the edge of a cliff just waiting to plummet. Max pops Kacey's fingers free, running his tongue across his teeth, smacking his lips lustily as he continues to hold my gaze. An unreadable expression on his swollen lips, his eyes hard to read.

"*Delicious*," he rasps, and my lungs suddenly remember how to work.

I choke on air, hot, sticky and humid, tinged with beer and sweat. My lungs squeezing painfully as my heart continues to pound like a wild deer being chased by a wolf. Kacey grips my chin. The predator in him not liking to share my attention too long, he did just make me come, he wants his reward.

Kacey's lips crash into mine, attacking my mouth with his. Beer and excitement on his tongue. I melt into him, my overwhelmed body flopping against his chest, relying on him to keep me upright. He licks into my mouth, long tangling strokes of his tongue. Worshipping my mouth like it gave him the very air in his lungs and the blood in his veins. I break away from him first, placing a soft kiss against his lips before I lean back in my seat. His hand dropping to my thigh, squeezing possessively.

Max's hand still clasped in mine, I flex my fingers, smiling as the little girl inside me squeals with happiness. I'm reluctant to let go, but only having one hand makes it difficult to do anything. Deciding on how best to grab a drink. I lean forward, opening my mouth wide, I take hold of a shot glass between my teeth. Throwing my head back quickly, the creamy, sweet, minty flavour burning its way down my throat as I swallow. My tongue darting into the glass, licking out the last drops before I spit it down onto the table. Huxley chuckles, Kacey shakes his head. I grin wide at Max as he gives me more than a frown for once, a little glint in his serious eyes.

"I'm gunna grab a smoke," Max announces, squeezing my fingers in silent request for release.

Reluctantly I spread my fingers, allowing him to pull free. Feeling *something*, I don't know what, not sad, just a little depleted?

Having his hand in mine felt like home.

He tasted me.

Huxley scoots over, standing up to let Max out of the booth. My gaze dropping back to the table, I give a soft shake of my head to myself. *Idiot.* He just thinks I'm some sort of desperate whore now, can't even have one drink without needing to get dicked down.

Fuck me.

"You comin', Princess?" his eyebrows rising on his forehead as he plucks a cigarette from behind his ear. Placing it between his teeth before producing another from his other ear, offering it up to me. "Smoke?"

This is his *olive branch.*

I nod once, a soft smile on my lips as Kacey lifts me clean off the seat. A squeal escaping me, he plants my feet down on either side of his wide thighs, holding me over him. His soppy grin wide as he stares up at me, his big hands on my hips.

"Let me down, Big Man," I laugh as he continues to keep me up above him.

He leans in, planting a kiss on my leather covered pussy. My cheeks heating as I hear someone across the bar wolf whistle before he's swinging me down into Huxley's waiting arms with a chuckle. Hux sweeps me into him, pressing a chaste kiss to my lips. Straightening my t-shirt so it covers more of my shoulders. He takes my jacket from where Kacey hands it to him, draping it carefully over my shoulders. I look past him to Max who's watching me with a look I can't quite decipher. My stomach bottoms out as he offers me his hand. Huxley instantly deciding for me, he takes mine and places it in Max's.

"We're okay with it, Darlin'," he breathes in my ear as Max starts to weave his way to an exit.

Pulling me behind him so I don't get crushed, I glance back over my shoulder at Huxley. His dark eyes twinkling, he winks and disappears from view. I swallow the dry lump in my throat, keeping close to Max's back as he grips my hand and pulls us through the swarm of people. It's even busier now, louder. Not that I'd noticed either of those things in the last half hour. Ignorance is bliss, and definitely not something I'm used to. I can't believe I let my guard down like that and in a pub of all places, especially one this busy. My hackles are usually up, my mind hyper aware of everyone and everything around me. But apparently, I came to a pub to get dick drunk above alcohol poisoning.

CHAPTER 12

KYLA-ROSE

Max pulls me through the crowd, pushing out of a fire exit into the alley behind. The cold December air assaulting my flushed face like hundreds of tiny papercuts as wind whips around us. I follow the alley down a short way, standing beside a large, green recycling bin. Cardboard overflowing from it despite its industrial size and piling up on the floor, but it helps stop the wind lashing at us on one side. Colourful graffiti covers the opposite wall, the bright green emergency exit light above the door the only thing allowing us to see. I kick my foot up against the brick, Max doing the same beside me. Offering me a cigarette, the white menthol stick pinched between his thumb and finger. I take it, our hands brushing.

"Thanks," I smile softly, quickly placing it between my lips.

"'ere," Max rumbles, flicking a little lime green lighter in my face.

The flame jumping around wildly in the arctic wind, despite his cupped hand around it. It finally catches as I inhale, the cherry burning brightly. I let my eyes fall shut, exhaling smoke through my nose as I lazily keep the cigarette between my lips. In through my mouth, out through my nose. Laying my head back against the wall, the vibrations of the music echoing through my skull.

"Lala, I wanna make shit right," Max sighs. I lazily roll my eyes over to him. "I wanna not have this," he grits his teeth. Motioning between us with his hand, "this tension, this angsty bullshit. It ain't fuckin' right, Lala, this ain't supposed to be us."

Inhaling deeply, I roll my cigarette between my teeth. Letting the smoke billow out from my lungs, puffing out between my teeth in gentle clouds. The wind whipping it away into the dark.

"What *is* supposed to be us, Maddox? I don't think we were *ever* on the same page."

I feel my insides twist, coiling like a viper ready to strike. My demon clawing at my chest. Her jagged claws slicing through flesh and bone, the hurt lodging in my throat. My memory flashing all those nights he'd be covered in love bites, stinking of someone else's shitty perfume, to the front of my mind. Drunk out of his mind, pounding on my window in the middle of the night. I always fucking let him in.

"I-"

"Do you remember the night that you came over? The one when you threw a handful of shingle at my bedroom window from next door's pathway and almost gave me a heart attack because it sounded like a pellet gun?" I interrupt him, cutting him off so I can make my point.

"Lala-"

"You hadn't so much as looked at me for three months, but that night you turned up at my house. I'd just scrubbed sick from the carpet; Mum had smashed my head into the bathroom door in a fit of rage. Splitting my eyebrow before she proceeded to chuck up all over the hall. I scrubbed that carpet so I didn't call you. I had to force myself to stop thinking about you, but every time something bad happened you're the one I wanted to save me. I wanted to run to you, have you take me into your arms and swear to me I never had to go back. Would never have to be away from you again," I stare ahead as I talk.

Not wanting to see his face as I travel back in time. My lipstick keeping my cigarette attached to my bottom lip.

"I showered myself in ice cold water. Using diluted bleach on my hands, trying to scrub the scent of sick from my fingertips before getting into bed. The electric was shut off because we hadn't paid our bill and I didn't wanna have to crawl to Dee and ask for money. I finally dragged myself into bed after two-am, my eyes just closing when something hit my window. And there you were, drunk off your arse all because

Henry Sawyer asked me to a party. Do you remember that night Max?"

"Yeah," he swallows guiltily with a nod.

"You fell into my bed, stinking of someone else. Covered in hickeys, lipstick on your skin and shitty perfume on your clothes. And you called *me* a no-good tramp, white trash, the likes of Henry Sawyer much too good for someone like me. He went to that fancy boys' school, you said he was only interested in handing me off to his pervert daddy, you remember that?" I question.

Ice pricking my skin but hot anger pulsing through my veins as I remember how much those words had hurt at the delicate age of fifteen.

"Yeah," he rasps.

"Then when you'd finished slurring venom at me you pulled me into your chest, cupping the back of my head and stroking my hair. Half pulling me on top of you in my single bed. You kissed my forehead. And I just remember feeling so, *so* fucking happy that you were there with me. Giving me your attention, despite the nasty shit you said. When you started snoring, I cried. I cried so damn hard that my body shook, and in your sleep, you shushed me. Soothed me with your presence, kept me close, held me tight so that all my broken pieces stayed in place just a little while longer. And then you mumbled that you loved me. You kissed my hair, telling me that you loved me. And you were drunk, of course you didn't remember, but I did. I remembered you telling me that as I woke up the next

morning without you again. Wondering if my imagination had conjured you up for comfort, summoning
the devil in my hour of need."

I swallow thickly, flicking my cigarette into the
darkness. The glowing tip quickly dying out in the
wind, reminding me of the fire in me as a teenager.
How it too, was snuffed out just as easily.

"You were just gone again, and I was alone, and
the thing is, Max. You continuously told me
throughout our entire lives that you'd never leave me,
time and time again and so now, how could I trust you
enough not to leave? Not to make me feel things for
you again, try to make this work, see where it goes.
How can we be happy in this life if I'm always waiting
for you to up and leave. For you to just pack up a bag
one day and walk out. I can't do it. I won't. You're not
stable, Maddox. You can't be what *we* need you to be.
Because it's not just me you need to be there for, this is
our family. Huxley, Kacey and I, we need stability,
and we have that together, but I'm unsure about you.
I don't know you anymore. You play dirty and you hit
harder and harder and harder and you're not Maxi
and I'm not Lala and the world is a mess. A giant
fuckin' mess where you and I are concerned. And I
just don't think I can do it again." I say, thumping my
fist against my belly.

"Kyla-Rose, I won't leave you," he rasps, his
usually smooth voice unsteady. "I'm never going to-"

A sharp whipping sound whistles past my ear,
brick behind my head exploding as a bullet lodges in

the wall. I drop down, Max ducking down with me, instantly drawing his gun.

"Fuck! Lala!"

"Shush!" I hiss.

My heart hammering in my chest, blood roaring in my ears. I strain hard to listen as my breath comes out in short, sharp pants. *Fuck*, if my assailant wasn't such a shit shot I'd be dead right now, that bullet wasn't even an inch from my face. My body heaving with breaths, Max tucks himself into me. Using the bin for cover, his crystal blue eyes wide as I stare back at him. A smile plucks at me, adrenaline roaring through my veins as I hear a single footstep.

I reach into my pocket, pulling free my little switchblade, leaving my gun in my waistband, because we absolutely do *not* need a shootout in central London, this ain't the wild west. Flicking it open, thumbing the edge of the blade, I hold my breath. Max stills, grip on his gun tightening like it's an extension of his arm, my focus enthralled by his fingers curling around the grip as I listen. My head tilting to one side, we stay crouched.

The shuffle of a foot, a mere few feet away. I gesture to Max, placing the blade between my teeth, using my good hand to lean on Max's knee for support. I start to silently pivot in place, working my feet in small circles. Turning my back on Max, I press the palm of my hand against the plastic bin. Steadying my feet and taking in a slow deep breath. We can't start a fucking shoot out in the middle of an alley, the attacker might have a silencer, but Max and I certainly don't and I'm not having the police getting involved. We'll deal with our own shit in the most English way we can.

A good old fashioned fist fight.

Guns are for emergencies.

I slap my hand against the bin, the sound echoing down the dark alleyway triggering another shot to whistle over our heads. I spring up, Max effortlessly boosting me up by my foot. Flinging me up into the air so I crash down feet first onto the half open bin lid. My booted feet pounding down onto it as Max darts out from behind it, distracting the lone shooter long enough for me to run at him. Throwing myself into him, I body slam him into the floor. The gun goes off, my ears ringing now that I'm in such close proximity, a silencer is nowhere near silencing, just lowers the usual boom of a gun.

I arc my knife down into my attacker's bicep, his head ricocheting off the concrete with the impact of my weight slamming into him. No more than a grunt released from his lips as Max kicks the gun from his hand, stepping onto the back of it, grinding it into the ground. Bending low he scoops up the gun. I stare down into the masked man's face, unfamiliar brown eyes glare back at me, not an ounce of fear in them. Nothing but pure unfiltered rage staring back. That's something I can understand, relate to.

Rage.

Such a beautiful fucking thing.

Excitement rides me hard, my body thrumming with exhilaration. I've fucking missed this the last few weeks. This used to be my weekly routine, every chance I got to get my hands dirty I'd be out with Charl, fucking shit up and leaving chaos in our wake.

I grin down at him as I carve my knife through his left arm, buried three inches deep in muscle I dig the blade through him. He hardly even winces, not bothering to try and get out from beneath me. My knees either side of his ribs, my weight seated on his stomach. Best position to be in should he roll, then I can get my feet under me and thrust up. I glance up at Max, jerking my chin at the guy's head. Max reaches forward, keeping the guy's own gun aimed on him as he crouches, gripping the black balaclava in his fist, ripping it free.

"Hello," I smile, getting a good look at his crooked nose and gaunt cheeks. "My name's Kyla-Rose, what's yours?" I ask like a kid in a playground, tilting my head.

"Fuck *you*," he spits through his gappy teeth, his scarred lip curling in disgust.

I laugh, "that's an unusual name, but I suppose with a face like yours, your mummy didn't like you very much." I shrug, squeezing my thighs hard, my bony knees grinding into his ribs. "So, *Fuck You*, why're you here?" I ask sweetly, my lashes batting dramatically, earning a scoff from Max.

The man stays silent, my blade still protruding

from his arm, his brown eyes narrowing as he glances at Max.

"Hey!" I snap.

Moving my foot to his sliced bicep, my finger and thumb digging into his cheeks as I grab his face. I squeeze hard, feeling his teeth carve against the inside of his mouth.

"Look. At. *Me.*" I demand, dragging his head up off the concrete before cracking it back down into the ground.

This time he groans, and I smile victoriously at the resounding smack.

"Now, let's try this again. *Why* are you here?"

The man's eyes roll into the back of his head, his eyelashes fluttering as he tries to stay conscious. I suppose his head must be spinning, I sigh heavily, such a shame when there's not much of a fight.

"Well, that was anticlimactic," I huff in disappointment, blowing a strand of hair from my face.

A suctioning squelch as I pluck my knife free from his flesh. I pocket it just as a stampede of heavy feet pound towards us.

"Spoke too soon, Princess," Max smirks, glancing up at the mouth of the alley where the footfalls encroach.

His hand reaching down for me, I shove up to my feet, my good hand gripping his, he tugs me forward. Hand in hand we sprint down the dark backstreet. The shadows becoming more than our friends as we run blind. Exhilaration tears through me, my legs pump harder, moving me faster. Our booted feet give us away, not that it'd be hard to find us, it's a straight alleyway. Both of us crouch low as a few lone shots are fired, weaving wildly down the narrowing passageway. Max's phone screen lights up as he places it against his ear, ducking and diving as we trample over black bin bags.

"Shooters!" he barks into the phone, his deep, commanding rumble making me fist his hand harder. "I don't know, enough," he grunts into the phone, narrowly avoiding a low angled shutter.

"Eight," I pant, "at least eight," I tell him, guessing the question from his mystery caller.

He glances over his shoulder, his shadowed turquoise eyes gleaming with pride.

"You hear that? Yeah. She's fine. I will," he confirms into the mouthpiece, shoving his phone back in his jacket pocket. "There's a wall coming up, I'm gunna boost you," he glances back at me as we continue to sprint forward. "You'll have to drop down the other side and roll. Think you can do that, princess?" he smirks.

"Of course I can fucking do that, arsehole," I bite out, gritting my teeth.

"Good. Tuck your bad hand and show me them moves, baby girl," he chuckles darkly as he begins to slow.

The echo of pounding feet behind us sends a thrill through me, it's all about the chase and it's been weeks too long without one. I'm not worrying too much about the guns, this is London after all, the Old Bill will be all over it like a rash and we do *not* need that right now.

"Ready?" Max barks over his shoulder as I quickly draw up alongside him.

"Ready!" I confirm as he cups his hands, fingers laced together, dipping low.

Before I even think it through, I trustingly jump into his hand and he launches me into the air. My feet scrabbling to make purchase, my good arm screaming as I heave myself up. My nails tearing into the brick, my fingers curling over the top of the wall. Max pops off a reluctant shot, forcing the echo of our pursuers to slow. Not enough, but it helps. Sweat rolls down my spine, my jacket dropping from my shoulders, thunking to the ground behind me.

Gritting my teeth, I slowly manage to heave myself up. My arm shaking so wildly I fear I'm about to fall when I find a foot hold. I breathe a rapid sigh of relief, swinging both legs up and over, but I don't drop down. I rock forward, my belly teetering on the walls edge, I stretch my arm down.

"Maddox!" I shout at him, not giving a fuck about being heard.

They know where we are whether they can fully see us in the dark or not. Max snaps his attention to me from his shielded spot behind a bin.

"Drop down, Lala!" he screams at me as a bullet *just* misses me.

"Come on, Max!" I bellow at him, my voice

cracking. "I'm not leaving you, hurry the fuck up!" I shout at him as our attackers move in.

Max growls wildly as he leaps at me, scooping up my jacket in the process, slinging it over the wall, I grip his hand in mine, leaning back further to heave him up with me. His use of both arms obviously making it easier. I pull back as far as I can, tugging his weight with me, gravity on our side as it pulls me towards the ground. He kicks a foot over and then we're falling. A ten-foot drop feels like fifty if you fall wrong, so I tuck my arms and roll. My shoulder slamming unforgivingly into the cracked pavement. My body rolling with the momentum of a free-falling sledgehammer, feeling every corner of upturned paving slabs dig and gouge at me. Max reaches out as we both roll, clawing me into his chest, rolling us to a stop, him above me.

Both breathing heavily, hearing shouts from the other side of the wall. His solid form blocking the night sky from view as he looks back to where we just came from. I glance to my left too, my chest brushing his, my injured hand trapped between us. We both pant to catch our breath. I look up at him then, a sigh of relief pouring from him as he looks down at me. Hands braced either side of my head, our lips dangerously close. His warm, sweet breath fanning over my skin, raven-black hair falling into his eyes. I lick my lips, my tongue catching his bottom lip as I swallow. Raising my hand, my fingers hesitant, I brush his hair back from his face.

"You good, Lala?" Max breathes.

I nod, "we should go," I murmur, glancing back to the dead-end alleyway.

Knowing it's only a matter of minutes before they circle around. Although they will have my whole security team to get through first. Max cups my cheek, keeping himself off my body, one hand still planted firmly to the ground. I inhale a small, shaky breath as his thumb brushes my cheek.

"You're not hurt?" he murmurs almost silently.

His eyes flicking between my own, his blue-green gaze running over my face.

"I'm fine," I whisper, my voice hoarse. "We need to go."

He nods, a soft sigh falling from his lips. He pushes to his knees, taking me with him as he gets to his feet. I move to grab my jacket, Max taking it from my hand, dropping it back over my shoulders. The back of our hands brush and like magnets our fingers snap together, interlocking. We hurry quickly down another side street, most of the street lamps out. The bulbs likely having been smashed out by kids, or they've died out through old age and the council just can't be bothered to replace them. We slip between parked cars, turning left then right, then another right.

Deep maroon walls, high, semicircle windows, a long, royal blue sign finally announces our arrival at Chalk Farm tube station. We jump the turnstiles, our booted feet pounding down the steep concrete stairs as our hands rejoin. The rush of hot air from the tunnels blows against us as we descend deep into the underground. I glance up at the overhead timing board as we hit the empty platform. Orange letters running across the screen, informing us the next train is in one minute. We hurry to the farthest end of the platform, ducking into an alcove as Max checks his phone.

The white tiled walls an ashen shade of grey from years of fumes. The thick heat chokes me as we finally stop to silently catch our breath. No matter the time of year these underground tube stations are always stifling heat. I avoid trains like the plague for that very reason. Plus, being stuck in the sweaty underground with only one fire escape route sets my teeth on edge like I've been scoffing sweets. I don't like being trapped.

My skin prickles uncomfortably as anxiety spikes through me. My chest tightening like a fist to the heart. I squeeze my eyes shut tight, trying to breathe through my nose.

"No signal," Max breathes, and I hear the creak of plastic like he's squeezing the phone in his hand in frustration. "Not that I thought there would be," he sighs, the zip of his pocket hissing as he locks the phone away.

I feel it then, without needing to look. His eyes on me, blazing a trail across my skin, goosebumps erupt-ing. Anxiety hits me harder, my breathing picking back up as I fight to keep my demon in check. Restless and pacing inside me, my skeleton her cage, my heart and lungs her target.

Endless long corridors of thick concrete, steel doors leading to six-by-six cells. Windowless, lightless, bleak grey space.

My chest heaves, my stomach twisting, a bead of sweat rolling down my spine. A knuckle tucks under my chin, my eyes squeezing ever tighter as another hand lays over my throat, the grip gentle but firm. Thumb brushing along my jaw, fingers flexing against my pulse.

"Breathe, Lala, I've got you," the devil breathes into me.

My soul soothes. Lying lips grazing over my ear, hot breath down my neck. The devil's hand tightening lazily on my neck like an inked collar of ownership. And I don't hate it. I *crave* it. My soul aches and flares all at one. Flames licking at my insides, heat coursing through my body as his fingers tighten further, my breath hitching.

"I've got you," he tells me, and, in the moment, he means it.

But for how long, Maddox? I want to scream at him, but I don't.

Instead, in this moment, right here and now, I eat it up.

I crack my eyes, his grip on my throat never wavering. I pull my bottom lip into my mouth, gnawing on it savagely.

"Don't do that," he scolds me.

His voice wrapping around me, pulling me under

the all-consuming wave that is Maddox fucking Sharpe. His free hand plants beside my head just as a sudden rush of air sends my curtain of silver hair flying up all around us.

"Our train," he breathes, his words against my lips as his thumb pops my abused lip free.

I nod, swallowing beneath his hand, it tightens once more, a split second before he releases me. Taking hold of my hand and tucking me behind him. His huge body shadowing me with protection. The devil leading the lamb to safety. What a contradiction. But then, I willingly gave my soul to him so long ago, of course he would never forget he owns me. Mind, body and wicked little soul. He's just waiting for the perfect time to eat me up.

The train comes to a stop with a drawn-out screech. Beeping alerts us that the doors are about to open just as feet hammer their way down the stairs at the other end of the platform.

"Wait," Max orders, his voice just loud enough for me to take notice of.

I suck in a sharp breath, my blood heating for an entirely different reason now. I love a good fight, but as I listen to the continued footfalls descending the stairs, I shake it off. Between us we have two guns, three knives and one arm out of action. We might enjoy a good fistfight, but these guys are playing big men. They're strapped up with fuck knows what, God only knows how many guns. So to even attempt a fight would be suicide, if their goal is to take us out. *Me.*

Which is when it hits me.

I actually *care*.

I care if I get into a fight right now. I know I won't win. I care about seeing my boys again, touching them, feeling them. They need me as much as I need them.

I care if I die.

"*Max*," I whisper urgently, and he hears it in my voice too.

The sudden panic in my tone, replacing the excitement, the rush. And then my insides are prickling for an entirely different reason. Something foreign. Something strange and indescribable works its way through my bones.

Realisation.

I need to be at home, tucked up safely in my impenetrable fortress, salaciously demanding the attention of my loyal hellhounds. Clawing at each other, breathing life into one another. Carving into each other's flesh, claiming souls with teeth and tongues and fucking. That's what I want. It's what we need. We can be each other's safety, the place we go when we don't feel our best. When we need to have difficult conversations and make hard decisions. Feel heat and passion and love.

My breathing speeds up as I hear the first warning beep of the train doors closing. Murmured conversation hits me next, far closer than I would like and my hand fists inside Max's, my fingers crushing his laced through mine.

"*Max,*" I hiss through my teeth.

The front of my body now flush with his back, my wounded hand clutched to my chest resting delicately between his shoulder blades. The warning beeping grows faster. And just when I think we're about to miss it, Max lunges forward. Spinning me and throwing me through the closing doors ahead of him into the end carriage. Slamming into me from behind, we both hit the floor, launching ourselves between the seats. He smothers me with his body, my wounded hand crushed to the floor. I cry out, gritting my teeth as my eyes squeeze shut. Max soothes me, his gentle shushing in my ear helps me breathe as the train pulls away. Juddery and uneven, but we're alone and there's quiet and I can't hear any voices. There are no stomping feet and no hail of gunfire.

Max rolls to one side as we're embraced in the darkness of the first tunnel. Shifting to a sitting position, he peels me up from lying on the filthy train carriage floor. Although, the familiarity of London grime helps me breathe a little easier. We're on home turf, *my* turf, I own these fucking streets, just as I own everyone in them.

"Lemme see your 'and," Max grunts with concern.

I look down to the fist clutched at my chest. Deep red blood stains the heavy white bandage, my fingers twitching with pins and needles.

"It's okay, we'll look at it when we get home. Are you okay?" my eyes check him, scanning over every visible inch.

"Yeah, I'm fine," he nods, his eyes on me for too long.

I resist the urge to squirm until his turquoise eyes finally divert. His gaze on the sign above my head, determining which train we're on and where it's going. But I don't care, I don't look, I just watch him. The way his jet-black hair hangs over his forehead. The grease he uses to push it back hardly doing its job because he runs his hands through it too much. The way his eyes flick over the map, rapidly taking in every detail, the way he just looked at me. *Seeing*. My heart squeezes painfully, needles prickling down the centre of my chest. Tears prick my eyes as I look at him. The little lines at the corners of his eyes, a pale scar in his cupid's bow, all things I'm unfamiliar with. Things and memories I'm not a part of and it stings, a lot.

We were always destined for this. This misery. Everything to be twisted and toxic and fucked up. The worst part is my sixteen-year-old self knew all of this and she went there anyway. And I'm trying so fucking hard not to make that same mistake ten years later. But when you're faced with the devil of your past, the man that haunts your dreams and nightmares in equal measure. A singular night playing on repeat in your mind's eye at all the inappropriate times of your life. How are you supposed to keep being mad? Keep being upset. Keep being this angry, frustrated, hurt little girl, just crying out for her lost love even when she shouldn't. Even when she knows this could never work. Because what is worse than having your love taken from you? It's when you know that they're still walking around somewhere, could be close by, could be far. But they're still *here*. On this plane, this dimension, living and breathing and smiling, just not at you, not *for* you.

They're still here, but they're not for you *anymore.*

"Well," he finally says.

But he is *here.*

You *are here.*

Together.

What the fuck are you doing, Lala?

"At least we're heading home. I say we get off at Leicester Square, jump on Piccadilly, get off in Knightsbridge," he rattles off.

I swallow thickly as he drops his gaze onto me. My eyelids burning, his muscular frame slumped. Ankle and knee of one leg resting against the floor. His other knee bent, foot planted on the floor, leg drawn close to his body, thigh to chest. His thick arm encased in leather perched on top, his hand lazily dangling over the space before him. My body is angled toward him, but I'm on my haunches, my feet tucked under my bum. Bleeding hand clutched to my chest, the other resting atop my thigh, palm down, fingers splayed.

"I'll call Frank to come get us. If we head up at Leicester Square for signal, I can pop off a message."

"Your boys will want to hear from you first. I'll

text Frank," he offers, a soft smile on those excruciatingly beautiful lips.

"They'll know I'm safe," I breathe the confession, the lights dimming as we shudder through another tunnel.

"Yeah?" Max hushes out on an exhale, all the while his eyes searching mine.

"Yeah," I confirm, swallowing hard. "I'm with you."

"I think you can more than look after yourself, Lala," Max whispers, his face suddenly much, *much* closer.

My breathing hitches at the same time his does. My chin dipped; I watch his hand lift to my face. Like fire to ice, scorching through every defence I've ever put in place. We won't be alone on this train for much longer. Not on Christmas Eve, Chalk Farm is a quieter station, a little removed, but the next stop is Camden Town, hoards will be boarding. The ice bricks around my heart start melting one after the other, my barbed wire wrapped heart hammering and bleeding. The evidence of it mixing with the river of ice water flowing from me. Tears, I realise, hot and salty, purging me of pain. Falling unbiddenly, they splash against his veiny hand, the hand that's all for me. Sliding down his thorn wrapped wrist, I heave in a shuddery breath.

The tears don't stop.

They don't stop when he kisses them from my cheeks, his tongue sliding along my cheekbone, lips sucking them from my skin. He slides forward, pulling me into the back corner of the carriage. He slumps us down, his back pressed to the corner. Sliding me between his legs, cradling my shaking body to his. They fall like April fucking showers come early, drenching my t-shirt, soaking my face. I lick them from my lips as I sniffle. Sending up a silent prayer in thanks for waterproof makeup and expert setting spray. Swiping hair back from my face, damp with my pain. Max just keeps me tucked up into him, even as his body trembles beneath mine. His strong hands sturdy and grounding, he anchors me here, to this, to him, to us. In this moment I don't need to be anything and it's the most freeing feeling in the fucking world.

Tormenting myself with possibilities, outcomes and consequences weigh heavily on me. My life was perfect less than three months ago. No men. No emotions. Just blood and carnage and games. Everything wrapped up in a pretty, blood-stained bow. The Chaos Twins slathering Southbrook in crimson. Drowning her in a macabre production. Hacking and slashing and vengeance. And then Big Man came bulldozing into my life, closely followed by my fearless counterpart and they smashed everything I thought I knew to smithereens.

"I've got you, Lala, and I'm never fucking letting you go."

Max kisses my hair, once, twice, three times. His strong hands clutching me to him so tight I can feel the bruises forming. The train comes to a stop, the doors slide open with a suction sound, feet, laughter, people. I hold my breath, I don't look up, trusting him. Max whispers reassurances against my temple, his lips brushing my hair and skin. His eyes seeing over my head, locked on the crowds as he speaks. His scorched black wings curl around us, protecting us from everything. His shadowed aura bleeding out into the space surrounding us, poisoning the air, keeping everyone at a distance.

The Devil really is just a fallen angel after all.

"No gunmen."

"No one's looking, Lala."

"The doors are gunna close."

"Ain't nothin' getting to ya."

"I've got you."

"It's you and me, Princess."

The doors beep, the sounds getting quicker, closer together, they close. I breathe. I press myself into Max's heat. His feet pressed flat to the floor, his thighs bracketing me in. My bum trapped between his legs, his arms wrapped around me. The tighter he squeezes the easier I breathe. My chest loosens, the tightness easing, I breathe deep, in through my nose.

"I don't think I wanna die anymore, Maxi," I barely breathe the confession, but that's what it is.

He's not who I should be telling.

But he'll understand it the best.

Better than anyone ever could.

Because we've been here before.

I see it then and my heart hurts, the decaying

organ batters against my insides as my mind travels back in time.

Rain pounds down, lashing my exposed skin. My bruises easing and aching all at once under its intense pressure. My booted feet pound against the uneven pavement, the puddles splashing up my legs Soaking through my torn tights, dribbling down my calves and settling into my boots. The wind whips my hair around me, but the rain starts helping by plastering it to my head. I swipe my forearm over my face, pushing harder, running faster.

Fucking Lucy Roberts.

I hate that nosy bitch, but her big brother Isaac told her to tell me to find Maddox. Isaac hangs in similar circles to Max. So, here I am. Because I've had this horrible feeling in my tummy all day. A twisting, something didn't feel right. It was my first day back to school after Christmas break. I was worried about Maxi the whole time. Since Gran's funeral he's cut himself off again, stayed away from me. Even after our moment, I thought we'd made progress. I thought we'd be okay, especially after we spent Christmas together. I broke us into Gran's, condemned it is, all boarded up, but Max didn't want to leave again after. He moved his shit back in, 'fuck the council, I'll be a squatter,' he said as he dragged his black bags of clothes back inside in rebellion, in grief.

It's January and it's freezing. The rain stings like razor-blades slicing into me as I run through it. It was supposed to be dry today, but typical English weather will always prevail. The weather forecast is pointless. It's always wrong.

I pound my feet down the back alley, twisting my ankle as I hit a pothole, but I keep going.

Something is just wrong.

I can feel it.

I trudge through the muddy grass, forcing open the unlocked back door as the wind tries to steal it from me.

I slow my pace, water dripping onto the kitchen floor. It's colder in here than out there. All the furniture removed. An entire person's life dismantled, shipped out in nothing more than a few boxes, the house is nothing but a carcass of a happy life once lived. I head for the stairs, my wet fingers gripping the creaky banister, my footsteps heavy as I ascend but my breathing stops. There is nothing. No sound, no movement, nothing.

Maybe he's left already.

I make it to the tiny landing, three closed doors leading off it, Gran's room, Max's, and the bathroom. I clench my fists, my fingers curling, nails digging into my palms. I inhale, soothing my trembling, I reach for Max's doorhandle, twisting the knob as quietly as I can. I push open the door, the curtains open, the miserable day outside infecting the inside with its gloom. The room is untouched, unlike the rest of the house, this isn't empty and bare. This room is lived in, crumpled sheets, jeans on the floor, a full ashtray by the window. Everything in its usual place but no Max. I pull my phone from my pocket, frowning at the screen. I re-lock it, seeing no notifications, I close my eyes, tapping the phone against my lips.

Where else would you go?

I move back onto the landing, closing the door softly behind me. I hesitate, looking down the stairs. I turn back to the doors. Shaking my head, I push open Ruth's bedroom door. Just an empty room, nothing inside it, but I swear I can smell her perfume, the sweet floral memory making me smile. I close the door, and stare at the bathroom door opposite. My stomach drops as I stare at it. My hand shakes as I reach out, my fingers sliding over the cold round handle, I twist and as the door opens my whole world falls apart.

"Max!" I scream.

His body slumped in the bath, a jean clad leg hanging over the side, wet boot on his foot. An arm flung out, fingers limp. My breath heaves in my chest as I look at his face. His eyes closed, his face black and blue, eye swollen and jaw slack. I step inside, closing the door behind me like we need privacy. I study his chest, my eyes burning in their sockets begging me to blink, when finally, finally, *his chest moves. But it's slow and lethargic and something's wrong.*

"Maxi?" I call, but my voice is barely a whisper. I get nearer, really looking at him, vomit down his t-shirt, on his lip, his chin. "Max!" I yell this time, my voice cracking as I see the pills, the half-drunk bottle of whiskey on the ledge.

I rush forward now, panic urging me to move. I drop to my knees beside the bath, my hands going to his face. He's cool but he's not cold. I exhale the breath I didn't realise I was holding. I slap his face, I slap it again, I feel his stuttered breath against my palm.

"MAX!" I scream in his face, rising up on my haunches, the freezing tiles grinding against my knobbly knees. "MAX! PLEASE!" I wail.

I stand up, my hands going to his armpits, I heave him up, so he's sitting more upright. His leg drops back into the empty bath with a thunk. The water's been cut off so I can't start the shower.

"MAX! Please, fucking please, Max!" I slap him again, this time it's angry, this time, I mean it.

He groans.

Using all my strength I push his heavy body forward, his head flopping, chin to chest. I clamber in behind him, letting his body slump between my bare thighs. I strain to sit up, my hands clinging to the bath edges. I grunt through gritted teeth as I finally get him sat up high enough. Working blindly, I force two fingers into his mouth, ramming them into the back of his throat, and he heaves.

"Yes! That's it, Max. Come on! Get it out, for me, please, please, please."

I push his body further forward, his back bowing, he retches. I push my fingers in farther, as far as I can and then he's sick. And I breathe, I hammer my other fist to his back as he groans.

"More, Max, more, come on," I murmur the chant as he continues heaving.

The sick keeps coming, I crane my neck, stretching myself so I can see over his shoulder. I press my fingers into it, feeling for pills, feeling for something.

"Come on, come on," I hush to myself, unable to see.

He's sick again and I feel them.

"Come on, Max, more!" I demand as he becomes slightly more coherent.

He can't have taken them too long before I got here. I'm used to shit like this since taking care of Mum, but this is Max. The panic is different, I care about the outcome.

He retches, dry heaving now. Eventually, nothing more to expel, he slumps back into me. His back plastered to my front. His weight makes it a struggle to breathe deeply but I'm comforted by it as his breaths fill his lungs and I feel them strong and steady through his back.

"Max?" I question quietly.

His breathing sharp, I press my hand to his chest, just needing to feel it working.

"I don't wanna die, Lala. I don't wanna leave you," he murmurs, sounding exhausted.

I feel the tears then. His splashing against my hand, mine against the top of his head, tucked beneath my chin.

"I'm sorry," he cries. "I'm so sorry," huge racking sobs, his entire body shaking between my legs, the vibrations of grief rolling through me, carving into my soul.

"It's okay, baby," I tell him. "I got you and I'm never letting you go."

CHAPTER 13
MAX

I don't think I wanna die anymore, Maxi.

That line running through my skull, relief and dread in equal measures race through my veins. I can't even begin to sort through that right now. Everything with this girl is so fucking raw.

"Next stop," I breathe against her hair.

Coconuts and lime, so familiar, yet not. I breathe her in, my arms her comfort. Her breathing regulates to match mine and I smile against the crown of her head, my chin resting atop. I let her slip into her memories, I keep her safe. I know what she's thinking about, when she found me, saved me. The only thing that made me throw up those pills, other than her fingers digging into my tonsils, was her softness. Her voice, her panic, her fear. I never want that for her. I was just lost for a little while. She found me. She always finds me. Like I'll always find her.

People stare at us as they get on and off the

carriage, a pair of demons sunken in the corner. Some are already in a drunken stupor, others eyeing me suspiciously. I glare at them all, tempted to flash my gun, maybe even pop a shot off. Instead, I just stare until I unnerve them enough to fuck off and mind their own business. No one will get within three feet of us. I won't allow it. I'll rip their fucking throats out if they so much as even try to approach.

"Okay," she whispers, stronger than before.

I can't stand to see her cry. It was always my weakness, my downfall, everything about her is my Achilles heel.

"You gotta make me a promise, Princess," I rasp against her head, her hair tickling my lip.

"What?" she whispers hoarsely.

"We go back to hatin' each other when we get home."

She glances up from beneath wet lashes, her grey eyes glinting with emerald, shining from tears. She frowns, her bottom lip pouting, a little crease between her brows. I smirk at her, keeping my lips to myself, knowing my self-control is in full force. I need to focus on keeping us safe. I *know* she can keep herself safe, but not like this, so I step up willingly. I'll kill anyone that so much as looks at her wrong.

She blinks up at me, and that innocent sixteen-year-old shines through, calling out to every broken part of me. Tugging on invisible strings I'd long forgotten.

"Deal," she breathes, a tiny smirk edging the corner of her red-stained lips.

"That's my girl," I wink, drawing her closer.

Clutching her to me, keeping her tight to my chest. Her injured hand trapped between our bodies, cradled by us both. I breathe deeply, her head dipped, tucked beneath my chin. I cling onto the seconds I've got left with her like this. I need to get her home to our boys, *her* boys, in one piece. I won't let them down. I should never have taken her out the back, shoulda smoked out front. But I wanted to apologise. Or something. Without an audience.

"Come on, Lala."

I shift beneath her, unfurling her body from mine. Climbing to my feet, I pull her up with me. Her good hand wrapped in mine, my hand easily double the size of hers. The train stops sharply, Lala's foot wrapped around the bottom of a pole, helping keep her upright. Her independence, even in something so small, makes my chest burn. She's had no one but her family to help keep her upright. Something so simple, I shouldn't have even noticed it, but I do and then I shake it off. I can't keep wallowing in the past. I gotta move forward, we've all got to move forward.

The doors slide open, I grip her hand tighter. Keeping her flush to my back, we move as one. Weaving through the crowds, my eyes scanning everyone we pass. Not that I know who I'm looking for. I didn't see anyone's faces, but I watch for people watching us and see nothing as we switch lines, change platforms, and duck onto another train. This one busier, as was expected, there are a couple seats I could sit her in, but I don't. Instead, keeping our backs to the corner, both facing out, we stand the four stops, cataloguing every face we see, silently watching. Every time the doors open and close again without incident, we both relax a little.

Knightsbridge Station.

We take the steep escalators, rising higher and higher as we both keep an eye on our phone signal. Our attention flitting between our screens and every-thing else happening around us. I get signal first, my fingers flying over the screen as we ascend, shooting off messages for a pickup point.

"I'm fine," I hear her exhale, my chest pinching uncomfortably as I hear Huxley's timbre through the phone.

Frank replies with nothing but a coded location which I clearly am not privy to. *Dragon?* Just another reminder of how far removed from her life I really am. I twist in place, flashing the phone to Lala, her eyes pinch but she nods. We push out into the cold. Lala shoving her phone back into her back pocket, her fingers linking with mine on instinct. Just like old times.

"Come on," she mutters, her too-large eyes flicking all around.

I let her lead, our feet working quickly to move us down the spit-shined pavement. God, how the other half really fucking live. I might have comfortable money now, but I grew up in a shit heap of a council house on an estate filled with screaming, fistfights, and drugs.

Skyscrapers tower around us, the windows immaculate, despite it being the middle of winter. Designer shops surround us on all sides, closed for the night but the streets still bustling with bodies. Red double-decker buses fly by, black cabs tooting their horns at cyclists and rogue pedestrians. Us Brits don't have much patience when it comes to driving. Road rage is real. We turn down a slightly quieter street. Large townhouses with private parking spaces either side of the road, we turn down a few more, suddenly appearing before *The Cadogan Hotel*.

The intimidating red brick building with white stone pillars is lit up and decorated for Christmas. Huge Christmas garlands dressed in red and gold wrap around the two huge pillars on either side of the entrance, glowing fairy lights intertwined. A huge round wreath hangs between, above the arched, glass door, a red velvet bow topping it. The doorman greets us with a huge white smile, his dark brown skin creasing at the corners of his warm eyes. Dressed in a deep red tartan coat, black trousers, shined black shoes and a black wool bowlers' hat.

"Miss Swallow," he inclines his head, he smiles and it's comforting, familiar.

"James," Lala replies happily, her voice soft. "I apologise for the attire."

"Miss, not at all. Patrick will see you up to your rooms."

"Thank you. You make sure you have a beautiful Christmas, James," Lala smiles warmly, folding a fifty into his leather gloved hand.

"Thank you. Merry Christmas, Miss, Sir."

He smiles at me, I offer one back, although my smiles are tight, I at least try.

We step through the black framed, glass doors. White walls and marble floors throughout, the ceilings high, the lighting homey. Armchairs and a roaring fire in the large foyer. A tall white man, whose back is as straight as an ironing board, greets us next. I can't help but look at him, his posture makes my back ache, he's never once slouched in his entire life, I shouldn't think.

"Miss Swallow," he bows, and I feel my head tilting to watch him, he bends like a folding switchblade.

"Patrick," Lala greets.

Turning to me next, "Sir," he says politely, "if you'll follow me, please."

Unsure of what's happening, I look to Lala. Her cheeky wink has me rolling my eyes, but I simply follow behind. Knowing I can ask questions once we're alone, but it's obvious she's a regular visitor.

Bypassing the front desk, we head down a dark, wooden panelled hallway. Pale flowers in the tiled floor, gold radiators beneath the windows. The hall opens up into what looks like a library, only the books can't be checked out, they're all decorative, an illusion. Patrick presses a gold button, a soft dinging has doors to a concealed elevator opening. The three of us step inside, Lala perfectly comfortable in the small space. We seem to keep going, the lift moving slowly. I'm sure we can't possibly climb any higher when we finally stop.

"The Penthouse, Miss Swallow, Sir," is all Patrick says as he hands Lala a key.

We both step out, the lift doors closing behind us, leaving us alone in the silent hallway. More rich wooden floors and wood panelled walls. Soft, orange light from sconces illuminating what I assume to be our destination door.

"What the fuck are we doing here, Lala?" I ask incredulously.

She turns her head to look at me, her large eyes glinting, her red lips curling up deviously.

"We're going to get changed and have a drink at the bar whilst we wait for Frank," she chimes, her voice melodic and sweet.

I raise a brow at her, "this is our *safe place*?" I deadpan, thoroughly unimpressed. "The coded location meant here?" I pull a face of confusion.

She chuckles, shrugging her jacket off and swiping our room key.

"'*The Welsh dragon battles for honour*'," I murmur Frank's message.

"Yes, Cadogan is Welsh," she grins at me, the door clicking. "Not every safehouse is a grimy old basement," she shrugs, pressing the handle down and pushing the door wide with her shoulder. "Now you know one of my secrets, you owe me one of yours," she taunts, winking salaciously before entering the room.

I rush forward, catching the heavy door and following her inside. Warm wood and beige walls, a pale grey runner lining the entrance. I feel so fucking out of place, everything's just so, *posh*. I walk through a living room, a lit fire crackling softly behind a grate, plush cream sofas surrounding it. Plum coloured throw cushions and soft beige blankets covering them. I follow the sound of Lala's boots being toed off, an *oomph* from her lungs. I pass the large dining area, and another sitting room before I reach the bedroom.

Similar colouring as the rest of the penthouse, the lights dimmed. Clothing bags, I assume are ours, hang in an open walk-in wardrobe. Lala lies on the huge bed in the middle, a carved wooden headboard against the far wall, covered in crisp white sheets. Her arm thrown over her eyes, legs crossed at the ankles. Her halo of silver hair fanning out across the wide display of throw pillows. She looks tiny, swallowed up in the centre of the mattress. Everything around her perfectly placed, an angel floating on a cloud.

"Do you think we could get away with just sleeping, Maxi?" she murmurs, sensing me in the shadowed room with her.

"Well, I'm not wearing a suit," I grunt in response.

Knowing that in a place like this, formalwear is the only acceptable attire to wander around in. The childlike giggle that explodes out of her throat has me blanching, the familiarity of it a haunting reminder of what was.

"You so *are*," she teases, knowing I will wear one, I just would really rather not. "Just come lie with me for a minute," she mumbles. "We've had a trying day," she laughs lightly but it's a heavy sound.

I hesitate, rocking on the balls of my feet. Unsure where to place myself. Dramatically dropping her arm onto the feather pillows above her head, she sighs.

"For fuck's sake, Max, get over here, I don't bite!"

"Oh, but you do, little demon," I murmur under my breath, staring at my boots as I kick them off.

Wondering what the hell I'm doing, I walk around the bed, she lazily watches my approach. Her too-large eyes tracking my every movement like the predator I know she is. Only I'm not prey, I'm a predator too. The way she's looking at me with intrigue has my cock hardening in my jeans, I will it to go down. That look though, she either wants to rip my throat out or have me mount her like a wild beast. Bruise her skin, my jaws locked on the back of her neck, rutting into her with wild abandon. Without thinking anymore into it, I throw myself onto the mattress beside her. Her laughter rings out into the room as throw pillows jump from the bed. A smile curves my lips as I look over at her, our faces turned toward each other.

"Thank you," she whispers.

"For what?" I frown.

"Keeping me safe."

"Lala, I-"

"No, you did, and I'm grateful," she swallows, closing her eyes for a brief moment. "And I'm sorry, for being a mess. You probably won't believe me when I say this because I feel like all you've seen of me as a woman is my breakdowns," she laughs lightly, but it's not real.

It's a false noise, something meant to comfort me.

"But I'm not usually like that." She glances away from me, she swallows, looking back. "Emotional, I mean. It just seems a lot's been happening lately and I'm not too stubborn to admit, it's a lot, and I'm struggling." She shrugs, smiling sadly at me.

I turn onto my side, palms pressed together beneath my cheek, her twisting to mirror my new position.

"You never have to apologise to me, Lala," I tell her honestly.

"Oh, but I do, Maddox Sharpe," she smiles.

Her eyes tracing the line of my lips, before blinking back up at me.

"If only for selfish reasons."

I hear what she doesn't say, *I need you to accept it.* I don't need or want an apology from her, but like she would for me, I accept it, knowing it's for her.

For whatever reason, I nod, my eyes tightening as I flex my jaw.

Her eyes slip closed. We lie in comfortable silence for a few minutes, allowing me a minute to just look at her, able to stare without anyone watching me watching her.

My breath catches in my throat as her eyes suddenly pop open. Lala's eyes are so fucking expressive, always were, we could have an entire conversation with them, no words need be spoken, but not tonight. Tonight I need to finally use my fucking words. I swallow down the lump in my throat, licking my suddenly dry lips. Heaving in a steadying breath I look at her, *fuck*, she's so fucking beautiful.

"I killed a man that night, that's why I didn't come back for you," I whisper, and she sucks in a sharp breath.

I'm sure her reaction is not about me killing a man but rather this is the last thing she expected me to say right now.

"I fucked it up and it took longer than I anticipated to make it back to you," I confess with a wince. "The night I came to you, I was supposed to be hunting Billy Cox." I watch her face for reaction, her eyes flicker between mine as she remembers why that name's familiar.

"He was one of mum's dealers," she whispers, and I nod.

"He was stealing, slicing a few grams off the top of his delivery. Taking profit that didn't belong to him. Anyway, I joined that gang to make fast money, I wanted to get us away from there, Lala. I wanted to keep you safe, I should have known that was a fucking stupid idea. But I was desperate, I hated your fucking mum, she was sucking the life out of you, and I hated what she was doing to you, you were so fucking tired, like a walking fucking corpse. Bony and malnourished, bags under your eyes, your hair a mess. Everything was spiralling out of our control, and I was scared, I didn't wanna lose you. Once I was a full-fledged member, I started earning a pretty penny, I shoved every quid away, every fucking one. Then I got a kill order, and you can't say no in that gang, Lala. You know as well as I do, once you're in, you're in, there's no getting out and no saying no to a task. I had to take out Billy, typical really, shoulda known everything always comes full fucking circle," I run my hands through my hair and sigh.

"I stopped by your place, I wanted to see you. Have you calm my fucking nerves, like you always fucking did. Even when you were mad at me for cutting you out, distancing myself from you. Every time I came back you were there for me. But when I knocked, your house in darkness, I went and checked your normal hidey holes. I checked the petrol station's roof, the old, abandoned gas works and then one of my boys said he'd seen you. That's when I found you at the warehouses."

I glance up at Lala, her eyes watching me. Studying me, taking in my movements, the look in my eyes, analysing my truth.

"I'm so fucking sorry I didn't get back to you in

time. I never should have left you. I should have just said fuck it all, grabbed you and run, we should have fucking run," I growl.

She sighs heavily.

"You and I both know they would have come for us, Max," she says gently. "We would have been dead before I was even seventeen," she reasons as I scrub my hands over my face.

"I'm so fucking sorry, so, so, *so*, fucking, fucking, sorry," I almost cry, tears prick the back of my eyes.

I feel like a fucking arsehole for explaining any of this, telling her at all, even trying to make her see, *understand*.

"*Maxi*," she whispers.

Tearing me from my troubled thoughts, my head snapping up. My eyes squinting to see her properly in the darkened room. My heart pounds wildly in my chest, the beats uncontrolled and out of sync.

"I forgive you," she tells me, so noiselessly it's almost inaudible.

My mouth drops open, my brow wrinkling in confusion.

"I think I forgave you the second I saw you again, but I felt like by letting go of ten fucking years of anger, *hatred*," I wince at that. "I was angry with myself for seeing you and letting my anger dissipate instantly as though it was never there to begin with," she swallows. Her eyes coming up to meet mine, "maybe it never really was."

God, I love this woman so fucking much.

"I love you, Max. I always have, I fear I always will," she confesses, dropping her gaze.

Large droplets falling from those big, grey doe eyes. Splashing against her high cheekbones, rolling down her curved jaw.

So fucking beautiful.

"I've spent what feels like my whole life waiting to hear those words, Princess," I rasp. "I have loved you your entire life, Rosie. I think I fell in love with you when you were two days old, thrust into my arms for a photograph. Even at three years old, I knew I held something precious. Little did I know *just* how precious. I was holding the other half of my soul. You've owned me your whole life, even when we were apart, you still had me. Nothing and no one could ever come close to what you mean to me. I've been dead inside for a really long time, Lala. Seeing you again fractured something inside me. Carved my soul up into irreparable pieces, just so you could put me back together, but with parts of you this time. Because there really is no me without you."

My voice thick with emotion, I cup her wet cheek. My thumb rolling through her salty tears, her dark lashes wet, they run down her face. She blinks up at me, her eyes glistening. She licks her lips, letting her eyes drop closed.

"We're inevitable, Kyla-Rose, you and me. But that doesn't mean I shouldn't have to work for you, earn your trust back. Show you, *prove* to you that I'm worth the risk, baby girl. I love you, Lala. I love you so hard it fucks me up. It makes me do and say stupid fucking shit because I don't know how to be around you without you being mine. Please, Lala. Take the risk. Leap and I'll fucking catch you."

She blinks her eyes open, tears cascading down her face, splashing onto the white sheets beneath her cheek. My eyes connect with hers; filled with tears and hope. That's all we ever had as fucking kids, *hope,* something that was foreign to us. Unfamiliar and scary as shit but we always had it, Lala and I.

She was hope for me.

My crumbling life, my bleak future, my broken heart.

All of it has led me here.

Back to her.

Before I can think too hard on it, before I open my goddamn mouth and say the wrong fucking thing and ruin everything. I move almost unconsciously.

I sit up suddenly, she twists to look at me with a small frown, wondering what I'm doing. My hands thrust out, my fingers latching around her dainty ankles. I get a solid grip and violently yank her towards me, a gasp escapes her as her back hits the mattress. I instantly cover her perfect figure with my large body, settling myself between her legs before she even has time to register what just happened.

God, she looks so fucking good spread out beneath me, I've never had her in this position before. The one and only time we fucked, I made goddamn love to her, it was sloppy and real and raw.

Everything about us together is just that, *raw*. Like the first snowfall of winter, those perfectly sculpted snowflakes that can only fall accompanied by the promise of a bitter wind. One that chills you to the bone and chaps your cheeks until they're pink and sore.

Her long hair fanned out around her slim heart shaped face like a silver halo. The dim lighting revealing one half of her, the other half shrouded in shadows. Her cheeks wet with tears, tears for us, what we had, what we could have had, what we didn't get. Everything we were and everything we've been since. How we fell back into each other's lives.

I drop my face, my lips hovering a hair's breadth from hers. My eyes bore into big grey orbs, cut with glittering emerald. She watches me. Her body trembling beneath mine as I gently graze my fingertips up her arm, goosebumps prickling her skin as my fingers climb. I trace over her t-shirt, up her throat, along her jaw until I've got my fist in her hair. She sucks in a sharp breath as I tighten my hold.

"I fucking love you, Lala. You believe that don't you, Princess?" I growl, my lips brushing hers with my words. She nods as much as she can with my fingers knotted in her hair. "Use your words, Rosie," I snarl, my top lip rolling over my teeth, I nip her bottom lip as she holds her breath.

"*Yes*, Max, I know, I know you do," she rushes out on a whimper as I grind my hips against hers in reward.

"Good girl," I bite out, my teeth catching on her tongue as she licks her lips, and that's what does it.

My restraint snaps, my lips slam against hers. My fist holding tight in her hair, my other forearm on the mattress beside her head as I hold myself above her. My kiss freezes her for a moment. Too stunned to react but then she's right fucking there with me and it's bliss. Her tongue lashing against my own, savagely attacking my mouth. Her delicate fingers entangle themselves in my hair, ripping hard at the root as she tugs me closer, demanding and taking. There's absolutely nothing gentle about our need for one another.

Fuck.

I tear myself from her lips as she skates her hand down my spine, fisting my t-shirt, motioning for me to take it off. I reach up, my weight balancing on the fist in her silver locks. I pull it over my head, threading it down my arm to my hand still wrapped in her hair. Her hand grips my back, nails ripping into the skin, burying themselves beneath my flesh like little razor blades. I hiss against her lips, nipping and sucking my way down her jaw, using my hand in her hair to steer her in the direction I want her. Nibbling her earlobe, the cool metal from her many piercings clicking against my teeth. I nip and suck a harsh trail along the left side of her jaw. Making sure I mark my way across her body, a roadmap of my travels, our journey together.

My teeth attack the column of her throat, her back arching up to press flush against me. Her legs coming up and around my waist, thighs clamping my raging cock against the molten heat of her cunt. And *fuck me*, is it molten. *Christ*, it's a raging inferno of heat that I can't fucking wait to slide into. I growl against the flesh where her neck meets her shoulder, the opposite side of where Kacey has his teeth marked in her. Jealousy soars through me, burning hot, my blood singing with fire. Groans and whimpers slip past her teeth as she drives her hips up into me, the heels of her feet digging into my arse.

Lala rakes her nails up my back, through my hair. Scratching and scraping at my scalp before fisting my hair and tearing my face away from her body.

"Fuck me, Max. I need to feel you inside me," she pants, my dick twitches in response to her snarled demand.

Leaning my weight back on my haunches I release her hair, grasping the neckline of her too big t-shirt, my eyes coming up to meet hers. I tear it sharply in half, the two pieces falling either side of her tattooed torso.

"Fucking Jesus Christ, have mercy, *fuck*," I ramble out quickly as I look down at her, my breath catching.

I know I've technically seen her naked, but I didn't look, I didn't take my eyes off her face. I watched every emotion slide across those beautiful features, I couldn't have looked away from those expressive eyes even if I'd have wanted to.

Her tattoos are a mass of black ink, covering her completely from the base of her throat. Her heavy breasts, perfectly pink nipples narrowed into fine, hard points, black metal bars through each one. I bite my lip so hard I draw blood. My eyes desperately try to take in every fucking inch of her like she may never let me see her again, like this, the body of a woman. *My* woman.

Fuck.

My eyes slowly drag up her body before they meet hers. The emerald green of her irises shining bright, her pupils blown as she looks at me. She doesn't try to shield herself from me or cover up. She lays perfectly still, other than her chest heaving with her elevated breathing. She gives me a coy, half smile letting her knees drop open for me.

So many emotions stir up inside of me, like a fucking cyclone ripping through every single part of me, my skin heats and prickles. I try to keep my control, but my resolve cracks and splinters.

And when she gives me that full smile, those deeply carved dimples in her pale face.

I fucking *shatter*.

I rear back from her, resting on my knees between her legs. I rip her leather trousers down her thighs, exposing her bare pussy to me, her wet folds glistening in the low light. Sucking in a breath through my teeth, I throw myself from the bed almost stumbling as my knees threaten to give out. I tear my jeans and boxers down my legs, kicking them off before diving back between her legs. Her knees open, the torn t-shirt still on her shoulders, laying open for me.

I lean forward, my teeth and tongue latching around her nipple. She arches her back, her head knocking from side to side like I'm performing a fucking exorcism as she cries out. I suck as much of her breast into my mouth as I can, my other hand massaging and kneading its way down her inner thigh. Her wounded hand lying safely off to the side, her good hand gripping and tugging at my head. I release her nipple with a loud pop, looking up at her from beneath my lashes.

Her eyes squeezed shut, her long silver hair fanned out around her face, her swollen bottom lip pulled in between her teeth.

How the fuck did I get this fucking lucky?

I shimmy my way down the bed, my mouth hovering just above her pussy. Breathing in the scent of her arousal, my mouth waters and fuck me, her cunt's just as fucking perfect as the rest of her.

"Such a pretty pussy, Lala," I whisper.

Blowing against her glistening folds, she sucks in a sharp breath, and I smirk. I drag a knuckle through the slickness of her pussy forcing me to grip the base of my cock. Giving it a squeeze to behave as it seeps from the tip, desperate to get inside her. I look up at her from my position between her creamy thighs.

"Lala," I demand her attention. Her eyes snapping open, she looks down at me. "Look at me, Princess. Watch me give this to you. I wanna feel those pretty eyes on me," she nods her agreement.

Looking down at me, me still watching her. I use

the flat of my tongue, running it up her slit, darting the tip between her folds, circling around her swollen clit. She cries out a whimper but keeps her eyes on me as I lick and suck and fuck her with my tongue. One of my arms curled beneath her leg, gripping her thigh in my thick hand. My other pressing down on her flat belly, keeping her in place as she writhes beneath me.

"You taste like fucking heaven," I tell her huskily.

My breath fanning across her sensitive skin, she groans low at my words before I'm dropping my mouth back to the wet lips between her legs. I lock my lips around her clit, sucking her into my mouth. Ravishing her with my tongue as I dive deep into her with two thick fingers. Her back arches, pushing her hot, little cunt into my mouth further. I groan against her, the vibrations making her thighs quiver. I thrust my fingers in and out of her at a rapid pace, dragging them down the inside walls of her pussy. Twisting and scissoring them inside of her and with one final suck on her swollen nub, she cries out. Wetness gushes from her, coating my fingers and my chin, but I don't let up until her body goes completely still. I continue licking and sucking, swallowing down everything she rewards me with before slowly dragging my fingers from inside of her.

I sit up on my knees, her wide eyes still on me, chest heaving with pants.

"Such a good girl," I murmur my praise.

Knowing how much she likes it after seeing the

effect it had on her when Huxley was fucking her in the kitchen.

Yeah, I have no qualms about watching.

Leaning over her, I offer up my fingers coated in her juices. She takes them into her mouth willingly, laving them with her tongue. Sucking them into the back of her throat, her cheeks hollowing. All without taking those fucking eyes from me. I used to think they were too big for her when we were little, they were always so wide and curious, trying to see and understand the world. But looking at her now, I realise that it's the world that's curious about her instead.

I groan as she wraps her tongue around my fingers. Her hand coming up gripping my wrist, she draws my fingers in and out of her mouth, fucking herself with them. Releasing her hold on my wrist, still sucking on my fingers, her hand runs down her heated body. Dipping low, she drags her fingers through her wetness. Watching her every move, I can't even breathe. Between her sucking my fingers and running her hand down her own body, I'm gunna explode before she even touches me.

Running her fingers through her release, I watch mesmerized by her every action. As I look back up to her face, my eyes locking with hers, her hand covered in her own juices closes around my hard cock. It pulses in her slick hand, seeping from the tip as she gives me a firm squeeze.

"*Fuckkkkk,*" I hiss through my teeth as she pumps

me a few times, gently, lazily but *God*, if I'm not already close.

Releasing my fingers from her mouth, she pops them free. I draw my hand back, covering her body with my own. Her hand coming up to grip my shoulder, I drop down on top of her. My lips crush hers as she writhes her bare body beneath me. The wet heat of her pussy against me makes my dick pulse and twitch painfully, desperate to find its way inside of her. I nestle my hips between her thighs, lowering myself, my tip finding her wet entrance like a homing beacon.

Lala's teeth score my bottom lip. She nips and bites until she draws blood, sucking at the wound, her nails biting into my shoulder. She tears her nails down my back as we fuck each other's mouths with our tongues. Biting and sucking and fighting for dominance, battling to own one another.

The heat from her pussy screaming at me to plunge inside of it, I do. I'm not gentle and I'm not loving but nothing about us coming together like this ever will be. We both need this, the rough, the pain, the *punishment*. Our bodies, knowing they never should have been separated, demand to be crushed together for all that lost time. All the times we should have been fucking, cuddling, laughing, lying in bed together, eating take out and watching shit TV. All of those fucking moments it should have been us, it all boils down to this moment, here and now.

My dick slams inside of her, hitting her deepest point. Burying myself to the hilt, we both moan at my intrusion. Immediately, I move, not giving her a chance to adjust to me. I'm aware I'm large and she's fucking *tiny* inside, if the vice like grip she has on me is anything to go by, but I can't stop. The animal inside me is running the show now. I fuck her relentlessly, the whole bed creaking as I hammer into her, trying to mesh our souls together. She clings to me as I bury my face into her neck. I strike like a viper, my teeth assaulting her throat, sucking and biting as she attacks me back, ravaging every inch of skin she can access.

Marking.

Claiming.

"*Mine,*" I growl between bites.

"*Yours,*" she cries, thrusting her hips up to meet every one of my punishing thrusts.

Coming together with her like this, free and savage and raw.

So. Fucking. Raw.

Everything about this is us coming full circle, we ended last time with a fuck not too dissimilar to this and now we're starting over. This is the start, our beginning, I can feel it, she can feel it, we belong to each other, we always have, and we always will because she is never getting away from me again.

From *us*.

"I'm never letting you go," I tell her through gritted teeth. "You're never getting away from me, ever a-fucking-gain, you hear me?" I growl, my hips hammering into hers, bruising her ruthlessly.

"Yes! Max, *fuck*, please, never. I fucking need you,

this, everything, I need your everything," she tells me breathlessly and it's my undoing because as she starts to freefall, I willingly go with her.

Pumping into her, her cunt clenches around me. Milking me for all I'm worth, I spill inside of her. My cum shooting into her, coating the entrance to her cervix, filling her up completely. She pulses around me, squeezing and tightening, sucking me deeper as we both ride out the colossal tidal wave of pleasure.

I drop down on top of her, panting in her ear. Burying my face in her hair, coconut and citrus filling my nose as I breathe in her sweet scent. Her delicate fingertips gently running up and down my sweat covered spine, her short shallow breaths fanning over my neck.

"I love you, Lala," I breathe against her neck.

"And I love you, Max."

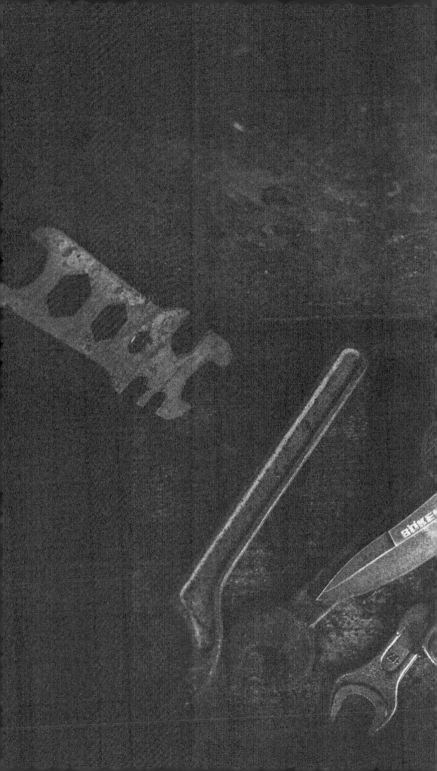

CHAPTER 14
CHARLIE

Christmas Day

A macabre symphony of cries is my only vice. I don't like a lot of other noise. I don't like to be around a lot of people. Humans, in my opinion, are scum of the earth. They take, they break and like a plague, they ruin everything they touch. Then there are those who are a special brand of evil, the ones who don't only ruin the earth but other humans too. They're my obsession, my poison, my antidote. I feed on their life force before I put them in the ground.

I protect what I love and destroy whatever tries to take that away from me; no one will ever steal what is mine.

My family business thrives on the certainty that

there are people on this earth who do bad things. Not one member of the Swallow family is innocent in this game we call life, we just play it differently.

Louder.

Bloodier.

Dirtier.

More *violently*.

Blood pools around his toes that barely scrape the floor. A man strung up from a meat hook like the filthy beast that he is. His arms stretching high above his head, bound together with rope, intertwined with barbed wire. If I just hook his hands up with barbed wire it'll slash his wrists from the weight of his body, killing him far too quickly.

I need to make him bleed.

Slowly.

Every inch of him is covered in glistening ruby, thick crimson coating his skin. Drying like scales, flaking off in some places, wet and dripping in others.

No.

I like the blood.

The smell, colour, texture, the *taste*. Everything about it has me lit up inside like that fucking monstrosity of a Christmas tree my dad has displayed upstairs.

The smell of the Norway spruce wafts through this daunting marble mansion in thick, cloying waves. It makes me think of the outdoors. The harsh howl of the winter wind, the setting afternoon sun low on the horizon. The feel of the damp earth squelching between my naked toes.

The want to run, the *need*.

To strip myself bare, thrash my way through the dense forest. The sharp pine branches lashing at my pale, inked skin. Beads of scarlet dripping down my chest, coating me in hot sticky claret. The bottoms of my feet splitting open, a trail left behind, *of me*.

Closed in, trapped. I don't like small spaces; I need large open areas. I need freedom, to stretch, breathe, to think. I sometimes feel so trapped inside this tight skin of mine that I want to dig my fingernails beneath my flesh and peel it all back.

Display my insides.

Tendon, muscle, bone.

I've seen it all. Felt it all. Exposed it.

I want to see my own.

Feel it, expose nerves and tug at veins, press my fingers in so deep I get lost inside myself and never find a way out.

The lone wolf.

Except, this wolf has a pack. Oftentimes feeling suffocated by it, all the while, still missing something, a single component perhaps. A feeling, an emotion, a *desire*.

A mate.

For my badly beating heart, for my *pain*.

Someone I could destroy as they destroy me. Someone else who has suffered the way I have.

Someone who wants to play in the dark with me, appreciate my art for what it is.

Necessary.

My bare chest already splattered with warm blood. I like the feel of it against my naked skin, it drives my hunger, soothes my soul. Rivulets of it drip down onto my face, falling from my shaggy blonde hair. I blink it free from my dark lashes, my nostrils flaring, I lick my metallic flavoured lips as I refocus on my prey.

This man delivered a threat to my family. He is connected to someone that's after my Kyla-Rose, and I will not stand for that. I will protect her with my life. She owns me you see, *understands* me, I only breathe to protect her. My life is hers to do with as she pleases. There is something almost pure inside her tainted soul that I must preserve at all costs. She is my other half, my reason to continue on in this sea of filth that I find myself endlessly floating in. She is the flicker of light in the dark. If she asked me to slit my own throat for her, I would do it, knowing that she would only ask it of me if it were necessary. She loves me too, you see, she would never harm me.

Therefore, I will never let someone take her from us.

From me.

The man hanging before me is short and chunky. He enjoys too many cigars, too much cognac and far too many rich foods. Looking at him makes me sick. Despite the shape of his body, he's a snake, slithering through life waiting for the right time to strike on unsuspecting prey. My cousin will never be his prey, as long as I have breath in my lungs, I will make sure of that. I'm under no illusions that he's the brains behind the operation, he's not. He's purely a low life, thrust into my eyeline by the higher powers. Yet, he still poses a threat, holding onto information I want, and I *will* get it.

She gave me a list you see.

Another small secret between The Chaos Twins.

As is our way.

Kyla-Rose's pretty handwriting, penmanship in blood red, neatly listing names. Things on that list to be hunted, to be captured, to be tortured and sliced up into tiny little pieces. Dragged down into my dungeon to do exactly as I please with them.

My only captive audience, Dillon, and he does enjoy a good show.

Sidney was the first to be struck off the list. I slashed through his name so hard my knife tore through the paper. You see when I sign my own name into things, I scratch it in. Carve line over line to bulk out my sharp letters. Obsessively scrape, dig and score my name into my prey. It's not often I sign my name with an actual pen, so it didn't occur to me to use one.

Which brings me, once again, to the final name on the list.

It's that name that had my head tilting when she presented me with it. There's always a little heart penned beneath the 'A' when she signs her own name.

Kyla-Rose Swallow.

Penned in cursive ink, that dainty red heart etched beneath the A.

Now, I didn't question that one. I just nodded. We'll get to that. But if she feels she needs to be on her own list, that's her prerogative. We'll get to the bottom of that when the time's right. For now, I hunt the rest. The most loyal, willing servant she'll ever have.

Regardless of my torture techniques over the last however many hours, he is yet to squeal like the pig that he is. He isn't a name on my list, but he is associated with at least one of them. I have more than enough time this morning to get what I want from him. I even bought him a drink. I threw an icy bucket of water over him; he could have stuck his tongue out or opened his mouth to catch some. I'm feeling generous today, I mean, it is Christmas after all.

"So, have you thought about what I asked?" I growl, my voice low and gravelly, holding the underlines of a threat in every word I speak.

The snivelling man is rasping for breath. Which is probably due to his multiple broken ribs and the punctured lung I gave him. The sounds he makes through his windpipe and nose are like music to my ears. These are the sounds I can tolerate, those of pain.

"What do you think, Dillon?" I direct my attention onto my stuffed, white feathered duck friend.

I've had Dillon for almost fifteen years now. He

wasn't always this way, though, on wheels I mean. He was my companion for eight years before that, without them. His beautiful, white feathers and brightly coloured, orange beak. Cocking my head, straining to hear his response, listening to his response, I smirk at his antics.

"Such a naughty boy," I wink at him conspiratorially.

Sitting beneath my table of tools, his little pully string tied around the leg of it; he can't be trusted. He likes to wander, and I don't like him getting his pretty feathers dirty. I spin back to face the snivelling man, cocking my head in the other direction, I sigh.

"I will ask you this question once more before I get a little irritated and I'm being patient with you because it's Christmas," I tell him calmly.

My head tilts to the left as my eyes rove over his torn flesh. There is nothing quite like admiring one's artwork the following day.

"Who sent you?"

The man hangs awkwardly from his right arm, his shoulder dislocated, ligaments in the elbow torn. I admire the uncomfortable angle as I restart the small blowtorch. The whoosh of heat and the soothing sound of its power thrill me as I work the glacial blue flame along the blade of my knife.

"You should be happy that it's me down here with you. My cousin is even less patient for information that threatens her family," I tell him as I carefully start to circle his groaning form.

I step up behind him. My cool breath blowing against the tender, raw skin of his back. I take my serrated blade, carving a deep line through the muscles between his shoulder blades. My heated knife burning and melting the flesh and tissue as I cut into him.

The smell is what hits me first, so familiar and comforting.

Then the silence.

That's what falls around me while I work.

I hear nothing until I hack away enough at my toys to finally enjoy the gruesome orchestra of pain. I ask my victims questions that I know I won't hear the answers to. The blood focuses me, driving me forward, there could be a room full of screaming, yet my ears pick up nothing.

I flip my attention to the front of his body. Slicing a nice, neat, surgical line beneath his lowest rib on the right side. Plunging my fingers into the wound, digging around inside him. Wriggling them around until my three thickest fingers wrap nicely around his bottom rib. Getting a nice solid grip on the slippery bone, I tug on it as hard as I can. I'm not the biggest guy, not like my younger brothers Cam and Eli. They spend a lot of their time in the gym, lifting weights and sparring. All my muscle is from running and chasing, digging graves and carrying corpses.

Sweat runs from my hairline, dripping down my forehead at the exertion. Mixing with the blood on my skin, creating a macabre cocktail of murder. I hold his body flush to mine with my free hand, his energy so depleted his legs hardly sway as he tries to kick at me. Continuing to flex the bone forwards and backwards inside his torso, I work tirelessly until it starts to crack. Eventually I feel it start to splinter, and with all my might, I tear the fragmented bone sharply towards me, snapping a part of it clean from his body. Raising it up above me, I examine the pretty treasure I've procured under the glow of the orange light.

I smile, my ears still deaf to sound. High pitched buzzing filling my head, like a swarm of bluebottle flies feasting on a rotting corpse. Laying their eggs in every crevice they can squirm into. Their fat, oil-slick coloured bodies digging themselves deep beneath the skin, the buzzing growing louder the harder they work.

"Did you know there are two-hundred and six bones in the human body?" I ask, flicking my eyes up towards his face, but not really seeing him. "I've just removed one of yours," *well mostly,* "and it took me roughly eighteen minutes. If I remove every single bone at that same speed, it will take me an estimated three-thousand, six-hundred and ninety minutes. That's the equivalent to sixty-one point five hours or two-hundred and twenty-one thousand, four-hundred seconds. How long do you think you'll last? Shall we make a wager? I'm not usually a betting man but I like my odds in this game." I release his body, letting it swing heavily back and forth from the hook, his unconscious weight tugging sharply on his bound arms.

He's passed out again, bleeding and pale, his breathing raspy and I can hear a gurgle at the back of his broken nose. It's so boring when they pass out. I grab a metal bucket filled with diluted household bleach. Tossing it over him, he startles awake with a scream of pain as my adrenaline lessens and my hearing fully returns. The thudding of my heartbeat and rushing of blood in my ears slowly dying away.

"Who are you working for?" I ask with a sigh.

I'm growing a little impatient because Dad demanded I be upstairs, clean, dressed and *blood-free* by eleven and we're definitely cutting it close to that now. The man's screaming, a sound I finally hear, so comfortingly familiar. I could drift off to sleep to it like a child would a nursery rhyme and that's quite a real possibility right now. I've been working on him for almost twenty-seven hours straight and I haven't gotten a single thing out of him, all he does is shake his head at me. Wordlessly mumbling over and over before losing consciousness again. I think I might have broken him. No superglue in the world is gunna fix this toy.

I prop my arse against the old wooden work-bench. Wiping a soiled hand off on a rag before petting Dillon gently on the head, caressing his pristine, white feathers. Crossing my bare feet at the ankles, I take a moment to just stare at the body hanging in the centre of the dark basement. My dad had this cave-like room built beneath the house, airtight and soundproof with a large underfloor drainage system, air vents and four thick steel security doors. Handprint scanners between this room and the stairs that lead up to the main house. Not that anyone survives down here long enough to even consider escaping, but it's always best to be careful.

I zone out, for how long, I'm unsure. But I'm suddenly back in the room when I hear the sliding of bolts in the third door away from me. My ears prick up like that of an African hunting dog, always pricked, alert, listening. Well, except in times of torture. I run my fingers along the rough bone of the rib still clutched in my hand as I study it in my thick fingers. Spitting on it, I rub my fingers over it, cleaning it off. Bones are a weird thing. Everyone expects them to be clean and smooth and rigid, but in reality, they're messy, rough and flexible. They get stiffer as they age but they're pretty pliable things usually.

The heavy door swings open. Kyla-Rose entering the room, her too large eyes finding mine in the dim light. A soft smile gracing her red lips when she finds me. She's the only person in this lifetime who could enter my space without needing my permission.

"'Sup, Charl? Merry fuckin' Christmas!" she cheerfully sing-songs from just inside the open doorway.

Her gentle husk immediately drawing and capti-vating the entirety of my attention. A white sequined, spaghetti strap, mini dress sits snugly on her lean body. The hem of it close to showing off something inappropriate. The top of it cut straight across her chest, the thin corded straps barely holding it up. The heavy sequins catch what little orange glow of light there is. Colourful patterns reflecting across the ceiling like rainbows, cutting through dense darkness as she struts further inside.

A demonic smile curves her plump red lips, it's sharp, threatening, *delicious*. I lick my own lips, tasting salt and copper. Tilting my head, my eyes tracking her across the short distance, she travels across the space gracefully. Her long lean legs carrying her further towards me, pin heels tapping against the concrete, vibrations echoing around the walls. She glides as gracefully and skilled as a gazelle, light on her feet, silent movements, but there's no gazelle underneath that perfectly imperfect skin, no. A demon lies dormant beneath, both savage and beautiful.

Deadly.

We are monsters.

Her and I.

Cut from the same cloth of fate, both travelling down the bloodiest path to hell.

Together.

But I don't mind, for thrones wait for us in those fiery pits, eagerly awaiting us to rule together.

She parks her perky arse against the workbench, our thighs almost touching but not quite. I let my eyelids fall shut as I inhale her familiar scent, vanilla, coconut, limes. She smells like her soul, soft, delicate, with a deadly sharpness that cuts through the creaminess of her. She reaches down, her tattooed arm brushing against my sticky blood splattered one. Her fingers lazily stroking Dillon's head. I almost frown when I see her injured hand bandaged and tightly tucked into her chest.

"Who's this?" she asks, drawing my attention away from her self-inflicted wound.

Cocking her head to one side, her grey eyes gliding rapidly over the bloody body suspended from the ceiling. Assessing, analysing every cut, bruise and detail she can lay her eyes on.

"A threat. I tracked him. For a name on the list," I grunt, not giving her anything else, that's enough, today anyway. "He's not talking," I growl lowly, the husk of my voice carrying through the silence, roughly vibrating through my chest.

Kyla-Rose looks at me from the corner of her eye and scowls. Her red lips pursing into a tight line, distaste at my lack of information. Effortlessly pushing herself up from the workbench, she takes a few slow steps forward, drifting in the direction of my prey. Victim is the wrong word to use. He is not innocent in this game. She circles the unconscious form, taking her time, narrowing her eyes in on particularly vicious wounds. Stopping just before him, her back to me, her knees bending slightly. Her head moving closer to the body, slowly tilting it again to one side.

Kyla-Rose glances at me over her shoulder, a slow

wink of mischief lighting up her grey-green eyes. Knowing I like a show, she steps to one side to not hinder my view. Her full focus now on the broken body, she reaches out. Her thin finger traces over the gaping wound -the place I removed part of his rib from- before thrusting her long taloned finger inside it. Shoving it in hard and deep, right up to her tattooed knuckle, harshly dragging her clawed finger-nails through the torn flesh. My prey snaps back to consciousness with a long low cry, snot and tears rushing down his face as he struggles pathetically against the damaging bindings. The irritated slices in his mangled wrists oozing and weeping. Even if he did get out of this, his arms would never work the same way again, the way the barbed wire is cutting into his flesh, the nerves will be destroyed.

"Hello, *friend*," Kyla-Rose hisses in a hushed menacing whisper.

Her viper tongue spitting venom with the friendly words. She plucks her delicate fingers from inside him. Smearing the hot, thick crimson across his cheek, marking him with his own blood. She smiles up at him brightly, an animalistic glint in her wicked gaze.

"How d'you feel?" she asks gently, softly.

The sound of her teasing forcing my blood-soaked skin to break out in goosebumps. A comical pout, a clownlike frown on her angelic face as she hides her true smile. Her goading kicks my heart into overdrive, beating uncontrollably inside my chest. My monster claws at my insides. This is a game. And Kyla-Rose is almost a better player in it than I am.

Almost.

The broken man shakes his head furiously at her. The waves of danger rolling off her like an over-whelming series of tsunamis, permeating the room with her anger. Even dressed up in her best clothes. A pair of three-thousand quid shoes on her feet. Hair and makeup groomed to perfection -you'd never know she has three-dozen hickeys smattered across her neck and jaw- everyone within a ten-mile radius could sense the threat of her presence.

Feel it.

Kyla-Rose reaches up suddenly, her hand snap-ping out at such a speed it's a blur. Her bloody fingers and thumb dig into his chubby cheeks. Squeezing so hard she forces his mouth open like a puckering fish, grunting at what she sees. Releasing her hold on him she pushes against his chest, sending him swinging back and forth on his hook. He rocks, his heavy weight putting even more pressure on his damaged body, he groans out in a chorus of anguished cries.

"Charl," she rasps softly, a small patient sound from her, created just for me.

It's what I need, her soft soothing tune to break through my darkness. A slender hand reaching inside my chest, caressing the half-living organ inside there, getting it to feel something.

She always knows how to speak to me.

We healed together, after all.

"Yeah?" I rasp.

"You've cut out his tongue," she tells me gently, her bloody hand coming up to rest against my bare shoulder, her crimson stained fingers squeezing comfortingly.

"I have?" I ask her with an exceptionally slow blink of my tired eyes.

She nods at me with that tender, loving smile. I just stare blankly at her angelic features.

"Want me to finish him off? Then we can go upstairs and open that tin of chocolates that Violet insisted I can't open without you," she winks with a broad grin.

I find myself nodding absently as she turns away from me. Lala approaches the weaponry wall. It's one long length of the room, various types of weapons hang there in different shapes and sizes. Everything clean, organised and immaculate. I spend a lot of time down here making sure all of my things are perfect and ready for use. I enjoy organising it and having control over the space. It's all mine.

This is the house Dad bought when Mum disappeared. We grew into men in this house. Kyla-Rose moved in when we brought her home from juvie. Dad taught her everything she knows too.

She came back from that place different.

Twisted.

More like *me*.

I was broken by bad men too.

Lala runs her ruby stained fingers over a long thin

scythe, examining it carefully. Running the pad of her thumb over the edge of the blade, snagging the skin but not drawing blood. Extracting it from the wall, testing its weight in her hand. Looking up at me, she flashes me that wild grin. The one that promises carnage, that's one thing people underestimate about Kyla-Rose, her violence is feral. Just because she dresses up like a demonic little barbie, doesn't mean she's afraid of getting her hands dirty.

She steps up behind the man, adjusting her body so she's poised with the weapon that will end his life. As she draws it back, I stop her.

"Wait!"

Her brow furrows, her slightly upturned nose wrinkling in confusion. I push up, grabbing a well-worn leather apron from its hook beside my work-bench. I move around behind her, placing it over her head, tying it at the waist. I untuck her long silver hair and step back, checking it's covering every clothed part of her.

"Thanks, Charl," she beams up at me before slashing through the man's thick jugular.

With one swift flick of the wrist, blood arcs, splaying across my already saturated body and I close my aching eyes with a sigh of relief as she showers me in it.

Stepping around me, Kyla-Rose places the bloodied weapon down. Turning away from me so I can untie the heavy apron. Lifting it over her head, I lay it down beside the scythe.

"Can we please go and open those sweets now?" she whines like a petulant child, not the demonic hellion that just killed a man.

Batting her eyelashes at me and jutting out that plump bottom lip again, gnawing on it like a crazed animal. It's a horrible habit, makes me want to cut it off so she can't do it anymore.

"You'll be sick like last year," I tell her on a grunt.

She throws her head back, infectious laughter erupting from her chest. She sniffs as she looks at me, wiping a finger beneath her smoky black eye.

"Cam's face really was a picture though, wasn't it?" she roars at the memory of her puking on my squeamish younger brother as I steer her towards the large steel door. "He was greener than me."

Fresh out the shower, smelling mundanely of soap instead of my favourite tangy, copper fragrance, I step into my bedroom. It's black. Black walls, black ceiling, red bulbs in all the lamps and fixtures, my eyes like the dark. I thrive in it, stalk the shadows, I'm a whisper in the darkness, a ghost, a malevolent spirit. My eyes run over the four-poster bed sitting in the centre of the room, all black, silk sheets with a crimson comforter.

Which is when I see it.

Stepping cautiously towards it, I stare blankly at the *outfit* laid out for me. Tight black slacks, a white long-sleeved dress shirt and polished black loafers. I grunt my disgust at the entire thing. There's no way I can wear any of it, not the way it looks now anyway. I pull on the too-tight trousers and slip my feet into the loafers, they're so shiny I can see my own fucking face in them.

God, I hate rich people clothes.

The shirt.

The too tight, overpriced, long-sleeve shirt.

It's not that there's anything wrong with it… I just don't want to be trapped inside of it.

Lifting the shirt, I cock my head, twisting my lips in contemplation. I hum to myself, snagging the shoulder seam with my teeth, I tear the arms from the shoulders. Ripping the sleeves off completely before pulling it on. Buttons left undone, the front of it gaping open.

Not trapped.

Looking in the mirror I ruffle my fingers through my wet hair. It's shaggy on top, hanging just above my eyes when it flops forward. Razor cut, uneven, blunt and jagged, just like the rest of me. Cam cuts it, I wouldn't have anyone else touch me, and even then, it's not always easy with him either. Enough length to it that I can pull on the ends in frustration. It's mussed up, sticking up all over the place, little drips of water sluicing over my face and lips. Dropping onto my soft white shirt, I look as good as I'm going to get.

At least I've got trousers on this year.

I shrug to myself, leaving my room by stepping into the overly white hallway. The thick carpet a subtle grey, the expensive kind your feet sink into. I drift down the grand split staircase. Coming from the left, where us kids have our suites, all except Jacob, he's on the right with our dad's rooms. My ridiculously priced shoes click against the cold marble as I make my way down, echoing obnoxiously in the silent space. The twenty-foot Christmas tree lit up, dressed in red and gold, sits centrally in the grand foyer, nestled between the mouths of the stairs.

This section of the house is open, all marble floors and tall glass panels, outside, the world is dull and lifeless. Thick grey clouds hang low with the promise of snow. It makes the house feel colder, if that's even a possibility, it's almost clinical this house, too clean. I like earth, that raw pungent smell of thick mud when its rained too hard. When the sun finally rears its ugly head and the dirt tries to suck up its rays. Looking for praise and affection from the sun, needing it to dry out.

I hate that. Everything always needing something else to survive, thrive. Although, it's a bit like I need my Lala, I suppose.

My ears prick at the first murmur of chatter, *people*. I tilt my head, stretching my neck, cracking the stiffness and flexing the tight muscle. Sighing heavily, I take in a deep breath through my nose, my nostrils flaring with the overwhelming stench of perfumes and aftershaves. The mixture of overpriced chemicals souring my stomach. I don't wear anything like that, I can't stand the chemical smells. They irritate my nostrils and burn the back of my throat.

Following the sounds of too many people, I travel through the empty hallways until I reach the grand reception room. It's too large and filled with too much unnecessary furniture but my dad likes it. And seeing as he built me my special room downstairs, I shouldn't be too harsh on his over-the-top tastes. Keeping to the farthest and darkest corner of the room I slink in unnoticed, scanning over the sea of faces.

Of course, I know them all, I make it my business to never forget anyone, but then I'm a supposed 'Super Recogniser', so that may have some part to play in that. I can recall the face of every person I've ever seen, with excessive precision. My defective brain is supposedly not so defective after all. I've been my eldest brother's fascination for as long as I can remember. When I was finally rescued from my captors, Jacob tried to hook me up to all these weird fucking machines to test my brain waves or some shit like that.

I bit him.

Well, I tore a chunk of flesh out of his shoulder.

With my teeth.

He needed nine stitches…

I don't like to be played with.

My emerald gaze roves over all the insignificant players in the room. First falling to Gremlin, he's speaking with Rubble and an overexcited woman. I tilt my head as I observe her interact, she's bouncing around like a yappy puppy. I already can't stand her. I wonder which one of them is fucking her. Unlikely to be Rubble, he fucks hard and fast and likes his conquests silent. I know because I've seen him and everyone he fucks he gags. I've seen everyone I know in compromising positions. You never know when you might need to use it against them.

Averting my attention to the far side of the room, my dad sits with his life partner Violet. Her petite frame nestled into his side. His thick arm tucked around her narrow waist protectively, drawing her into his side with obvious affection. Violet's chestnut hair falls around her slim shoulders in shiny, soft waves. Her large, brown doe-eyes crinkle at the corners as she laughs at something Dad says to her.

I like Violet.

She always smells nice, warm and floral, not that artificial bullshit either.

Plus, I kinda liked her as a mother, if I needed one, which I don't.

Cam and Eli are standing a few feet to their left, speaking with some of Dad's personal circle. Cam isn't much of a talker, he nods, he smiles -what he thinks is a smile- at the petty bullshit that spills from their corrupt mouths.

Jacob is being Jacob. He's getting on my nerves a lot lately, my eyes automatically dismiss him. I don't give a fuck what he's doing today, as long as he stays the fuck away from me. I love my brother, but I also hate him sometimes. Now is one of those times.

Frank and his wife Carol are sitting on another ostentatious sofa. The fabric lavish and too bright, everything in this fucking room is too bright. My eyes ache just standing in this darkened corner. Kyla-Rose is nestled between them, looking happier than ever having Carol gushing over her, as she does at every family event. She can be a charmer when she's not slaughtering grown men three times her size. Carol reaches up cupping Kyla-Rose's cheek, her thumb caressing her soft skin, I growl lowly, my chest vibrating. I know she's not a threat, but one can never be too careful.

Kacey, Huxley and Maddox stand sentry at the side of the couch. Their imposing frames keeping everyone else a good three-feet away at all times. Their collective gazes monitoring every guest, every staff entry and exit. Stances ready to pounce should the need to protect my cousin arise. I feel my lip twitch in amusement. They needn't worry, no one shall get to her whilst I'm here. Although, I'm glad to see them taking the job of protecting my other half seriously.

Stealthily I move through the room. My movements causing an automatic ripple effect through the groups of people. Simultaneously they shuffle out of my way, ensuring they give me enough space to pass through without the need to touch any of them. Keeping to the edges of the room, I approach my cousin's men. I move as delicately as possible before stopping still behind none other than Maddox fucking Sharpe.

His spine goes rigid at sensing my presence, and I have to banish the slight tilt of my lips from my stony face. I'm going to intimidate this man into making sure he doesn't upset Kyla-Rose. Although, the big one with the tattooed head growled at me over him the other day. That was an interesting development. But I won't watch her hurt over him. She's done just that for the past ten years and I refuse to see it happen again.

Perhaps I should lure him out and kill him now, make it quick and bury him in one of Violet's many flower beds. I could do all of that before dinner is served, I'm sure of it. The ground is hard but that's never stopped me before. I could always chop him up and dump him in the bottom of the compost heap. I wonder how long it would take for him to rot in this cold weather. In fact, I could dispose of all three of these men without anyone but Lala ever noticing.

Perhaps that would make her cry, or perhaps I could distract her enough that she wouldn't notice them gone. We could play lots of games and brutalise lots of bad people to keep her occupied. She would notice them gone *eventually*; she's smart this one. Plus, I don't think I even need to worry about the other two. The fighter worships her, an idiot could see that, and the dark eyed hacker is quite obviously besotted.

I shall leave them alive.

For now.

"Maddox," I growl, my sharpened fangs almost brushing the shell of his ear before I step back and raise my eyebrows at the other two in greeting.

"Charlie," Max grunts in return.

I watch him from the corner of my eye, his face hard and unyielding. The man is by no means frightened or even concerned with my presence but I sure as shit will try my very fucking best to change that. I love a game. I can see why my cousin is drawn to him, his soul is pitch black and familiar, it calls to hers, I can almost feel their pull to one another, it's magnetic.

"Report," I order, shoving my tatted fists into the overly tight pockets of my slacks, eyeballing the three men.

"Nothing since the bird, and obviously the pub incident last night," Huxley tells me as he switches from civilian to soldier.

His spine straightens, his arms hanging by his sides in a comfortable but formal stance. You can take the soldier out of the army, but you can't take the soldier out of the man. I nod, sliding my view over to Kyla-Rose. Her misty emeralds narrowed in on me, I smirk at her with a wink. She knows I'm checking up on her, but I'll never stop. I will die for her if I need to. Slit my own throat and offer myself up in sacrifice.

"You sorted your shit out with her yet?" I pry gruffly.

I needn't say more, they all know who my question is aimed at.

Maddox grunts in response, but there's something

in his eyes that has me narrowing mine in on him. I tilt my head, his large, tattooed hand runs over his raven-black hair, curling into a fist as he tugs his fingers through the length. I raise a single brow at him before shifting my gaze to the lesser of evils, the hacker and the fighter.

"You gunna share her with him if he ever pulls his head out of his arsehole long enough to make it up to her?" I deadpan.

Huxley erupts into uncomfortable laughter. As is his way, being the comedian of the group to shield your feelings seems like a lot of hard work. Kacey narrows his eyes on Maddox before sliding his gold gaze back to me.

Interesting.

"That's not up to us, it's up to Kyla-Rose," Kacey huffs, shoving his hands into his pockets.

His answer more than perfect -not that I'll tell him that.

"You three better not fuck up, I've got very creative ideas on how to end you and ensure you're never found," I smile at them, a devilish grin that makes Huxley shudder, my smile widening accordingly. "I even have mood boards for each of your deaths," I smile broader, my sharp fangs glinting in the light as I turn away, heading straight for Lala.

"He scares me," I hear Huxley whisper and this time I can't stop the grin that engulfs my face, twisting my features into something downright petrifying.

Approaching the couch where Frank and Carol

are still doting on Kyla-Rose. I slow my pace, watching as Carol caresses my cousin's cheek, taking any and every opportunity she can to touch Lala's face or hair. I'm pretty sure Carol would adopt her if it was a possibility. She would have made a much better mother than the one Lala was stuck with.

"Frank," I greet with a firm nod of my head.

"Merry Christmas, Charlie," Frank smiles, knowingly keeping his hands to himself, I don't do handshakes.

"'Appy Christmas, Carol," I offer, the smallest, most genuine smile I can muster tilts my lips.

Knowing that it'll make my cousin happy if I'm polite.

"Merry Christmas, Charlie," she smiles at me, and I feel warmth bloom in my chest.

I like Carol, she's kind and she means well. She has a big heart. It's a shame this world likes to snuff out people like her.

"I'm sorry to interrupt, but I've come to kidnap my cousin," I wink, only half joking.

I sometimes think we'd be better off somewhere far away from here.

"Oh, of course! I've been hogging her all to myself!" she laughs, her cheeks turning a soft shade of pink.

"You can have her back soon. I won't keep her long," I promise with a sly smirk.

Taking Kyla-Rose's small hand in my large, rough one, I pull her up from the couch.

Tugging her tightly behind me as I start to lead her from the room.

"Charl?" she questions as we pass her trio of men, all of whom follow her with their eyes.

Good.

Tightening my grip on her delicate fingers, I crush them between my own. Dragging her behind me, her too-high heels clacking against the white marble floors. I weave us through the large dining room. Working my way between the busy catering staff currently filling the buffet table with a feast. I whip us out of the archway, around the corner and slam her back into a darkened alcove with my forearm across her chest.

"*Charlieeee*," she whines, her eyes sparkling with mischief. "Dee's gunna be so, *so* mad if we play a game right now, the house is full of people," she pouts, biting her bottom lip to hide her smirk.

I can see in her eyes she wants to play, they're filled with excitement. Her demon rearing its head, her pupils blown with deviant ideas. She's been out of the game for a whole fucking month, I can see how desperate she is to do *something*. Anything to wreak havoc or make a *bloody* mess. I didn't drag her out here to play... but maybe later.

"No games," I growl, making her smirk grow, her lip popping free from her teeth. "I wanted to give you your gift," I hiss at her and her eyes gleam.

"What did you get me?" she whispers curiously,

her head tilting in wonder, those too large eyes peering into my own.

Without taking my eyes from hers, I pull out the small vile from my trouser pocket, holding it up to her face.

"Venom." I answer coolly, my expression stoic.

Her large grey-green orbs blink at me slowly, once, twice.

"Is that? Charlie is *that*... no fucking wayyy," she whispers, her awed gaze flicking between my eyes and the small vile.

She swallows hard, her tongue darting out to lick her red lips.

"Inland Taipan."

"NO FUCKING WAY!" she squeals.

The high pitch ringing through my ears, my eyes narrowing as a growl stirs in my chest at the discomfort. She screams quietly through her gritted teeth. Her long, black nailed fingers gripping my bicep as she jumps up and down in excitement, just like a kid on Christmas. I smirk at the thought.

"How in the fuck did you get it? That snake is just- when can we use it? How long does it keep for? *Fuck*, Charlie!" she asks me too many questions, her husky voice low and breathy.

"It doesn't matter how, but it needs to be kept in the freezer, I just wanted you to see it first."

"Can I?" she asks innocently, her small uninjured hand reaching up to take the vile from between my fingers.

I offer it up to her. Gently lifting it up towards the light from the hall. Her head tilting as she looks up into the bottom of the vile, her lips kicking up at the corners.

"Thank you, Charlie," she whispers.

Stretching up on tiptoes, she places a soft kiss on my cheek, wrapping me up in her soft coconut scent. I take the vile back, stepping out of the alcove and into the hall. Heading in the direction of my dungeon.

"I love you, *brother,*" she breathes that last word almost silently.

My steps nearly falter but I don't let it show in my confident stride.

"I love you, too," I whisper in return.

That, she doesn't hear.

CHAPTER 15
KYLA-ROSE

Leaning my weight back against Huxley's firm chest, his arm banded around my waist. I sip my champagne, my eyes scanning over the faces of close to a hundred people. I definitely prefer when we would have smaller Christmas celebrations. Not that I'll act any differently, I'm not working today. No one in attendance is, though, it can be hard to switch off entirely. Charlie skulked off to his torture chamber, muttering about too many people. He's not keen on having intruders in his space. He'll likely be sitting with Dillon, stroking his feathers to calm his stress. I'll go and get him back in a bit, God forbid Jacob goes down there, I shudder at the thought.

Huxley presses a kiss to the top of my head, drawing my attention back to the room. I glance up at him, pressing myself further against him. He was weirdly happy about Max and I when we told him.

Frank came to get us from The Cadogan, the car

journey home was an anxious one. Both of us feeling out of sorts. We held hands, our entwined fingers resting on the centre seat. The pair of us lost in thought, staring out of our respective windows. My mouth dry the entire journey, as thoughts of my boys walking out on me filled my head. I know they said they were okay with it, but were they really?

When we got in, Huxley was waiting in my entry-way. A small grin on his face as his dark eyes roved over my new love bites, my heart lodged in my throat. He stepped forward, his lean, muscled arms opening wide for me. I stepped into him. His scent comforting me, he kissed the crown of my head as I buried my face in his t-shirt. I felt the moment my beast joined us, the air shifted, my skin prickled with goosebumps. I peered over Huxley's shoulder, my body taut with worry as I locked eyes on glittering gold ones.

Kacey's face was pulled tight, little lines of stress at the outer corners of his beautiful eyes. A sob caught in my throat as he nodded and turned away. Huxley told me to leave him be, that he was okay with it, it was just an adjustment. Conflicting feelings ran through me. Fear, heartache, love. I felt like I might burst, I trembled in Huxley's embrace, his long fingers smoothing up and down my spine. My face buried protectively against him. His hand cupping the back of my head, keeping me flush to him, I let out a shuddery breath. Max went off to the room he's been using as his, kissing me softly on the lips as he passed, leaving me alone with Hux. I blinked up at him, my eyes filling with tears, my heart clenching painfully in my chest. He soothed my fears, murmuring reassurances of love, on behalf of him and Big Man.

Kacey didn't come to bed with us last night. Angel even left his spot open, her whining when she realised he wasn't coming broke something inside me. The angry bitch hates everyone, but she's just as attached to these two men now as I am. It makes me worry about what I'll do if Kacey doesn't want this anymore. I fear I don't think very rationally when it comes to Kacey and Huxley.

Charlie asked me early on if I was sure this was love or if it was just obsession. I said I couldn't be sure, but that sometimes it hurts inside my chest when I think about them. After discussion we decided our past obsessions hadn't ever caused us any pain, so it must be love. I can be very certain of one thing, obsession or not, I am in love with these men. Painfully and frightfully so.

"What you thinking about, Darlin'?" Huxley rasps, his teeth grazing the top of my ear, the ball from his tongue bar running along my cartilage piercings.

A shudder rolls through me, my thighs clenching, I release a stuttered breath.

"Nothing," I breathe the lie, his grip pinching my waist as he tightens his hold.

"Tell me," he orders, that stern, take-no-shit tone making me breathy.

"Kacey," I whisper as my eyes lock on his huge body across the room.

There he stands, dressed in all black, tight black slacks, a long-sleeved, button-up black shirt. The top button flicked open, the thick scar across his throat shining under the bright lights. My fingers twitch, aching to trace it, kiss the underside of his clean-shaven jaw, bite into his neck like a savage.

"He's not upset with you, Darlin'. He's talking to Nox," Huxley shrugs.

I glare up at him, "he punched him in the mouth, Huxley."

He chuckles, "well yeah, Nox fucked our girl."

I frown, my eyebrows knitting together, my expression sharp enough to cut. I drag my gaze back onto Kacey, Max beside him, dressed identically, a fresh split in his top lip, a soft smirk on his face. I sigh, leaning farther back into Huxley. Oranges and sandalwood wrapping me up, I breathe easier, even while I pout.

Indecision warring inside me. Half of me wants to storm over there, press my knife into his neck and demand he drop to his knees before me. Ravish my cunt right here and now and beg me to forgive him for abandoning me last night. The other half of me, the smaller half, the saner half, is telling me to wait it out, give him the space he's obviously needing, leave him be and tackle the conversation later. Apologise and beg for forgiveness, see where he stands on this now, on us, if he's changed his mind. My chest aches, prickles running through the centre of it. I knock the rest of my champagne back, dumping the glass on a passing waiter's tray, declining another.

I try to avert my attention. Listen to what Huxley and Eli are currently yammering on about, something about security cameras and some weird fucking x-ray bullshit. All these weird techy things make my teeth grind, I can barely use the TV remote, but I *can* rapidly disassemble and reassemble a Remington 870. So, I do have my uses.

My other two men still in my peripheral, the bigger of the two shifts, my gaze slides back over. Kacey slaps Max on the back, handing off his glass of scotch. I wriggle free from Huxley's hold, his grip tightening as I huff.

"Where you goin'?" Huxley teases, knowing full well what I just witnessed.

He keeps them in his peripheral at all times too.

"Let me go, I just need to talk to him," I say quietly.

Eli's attention flicks between the two of us.

"Somethin' wrong, Lala?" he murmurs, a blonde brow raised as I glance at him.

"No, nothing wrong. Just need to talk to Kacey about something," I struggle against Huxley's forearm as I lose sight of my golden-eyed beast slipping from the room. "Huxley," I hiss, his arm releasing me.

"Go on. Be good," he murmurs, a smirk on his peach lips.

Fingers latching around my arm. Quickly pulling

me back into him, he presses a scorching kiss to my lips, I sway on my feet as he finally releases me.

I hurry across the room, darting around people, my heels clacking against the marble floor. I pass through the large, open archway, looking left then right. Catching sight of Kacey's large frame turning at the end of the corridor. Shamelessly I rush down the empty hallway, guest rooms and bathrooms, the only thing leading off this hall. A smoking room at the very end. As I turn the corner, I see Kacey closing a bathroom door. I throw myself forward as fast as my feet will carry me. My palm slapping against the solid wood door, my heeled foot sliding in the tight space. He stops trying to close the door, his eyeline on my foot, before he draws his gaze up, his frown dissipating as his eyes lock on mine.

"Sweetheart?"

"Big Man," I say, forcing my way into the room.

Kacey backs up, allowing me entrance, still looking a little confused as to why I've followed him into the bathroom. I close the door behind me, the automatic LEDs around the mirror flicking on as the lock engages. I rest my back against the wood, my good hand between me and the door, my feet crossed at the ankles.

"Talk to me," I demand, "tell me what's wrong, tell me, Kacey." I swallow, licking my lips, the waxy texture drying my tongue.

"Kyla-Rose, nothing's wrong, I'm fine," he sighs heavily, running a large hand over his tattooed head, the hair shaved away completely so you can see the intricate ivy design.

"Don't lie to me, we're way past shit like this," I squeeze the words out through my tight throat.

Kacey's eyes lock on mine, his shoulders deflating, his head dropping forward. My heart squeezes as I hold my breath. This is it. He's going to tell me we're over. He finally looks up at me, and my breath rushes out of me.

"You're going to leave me, aren't you?" I hush out, my chest heaving.

I uncross my ankles, straightening from my leaning position against the door. Pain tears through me, I pull my top lip between my teeth, biting down on it so hard I have to swallow blood. My teeth tear into my cupids bow as I stare at a piece of my soul slowly disconnecting from me.

His gold eyes flash in the dark, sweet honey and warm amber, the eyes of a bloodthirsty beast. *My* bloodthirsty beast.

I go to take a step towards him, "Kacey, *please-*"

"I'm not leaving you," he growls, cutting me off.

I roll back on my heels, keeping my distance. He sighs heavily, dropping his head back on his shoulders, his eyes closed, facing the ceiling. He reaches up, pinching the bridge of his nose before rolling his head on his shoulders. His eyes opening to look at me. His expression unreadable, my heart battering against my ribcage, trying to break free of its boned prison. I press my wounded hand to my chest. My aching fingers curled into my palm, nails snagging my bandage. Blood rushing to my head, my ears buzz, I blink rapidly, trying to calm down. My breath comes in short rasps, my body trembling as he cocks his head.

"It's not you," he sighs, lacing his fingers together and planting them on the back of his head, he shuts his eyes again.

"*It's not you, it's me*, right? You're gunna spin me that bullshit, Kace?" I snap out, but it doesn't have the desired effect, because my voice cracks on his name.

His eyes pop open, his brows knitting together, he drops his arms. My bottom lip trembles.

"What can I do to make you stay with me?" I whisper, my voice grates out like sandpaper's been taken to my vocal cords.

"What?" he frowns.

"Just, tell me, whatever it is, I'll do it, Kace. I'll beg if you want."

I lick my lips, readying to do just that when he rushes me, slamming me back into the door. I wince, waiting for my head to slam into the wood, but his hand slides effortlessly to the back of my skull, his huge hand cradling my head. His hips pinning me in place, his other hand cupping my face, his thumb sliding over my top lip. He sweeps it across my torn flesh, bringing it back to his lips. Keeping his eyes locked on mine, he sucks the little trace of blood free from his skin.

"I'm not going anywhere, Sweetheart. I'm just, I'm *adjusting*," he almost chokes on the word.

I screw my face up, shaking my head, "I don't understand, I thought-"

"I'm jealous, baby girl," he sighs heavily, cutting me off, his breath on my lips.

"Last night, you didn't come to bed," I whisper.

My eyes staring up into his, not understanding how these things are supposed to go.

"I went to the gym with Cam, I needed to hit something, and I didn't wanna upset you by messing up pretty boy's face."

"But you did hit him, Kace," I say quietly, confusion still steadily working through me.

"Well, yeah, he fucked my girl, but I didn't kill him," he shrugs nonchalantly.

I can't help the small smile tilting my lips.

"You're my girl, and he's my boy. I want him on board, I do. I want it to work, the way it works with you, me and Huxley. *Fuck*, I encouraged it. I'm just jealous. And I've never really been jealous before, so I don't really know what I'm supposed to do with all this- this anger," he sighs heavily again, dropping his face to the crook of my neck.

I exhale a soft breath, my tense shoulders relaxing a little.

He's not going anywhere.

"Kacey," I murmur, running my fingers through his flop of sandy blonde hair. "You share me with Hux, and you've never got upset like this before," I say softly, his grip on my hip tightening as I gently claw over his scalp.

"Me and Huxley were on the same starting line. Nox has like twenty fucking years on us and it's not-we aren't on equal footing anymore, are we? He's so far ahead, we'll be playing catch up for like, well, our whole lives." He looks up at me, my fingers twisting in his hair.

"I love you. Do you love me, Kace?"

"You know I do," he murmurs, making me smile.

"Do you trust me?"

"With my life," he answers without hesitation.

"I will *never* love *anyone* more than I love you." I swallow, his eyes flicking between my own. "I love you. You were-" I swallow hard, averting my gaze to steel my spine. "You were the first man I've had sex with, that I wanted to, since Max. Someone I had actual feelings for. Do you understand what I'm saying to you, Big Man?" I blink up at him. "I chose *you*, no one else, just you. You caught me when I was falling and I would choose you again. *Every single time.* You make me feel," I pause, looking into those beautiful gold eyes. "You make me feel worth it," I whisper, the words clawing their way out. "You made me feel, feel something, for the first time in a long time. It was *you*, Big Man. You made my heart beat, you resurrected this dying, broken girl. You gave me life, Big Man. You gave me *me* back. I will love you for the next thousand years, and the thousand after that and after that. I will stalk you through shadows, hunt you down day or night. You own a piece of me, Kace. Mind, body and bleeding fucking soul. You are it for me. So, please, don't ever leave me." I swallow nervously.

My heart thunking like a slow hammering gavel in a courtroom, Kaccy holding it in his big hands, deciding my fate. A life sentence spent together or my death.

I'm throwing it out there, pure vulnerability oozing from me. But I do, I love him so much, I'll bare myself to him in my rawest form if that's what it takes. I need him to see what he means to me.

"Sweetheart, *fuck*, you have no idea, do you?" he laughs humourlessly.

Drawing back from me, his hips still holding mine flush to the door.

"What?" I whisper, anxiety tightening my spine.

"*God*, Kyla-Rose. When I first laid eyes on you, I just knew, my *soul* just knew. You were the stranger it recognised. I'd do anything for you, *anything*. You wanna lock a collar around my neck, drag me around on a lead? Do it. Whatever the fuck you want or need, I'm gunna get it for you. I'll pluck the stars out of the sky and trap them in a jar, so you never have to live in the dark again. I'll take out your enemies and bring you back their hearts. I'll give you mine. I'd drop to my knees right now, cut it from my chest and fucking offer it up to you. You own it, Sweetheart. I'll do anything you desire. I love you more than I could ever love anything. You've infected me like the sweetest poison, you're all I think about. You've got inside me so deep, baby girl, I'd have to turn myself inside out just to find the littlest shards of you. I'm not going any-fucking-where."

I swallow, his eyes moving between my own, his hot breath against my lips, I let my eyes slip closed. Exhaling a long breath. The backs of my eyes prickling, I lick my lips.

"Please don't punish me like that again," I say quietly, thinking of how painful it was not to have him hold me last night.

"I won't, it wasn't my intention, and I'm sorry for that," his deep voice rumbles earnestly.

"You swear it, Big Man?"

"I swear it, Sweetheart. Look at me."

I open my eyes, his hand cupping my jaw, thumb caressing my cheek.

"No more, I promise. I'll get my shit together, I've got it together, I want this to work, it's not a *you* problem. It's just a *me* problem, I'll fix it," he promises.

I arch up on tiptoes, my lips pressing against his, my eyes slip closed as I hum into our kiss. His lips open, allowing me entrance, I slide my tongue over his, slow, teasing licks into his mouth, his lips working against mine. His teeth nipping at me, his tongue gliding against my own. He draws me into his big body, my back arching as he slowly starts to fuck my mouth with his. My fingers slide up the back of his head into his hair, tangling in his length, tugging at his roots as he devours me with his lips.

Sliding a hand down my spine, stopping on my arse, he grabs a handful, dragging me even closer. My front plastered to his in a heated kiss and I know I'm exactly where I'm supposed to be.

Breathlessly I pull back, stumbling from suddenly having to support my own weight; Kacey releases me, dropping his hands down by his sides.

"I want you," I tell him confidently as his gold eyes attack my body with a hungry gaze. "Come here," I instruct.

My hand held out between us, he laces his thick fingers through mine. I tug him sharply, his body pressing up against me. Spinning us around, I shove him, slamming his back against the door. I grind into him, rolling my body, undulating my hips against him.

"Sweetheart," he growls in warning.

I stare up into his eyes, the gold glistening with only the artificial glow from the mirror. I flick his trouser button open, dragging the zipper down slowly. Never taking my eyes from his, a small smirk curving my lips as I hear his breathing hitch. I love that I have this effect on him. Sliding my hand over his hip, fingers diving beneath the material of his boxers, my palm running over his heated skin. I slide his boxers and trousers down in one, dropping to my knees with them. My eyes still firmly on his, he stares down his muscled body at me, his chest heaving with every desperate breath.

The look on his face, in his eyes, the way he watches my every move, every breath, every sigh, every swallow and blink of my eyes. He tracks it all with a gaze that devours my fucking soul. Tracing my hand up his thigh, leaving a trail of goosebumps in my wake, I grip the base of his already hard cock. Darting my tongue out, I lave my tongue over his slit, lapping at the bead of pre-cum. My teeth tug the piercing through his tip, making him groan, his rock-solid body shivering as I suckle on his head. Drawing back, I smile up at him. Gently pumping him with my hand before opening my mouth and letting the heavy head of his cock lie on the flat of my outstretched tongue.

I take his swollen head in, locking my lips around his thick length and I can't help but groan in sync with him. Fuck, I love doing this to him. My red lipstick stains his skin as I take him deeper, drawing him in and swallowing around him. I run my tongue along the underside of his pulsing flesh, lazily dragging my lips back and forth as my tongue dances erotically around him. His head thumps as he drops it back heavily against the door, his hand coming up to cup the back of my head. His thick fingers massaging my scalp, knotting in the back of my hair as his grip tightens and he starts to coax me to take more of him.

Hollowing out my cheeks, I pick up my pace. Working my mouth and hand in tandem, twisting my fist around his wide base. I run my tongue around his tip, swallowing down the next drop of pre-cum I'm rewarded with for my efforts.

His cock twitches on my tongue. His large hand

gripping the base of my skull, his hips rocking into me, he starts to fuck my mouth. I move my hand, gripping the back of this bare thigh, my nails digging into his firm flesh, pulling him closer to me, I swallow around his tip as I take him as deep as I can.

I want to make him feel good. I don't want Kacey, *ever*, thinking he means less to me than someone else. I fell in love with him, my first true love as an adult and I honestly don't think he'll ever realise just how special that makes him to me.

Kacey grunts, his fingers locked in my hair pull my head back sharply. Forcing me to release him with a loud pop, a mixture of spit and pre-cum dribbles down my chin. Before I can even blink, Kacey heaves me up under my arms. My heeled feet hovering above the floor, he flips me around, bending me over the marble sink. Then his big hands are there, tearing my white, lace knickers down my legs, bunching at my ankles. Thrusting my tight dress up and over the curve of my arse, the sequins scraping over my flushed skin, exposing me to him.

"I fucking love you in white," he rasps in my ear making me tremble.

One of his large hands presses the side of my face down onto the cold, marble countertop. Holding me down, he lines himself up with my soaking wet entrance, brutally slamming his way home.

I cry out at the invasion as my pussy tries desperately to accommodate his large size. But before I can even attempt to catch my breath, he's fucking me, and

I can feel him *everywhere*. My skin ablaze, heat soaring through my veins with every brutalising stroke of his cock, scorching me, claiming me, fucking owning me.

"I know you do," I pant. "I wore this all for you, Big Man," I tell him truthfully, earning me a strangled grunt from deep within his chest.

A harsh slap with the flat of his hand to my bare arse, all things I think are his approval. The sting of his hand and the heat of his cock, the pain and pleasure has me crying out for more.

Hard, unrelenting thrusts have his thick cock dragging deliciously through me as he pulls out and slams back into the hilt. His large hand still splayed over my cheek, pressing my face into the countertop. I willingly let him have complete control over me, dominating me in every way he can.

I lick the pad of his pinkie finger that rests against my lips, biting down on it, *hard*. Sucking the wound, swallowing his blood, my tongue caresses him, laving the sting away. I continue sucking and licking the tip of his finger, taking even more from him, I need everything he has to give me and *more*. Always more.

"So. *Fucking*. Perfect."

He growls out, pronouncing each word on a thrust that slams my body into complete oblivion. My fingers curl around the edge of the counter. All I can do at this point is hold on. Kacey drapes his huge body over mine, tossing my hair over one shoulder, he bites and sucks a painful, lust-filled trail up my spine to the nape of my neck. Leaving a possessive line of bruising in his wake. He reaches his thick arm around us. The pad of his thick finger instantly finding and rubbing my clit in dangerously fast circles as his thrusts get harder and harder. My hips slam into the solid marble surface, ensuring he leaves me with nothing less than bruised bones.

That pure bite of pain mixed with pleasure sends me free-falling over the edge. I cry out his name as I come on his cock. Wave after wave of heat laps at my scorching skin as he continues to demand more and more from me, forcing more pleasure through me. With another punishing thrust and my name barely a whisper on his swollen lips, he detonates inside of me. His cock pulsing, filling me with lashings of his hot cum.

Resting more of his weight on me, his breath fanning across my flushed face, he moves his hand from my cheek, kissing my temple as he stands. He pulls himself out of me, stepping back to give me enough room to attempt to stand on my jelly legs.

"You're something else," he beams. "*Fuck*, I'm lucky," he pants out between breaths, running his thick fingers through his tousled hair.

"You're quite something yourself, Big Man."

I smile back at him, the reflection in the mirror over the sink. He tucks himself away, re-buttoning his trousers before cleaning me up with a wet washcloth, *ever the gentleman*. Kacey insists on re-dressing me. Kneeling on one knee, his hands finding my lace knickers wrapped around my ankles. He threads them seductively slowly up my legs, smoothing my dress next. Standing, he runs his big hands through my hair until his fingers get knotted in the ends. He holds his hands out with my silver strands still entangled around his thick fingers.

"I was *trying* to be helpful," he grimaces at the tangles, and I laugh.

"It's fine, there's '*after-sex kits*', under the sink for this very occasion," I laugh as he gapes at me in disbelief.

Proving my point, I bend down, pulling open the cupboard beneath the sink. Removing a little woven, wicker basket filled with plastic wrapped combs, mini-hairbrushes, condoms, sachets of lube, mouthwash, and make-up wipes, among other essentials. I present him with the basket with a big grin on my face and he laughs loudly, shaking his head in disbelief.

"I think I love your uncle," he booms on a laugh.

"He has four sons, Kace," I remind him with a simple shrug as I unpackage a little blue hairbrush and start to unknot my silver mane.

Kacey laughs again, coming up behind me. I eye him in the mirror as his hands slide around my waist, he drops a kiss to my bare shoulder.

"I love you, Sweetheart."

"And I love you, Big Man. More than you will ever know."

CHAPTER 16
HUXLEY

Christmas Day at my parents' is a political, extravagant affair to the nth degree, but *nothing* is quite like the circus that is here today at the Swallow's. Dee has got his fingers in some fucking pies, that's for damn sure. There is a fuck load of people here, who in the normal world would *not* be mixing together. There's Italian mobsters, mafia Dons and a fucking *Prince* from somewhere in the Far East. Those are just *some* of his special guests, I can't even begin to dissect what this could mean for my girl's future.

I haven't taken my fucking eyes off her, not trusting anyone in this fucking room. Not that I think any of these fuckers are current threats, especially not in her family home, but in this life, people switch sides at the drop of a hat.

Kyla-Rose may be in business with these fuckers,

but outside of this room, it's a dog-eat-dog world. Though, if they mistake my girl for a kitty cat, they'll learn very quickly she's not to be fucked with. Having Kacey, Nox and I at her back too, we may look like nobodies, but we far surpass that. We own a private security company, sure, but there's a lot more to that than meets the eye. Even Eli was impressed by just how far our reach goes when I gave him a little insight into what we do on a daily. We take on all sorts of jobs, hired guns, security, protection detail, torturing, information gathering, the occasional assassination. We're mercenaries I suppose, if you had to define it. We don't take on everything tasked to us, we delve into it first and decide what we want to do. We might live outside of all this political bullshit, but we see enough and deal with enough of it, to understand how it works. I mean we've carried out jobs for half the families in this room.

Across this ridiculously huge ball room-esque style lounge is Dee, standing with his partner Violet, talking to *Vito Gambino*.

Vito, Italian Mafia Don, thirty-five, six-foot-four, as wide as he is tall with thick black hair as dark as his reputation. Matching eyebrows dropped low over menacingly pale blue eyes. He's a dangerous fucker, brutal and ruthless but with a charm all the ladies seem to be drawn to. Sensible women? They'd run a mile when they saw him, not drop their fucking knickers, but such is life. Anyway, my point is, he's been eyeing up my girl like she's his next fucking meal and I will not hesitate to knock his front teeth down his fucking throat if his filthy gaze lands on her once fucking more.

My girl though?

Completely.

Fucking.

Oblivious.

As per fucking usual.

She's within reaching distance of me thankfully, her head dropped back against Kacey's chest, his arms around her waist. She roars a laugh at whatever Eli's telling her as he tosses back handful after handful of peanuts. Completely and utterly, blissfully unaware she's being eyed up by a predator. Nox, Kacey and I? We noticed the second that slimeball stepped foot in the fucking building, my hackles rose and my body locked itself into high alert mode.

Nox and Kyla-Rose might be in a bit of a weird place right now, but we'll figure this shit out. And now that the three of us men have had a little chat, Kacey admitting to still feeling jealous, warning Nox that he can't take Kyla-Rose away from us, which honestly, I had never even considered. Nox loves us both too much to ever cause such harm but that apparently hadn't stopped Kacey from worrying about it.

Anyway, we've cleared the air. And I just want everyone to be happy.

"He's looking at her again," Nox hushes in my ear as he steps up beside me.

He's dressed head to toe in black, matching mine

and Kacey's attire, as per our queen's request, of course.

His black hair is, as usual, a shaggy mess from running his nervous hands through it so much. It's a decent enough length that he can style it back from his face. When he does, he tends to wax it back like a greaser from the fucking fifties, nine times out of ten he fucks it up within ten minutes with anxious fingers. And then the classic cigarette behind the ear, that he often removes from its resting place, rolls between his teeth, then places it back behind his ear. I always thought it was a weird habit, I've never been a smoker myself, so I paid it no mind. However, I know a certain young woman who happens to do the very same shit with hers. Honestly, two peas in a fucking pod.

"I know," I say in response, almost silently through gritted teeth.

I swirl my honey-coloured drink around in the crystal cut tumbler. Knocking it back with a grinding of my teeth and like a stroke of magic, my empty glass is removed from my hand and replaced with a full one.

The team of staff around this house are silent, but fuck me, are they fast. I can see why the stories of these Christmas day parties end up in orgies and drunken fuckers waking up the next day in various bushes and shrubs around the property. You don't have time to realise you've finished what's in your glass before it's replaced. Not that I'm complaining, I'd really love my night to end with an orgy if I'm honest.

"What we gunna do about him?" Nox grunts.

He's a possessive fucker, especially now he's sealed the deal, but I can relate. Since I met Kyla-Rose, I realise I am too. I guess that happens when you meet the right woman.

I shrug, swallowing my fresh drink.

"We can't start shit with him, Maddox," I warn. "Just play it cool, he likes games. He'll see this shit as a challenge if you start marking your territory and pissing all over her." His sea-blue eyes snap to mine and narrow on me as I scoff a laugh. "Chill the fuck out, bro. She can handle herself just fine. But we won't let her out of our sight," I promise, clapping him on the shoulder. "Plus, can't see Dee letting anything happen under his own fucking roof, can you?"

He grunts in response, tightening his grip on his glass, his lips pursed.

The tapping of metal against a glass gets every-one's attention. All turning to face Dee standing in the centre of the room with a big smile on his face.

"I just want to thank you all for coming today. I know most of you have attended these holiday parties before, so welcome back and to those of you who are new this year, welcome! Now, I hope everyone has had a good day so far and you've all had plenty to drink!"

a few cheers sound out around the large room at that, before he continues. Dec laughs, "now if you would all care to join me in the grand dining room for dinner and more drinks," he winks at Carol, who blushes. "It is my pleasure to have your company on one of my favourite days of the year," he finishes.

People clap, everyone smiling as he starts to make his way out of the ballroom, leading everyone into the dining room.

"No puking this year, Ky," Eli smirks, elbowing Kyla-Rose in the ribs as he drops into formation around her.

"Fuck you," she snaps back with a scowl. "It's your fucking fault I even got sick, fucker."

"Hardly!" Eli mocks, "you and Charl shouldn't have eaten so much fucking chocolate after stuffing your fat face with turkey!" he screeches with a snigger.

Kyla-Rose punches him on the shoulder, "what-the-fuck-ever," she rolls her eyes, flashing him a wide, feral grin.

Charlie leads, having apparently apparated from the shadows. Eli and Cam flanking either side of her. Kacey, Nox and I dropping in around her back as we move into the dining room.

Cream walls, gold accents and chandeliers, every inch decorated with extravagant art. Long buffet tables line the back wall, mountains of food piled on top. Large, circular tables fill the rest of the space, everyone helping themselves to food, waiters and waitresses rushing around with drinks. The smells alone make my mouth water.

Everyone serves themselves, Charlie, choosing to forgo the food all together, stalks back into the quietest corner of the room. Kaccy fills Kyla-Rose's plate with more food than I think I've ever seen her eat. She points to what she wants, and he hefts mountains of it onto her plate with a grin. She must feel me watching them because she tosses a look over her shoulder, throwing me a sultry smile. I shoot her a wink as Kaccy hands her the food. She practically prances over to an empty table, dropping her plate down atop it, her perky arse sliding into a velvet chair.

I watch her from my position, my gaze flicking between the food selections and her. When I glance back and see who's seated next to her, I grind my teeth so hard I crack my jaw.

"What the fuck is that about?" Nox hisses, threatening blue eyes locked on the threat.

"Dunno," I shrug, my shoulders tense as I watch Vito Gambino lean into our girl.

"Let's get over there before the fucking viper strikes," Nox grunts with irritation.

I slap my hand against his chest, stopping him as he goes to bypass me, his narrowed eyes sliding over to me.

"*Easy*, think about where we are," I warn him quietly. "You've only just made it into her good graces. Don't go all Kaccy caveman on this shit," I roll my tongue over my teeth, trying to keep my cool. Ever the sane one out of our little trio, "okay?"

Nox wrinkles his nose is irritation, his dark brows pulled low over his bright eyes. Danger wafting off his body like a rolling heatwave.

"Yeah, okay," he nods.

I drop my hand from his chest. Taking the lead, I stalk towards our woman with intent. I drop down into the seat beside Kyla-Rose, Nox on my other side. She tosses her head back, a raucous laugh leaving her open mouth, her eyes squeezed tight, she rocks with laughter. My brow furrows as she wipes tears from her face. My eyes tightening, I look at Vito, a smug smirk on his playboy mouth, he winks at me.

Nox shifts beside me, I clamp a hand to his thigh beneath the table. *Not now,* I silently tell him with a sharp look. He swallows hard, giving me a subtle nod.

Breathe.

"What's so funny?" Nox growls, unable to bite his tongue.

I sigh as Kyla-Rose shoots him daggers.

"Just an old story, nothing important," Vito purrs, his Italian accent thick.

That sound alone gets my fucking back up. Let alone the way he purposely avoids looking at either of us when he answers, dismissing us completely.

"Oh, I love old stories. Do tell," Nox continues, a raised brow.

"We were just discussing a masquerade ball we both attended at Vito's father's home in Italy," Kyla-

Rose says gently, her eyes flicking between us both in silent warning.

"Who are these men to you, *Rose?*" Vito asks blandly without looking at either of us.

His pale blue eyes undressing her with his gaze. The nickname rolling off his vile tongue like they're familiars makes me murderous.

"These are two of my boyfriends," she announces proudly, making Vito lean back slightly in his chair.

I'm sure if Nox wasn't so focused on trying not to choke the piece of shit mafia Don, he'd probably have had a stronger reaction to Kyla-Rose calling him her boyfriend. Although the words must have penetrated his thick skull somewhat because he grinds his teeth, his gaze softening ever so slightly when he locks eyes with her.

"Two of?" Vito questions for confirmation.

His eyes narrowing slightly on her, probably calculating how easily he could dispose of us.

"Yeah. Two of three," she says, straightening her spine.

She peers over her shoulder, searching around the room, looking a little like a meerkat. Her delicate hand stretches between their two chairs, her body twisting dangerously close to the mafia prick. She points out the big blonde fucker standing at the buffet.

"That's Kacey, he's my other boyfriend," she emphasises with pride in her voice, a glint in her eye.

Kacey catches sight of her and when their eyes

lock, he throws her a smirk and a dirty wink, causing a pale blush to tint her cheeks.

"It takes a few men to entertain her," Charlie rasps, dropping into a chair on the other side of Gambino, a seat separating them on the curve of the table.

Brandishing a knife between his tattooed fingers, his shirt open, the sleeves torn off, his bare chest on display, he stares at Vito.

Is he never cold?

Vito's head practically does a three-sixty at the sound of Charlie's husky growl in such close proximity.

"Oh, I'm sure," Vito smirks, regaining his relaxed, over-confident composure. He rakes his filthy eyes all over our girl, "you're a very impressive woman, Miss Swallow. I would expect nothing less from the *queen* of the underworld," he smiles, his gold tooth glinting in the chandelier light as his smile widens.

"Mm," Kyla-Rose hums, tapping her long, black nails against the wood of the table.

My hand slides down her thigh, my fingers squeezing her knee. She turns into me, a coy smile on her face. I wink down at her, placing a kiss to the bridge of her nose. She inhales deeply, rolling her neck, turning back to the table.

"It was good to see you, Vito," she smiles gracefully but I don't miss the dismissal in her tone and neither does he. "I look forward to the new year and the business prospects we will endeavour to pursue," she bows her head slightly.

He stands, Charlie watching him like prey, he flicks the gold steak knife between his fingers.

Tongue in cheek, Vito says, "me too, Miss Swallow, me too," before walking away and approaching Dee.

"I don't like him," Nox announces on a hiss making Charlie release a gravelly laugh, I smirk in agreement.

"He's a creep," Kyla-Rose hums. "But he knows his place, he's a dog, I'm the hand that feeds him. He won't bite it off unless he wants to starve," she murmurs casually.

Her beautiful storm-green eyes lock on mine, her delicate fingers sweeping across my cheek.

"We'll have to watch him," Charlie growls as he and Kyla-Rose share a look.

"Kyla-Rose," a deep, gruff voice speaks from behind us, "Charlie."

The entire table looks up at the stranger. Kyla-Rose spins in her seat, her eyes finding the owner, she squeals. Like, literally squeals, the noise makes everyone cringe including the ridiculously tall stranger, he must be nearly seven-foot. She dives out of her chair, flinging herself at him, an *oompf* escapes him as he catches her.

"Dominic! What in the fuck are you doing here! Where's Scarlett? Did she come, too? Ashlee?

Gabriel?" she rattles off without taking a single breath.

"Dom," Charlie greets, moving up and out of his seat to greet the newcomer.

Seeing the three of them together, you can instantly see the similarities. Dominic is possibly the tallest man I've ever met, he towers over everyone, standing at least a foot above the rest of the room. Tall and lean, icy white skin, just like the Swallows either side of him, grey eyes and pale blonde hair. Everything about him is right on the Swallow family brand.

"I came with Ashlee," he states emotionlessly, dropping Kyla-Rose back down to her feet. "She's around here somewhere, you'll probably hear her before you see her."

"You're a dick, Dom," Kyla-Rose laughs before turning back to us. "This is Huxley," she introduces, a big beaming grin on her face. "Hux, this is Dominic Montblanc, our cousin."

Another cousin, *interesting*. Just how big is this family?

"'Sup, dude," I greet, reaching over the back of my chair, offering my hand.

Dom gives me a nod, shaking my hand before tucking his bony hands back into his black slacks.

"You know, Maddox," she says quietly, turning her gaze back to Dom.

Dom nods, his face stoic and expressionless. His grey eyes like endless puddles of rainwater, something cold and vacant in his gaze. He sits down in Vito's vacated seat, clasping his hands on the table as everyone sits back down. The cousins catch up. He reminds me a little of Charlie and Jacob mashed together. The man's got control over every tiny movement he makes, everything calculated even with his own family.

I hear Kacey's rumble of a laugh as he approaches. A tall, slim brunette and a big burly guy, heavy muscles packed beneath his dark skin, in tow. He's more or less the same build as Kacey, another guy who likes to punch things, if I had to guess.

Kyla-Rose snaps her head around at the sound of *her* big bad fighter and then her mouth gapes open.

"Dominic!" she shrieks, backhanding his shoulder as she twists in her seat. "You said you only came with Ashlee!" she glances at him, disbelief written all over her face. "Ronan *and* Ashlee, you little fuck."

"I said I came with Ashlee, I didn't say only," Dominic shrugs emotionlessly.

The big guy barking a laugh, his deep brown eyes crinkling with humour.

"You're a fucking prick, Dom," he says in a deep American accent. "We're *boyfriends* now. It hurts my feelings that you're embarrassed of me enough to not even tell my cousins-in-law that I'm here!" he cries with what is very clearly mock outrage, a large hand splayed over his chest in faux shock.

"You are not my *boyfriend*, you fucking heathen,"

Dom hisses, glaring at the hulking figure standing over him.

"Dude, my dick has touched your dick, we're totally boyfriends," he barks another raucous laugh. Taking the empty seat between Dom and Charlie. He leans across a very, *very* pissed off Dominic, his hand outstretched, he introduces himself to the table as a whole. "I'm Ronan. We're both fucking Ashlee," he says honestly, waving his hand between himself and Dom.

I snort a laugh, my beer working its way up the back of my nose. I splutter a cough and shake his hand, half-gasping out my own name in return as I choke on my backed-up drink. Kacey dumps his mountain of turkey down, slumping into the seat beside Nox. I stare at his plate with a slight head tilt as I catch my breath.

"Kace, what in the fuck, is that *just* turkey? Where's everything else?" I wrinkle my nose, raising a brow at the giant fucker.

The buffet has just about every food choice you can imagine. Kacey has not even one percent of the choices on offer.

"Protein," is all he says in response.

Health nut.

Our girl stands, pulling the leggy brunette into a tight one-handed embrace. The woman closing her eyes, a soft smile on her face, her chin resting on Kyla-Rose's shoulder as she hugs her back.

"Dom told me it was only you and him," Kyla-

Rose smiles, releasing the brunette and dropping back down into her seat.

"Dominic is still *adjusting*," she emphasises with a smirk, pressing a gentle kiss to Dom's cheek before sitting herself in Ronan's lap. "I'm Ashlee," she smiles happily at the rest of us.

"So's Nox," I chortle in response to her first comment.

Ronan beams at me, gripping Ashlee in one arm. He reaches his other fist across the table, with a waggle of his eyebrows, I pound my knuckles into his. Both of us laugh as Nox elbows me hard in the ribs.

"So, how long are you staying?" Kyla-Rose asks, looking between the three of them.

Ashlee frowns, Ronan drops his head back, releasing a heavy sigh. Everyone's attention diverting to Dom. He chews slowly, swallowing his mouthful, wiping at the corners of his mouth with a white napkin. Carefully, every movement meticulously controlled.

"We leave tomorrow night," Dom announces.

Kyla-Rose tilts her head at him, the same time that Charlie does. Their movements so cleanly in sync, I'm not sure I'll ever get used to it.

"Why?" she asks.

"Because we have things to do," Dominic states blankly, his eyes slowly rolling onto the other two people in his relationship. "And these two think our lives are parties. Which they are not."

I raise my brows, biting my lips to stop my smirk, I

drop my gaze to my plate. Everyone's quiet for a moment, picking their cutlery back up, resuming their meals in silence.

"Okay," Kyla-Rose says after a minute, her head lolling on her shoulder before she rights herself and nods. "Ash?" she calls, Ashlee's big blue eyes snapping up. "Fancy hitting The Pit tonight?"

Loud *no's* echo around the table instantly, over-shadowed by Ashlee's squeals.

"Yes! Yes, *yes!* Fuck, we haven't been there for ages!"

Ashlee wriggles with excitement in Ronan's lap, his eyes widening just slightly before he clamps a large dark hand down on her squirming tanned thigh. Dropping his lips to her ear, he whispers, her cheeks turning pink.

"Cool, we'll go tonight. Huxley's always up for dancing, aren't ya?" Kyla-Rose beams up at me, my eyes narrowing.

"Dancing is not what happens there, you and I both know that," I raise a brow, her dimples puncturing her cheeks as she smiles wider. "And this is not a good idea." I finish.

"You'll all be there, it'll be safe, they're only here one night! One sign of danger and we'll come straight home, I swear!" Kyla-Rose pokes out her bottom lip, pouting at me, she bats her eyelashes.

"We could gear up, you know your way around down there, Hux. It's Christmas. Give our girl what she wants," Kacey throws in, seemingly unphased by all the shit that could go wrong, like being stuck in an all-out war *underground.*

Why am I suddenly the only sensible one?

"Don't be scared," my girl whispers, a dangerous glint in her eye as she presses a kiss to my throat. "We can have fun, it'll be like going back in time. You and I, dirty dancing," she rasps, her lips trailing up my jaw, my dick thickening in my jeans.

"With everything going on, I'm heavily against this idea," Dominic pipes up.

"Shut up, Dom, you're *heavily against* everything fun. You're like a fucking vampire, but you suck fun instead of blood. Well, probably a little of both," Ronan chuckles. "Right, baby?" he growls huskily against Ashlee's neck, biting into her throat.

She giggles, Dominic sighs and my girl continues to pout. I turn to look at Nox, a scowl on his face, his eyes locked on our girl.

He licks his lips, "maybe we just go for a little while," he utters absently.

"Yay! It's settled, we're going," Kyla-Rose announces smugly, kissing the underside of my jaw before returning her attention back to her plate.

"Fucking hell," I groan, pinching the bridge of my nose.

Looks like we're going to a rave.

The Pit is just the same as always. I haven't been in a long while. I used to come when I needed to clear my head, which seems like a weird thing to do in an underground rave, but it is what it is. Sometimes my head is just too quiet.

We pay the guy on the entrance. Trudging through the dark concrete tunnels, following the echoing thumps down the winding passageways. Nothing but battery-operated push lights and glow-sticks strewn along the floor, lighting the way. The deeper we get, the hotter it grows, sweat pricks the back of my neck, my curls already damp. The music becomes clearer. All of us quiet as we work our way towards the main room.

Ronan, Dom and Ashlee. Me, Kacey, Nox and Kyla-Rose. All of us changed, or rather, we took some clothes off. Kacey was just happy he didn't have to wear a shirt, any excuse to show off his hulking frame. Ashlee slapped some leftover UV body paint she stole from Eli across us all. Pink, yellow and orange hand-prints, splatters and the occasional lip print, courtesy of my girl of course, cover our naked torsos. The girls choosing to go for a slightly different look.

Both opted for matching latex dresses, the top half of their hair up in something called space buns. Yeah, I know, tell me about it. Tiny body-clinging, black latex, the material glued to them like a second skin, making it obvious they're both completely bare beneath. I swear I can't take my eyes off her, even more than normal. The dress hits just below the curve

of her arse. A deep sweetheart neckline, her tits
pushed up high, nipple piercings clearly outlined. It
leaves nothing to the imagination. *Nothing.* Jacob
nearly had a heart attack when he passed us in the
hall on our way out. A vein pulsed in his temple so
hard I thought it was gunna explode. I would have
laughed if my cock didn't hurt so much. It's been
hard for over a fucking hour, refusing to go down until
it sinks inside her tight, wet heat. The second she
grinds that perky arse on me I'm gunna come in my
jeans. I just know it.

God, what a lucky son of a bitch.

The tunnel starts to widen, opening up to the
huge open space used as a dance floor. Hundreds of
people grinding on one another, heavy bass pounding
through the speakers. Concrete floors, walls and ceiling, nothing but strobe UV lighting. The DJ booth on
a platform in the centre of the room, the room thick
with fog and smoke. Clouds of smoke float toward the
ceiling from cigarettes and blunts. Fog from the smoke
machines drifting around our ankles. My eyes try to
take it all in, but it's impossible.

"Come on, Hux," Kyla-Rose shouts, her delicate
fingers twining through my own.

Kacey slaps me on the back, a huge grin on his
face as he backs his way into the bustling crowd. Nox
steps up beside me, his hand firmly clasped on my
shoulder. I look down into big grey orbs, swallowing
my worry, she thinks I'm not afraid of anything. I hide
it well, but I just don't think this is a good idea. I nod

my head anyway, pulling her through the crowd after Kacey.

Within seconds we're in the centre of the room, bodies slick with sweat on all sides. Her arm slung over my shoulder, fingers tangling in the sweat drenched curls at the back of my neck. Her nails clawing at my nape piercing. She presses into me, my hands on her hips. Kacey's hand lands on my hip, his other locked just below her breast, trapping her between us. Her eyes drop closed, head against Kacey's chest, her fingers gripping the back of my neck, she grinds her lithe, little body between us. Her lips slightly parted, a droplet of sweat running down her chest, disappearing in the valley of her breasts.

I lean forward, my lips latching onto her jaw, she hums her approval, her grip on my neck tightening. I run my tongue down the column of her throat, nipping at her flying pulse point as I pass it. She pants, her short breaths against my ear. Kacey's lips and tongue attacking her right side, his teeth digging into his own mark. I run my tongue across her collarbone, laving the flat of my tongue over my carved initial, the ball of my piercing catching the torn skin. I draw back slightly, peering down at it. It's angry and red and raised. I'm positive I've never seen anything more fucking beautiful.

A shadow descends over us, Nox coming up on my left. Confidently, he slides a hand between our joint pelvises, the back of his hand grazing my bulging erection as he grabs the inside of Kyla-Rose's thigh. Forcing her and I apart enough for his hand to settle between her legs. His other hand grasps her face fiercely. His thumb and finger carving into her already deep dimples, he pops her mouth open. Her eyes bore into his as his face closes the space between them. He opens his mouth, his lips barely brushing hers, his tongue tracing her bottom lip, then the top. She whimpers as his tongue dives deep, long, lashings of his tongue over hers, their lips seal. She bucks her hips into me as Nox removes his hand from between us. Kacey pushing in closer as my hands run over her body. Fingers tweaking her nipples, squeezing her waist.

The four of us locked in a filthy display of romantic carnage. We never did play by the rules, why start now.

Kyla-Rose thrusts her hips against me, grinding her pussy against my hard cock. Kacey's hips rocking into her from behind, forcing us closer. Nox releases her face, sliding his fingers down to her throat. He squeezes tight, pillaging her mouth with his tongue. Her eyes snap open, not a hint of fear in her grey orbs despite her lack of breath. She lazily winks at me, her lips still working with Nox's, the corner of her mouth tilting up.

Any remaining blood left in the rest of my body rushes to my already aching cock. My head spins, my dick pulses against her and it takes everything in me not to take her right here. Although, it seems not everyone in this little foursome is on board with that notion as Nox's hand disappears back between us. I angle her body towards him slightly giving him better access.

Kyla-Rose's head drops back. Her throat bared, lips parted, a stuttered gasp leaving her swollen lips. Kacey's teeth latch onto his bite mark in her shoulder. Nox draws back half an inch from her face, a cocky smirk on his lips as pumps his fingers into her, right here in the centre of hundreds of people. All covered in UV paint, sweat slicked brows, hard dicks and wet pussies. It should be wrong, but nothing else matters, it's *so*. Fucking. Right.

Kacey's grip on my hip tightens. Nox's fingers clasping our girl's throat so intensely her face reddens. His knuckles blanched white, digging into her pale flesh, intensified by the blue strobe lights, but still no panic.

She trusts us.

All of us.

My hand on her hip slides down, slipping beneath the raised hem of her latex dress, my knuckles grazing Nox's. Nox chuckles darkly, a look of pure ecstasy on his face, knowing my intention. Kacey bites into her harder, his teeth savagely attacking her skin. She doesn't even flinch, blissed out in another world entirely. My fingers slide against Nox's slippery ones, drenched in her wetness. He pulls out slowly, waiting for me to join him. Our palms pressed together, middle fingers perfectly aligned, we slip inside her wet heat. She pants, turning her face, her head lolling to her left. She licks her lips, her eyes summoning me closer.

I oblige. My lips meeting hers, my breath greedily stolen as Nox lets up his grip for a split second. She sucks the life from my lungs as I kiss her. My tongue running over hers, massaging and taking. The faintest hint of a cigarette on her breath, something sweet, something sharp. Her teeth bite into my bottom lip, tugging and pulling on it as she comes. Kacey squeezing us together so hard, my bones ache but I've never wanted to be a part of anything more. Her slim body trembles between the three of us, shielded from the room by our towering bodies. Safe to be vulnerable in the middle of us. Always her protectors.

Her grip on my neck flexes, her fingers twisting in my hair, tugging on the strands. A breathless, choked cry leaving her lips as she comes around our joint fingers. Her cunt squeezing and sucking, crushing our bones inside her tight pussy as we continue pumping into her, letting her ride it out. Her release coating our hands, we withdraw them from inside of her.

Nox keeps our hands together, lacing our fingers, keeping our middle ones straight. He releases her throat, instead gripping the back of Kacey's neck. Clamping hold of him like the scruff of a dog, he drags Kacey away from Kyla-Rose's shoulder, thrusting our wet fingers into his mouth. She watches him intently, her head thrown back against his shoulder as he sucks her from our fingers. All of us watching her as she pants, her chest rising and falling rapidly. Her body still trembling between us, Kacey rolls his hips against her arse, releasing our fingers with a pop. She starts to grind against us, her arm thrown up, wrapping around Kacey's neck this time. Her lips peppering sloppy kisses against his jaw, as we all continue to move together.

Song after song, beat after beat, we switch positions, hands, tongues and mouths trailing all over the girl at our centre. The centre of our universe, the missing piece to our messy lives. Everything about this woman has me in awe.

I'm glad, when I think back to the first time I ever laid my eyes on her, here in this very space, that we didn't take things further. I think it would have changed this. What we have, it wouldn't be the same, nothing could ever be any better than what we have with each other now.

Someone knocks into the back of me, shoving me forward, Kyla-Rose's eyes snap open as I jolt her back into Kacey. She frowns, I shrug, offering her a small smile. We're in the centre of a rave, we're nobodies here, we're not untouchable, it's expected. Either way, it's the push I need to check the time.

"We should find the others," I shout in Nox's ear, twisting my wrist so he can see my watch.

He nods, shifting his position to speak in Kacey's ear, their heads pressed together. I cup Kyla-Rose's face, thumbing her plump bottom lip.

"You ready, Darlin'?" I shout, her tongue poking out, tracing the pad of my thumb, she nods.

I step into her, my arm snaking around her waist, dragging her protectively into my side. Keeping her wounded hand shielded from being jostled. I start to lead us out of the masses, my eyes scanning the crowd for her cousin, and his family. Kacey and Nox at our back. Kacey's hand on her hip, Nox's chest almost flush with my back as we work our way out of the crowd.

I spot Ronan first. His huge body slathered in orange and pink paint, glowing starkly against his dark brown skin beneath the blue and red strobe lights. He nods over the crowd, getting the attention of Dom and Ashlee. He too, starts to lead them out of the hordes of people.

"Woah, easy, dude," Kacey grunts as someone slams into him, jerking my attention to him.

We keep pushing through. Kyla-Rose wedged between the three of us, her hand in mine. People knock into us more and more as we get closer to the edge. My hackles rising, uneasiness prickling through me. I reach behind me, my fingers closing around the grip of my Glock 19, fifteen rounds sitting snugly inside it. I breathe a little easier as I hold onto it. Something spikes anxiety through me, my eyes scanning through the smog. I feel my boys close in on me. I think of Kyla-Rose unarmed, the first time since I've known her, all because of her tiny dress. *'I'll be fine,'* she had said, *'I'm with my boys,'* she told me confidently. A coy smile, a one shouldered shrug. Pride made me puff up like a peacock, hearing her confidence in us, I went with it.

Stupid.

Fucking stupid.

We make it to the edge of the crowd, her grip on my hand intense. Ronan, Dom and Ashlee already by the exit tunnel. I lead us toward them, picking my way through the stragglers on the outskirts. I walk with intent, nodding at Dom, his eyes over our shoulders, watching our backs.

"Problem?" he asks blankly as the three of them fall into step with us.

"Not yet."

"I feel it too," Dom says emotionlessly, his tall stature working like a looking tower, high above us all.

"I just have an uneasy feeling. Let's get out of here," I say, just loud enough for Dom and Dom alone to hear, he nods sharply.

Taking point on our little group, I hurry us through the inclining dark tunnels. Knowing there's no way out of here except the one route we're already following. We twist and turn through the passageways, half of the lights that were here on our way in, now dead, meaning more darkness. The heavy bass fades until it's barely audible, my eyes adjusting to the thick darkness. Our collective breathing suddenly the only thing I can hear. I know we're almost out of here, it's a long way, though. Almost a quarter mile of dark tunnels.

"Is everything okay?" Ashlee asks softly, her sweet voice breaking the silence first.

"Everything's fine, babe," Ronan's gruff voice tells her calmly, reassuringly.

No one speaks after that. And then we're at the exit, the iron gates swung open on the cave-like entrance. I step out first, a single street lamp flickering across the empty street, our car parked just past it. I suck in a deep lungful of winter air, not realising just how starved of oxygen I was. Unintentionally holding my breath more or less the entire journey back up here. A shiver racks through me, the icy December air has goosebumps erupting all over my skin.

Kacey moves ahead, digging in his jean pocket for the car key. Having decided he'd drive, the only one of us being under the legal limit. None of us wanting to drive under the influence, especially not with Kyla-Rose in the car. We have enough blood on our hands as it is. The blacked-out Mercedes-AMG GLS beeps as Kacey unlocks it, the lights flashing. All of us climbing in, the two girls in the very back, being the smallest. Kacey and Ronan up front, Dom, Nox and I in the central seats.

Kacey starts the engine, pulling us out onto the road, everyone sitting in silence, my body tense, the girls quiet. Nothing like the journey on the way here. We had music pounding through the speakers, the windows open, the girls laughing and throwing back little cans of pre-mixed cocktails.

The silence now is deafening. No one daring to

breathe too
on edge.

I breat
main road
ering it's j
cabs about

It's on
everyone s
tions starti
window.

CHAPTER 17
KYLA-ROSE

I mpulse has me grabbing the back of Ashlee's head and slamming it down between her knees.

"Stay the fuck down," I shout at her. Ducking low, my eyes trained up front, my hand rummaging around in the seat pocket for a gun. "Kace?"

"I got it, Sweetheart," he yells back, his foot slamming onto the accelerator.

The car purrs beneath us, sharp turns have me unclipping my seatbelt so I can reach across Ashlee. My hand sliding into the leather seat pocket in front of her. My fingers finding nothing. I huff in frustration, a bullet hits the rear window again, not penetrating the reinforced glass. Ashlee turns her head, her cheek on her knees, blue eyes wide, I nod. There're no words that can make a situation like this any better. But she knows what I'm silently translating. We're gunna get out of this, and she's going to be fine.

"Someone give me a gun," I hiss in frustration.

Internally cursing my recklessness in choosing such a tiny fucking outfit. The car careening wildly, left to right. The back tyre taking a hit, I send thanks to whoever invented run-flat tyres as we tear down the road at high speed. I reach my good arm over the seat, grabbing a fistful of Max's t-shirt. He turns his body coiled in a hunched position.

"Get me a gun. There should be one in every seat pocket, there's none back here." I jolt, another bullet hitting the back window, another, another. "*Fuck*, Kacey!" I almost screech knowing this is absolutely *not* good.

"I know, baby girl," Kacey grunts back, the car taking a screeching right turn.

I fall to the left, my body bumping into Ashlee. Her hands steadying me as I sit up onto my knees. The back window cracks, the glass spider webbing as bullet after bullet collides with it. I hear Ronan from the front seat, on the phone, barking about shots fired and my lungs scream as I hold my breath. Max passes me a gun, the magazine fucking empty.

"What in the fuck?!" I screech in anger, my eyes squeezing tight for just a second. I breathe through my nose, "how many are on us?"

"Four," Dom states clinically, slamming a fresh magazine into his gun. "Crawl through, Ky," he instructs me.

I slither over the back seats. Max rapidly pulling me over his shoulder, I land across their laps, my head in Dom's lap. I look up at him, his startling grey eyes on mine.

"Sunroof," is all he says, I nod.

Max's grip tightens on the back of my thigh.

"No," Max threatens, danger emanating off him in thick plumes.

"I got this," I tell him, *promising* him. "Trust me," I murmur, Huxley hauling me up to sitting by my calves. "Kacey, can we take a sharp corner?" I shout forward.

"You got it, Sweetheart!"

Ronan looks at me over his shoulder, a wide grin on his face.

"This is the family reunion I was fucking waiting for! Fuck yeah!" he slaps his huge thigh.

His finger pressing the button to open the sunroof, it starts to crawl open. The last time we were all together like this was Italy a few years ago, fucking up my cousin, Scarlett's, ex, Jameson Bianchi. The slimy little fuck. It was the best holiday of mine and Charlie's lives.

I squirm up onto my knees, Dom handing me the loaded weapon. I frown at him as he rolls his window down.

"I brought something of Eli's with me," he says, so blankly, so stoically. "When in London," he shrugs, and I want to laugh as he ever so casually pulls a sawn-off shotgun out from beneath Kacey's seat.

That is *very* Eli.

Eli thinks of himself as some sort of British thug

393

from the sixties, he's not about the automatics, not even the semis. Give him an old cricket bat, some brass knuckles, and a sawn-off shotgun any day and he's happy.

Huxley readies himself, unsnapping his seatbelt. His window opening, the arctic wind slapping my skin. He twists, his body ready to hang out the side window.

A smile twists my lips, my tongue darting out to wet them. Even though I know it shouldn't, excitement thuds through me. My skin prickling in anticipation. I shake my head at myself.

Focus.

I take a breath.

"You have to help me," I tell Max.

Huxley nods, his dark eyes on mine, he knows whatever I'm going to do is going to happen, they may as well help over hinder. I straddle Max's lap, my chest to his, his hands on my hips, my booted feet on the seat.

"Ready?" Kacey hollers, his deep timbre rattling my insides.

"Ready!" I shout back, the wind whipping through the open sunroof.

I look to my cousin, he nods. Kacey spins the wheel, the car jerks violently, I spring up through the sunroof as we hit the corner. Max's hands firm and steady on my thighs. I hear the screeching of tyres as we race down a dark backstreet, every other street lamp out. My hair flies like silver streamers behind me, the arctic wind making my eyes stream. But I focus.

Inhale.

Squeeze.

The first car chasing us skids around the corner.

Aim.

The windscreen tinted so dark; I know that shit's not legal. But I aim for the driver I can't see anyway. Firing once, twice, three times. The car veers off to the left, cutting off the car behind it, slamming into the brick wall. The crunch of metal echoes around me.

Exhale.

Dom takes out a guy stumbling from the crushed car, the boom from his shotgun, the click. Bullets fly, I drop down inside the car, my chest heaving. Max's grip moves to my waist.

"You okay, Princess?" his fingers flexing on my ribcage.

His grip so tight it feels as though he's bending the bones into my thrashing heart.

"I'm good," I smile confidently, toothy and wide, deranged most likely.

He chuckles darkly. Hefting me back up, clapping his big hand on my latex covered arse.

"Good girl," he rasps, goosebumps smattering over my skin at his praise.

Kacey spins the car in the opposite direction this time. Huxley ducks back inside at the same time Dom does, reloading.

"Fuck!" Kacey grunts, slamming his fist into the dashboard, the car slowing.

I whip my head over my shoulder, seeing the problem.

"A skip?" Ronan scoffs the question in disbelief. "Dollface," he barks next, turning to peer in the back where I left Ashlee.

I suck in a sharp breath, calming the adrenaline rushing to my brain as the boys start to pull Ashlee through the seats. I feel almost drunk. The alcohol I consumed hours ago no longer prominent in my system, but the high is there. That floating feeling where you teeter between reality and somewhere else. Excitement runs through me like a fast-acting poison. My demon snarls, clawing at my insides, she purrs, encouraging, wanting, she knows.

The car stops.

I smile.

Max frowns.

I laugh.

The unhinged chorus bursts free. I thrust myself up, my good arm slapping down on the roof. My fingers curled around my gun as I thrust my body up and pull myself through the sunroof. Max snarls below me, his thick fingers latching onto my dangling ankles, but I kick out at him. He lets go, I draw my legs up and out, moving fast.

The winter wind no longer feels cold, my skin so hot, steam practically emitting off of me. I skate down the windscreen, my booted feet hammering across the bonnet, I jump down, crouched low. More car doors open, some slamming shut. Ronan throws Ashlee down beside me. His huge body crouching over the top of her, his spine curved, protecting her like a mother would their cub. His huge, muscled body, dark and light. The electric UV body paint against his beautiful ebony skin. His rich, brown eyes on his woman. My heart clenches.

"Stay here," I tell him, and for once, the big joker doesn't argue, just looks up and nods, his grip unyielding on his love.

I shuffle forward, the arches of my feet screaming. Silence. Kacey looks through the windscreen at me, his gold eyes the only thing I want to see in the dark. A shadow moves behind our car, my eyes flicker to behind him. Just as I'm about to rise out of my position, Dominic's door flies open, his alabaster skin shining like the face of the moon. His giant height solid, his stature straight. He starts walking forward, he fires his shotgun, seemingly unphased with being so exposed. Huxley moves in behind me, his palm freezing against my scorching skin. He kisses my shoulder; bullets start to fly and then we both move. Blowing our cover for the sake of taking down our enemies, to keep our family safe. Max pops up through the sunroof, sliding down the side of the car. Kacey climbs out, a tyre iron in his hand.

We rush forward, an impenetrable wall, but for how long? We have no reloads, other than Dom's shotgun shells. That counts for nothing if they're geared up, and why wouldn't they be? This was their purpose.

We've been hunted.

But I never really was very good at being prey.

My eyes adjusting to the darkness, I know I only have seven or so rounds.

Better make them count.

We pass the crashed cars, the windscreen shattered, a man slumped over the steering wheel, my bullet in his face. I count five bodies. Two cars block the road, all the doors open, that could mean up to fourteen men. Maybe more. The odds aren't in our favour but when have they ever been.

A smile touches my lips as I think of Charlie. Knowing how pissed he'll be that he wasn't here. He may be on his way after Ronan's phone call, but he won't get here in time, not now. My body thrums, adrenaline smashing through every part of me. My demon stretching, her jaws gnashing as I give her the freedom to play.

Dominic drops the first guy to pop off a shot. Slamming the butt of his gun into his skull, blood splatters as he hammers into him, over and over. My cousin may be stoic, cool, calm and collected, and he may be a Montblanc by name. But there's still that deadly Swallow blood running through those veins, something violent and brutal. I smile as everyone suddenly leaps into action. Men swarm, balaclavas on their heads, their faces covered, just like last night outside The Black Heart.

A guy rushes me from the left, my right hand lashing out. The heel of my good hand slamming up into the base of his chin, my fist and the gun impacting. Blood instantly leaks from his lips, I twist my body, firing a bullet into his chest, sweeping his legs out from beneath him. His body collapsing in a heap, I step over him. I shoot two more. Three men are on Kacey, he headbutts one of them, then smashes the one behind him with the back of his skull. I smile, my thighs clenching. This is what gets me off, I don't care what anyone says about me, this is who I am. It's in my fucking DNA.

Sometimes we're thrust into violence and it stains, scars, seeps deep into those cracks and crevices you didn't even know were there. It hibernates then, lying in wait, waiting to be needed and when you finally let it out to play. It's fucking beautiful. Thing is, you need to be prepared for what you release, 'cause once you set it free, it ain't never going back.

I crack a guy in the ribs with my elbow as he goes to grab me. His fingers attempt to grasp my dress, it's so skin-tight he stands absolutely zero chance. I laugh at him, a quick bullet to his head. Why the fuck do these people think I'm not going to shoot them? I'd rather be in a fist fight, but we all deal with the hand we're dealt, regardless of preferences, and we need this to be over quickly.

My eyes scan over the brawl. Skin slapping, thumping, grunts and groans, but not many guns firing, thankfully. I hear sirens in the distance,

K.L. TAYLOR-LANE

signalling our game is almost over, but I don't want any of these fuckers getting away.

Kacey bends low. Throwing the guy behind him over his back, down to the cracked tarmac at his feet. Max and Dom back-to-back, each of them holding their own, easily surrounded by seven or eight men.

I look for my Huxley. A man, gun in hand, his arm coming up, his aim on the back of Huxley's head. I don't think, I run. Everything seems to play out in slow motion, someone hits me from the side, rugby tackling me to the ground. The air knocked from my lungs, my gun skittering across the tarmac, my skin grazing as I slide across the ground. I kick out, catching my attacker in the thigh, but his grip doesn't loosen, it tightens, my bent leg trapped between us.

"HUXLEY! DUCK!" I scream, my lungs wailing with the sound.

His head snaps up, his body dropping down on instinct as the gun behind him goes off. I cough my relief, watching as he takes his shooter out. His leg sweeping out from his crouched position, he pounces on his fallen attacker. One, two, three bullets to his chest, before spinning on another.

I slump into the cold ground, the man on top of me, his arms banded around me has me panting for breath. He half crawls over me, a glint in his murky brown eyes. I buck up against him, using my trapped leg, my knee digging into his stomach. I push it up, grunting with exertion. This guy is fucking heavy. He grins, his teeth perfectly straight, stark white against his black mask. My wounded hand on fire between us, I grit my teeth. Using my free hand to grab his throat, my thumb in his windpipe, he laughs, sneering as I push harder.

He rears back, throwing his head forward, his forehead slamming into mine despite my hand around his throat. A loud crack, my ears ringing, teeth clashing with my lip, my mouth filling with blood. My eyes blur, white spots dancing in my vision, he grins wider. I swirl the blood in my mouth, spitting it in his face, he punches me in the side. I grunt, my ribs screaming. I re-angle my knee, he rears back again, readying for a second headbutt, I can't take another one.

God, is his head made of fucking steel?

I crane my neck as his head comes forward. Unfortunately, all that happens is he headbutts me in the side of the throat, my windpipe crunching. He hits me, again and again. Landing blows across my torso, my face. He lets up, I cough, my lungs heaving. He laughs then. A loud, deep chuckle, but it's enough to have me blinking through my pain. I breathe heavily through my nose, sirens getting nearer. He leans his weight back, reaching for my gun. Motherfucker. I release his throat, knowing that's wasted energy, he has the upper hand. His free palm splayed over my chest, forcing my spine to the ground. I wriggle my knee, curling my knuckles, he looks down at my leg, tutting like the cocky fucker he is.

So. Fucking. Confident.

I smash my fist into the front of his neck. His hand on my chest automatically going to his throat, clawing at his skin. I half launch myself up, my teeth nipping at his neck. My leg still trapped between us, he grabs me again. Slamming me down, my head ricocheting off the tarmac. I see stars, my brain rattling around inside my skull, my mind screaming at me to push up, anything. Heat rushes through my limbs, keeping them down, my stomach lurches, I gag. My attacker laughs, getting in my face, his lips a hair's breadth from my own.

"Game over, *Your Highness*," he chuckles, the sound racing through my head.

My arm lying limply beside me, pins and needles rushing through my body.

"You're just a weak, pathetic, little bitch," he taunts, my eyes struggling to focus. "I don't see what all the fuss is about, having all these men come for you," he spits.

His mask grazing against the side of my face, the material rough as he drops his lips to my ear.

"The way I see it, you're just some dried up, useless cunt," he huffs half a laugh, his breath in my ear.

I struggle to laugh, it's quiet and raspy, strained, but he hears it.

"Summin' funny, darlin'?" he snickers in my ear, his teeth against my lobe.

"Yeah," I rasp out.

"What's that then?"

"You," I deadpan the whisper.

Opening my mouth as wide as I can, I bite into his throat, sinking my teeth in. He grabs hold of my head, frantically trying to pull me off. I lock my jaw. My teeth sinking in deeper, blood gurgles in the back of my throat as he thrashes against me, his fist hitting me everywhere he can reach. I've been trained to ignore the pain, channel it into rage, doesn't mean I don't feel it, just means I can push past it, *usually*.

I am good for something.

Violence.

My good arm comes up sluggishly, my hand latching around the back of his neck, pulling him flush to me with all the strength I have left. Stopping him from punching me in the head without catching himself in the process. I swallow the mouthful of blood, my stomach rolling. Biting down harder, my teeth deep in his flesh like sharp, little barbs. He stops struggling so hard, blood overflowing between my teeth, I choke on it, feeling it in the back of my nose.

Swallowing as I keep biting, I don't let go, even when he goes completely limp above me, his huge weight slumping into me. I bite harder, swallowing and swallowing, gagging on the hot liquid as it runs down the sides of my face, blurring one of my eyes. My teeth still locked in his flesh I throw my head to the right with everything I have. My cheek smashes into the tarmac, my teeth taking part of his throat with me. I spit the chunk of flesh out, my head lolling to the side, my eyes blinking hard as his body is torn off me.

Big hands slide beneath my limp body. They're warm and wet, but I don't struggle because I recognise them. Even in this state, I'd know him anywhere. His smell overpowering the pungent copper filling my nostrils. Flooding me with that undercurrent of raw earth, bergamot, a hint of mint. I groan, letting my head loll in the crook of his elbow, knowing I'm safe. Drawing me into his bare chest, his skin cool beneath my hot cheek. My head spinning, ears ringing, he murmurs something to me, *an apology*. I wince as he starts to run, jostling my aching body. I splutter a cough, blood backing up my throat, I spit it down my chin, unable to turn my head the other way. My nose burns, making me snort, so much blood, I gag, I can't help it.

Doors slam, sirens screech, the sound piercing through me.

I'm passed into different hands, long fingers wiping my blood-filled eye, the scent of oranges overwhelmed by something sulphuric and musty. Lots of talking, too much noise. I groan as the rumble of the engine reverberates through me. A rough hand cupping my aching cheek, tobacco, something sickly sweet.

And then it's lights out.

"**W**hy were there no weapons in the car?" I start, late that afternoon.

Boxing Day, the family gathered around the long breakfast table in Uncle Dee's sunroom. Snow beyond the glass walls, we knew it was coming, the clouds were heavy and low all day yesterday. We woke up not even an hour ago to half a foot of the stuff. It's five-pm now, a feast spread out before us. Platters of fruits, sandwiches, soups, and cheeses, there's even milk and cereals. A huge variety of juices and waters, sparkling and still, some with lime, some with lemon. It's really just a big brunch, but at teatime.

"Who the fuck disarms a family vehicle?" I spit out again.

Unsure where the fuck I should be directing my anger, it's not even really anger, I'm just, I don't know.

"I don't know," Dee sighs, echoing my thoughts, his voice sounds exhausted.

It's an unusual thing to hear from him. He pushes his hand through his slightly greying hair. Trimmed to perfection, styled just the same. Everything about him impeccable as always, even in casual clothing, dark blue jeans, and a white polo shirt. Him at the head of the long rectangular table, Violet on his left, Jacob to his right. Bone china plates and polished silver cutlery sit empty before him. Even his usually filled glass is dry.

"We've got someone on the inside," Jacob growls.

His white-blonde hair cropped short, those emerald eyes, the centre circled blue, so different to the rest of us, glistening with anger. Jacob slams his palms down on the table, the jugs of water clinking with the force. Violet jumps, her hand flying to her chest.

"Elijah!" he barks. "You said we were fucking solid!" he roars, spit flying over the croissants.

Leaning over the table, one hand still splayed against the tablecloth. The other now outstretched, his finger pointed at his youngest brother down the table. A blue vein jumping in his temple, he grinds his jaw, veins poking through his neck. I watch his pulse hammer, my head tilting in fascination. Jacob never does this. He's the calm one. The detached one. From this life, anyway.

"Seriously, I- I don't understand." Elijah shakes his head, blows out a breath. "The cars were all checked, the boards were fucking signed." He sighs, referring to the stock checks that happen wherever we have weaponry anywhere, a signing in and out sheet if you will. "It's impossible."

"Well, it's clearly not fucking *impossible,* is it, Elijah! Fuck me, LOOK AT HER!" he screams, gesturing wildly at me.

Bellowing so loudly that even I visibly shrink back. His fists coming back down on the table, water sloshing over the side of his glass. His entire body trembles, the muscles in his exposed forearms strain- ing, the colour of his tattoos looking too bright for his temper. His face reddening the longer he stares down the table at his brother.

"I don't know what you want me to fucking say!" Eli suddenly yells back. My head snapping in his direction, my neck screaming with the motion. "I'm doing my fucking job! Unlike you, you fucking cunt!" Eli hisses. "Where were you when I was interviewing for security? *Huh?* WHERE WERE YOU?!" he roars. I don't think I have *ever* seen either of these men behave like this. "Don't walk back in here, holier than fucking thou," he spits, venom shooting from him with every word. "You're too fucking good for us, *remember?* You're better than this shit! *You* fucking said that! *You* did! A *surgeon!*" he scoffs. "Fuck you, J! Just fuck you, you fucking arsehole, I'm fucking done listening to your shit. We're the ones knocking our bollocks out, grinding harder every fucking day to make this family safe and our businesses run smoothly.

You think you can do a better fucking job, you fucking do it!" Eli slumps down into his seat, breathless and red-faced.

"Well, looks like I'll have to, doesn't it," Jacob spits back, not letting this go. "Who signed the clipboard last? Which guard?" he questions, still staring down the table at Eli. "I'll have him dragged downstairs for Charlie to question, and-"

"No," Charlie pipes up, "you won't," he rasps, his voice strained. "You don't dictate here, Jacob, I'm not even sure why you're a part of this conversation."

"Charlie," Dee starts to say but Charlie cuts him off.

Another thing that's unheard of, Charlie never involves himself in arguments.

"No, Dad. He didn't want this; Jacob didn't want to be a part of the family business. He's allowed to change his mind, we would welcome him with open arms, but he hasn't done that. Have you, J?" Charlie rasps, his voice melodic yet gruff, the volume getting quieter the more he strains his damaged vocal cords.

He cocks his head, white-blonde hair falling into his emerald eyes, looking down the table. Guiding his line of sight past Eli and Cam, both between him and Jacob. In fact, there are two empty seats between Cam and Jacob too. Eli right beside Cam, Charlie the other side of Eli.

"I've not changed my mind," Jacob says calmly.

Smoothing his hands down the front of his shirt,

still in a dress shirt. Black, the top two buttons open, sleeves folded up to his elbows.

"Then sit down, and be quiet," Charlie finishes.

The table in silence. Jacob still standing. Charlie reaches forward, his fingers sliding around a glass of lime water, condensation sluicing down the sides of it. He lifts it to his lips, swallowing half the glass, nobody speaks. He puts the glass down, eyeing it for a moment.

"Kyla-Rose made a decision." Cam, the most silent member of our family speaks next. His dark blonde hair pulled back into a bun, the sides and underneath shorn. "Knowing full well she could be putting herself *and* others in danger. She did it anyway. Kyla-Rose is an adult, the people she was with are adults. They all made up their own minds. Nobody was coerced or forced into the situation. It was of their own accord. She got hurt. We know, this life is dangerous, but we can't stop living it because someone, may or may not be, out to get us. Jacob, you're not actively involved. You can't pipe up with an opinion when you have no idea what we're all dealing with on a daily basis. You're upset she got hurt, so am I, so is Charlie, Dad, Eli. We all care, this isn't about that. It's about discussing what went wrong and how, fortunately, we can learn from it. Okay?" Cam says calmly, ever the mediator when he does decide to put his two cents in.

I lick my lips, my thigh vibrating with anxiety beneath the table, jumping violently. I eye Jacob, still standing, his fingers curling and uncurling into fists at his sides. His teeth clenching, jaw grinding, I bite my lip. I think of the already torn skin, I bite back into it anyways, never able to stop myself. Max clamps a hand down onto my thigh, his grip firm but gentle, careful of my hideous bruising and road rash. Kacey's hand sliding up my other, his fingers circling the purple, mottled skin. My gaze still laser focused on Jacob, I suck my lip into my mouth, the tang of blood making me want to heave again. But I don't, I hold it in, swallow down my anxiety.

"If I can just say-"

"Shut your fucking mouth!" Jacob spits at me, his eyes wide.

My mouth drops open at his outburst, Charlie silently stands.

"Don't fucking speak to her like that," Kacey warns lowly, getting to his feet.

One giant hand splayed out on the table, his shadow towering over me.

"Watch how you fucking talk to her," he points a thick, tattooed finger at my eldest cousin.

My tummy flip-flopping at having him stick up for me.

"Oh, fuck off, *Kacey*, put your overgrown ape bull-shit away, no one gives a fuck what you have to say." Jacob scoffs, "you've not got enough going on upstairs to be a part of this conversation," tapping two fingers to the side of his head, he chuckles caustically, the air around me grows finer, making my lungs ache.

"Jacob!" Dee scolds, his bark biting, like a whip cracking through the room.

"No! No!" Jacob shouts, "*this* is exactly the fucking problem! She gets away with EVERYTHING! Where is the *punishment?!*" he bellows.

"You're behaving like a child. *Enough.* Sit down, *now.*" Uncle Dee commands, his voice brokering no arguments, a low growl in the back of his throat.

Kacey glides back down into his seat beside me, Charlie silently retaking his.

Dee may be slowing down on the work front now that us kids are slowly taking parts of it over, but he is still the patriarch of this family. Always will be, until his dying day.

"Now, I feel this has been discussed enough for one evening. Eli, I trust you'll look into the situation with the weaponry in the cars," Eli nods firmly. "And Cameron, you will aid your brother in any way you can, between now and New Year's." Cam nods in response. "The fights will be open for our largest event of the year, we have five days before then, that's a lot of work and with Lala out of action because of her surgery tomorrow-"

"*Possible,*" I cough the correction, "*possible* surgery." I confirm quietly.

Dee offers me a wink, "with Lala's *possible* hand surgery tomorrow, we need to work extra hard and help each other. You boys can do it. Charlie, you know what you're tasked with. Try to keep it clean, my boy," he raises an eyebrow, a slow smirk working its way onto Charlie's lips.

"Kyla-Rose can help me downstairs during her recovery," he rasps, a shiver rakes its way down my spine. "Just to keep her hand in," he cocks his head, his big green eyes on his dad.

"I agree, it'll be good for you," Dee says after a beat, nodding his head at me.

The look Charlie gives me next has me licking my lips, a tremble rolling through me at the prospects.

"I wanna be at fight night," I announce next.

Jacob finally slipping into his seat. Violet reaches across the table, patting the top of his hand, he doesn't look at her.

"Any room for me on the card, Cam?" Kacey asks conversationally, the pair of them slipping into easy discussion.

Charlie scrapes his knife across the tablecloth, his mind focused elsewhere as Huxley piles food on his plate. Everyone now helping themselves, Max slides me a cheese and tomato toastie, dolloping a heap of mayo on the side of my plate. I smile, looking up at him from beneath my lashes. He winks and I have to avert my gaze as my core tightens, heat licking at my insides. I dip the corner of my toastie in the mayo, taking a bite, licking at the corner of my mouth. Max reaches over, cupping my cheek and thumbing my lip instead, wiping the mayonnaise off, sucking it into his own mouth.

"Not at the fucking table," Eli roars, cackling,

head thrown back, his mouth full of cereal. Milk dripping down his chin. "It's bad enough we have to watch her grinding on these two," he laughs, gesturing to Kacey and Huxley on the other side of me with his spoon. "Now you too?" he swallows, shovelling another spoonful of chocolate cereal into his mouth. He points his spoon at Max, "you hurt her, you die, you got that, Sharpe?" Eli crunches his mouthful, making me smirk, Max nods. "Gooood," he drags out. "Charlie's already got his hands full enough as it is, without having to add your ugly mug to his kill list. Ain't that right, Charl?" he snickers, Charlie rolling his gaze onto his youngest brother, chin dipped.

"Mm," he agrees, going back to his knife carving in the table.

He's carved his way through the fancy tablecloth now, scratching his blunt blade into the polished wood. No one gives a fuck though; Dee will just get it fixed. I think they're all just happy to have Charlie at a mealtime without being covered in blood. Eating my sandwich, I glance down the table, Dee in hushed conversation with his eldest son. Jacob's head bent low; eyes locked on his still empty plate. Dee's hand clamped on his shoulder. Violet's warm smile on them both. She practically raised the boys; their birth mum having left them when Eli was just six-months old. I wasn't born yet, so I didn't know her, but I've known Violet my whole life. Her and Dee have been together for twenty-seven years. I like her. A lot.

Dinner wraps up, Charlie skulking out in the shadows. A hushed goodnight on his lips as he heads towards his dungeon. Eli sits, hunched over his phone, fingers flying across the screen, a small smirk on his lips growing by the second. Guess he just found his last-minute booty call. He gets up without a word, a silent salute as he exits. Cam's next, muttering good-night, he tosses a grape up into the air, catching it in his mouth on his way out.

"Kyla-Rose," Jacob's broken voice calls me, I snap my attention over to him.

He opens his mouth to speak, I shake my head. Pushing up from my seat, I make my way around to his side of the table, no one else needs to hear us. My three boys say their thanks to Dee and Violet, exiting the room as I make my way over. Jacob twists in his seat, holding his hand out to me as I step up beside him. I lay my hand in his, he draws me closer so I can sit on his lap. Curling my arm around his neck, I look down at him, his big eyes on mine.

"I'm sorry for lashing out," he apologises, and I smile.

"It's okay, J, I'm sorry too."

"What the hell are you sorry for?" he blanches, drawing back to look at me.

"Scaring you." I shrug loosely, "I'm impulsive."

He swipes a hand down his face, the bags beneath his tired eyes are dark.

"I love you, is all, I want to keep you safe," he sighs heavily, his grip on my waist tight, secure, safe.

"I know, I love you, too. I want to keep you safe too," I smile, meaning every word.

"I'll apologise to Kacey," he swallows, his eyes hitting Violet's for a split second, "I lashed out."

"You did, and Kacey isn't stupid, J."

"I know," he agrees with a short nod. "We're okay?"

I nod, touching my forehead to his, "we're okay."

He sighs heavily, his muscular body shifting beneath me, muscles uncoiling.

"Go to bed, Lala," he murmurs.

I nod in agreement as he helps me stand, I'm dead on my feet.

"Goodnight, J," I press my lips to the top of his head, his arm around me squeezing gently in a hug.

"Goodnight, Ky."

I slip from his lap, rounding the table, kissing Violet on the cheek, Dee squeezes my hand.

"Goodnight," I call over my shoulder as I hit the empty hallway.

I pad my bare feet down the darkened hallways, the marble cool beneath my feet. Tracing my fingers over the banister, I start to ascend the stairs. The wall sconces just barely lit, leaving everything in deep shadows. I drag myself down the hall, utterly exhausted, I can't wait to fall into bed. I push my bedroom door open, black carpet, ivory walls. The corner lamps switched on, violet bulbs in each, bathing the room in a pale purple light. My bathroom and walk in wardrobe to the left, a curved desk in the corner. The back wall made almost entirely of glass, twin double doors leading out onto the carved stone balcony.

It takes my tired eyes a second to adjust, blinking heavily as I try to keep them open. I glance to my right, the huge bed dressed in white. My mouth drops open, my eyes now blinking rapidly as I take in the scene before me.

Kacey, Max and Huxley all lying on top of the covers, an arm propped behind each of their heads. Nothing but their boxers covering all that tight, inked skin. I swallow. *Hard.*

"Um," I say, my mouth suddenly *very* fucking dry.

I back up a step, bumping into the dresser as Kacey smirks, that predatory glint flashing in his gold eyes.

"Where you running to, Sweetheart?" he coos, the beast in him crying out for a chase.

"Nowhere. I just, um, have to go see something, that's not in here, right now," I stutter like a fucking moron.

Unsure what the fuck I'm doing as I slowly back towards the door.

"Uh-uh," Kacey smirks, his face cast in shadow as he flips himself onto all fours.

My heart flip-flops in my chest as I watch him slowly crawl to the end of the bed, his fingers curling over the footboard. His knuckles blanching as he flexes his fingers, testing his grip. I stop moving, every single nerve ending in my body screaming at me to run. I lick my lips, Huxley and Max unmoving, but their eyes on me. Their gazes devouring me inch by inch as they look their fill. Kacey's laser focused on mine, the gold bleeding into the black of his pupils, making him look like some sort of demon. His smirk slowly morphing into a grin, toothy and wide and wild. My mouth open, my breaths panting, I feel myself getting wet for him. All my aches and bruises disappear, nothing left inside me but a delicious mixture of fear, desire and anticipation.

I back up another step, this one confident, more deliberate. Kacey's eyes flash, my breathing hitching, my chest rising and falling dramatically as I study him. Waiting. He tilts his head at me, his flop of blonde hair falling over one eye.

He dips his chin, purring, "don't run from us, baby girl."

My heart stutters in my chest, the rumble from his chest hitting me like a knife to the heart. Everything in me telling me not to move my feet, I shuffle back half a step. A second later he's launching himself over the footboard, I spin around. My fingertips just brushing the door handle when a large hand fists my hair.

Wrenching my head back, my neck arching, I look at him, my view upside down. A sick grin on his beautiful face, one that should send a shiver through me for a completely different reason than the needy one currently rolling through me. His other hand planted flat against my belly, his thumb stroking the base of my sternum, he gently pulls me against his huge, muscular body. His head bent, his stubbled cheek grazing against mine, his lips at my ear, hot breath on my neck.

"I'm never gunna let you go, baby girl. I'll chase you, wherever you are, Sweetheart. I'll always find you, even when you run from me," he growls before his tongue is pillaging my mouth.

Kacey's lips smash into mine, my teeth knocking into his as his tongue dives deep. Long, luscious licks into my mouth have me panting, my good hand threading up and around the back of his neck. My head still angled painfully, he fists my hair harder, ripping strands out at the root. I whimper into his kiss, my body thrumming with need. He tears his mouth from mine, nipping at my raggedy bottom lip savagely. Pulling back so he can look into my eyes, he flattens his tongue. Making sure I watch as he laps at my chin, the trickle of blood from my torn lip devoured by his mouth. His lips lock onto my lip, sucking it hard into his mouth, releasing it with a pop.

"You taste so fuckin' sweet, Kyla-Rose," he rumbles as I pant, my breath against his mouth. "I'm going to devour you," he promises me.

Suddenly he pushes me forward, twisting me around and slamming me into the door. He rolls his firm body into me, his hard, thick cock burning against my core. I groan as his hand comes to my throat, his thumb pressing into my pulse point. Dipping his head, his tongue running up my throat, his teeth tugging on my earlobe. I desperately rub my thighs together. His hard cock digging into my lower belly.

"No," he snaps, his face suddenly in mine, his nose softly nuzzling my own, something so gentle. "No, you do not get relief," he barks huskily.

My entire body trembling at his sudden switch, his actions and tones all conflicting.

"Girls that run get punished," he breathes against my cheek, making me sag against the door, his grip on my throat the only thing keeping me upright.

He inhales sharp and fast, running his nose up the column of my throat, his lips to my ear, I shiver.

"You're going to be a good girl for us, aren't you, Kyla-Rose?"

The way he says my name has me practically melting to the floor. I tremble so hard, my teeth chatter.

"Yes," I whisper.

A smug smirk working its way to his lips, that devilish glint in his gold eyes.

"Good girl," he purrs.

His thumb sliding over my pulse, his fingers loosening their hold.

"Now get on your knees and crawl to your masters," he finishes, roughly throwing me down onto the carpet.

My knees hit first, my palm landing next, my wounded hand, thankfully, still tucked into my chest. Not that I'm worried, I know Kacey wouldn't have let me hurt myself. I suck in a sharp breath, my head spinning. Kacey's huge shadow falls over me in the dim purple light. My eyes on the floor, I start to crawl forward, my cheeks heating as I go. I slide my hand forward, my knees moving me closer until I get to the end of the bed. I sit back on my haunches, tipping my head back, my eyes on Kacey. His chest heaving with every breath, he reaches down, his thick fingers once again clasping my throat like a possessive tattooed collar. He tugs me up, my feet scrabbling to get under me. He stands behind me, his hands sliding onto my hips, his fingers slipping beneath the hem of my black, silk pyjama shorts, his calloused fingertips grazing my flared hips.

I stare at the two men on the bed.

Both of them now rock hard, the undeniable evidence is in each of their hands, boxers discarded. Huxley tugs lightly on the piercing in his tip. I bite my lip, my heart hammers against my breastbone so hard it feels like my ribs are curling into it every time I inhale.

Max sits up first, his turquoise eyes shining brightly in the soft glow of lilac. He scoots forward until he's sitting before me. His legs hanging over the low footboard, his big hands on his thighs. He cocks his head, a soft smile on his face as his eyes rake over me. His muscular thighs spread, his thick length bobbing between us.

I shiver, Kacey's fingers dipping lower, Max's moving to my waist. His fingers brush over Kacey's as he glides his big hands beneath my loose t-shirt. Sliding up my body until my breasts are engulfed in his hot hands. I groan, my eyes slipping closed. My head dropping back against Kacey's chest, directly over the initial I carved there. Kacey slips his hands down my shorts, his hands on my thighs as the material passes over us, letting them pool around my ankles. Max lifts my t-shirt, both men working together to gently work my wounded hand free. But that's where it ends. The softness and gentleness vanish like it never existed as my t-shirt hits the floor.

Kacey grabs hold of me. His hands cinching my waist, pinching the soft skin, he heaves me up, dropping me down onto Max's naked lap. My eyes go over his shoulder, Huxley propped up against the headboard, one arm still folded behind his head. A smug smirk on his lips, heat in his gaze, he shoots me a wink and I feel my arousal drip from me straight onto Max's throbbing cock.

When I glance back at him, his eyes focused on the space between us, I know he sees it, *feels* it. My cheeks heat, my gaze dropping, eyes sliding shut, I steady my breath.

"God, you're so fucking perfect," he rasps quietly. One hand coming up to pinch my chin between his finger and thumb, forcing me to look at him. "I want you to ride my dick, Princess," he informs me gruffly, a dark chuckle escaping him.

Max urges me up. Lifting onto my knees, my hand on his shoulder, steadying myself. I lick my lips, nervous energy rushing through me as his hot dick is flush with my core. Using his hold on me, he works me over his length, his hard cock slipping and sliding between my wet folds, I groan as he bumps my clit. His grip on my waist tightening, he moves me faster, electricity pulses through me. My head dropping forward as he uses me to coat his dick with my wetness, never pushing in.

"Max," I moan.

Everything he's doing to me has me panting harder and faster, my core tightening as he glides me over his cock.

"You need something, Princess?" he chuckles.

I groan as his thick cock finally nudges at my entrance.

"*Yes*," I hiss, the sound barely making its way through my teeth.

"Yeah?" he mocks, making me want to punch his front teeth down his throat.

"Yes!" I screech as he mercilessly slams his way home.

I can feel him in my goddamn throat as he thrusts me down on his cock, my breath rushing out of me. Between my heat and his thick length, I could come already.

"Jesus fuck," Max hisses, his head thrown back, his grip on me crushing. "You feel so fucking good, baby."

Using my grip on his shoulder, I rise up, leaving just the tip inside me before dropping back down. He grunts as I do it over and over. My walls sucking and pulling at his length as I slam myself down onto him.

Kacey steps around the side of the bed, my attention snapping to him. He watches me with hunger as he too, slips his boxers down his thick thighs. I watch enraptured as he fists his cock, squeezing the base, flicking the metal bar through his tip. Then he's nudging his free fist against Huxley's knee, prompting him into action. Huxley jumps off the bed, stepping up behind me, my pace slows. Max's eyes snap open, starting to grind up into me. I twist my head, turning to face my caramel skinned demon.

Huxley strokes my face, thumbing my bottom lip, he drops his mouth to mine. His tongue sliding effortlessly into my mouth, his tongue bar clinking against my teeth as he caresses my tongue, his lips massaging mine. His hand in my hair, fingers kneading my skull, I relax into him. The unmistakable click of a bottle has my eyes snapping open. Huxley's lips still attached to mine, I watch Kacey step up beside us, his huge body casting the three of us in complete shadow.

Max continues to grind up into me, his pace slow, but deep. My insides all twisting, heat licking my skin, a thin sheen of sweat slowly working its way across my body. Huxley pulls back, my swollen lips already greedy for the return of his. Kacey smirks at me, his face reading nothing but savage intent as he presses a soft kiss to my lips.

"You're hurting, Sweetheart," he whispers against my mouth, my eyes flicking between his caring amber orbs. "But you're going to take us all, aren't you, baby girl."

It's not a question.

My core tightens in answer, Max grunts and then everyone's moving all at once. Max's back drops flat to the mattress, his arms banding around me, his tongue plunging into my mouth. He nips and sucks at my lips, my tongue licking into his mouth. He spreads his thighs further apart, making me flatten against him as my legs are drawn further apart. My thigh muscles burning. Max's hands hold my face, another pair of warm palms flattening on my shoulder blades. Fingers dragging torturously slowly down my spine. Long fingers gripping handfuls of my arse, spreading me wide. I gasp into Max's mouth as cold liquid hits my arse, dripping down onto Max beneath me. A shiver working its way through the both of us, I press my face into his chest. Huxley's hands massaging the globes of my arse, his thumbs in my crack, pulling me apart.

I hiss through my teeth as his steel cock slides effortlessly between my cheeks. The cold metal of his piercing like ice against my heated skin, the lube making it even colder. His cock slippery and cool, he rocks against me. His hands still firmly on my cheeks, Max's on my face. Kaccy's palm lands on the base of my spine, his thick fingers splayed.

"Be a good girl, Kyla-Rose," he grunts, my eyes flicking over my shoulder.

The angle I'm at, I can't see anything, but I can

feel exactly what his intention is when his slick thumb thrusts unceremoniously into my arse.

"Jesus *fuck!*" I shout at the sudden intrusion.

Lurching forward, my tits in Max's face, Huxley's grip tightening on my spread cheeks. Kacey's thumb twisting ever deeper, he works it into me. my pussy clamping down onto Max so hard, he squirms beneath me.

"Christ, Lala, stay still," he hisses between his teeth before biting down on my nipple.

Kacey's oversized thumb fucking into my arse. I throw my head back, panting as he switches it out for two fingers. Huxley's monster cock nudging against Max's, I tense up.

"Don't you dare!" I squeal, Max's tongue flicking over my nipple, his teeth tugging on the piercing.

Kacey chuckles darkly, my eyes narrowing as his free hand whips out, gripping my throat.

"We can do whatever the fuck we want to you, Sweetheart. We own you. Tell me you don't want this, tell me to stop," he dares me, a devilish lilt in his deep voice.

Gripping my jaw, dragging my head backwards, my neck arching until my eyes water at the pinch. He moves me, but I don't say stop. Even as Huxley's slick cock pushes against Max's with harsher intent. Kacey thrusts his fingers into me harder, scissoring them inside me, stars explode behind my eyelids as I slam them shut. His grip on my jaw crushing, my teeth carving into my cheeks. Huxley moves his cock, and I pant out relief, but then his fingers are there. Slippery and wet, he slides one inside my pussy, alongside Max's cock and I just stop breathing.

They move in tandem, my body twisting like a goddamn contortionist. Max groaning against my chest as he laves his tongue all over my tits, nuzzling his face between them. Huxley pushes another finger in, my lungs constricting. Both boys stilling as I lift up, lube mixing with my arousal helping ease me back down. I tilt my head, completely unsure if I feel too full or not full enough. Never having felt anything like this before.

Kacey and Huxley together is different, I'm used to them, but Huxley's cock is a beast of otherworldly proportions. I haven't even let him near my arse yet through fear of being split in half. Kacey's not small on any account, but he's a little smaller than Hux. But Huxley and Max, both, in my pussy. I don't know if I'll love it or already hate it and they're not even both inside of me yet.

Pushing myself up a little, my hand on Max's chest. Kacey continues his ministrations, adding a third finger making me wince as Huxley adds a third too. And I suddenly just can't breathe. Everything is just too, too full and my insides feel like they're jumping into my throat. Desperately trying to make space for these three men that own every single piece of me. Max thrusts two fingers into my mouth.

"Suck," he demands.

I swirl my tongue around them, sucking them into

my mouth, my tongue lapping over them. He pulls them free, instantly pressing them to my clit.

"Oh, fuck, fuck, *fuck*," I chant, over and over, my voice ringing out raspy and thick.

Huxley slowly withdraws his fingers, the head of his slick cock instantly replacing them. And I can't find it in me to do anything but tremble between them as he pushes inside, slowly, inch by inch until I'm completely full. Max relentlessly grinding his fingers against my aching clit, my legs shaking violently. Huxley grips my hips, his pelvis rocking gently. Max laces their fingers together, their grip punishing on my hips. Kacey still pumping his fingers in and out of my arse, I reach across, taking his hot length into my hand. He twitches in my palm as I encircle my fingers at his base, running my soft fingers along his silky skin. Teasing the foreskin back, my thumb flicking over his piercing, dragging the glistening pre-cum down his length.

Using his grip on my jaw he rolls my head back, him bending down until we're face to face.

"Open your mouth," he commands, and I do it without conscious thought. "Stick out your tongue," he grunts.

His fingers inside me speeding up as my other two boys start to move me on their cocks. I gaze up into his golden eyes, the demon in him screaming at mine to submit. A strangled sound gets caught in the back of my throat as Kacey spits in my mouth.

"Swallow," he growls, forcing my jaw shut.

I swallow, his eyes on my throat working his saliva down.

"Again."

I open my mouth, my tongue out, waiting for his next move. He leans in, the flat of his tongue lapping over mine, he devours me with an uncontrollable kiss. It's sloppy and wet, colouring outside of all the lines. He eats at me, my lips, my tongue, his teeth clashing with mine. He feasts on me as the three of them start to move faster. I pant, my eyes squeezed shut. I grip the cocks inside of me like a vice, trying to keep them in, trying to push them out. Everything is so distorted as I squeeze Kacey in my hand. My nails grazing his balls as they draw up, my fingers flexing on the silky steel of his cock. I work him over, smoothing pre-cum down him, corkscrewing my fist.

Huxley's teeth graze down my back, his cock slamming into me. Max's hips thrusting up into me harder and harder, the pair of them working in perfect sync. Their joint grip on my hips crushing to the point I'm sure they're grinding my bones into dust. Kacey's tongue smothers me. His lips sucking across my cheeks, down my jaw, back to my lips, his fingers still twisting inside of me. I can do nothing but hold on. My fingers squeezing his cock hard, working him over, he bucks into my hand, his tongue fucking my mouth.

Max's fingers finally find my clit again and I deto-nate. My breath held, I come, my entire body writhing between these three men as they completely consume me, mind, body and fucking soul. Kacey's cum splashes up my forearm, his fingers stilling inside me. Grunting in my mouth, he breathes the life back into my lungs. Then the two men inside of me together are coming too, coating my insides with the evidence of what I do to them. The power I have over these monsters has my heart hammering in my chest, smashing against my ribcage like a bird trying to fight its way free.

Kacey pulls his fingers free as I fall forward. Max's hand trapped between our bodies as I lie on his chest. Huxley flops down onto my back, both men still pressed together inside me, our joint release dripping between us, but no one seems to care, so I don't either. Kacey bends low, his dick still in my hand, crushing his lips to mine for another filthy kiss. His tongue lazily licking into my mouth as he squeezes my jaw.

"Good girl," he rasps, drawing back, his words making me tremble.

Placing a delicate kiss to the tip of my nose, his big hand cupping the back of my head, his fingers tenderly stroking my hair.

"So fucking beautiful," Kacey praises.

"Perfect, isn't she," Huxley agrees, his voice breathless.

His lips finding my neck, peppering kisses on every patch of skin he can reach without pulling out of me.

"Princess," Max's husky voice has me blinking as I

turn slightly to see him. "I love you," his eyes alert, flicking between my own.

"And I love you," I tell him truthfully, my chin resting on his chest, his heartbeat vibrating through me.

"And I love you," I tell Kacey, squeezing his softening cock in my hand.

"I love you, Sweetheart," he chuckles, his hand still holding my head lovingly.

I twist as much as I can, the awkward angle I'm crushed at making it a challenge to see my fearless lover. He cranes his neck over my shoulder, his lips brushing my ear.

"I love you, Hux," I tell him quietly, always anxious with vulnerability.

Even now it's sometimes so easy and simple to declare my love for these men that the words fall freely from my lips without any conscious thought. And other times, I have a heavy ball of rejection waiting in my chest, compressing my heart and making my brain ache. But then one of them will reassure me and I'll be better, feel better.

"I love you, Darlin'," Huxley whispers into my hair.

And with that I breathe out a soft sigh of relief, letting my eyes slip closed, I fall into a blissful slumber.

CHAPTER 19

KYLA-ROSE

"Y ou don't need a gun in the hospital, Kyla-Rose," Max tells me for the trillionth time, snatching the SIG Sauer P365 I was trying to hide, out of my palm.

I huff in frustration, trying really fucking hard not to stamp my foot like a bratty toddler.

"Isn't it enough making me go to the hospital in the first place? Now I can't even have a teeny, tiny piece of protection for myself either? What is this, pick on Kyla-Rose day or something?"

"Stop pouting. Huxley will be there," Max calls over his shoulder making my eyes narrow.

If I could pinch him in just the right spot on his neck, he'd be out cold. I could pack the shit I want to pack and maybe, just *maybe*, I'd let him live.

"Stop plotting my death," he scolds as he disappears back inside my en-suite.

I'm going to bury him.

My eyes narrow until they're nothing more than slits. I follow him with rapt attention from my spot by the dresser as he comes back into my bedroom, thrusting a toothbrush into my duffle bag.

"I can pack my own bag, Maddox," I snarl, agitation riding me hard.

He cocks a brow, the start of a smirk on his face as he looks across the bed at me.

"You're going to the hospital, not on a murdering spree. What do you think you'll need in the hospital, Princess?" the lilt in his tone mocking.

Regardless of whether or not I know what you need for a hospital visit, possible stay, I'm not completely stupid. He's lucky he snatched that gun away from me when he did, or I might punch a couple bullets in his brain. Well, maybe not his brain, but somewhere shitty at least, like his foot or his shin.

"Earth to Kyla-Rose," Max clicks his fingers in front of my face, regaining my attention. "Where'd you go?" he asks, his voice steady and even, the sound wrapping around me like the finest silk making me shudder.

"I was thinking about somewhere painful to shoot you. Tell me, Maddox, ever taken a bullet to the shin?"

His hand flies up, his fingers gripping my throat, he clucks his tongue.

"Bad girls get punished," he rasps in my ear.

Goosebumps breaking out over my skin, my pulse kicks up, thumping against his hand. Stepping into

436

me, his ripped body flush with mine, he chuckles, the sound vibrating through me.

"Behave," he warns in a threatening tone, the word rattling around inside my skull.

I lick my lips.

"It's just not in my nature," I breathe against his mouth, my tongue swiping over his bottom lip.

He lunges forward with a snarl, crushing me against the dresser, he devours me. His tongue assaulting my mouth, like he'll never get another chance. All too soon he tears himself away. Leaving me panting and breathless and feeling all kinds of empty as he releases my throat and takes a step back. I sag against the dresser, my palm splayed on the wood.

"Pack the gun, Maddox," I order but all he does is laugh, zipping up the bag without it and tossing it over his shoulder.

"Come on, Princess," he rolls his eyes.

A smug smirk on his swollen lips as he throws his free arm over my shoulder and guides me from the room.

After saying goodbye to the entire family at least four times, Huxley finally catching onto what I was doing. Stalling… I'm forced into Frank's car and kidnapped to the hospital. I know I'm dramatic but what the fuck ever, I hate fucking hospitals.

I'm taken in through a back entrance, avoiding any and all public areas. Rubble and Gremlin keeping Huxley and I between them. We've kept this little trip on an absolutely need to know basis. After everything that's been happening over the last few days, we thought it best not to risk it. Despite recent events and Jacob's, more than likely very accurate, suspicion that there's someone on the inside supplying our enemies with information. I trust Grem and Rubble with my life. So no one outside of the family, these two, and Frank, has any idea I've even left Uncle Dee's mansion.

The halls are white, pale blue lino beneath our feet, overly bright strip bulbs overhead. My heart drumming in my chest, anxiety clawing at my insides. I'm unsettled, and the smell of bleach and antiseptic mixed together makes me want to heave. Huxley's fingers comfort me, even as mine threaten to break his knuckles, he doesn't seem to mind.

Even during my x-rays, ultrasounds, CT scan and an MRI, he stays with me, keeping his hand firmly in mine or watching from behind the protective glass. His thumb traces over the back of my hand as the doctors confirm I need surgery and that it'll happen today.

I tremble trying to kick my boots off, my legs shaking as I try to toe my feet free. Huxley drops down, sliding my boots off. The rest of my clothes already discarded, a scratchy blue gown in its place. My hair tangled up in a bun on the top of my head, a red scrunchie keeping it tamed. My piercings all removed and tossed in a little cardboard tray. Huxley threads red socks with rubber grippers on the soles onto my feet, I wrinkle my nose in distaste. He smiles up at me from his place on the floor. His navy-blue scrubs tight across his muscular chest and tight lean body. He stands up, leaning forward, hands either side of my thighs where I sit on the bed, his face close to mine.

"I'm not going anywhere, I promise you," he tells me, brushing a gentle kiss against my lips.

I nod against him, our lips still connected, my hand coming up to cup his cheek. He draws back a little.

"You're so brave, Darlin'. I know you're scared but I'm here and it's going to be fine, you'll have the use of your hand back before you know it."

The doctors said they're confident that the surgery will go well. The damage not as excessive as they originally thought. Which is good news, but I still don't like hospitals. Having spent way too long in the accident and emergency waiting room as a kid, waiting while they pumped my mum full of Naloxone.

But that's not me.

I nod again, his forehead to my own. A knock on the door has us separating and then I'm going into surgery.

Warm fingers brush over my forehead, my eyes feeling like they're glued shut. A brass band smashing cymbals and banging drums inside my skull has me groaning. Lolling my head to the right, I take in a long deep breath through my nose. My tongue trying to put moisture back into my very dry lips.

"I've got you, Darlin'," that beautifully familiar voice assures me.

A slim cardboard tube pressing against my mouth, I part my lips, a straw pushed between them. I suck up the cool water, my throat dry and scratchy, I swallow it down greedily. My eyes still closed, I release the straw. His hand comes back to my face, his long fingers smoothing over my cool skin.

"I'm not dead then," I croak out, his hand vibrating against my cheek.

"You're not dead. In fact, you're good as new. My afro on the other hand..." he chuckles softly, the sound bringing a smile to my cracked lips.

"After twelve long weeks and then physio," I mumble, "and your hair is always beautiful."

"Oh, stop it," he laughs. "And you know it was worth it," he scolds me, his voice deep but light in tone.

"Kiss me," I smile.

"As her majesty wishes," he whispers, his lips instantly pressing against mine.

Nothing more than lips on lips, but it has my insides warming all the same, not in the usual lust filled way. In a way that soothes my soul, softness that strokes my demon into submission. Making my heart thump harder, expanding, beating the way it should, alive.

"Tell me a story," I murmur against his mouth, the drugs in my system making me groggy.

"A story? Okay, what sort of story do you wanna hear?" he asks quietly, his voice a caress.

"Anything."

He thinks for a moment, his eyes on the far corner of the room. A soft smile flitting to his face, he looks back at me.

"Well, I took Kacey and Nox to Zambia to meet my gran and my cousins a couple years back. My gran is absolutely not a fan of Kacey, he ate her out of house and home," he chuckles.

My lips kick up too as he gently lifts my hand, placing it in his. The cannula in the back of it uncomfortable but with Huxley's touch it almost doesn't exist anymore. My other hand in a weird box-brace thing, perched on a pillow.

"We did a walking safari. The sun was so, so hot, you'd have hated it," he tells me, and I laugh knowing he's absolutely right. I'm not good in the heat. "Nox got chased by a Bushpig and ended up in a tree. Kacey laughed so hard he nearly cried, we had two weeks of our trip left and Nox just refused to leave the house for anything but the safety of a vehicle and a trip back to the airport after that."

He chuckles wickedly and I feel my lips pull into a wide grin.

"Max is a pussy," I rasp, making him laugh harder.

"He is, Darlin', he is," he hums.

We fall into comfortable silence, his hand in mine, skin like the finest silk. My eyes slip closed, a smile on my lips, until he speaks again.

"Can I tell you somethin', Darlin'?" he asks me softly, his voice unsteady.

I crack my eyes open, my head resting on the pillow. I nod at him sleepily.

"Anything."

He swallows, his dark eyes dropping to our joint hands. His thumb tracing soothing circles over my knuckles. His dark curls wild and untamed. His thick lashes brushing his cheekbones, he looks up at me. Something uncertain in his eyes. I swallow the pain in my chest, something about the look in his eyes making my heart constrict.

"When I was young, my mum and dad worked a lot. Ya know, Mum's a politician, Dad's her bitch," he shrugs casually. "I had nannies," he swallows, his tongue darting out to wet his lips. "When I got Phoebe. She was young, only fifteen years older than me. She was fun and smart, always helping me with my schoolwork and projects," he laughs awkwardly. His eyes glassy, something akin to sadness in his onyx gaze.

"I was thirteen, all my friends would comment on how she was a MILF, and I should screw the help. Ribbing me, teasing me, always asking me if I was fucking her," he shakes his head. "Typical pubescent teenage boy bullshit, ya know, the peer pressure was real. I was in a private school full of rich white boys, all these blue eyes and blonde-haired heirs to their families' thrones. And I was just trying to fit in. I just wanted to be cool." Huxley sucks in a shuddery breath, one that makes even my lungs ache, he drops his gaze.

"So, one day when I went home from school. Some dick in my class had stuck gum in the back of my hair, and I knew it'd have to be cut out, and I was just miserable. Phoebe and I were home alone, much like every day, and I told her about the shit that was happening at school. Not the comments about her, just the bullying stuff, and it wasn't really bullying. I think, maybe I was soft. I dunno. Anyway, she put an arm around me, pulled me into her side and told me to ignore them. She managed to get the glob of gum out of my hair with ice and a fine comb, she just made me feel better, ya know."

His eyes draw back up to mine and I nod, unsure where exactly this is going.

"That night we ate dinner together at the kitchen counter, like we always did. I was telling her a story about something I'd read in a magazine, wondering what she thought about it, and her hand-" he pauses, taking a deep breath, tears spring to my eyes.

"Huxley-"

"No, let me, I'm okay," he promises, his eyes glistening. "She put her hand on my thigh, high up. Her little finger was near me, and I froze, I just froze, and I let her, and I didn't hate it. So I just fucking *let* her," he shakes his head, grinding his teeth. "And that just escalated, every week something more, something new. I turned fourteen and she said I was a man now," he laughs bitterly, the sound grating. "It was time for us to make our relationship real, and I was so scared, but I didn't want to let her down. She kept telling me how much of a man I was and how good I felt. After that night she convinced me we were in a relationship, but that we had to keep it a secret or she'd be made to leave and by this point I just wanted her. I didn't have anybody else, and she was mine. And even if no one else knew, I knew how cool I was. How grown up and how much of a man I really was. It gave me the confidence to tell everyone else to go fuck themselves."

He looks at me then, his dark eyes filled with shame, a tear slides down my cheek, a matching one on his.

"I never told anyone. She left when I was almost sixteen. I never saw her again, but the things she'd made me do by then, it was just, I dunno. I thought it was okay. Then I thought even if it wasn't, it was my fault anyway, it was me who let her. I asked for it, I *enjoyed* it. Do you think I'm- do you find me-"

"Huxley," I whisper.

Cutting him off, he swallows hard. My fingers squeezing his, my stomach churning.

"She raped you, baby. It wasn't you, it wasn't your fault. You were a *child*." I blink back tears as he just stares at me, so vulnerable and unsure, he bites into his lip. "You didn't know, baby."

I shuffle over to the left, my arm in a stupid box, propped on a pillow. I shove it all out the way.

"Come up here with me, Hux," I say quietly, his dark gaze boring into mine. "Please."

He shifts from the chair, collapsing the bed bar down, he climbs up beside me. Curling up under my arm, his face buried in my neck.

"I love you more than anything, Huxley. You are the bravest, most fearless, loving, caring, amazing man I know," I tell him honestly. Even as tears sluice down his face, he's beautiful. "I don't know where I would be if I didn't have you by my side, protecting me and loving me. You do it so, so well. Let me take care of you now," I whisper against the top of his head, his tears soaking through my thin gown.

I run my fingers through his soft curls, lightly massaging his scalp with my fingertips. I press my lips to his head, over and over until I feel him finally go still, his breathing heavy. I let my eyes fall closed, succumbing to the darkness. I let it drag me under.

A clicking noise in my ear pulls me from my slumber, my eyes heavy. I try to blink through the fuzziness inside my head. The brass band from earlier are at it again, only this time they're all out of tune and extra loud. I groan, bringing the heel of my hand to my forehead, pressing against it as if that'll make the pain vanish.

"Get up," an unfamiliar voice barks.

My eyes snap open instantly, my vision blurred, my head spinning as I shoot upright.

"Now!" the male voice demands, my stomach rolls as a hand grabs my wrist.

I try to pull back, but my strength is non-existent.

"Huxley!" I try to shout, but my words come out all wrong, too quiet, my tongue thick in my mouth.

"Shut the fuck up and move. He's not coming for you, he's the one that let me in," the man mocks, a deep chuckle rumbling from his chest as he rips the cannula from my hand.

What?

I flop out of the bed as he tugs my arm sharply, my legs not knowing how to work properly. He huffs at me impatiently as I fall to my knees. My bones smashing into the hard floor. Without the use of my injured hand and the other held hostage by my possible kidnapper, I fall forward hard. My chin ricocheting off the linoleum, my teeth crashing together, blood pooling in my mouth. I gag as my head spins. The man pulling me up sharply, my shoulder cracking. I try to spit my mouthful of blood out, but I can't even manage that. Instead, it all just dribbles down my chin.

Blinking hard, still trying to get my eyes to actually see, I'm dragged down the corridor. My feet still working to get under me. Where is everyone? I swing my head side to side, looking for someone, something. A person, a weapon, a fire alarm. My eyes hazy and unfocused, the room spinning, my brain like mush. I heave again, nothing in my stomach to come up, acid burning my chest. My vision getting worse instead of better, the more I blink the hazier everything gets. The light burns, the darkness threatens.

Cold air blasts me and I'm falling again. Murmured voices surround me, my cheek pressed into cold concrete. Why can't I move? *Come on, come on, come on.*

My mind wanders as my hearing finally disappears. Why would Huxley let a stranger into my room, he wouldn't, this man's a liar. Huxley will know I'm missing by now and he'll find me. He would never let anything happen to me. I just have to wait, I trust him to come. I'm not alone anymore. And I have something to live for, and I will live for them, for us. Because they need me as much as I need them. And if one of them were missing I'd burn the whole world until I found them. I know they'll do the same for me.

My lungs constrict, air bubbling out of me, ice water smothering me, I'm thrown to the floor. A different floor.

What the hell?

"Rise and fucking shine, little love," *his* voice mocks.

This one is familiar. Eerily familiar. Something inside my mind crumples, years of abuse burned his voice into the inside of my skull. I could never, *ever* forget this evil.

I gasp for breath, spluttering up water from my

lungs, burning its way up my throat. I lurch forward on all fours, crying out as I land on my newly braced hand, the big clunky box it was in now gone. Hands grab me. I kick and squirm to get away from him, but everything is too slow, my limbs heavy and weighted. My spine slams into a wooden chair, pain screaming through my veins, I grit my teeth. Someone else's hand wrapping around my throat. I suck in one last lungful of air, blinking my eyes in the dark room.

My wet hospital gown freezing me to the bone. I shiver and shake as rope is wound around my body, thick and rough and tight. Too tight. The fingers at my throat release, my head flopping forward. Too heavy for my fragile neck to hold up, spit dribbles from the corner of my mouth, my breathing ragged. A hand fists my hair, yanking my head back. I groan, the reaction delayed even to my own ears. My neck arched back painfully, my spine threatening to pierce through my throat. I look up into an all too familiar pair of beady brown eyes, gaunt cheeks and thick eyebrows, hair that needs a good wash. *He* grins at me. My former personal officer from juvie, also known as my rapist.

"How you feelin', little love?" he cocks his head at me, a silver capped tooth glinting in his ugly smile.

"Fuck. You."

With that, using all the strength I can muster, I spit in his face. His hand ripping my hair from the root.

"They said you'd be hard to break now," he

muses, almost happily. Using the back of his other hand to wipe my saliva from his cheek. "But the difference is, I know all the nasty little things that can really make you scream. Don't I, little love."

I want to whimper, break down and cry. Remembering what teenage Kyla-Rose suffered through. Adult Kyla-Rose swearing never again. And now I'm back there, with *him*. Haven't I suffered enough yet?

When will it ever be enough?

He shoves my head down, my chin slamming into my breastbone. Tearing his hand away, what feels like half my head of hair going with him. He shakes out his hand. I watch from beneath my lashes as my long silver strands drift to the floor when his hand snaps out. His fist connecting with my face so hard I momentarily see stars as my face flies to the right. I work my jaw, righting myself as much as I can. My ankles tied to the chair legs, my arms and torso bound to the chair back. Not that I could move, even if I weren't, even if I wanted to. I've been drugged, that much is obvious. I can hardly keep my head up on my own shoulders.

"I think we could go a few rounds before the real fun starts," he sneers.

That evil glint in his eye, like he's reliving every sick depraved thing he did to me way back when. Sniffing, he pulls his arm back again, his fist connecting with the same cheek.

Once he feels he's beaten my face a sufficient number of times, stopping only before breaking my jaw. He splays his hands over his thighs, his rancid breath in my face. I defiantly lift my head, my brows pulled together, a sneer on my face. He smiles, caustic and challenging, he thrives on defiance.

"How you feelin' now, little love?"

"Fan-fucking-tastic," I laugh, spitting one of my molars to the floor in a puddle of blood.

He sneers, his fist connecting with my stomach, my body wanting to curl in on itself, unable to because of my bindings. I breathe through the pain. He paces in the space before me, the room bare, concrete, no windows, a single door, that I can see anyway. I don't know what's behind me, I imagine a bath of water somewhere. I did wake up half drowning.

"Tell me somethin', little love. Why d'you think you're here?"

I shrug, as much as I can, defiance only growing the more he tries to break me.

"Okay, don't tell me." He shrugs then too, "we're not that bothered." Stopping before me, he taps his foot. "I'll just spend the next few hours torturing you. Playing with you before carving little pieces of you up until you eventually bleed out. How do you think your family will survive without you? Isn't it your damaged little soul that holds all of those psycho Swallows together?" he tilts his head at me, and I think of Charlie.

Imagining his glaring green eyes, his white hair. How he looks simply ethereal dripping in crimson.

Red is Charlie's colour, when I get out of here, I'm gunna get him a scarlet red leather jacket to match mine. The Chaos Twins really will twin. I smile at the thought.

"God, you are fucking crazy," he tsks, like it's a bad thing.

"Yeah, I fucking am," I agree, a grin stretching across my battered face, despite my words slurring. "Do your fucking worst," I hiss.

And he does.

My limp body untied; I flop to the floor. Nothing to break my fall, I land in a boneless heap. The chair flies across the room, I hear it thud as it lands. *His* heavy footsteps echoing towards me. That's when I crawl into the darkest recess of my mind and stay there.

I don't know how much time passes. How many times I'm knocked unconscious, or how many times he forces himself on me. But eventually pain overwhelms all of my senses, forcing me back into the room. My breathing raspy, ribs cracked. Eyes swollen to the point I can hardly see.

All I cling onto now is knowing that my boys will come for me. My hellhounds will scent blood and track me down. Whisk me away from here and love me regardless of what's been done to me today. Hold my broken body close and kiss my face, stroke my hair, and keep me safe. Tattooed arms and muscular chests, big hands and warm smiles, all of that reserved just for me.

Retied in my chair, my naked body bloody and broken, I'm left alone. I fight to stay awake, but I can't. I drift in and out of consciousness. Only images of my lovers bringing me back into the present. Thoughts of them giving me just enough to hold onto, to keep me here. Stop me from falling into that endless black abyss.

I hear the shuffling of papers, something slapping down at my feet.

"This is something my boss wants you to know before I kill you. The real reason you're here," my attacker scoffs.

He crouches down before me, scatterings of papers between us. He cocks his head, a sly, crooked grin on his thin lips.

"You let professional devils into your bed. Like a desperate whore, you invited them into your home, into your life, your *cunt*. Let them in on family meals, have access to your private files, let them roam your house. And all because you were so fucking desperate for love. That's what's wrong with women in this line of work, always letting your emotions lead you. Well, luckily for my boss, that's true, int it. It worked, you fell for them hook, line, and bloody sinker. I probably should have showed you this before I fucked up your pretty little face, but I got a bit carried away, sure you understand, little love. It's been so long since we've been together, I wanted to make the most of it."

He cups my face, his thumb smoothing across my swollen cheekbone. Gently, lovingly. It makes me sick.

"This is all the evidence you need; my boss didn't think you'd take my word for it. I wasn't so sure, I mean, if you were dumb enough to fall for this shit, you'd probably take anyone's word for it. But alas here we are, just doin' as I'm told," he mocks, a dark chuckle falling from his chest.

I strain my eyes open as much as I can, taking in the, what must be, hundreds of photos at my feet. Photos of me, of Charlie, the warehouse, the tower. Anyone could have taken these shots but what has my heart shrivelling up inside my chest is the handwritten notes accompanying them. Kaccy's graffiti style lettering, Huxley's private education cursive. Even Max's chicken scratch, all stapled to pictures of me. Images of me from the summer, even earlier. All before we ever met. Floorplans stolen from where I kept them in my bedroom. Photographs of schedules and timetables of shippings taken from my at home office. Dock timetables that I had taped inside my gun safe, the same safe I gave Max access to on Christmas Eve. Places that no one has had access to but my three boys. There's even photos of me in bed, nights that I spent with more than one of the boys, only the photos show only one of them with me... Meaning it could have been them taking the pictures.

No one else knew I was in that hospital.

"Your dead bird was courtesy of your boy Huxley, did you screech like a little girl when you saw it?" he mocks. "Kaccy randomly finding you the morning after the fights, you thought that was just a coincidence? Persistent wasn't he, did you think you were that alluring that he'd chase you around like a little lost puppy just to get into your bed?" he tuts at my stupidity as though it disappoints him.

My eyes blur with unshed tears.

"Oh, don't cry, little love, they're not worth your tears. You held yourself together so much better than you used to. Don't ruin it for yourself now," he chuckles, the sound dark and laced with poison.

My stomach twists painfully, the longer I look, the more I see. And although I can't see what their words say, it is very clearly their writing. Even with my eyes half swollen shut, I can see that. They are all so unique, and even if they weren't, I fear I'm so completely besotted, wrapped up in them all so deeply that I'd know anyway. Even if it looked just like everybody else's.

I can't hold back the sob that tears free from my abused throat, the sound fractured and raw. Everything inside me shattering into pieces, the sharp shards piercing me from the inside out. My body shakes violently, the pain of my injuries dissipates. The pain in my heart cancelling out everything else, the organ I thought had been revived starts to die all over again. My soul feels like it's lifting free of my body, disappearing like a cloud of thin smoke to the wind. Nothing on this green earth enough to tether it down. Tears pour down my face. The strangled sounds ripping free from my chest aren't familiar even to my own ears. Even after everything I've been through. This betrayal hurts the most, cuts the deepest, stings the harshest. It completely destroys me in every single way.

I thought I'd finally found my happiness.

I sob until I can't breathe and even then, I can't find it in myself to stop.

"Well, it's been fun, little love," my abuser sighs, standing as he does. "But all good things must come to an end, and my time is up. I must say I did enjoy reacquainting myself with your tight little body again. Shame that'll be the last time," he shrugs nonchalantly.

Strolling over to me, he lifts my chair, and I don't struggle. I go lax in my bindings as he hefts me in the chair over to a huge tank of water.

"Someone really wanted to hurt you before they took you out, enough to send me. Given up now, little love?" he cackles, lifting me up high. "Sweet dreams, *princess*," he hisses, dropping me face down into the freezing tank of water.

Bound to my chair, the icy water feeling like a thousand knives assaulting my skin, I sink to the bottom. My eyes closed, my lungs burning with what tiny amount of oxygen they have left inside them. I think of Max's bright sea-blue eyes, his tattooed hands laid atop ivory piano keys. Huxley's fearless nature, his sly winks and comforting hands. Kacey's teeth in my neck, his big body curled around mine protectively. All the sweet things we laid in bed whispering to each other, stayed up late and talked about.

The ways they took care of me, all the smiles and affection.

The love.

How all of it was lies.

How they stitched my heart back together between them. Replacing little missing pieces with some of theirs, completing me with their devotion. Only to smash their collective hands inside my chest, grip my mended heart in brutal, unforgiving fists and tear it out. Ripping it into irreparable little pieces and setting it on fire.

I slowly release that tiny bubble of oxygen left inside my lungs, think of all the ways they ruined me, and inhale a deadly amount of water.

Afterword

How are we feeling? I KNOW! And I'm not sorry… Thing is, I thought I'd never finish this book. It was torn apart SO. MANY. TIMES. Characters changed, arcs changed, the entire plot changed… But I'm so glad it did. I mean, I never thought I'd love Max. I was almost *determined* to hate him. But, well, I guess we'll see how I *really* feel about him in book 3, won't we? Huxley just wants to be loved and how can you not? Kacey, Big Man, he really just needs to let that inner beast roar, baby.

I think I've grown a lot as an author *and* a person since I wrote Purgatory. Kyla-Rose has pulled me in so many different directions. Literally through Hell and back. She grew, I grew with her. She fell apart, I fell with her, and sometimes it was really hard to claw my way out of that hole. But we did it together, and she has my whole heart. And let's be honest, she really needed to fall apart. A bit like my brain whilst writing this. I'm not normally an emotional person. Certainly not a crier… I legitimately cried when I finished this book. And I still don't really know if they were happy tears or sad.

A lot of healing started to happen here. Retaking control when you feel as though you've lost it forever can feel impossible. You may not have yours yet and that's okay. But just, don't stop looking for it okay? I promise it's there, just be patient with yourself.

Acknowledgments

Mark, you honestly will never realise *just* how much I love you. There is nothing more I can say.

Kendal, you're my hero. You don't understand this yet, but I promise someday you will. I love you with my whole heart.

Mum and Dad, thank you for everything you do for me. I Love you both so, so much.

Laura, wife, soul sista, there are not enough words to explain how I feel about you. Thank you for getting me through this book. I could not have done it without you. For taking my emotional phone calls, tantrums, tears. For replying to my 300 voice notes the morning after I've spewed shit at you all night. For being my best friend and bringing me endless, endless joy. How did I ever survive 28 years without you?

Selina, wife, *daddy*, I love you so much it hurts. Your TikTok bollocks never fails to bring a tear to my eye and an ache to my lungs… from laughing at all the ridiculous shit you send us. Your voice notes and poetic, sick shit. Your compassion, your kindness, your heart, I am so lucky to have you. I couldn't imagine life without speaking to you every single day, it just wouldn't be worth it.

Blossom and Buttercup, I never want to have to spend a day without you both for the rest my life.

Kristen, where do I even start? I honestly don't remember not having you… I feel all out of sorts if we go more than a day without some sort of communication with one another. I think that's called dependancy and some would say it's not good. But I say fuck those people, am I right?! I'm so grateful to have you on this journey with me. For sending me music and videos and memes. For talking shit through with me, fixing sex scenes with 857 hands, sending me photos of poorly plants you're going to *doctor* and tagging me in duck videos. I love you.

Michelle, you are *the* boss bitch to end all others! You are so confident and *organised* and kind! You have a heart of pure gold and I am so happy you found me! I could never thank you enough for everything you do, and help me with. I feel so very lucky to have met you, I'm so grateful for your friendship. And I hope you'll still talk to me after that ending…

Kalynn, I can only apologise for my excessive use of punctuation. Wording everything in an odd fashion and throwing commas in where they don't need to be just cause there hasn't been one for a while! I am endlessly grateful for everything you help me with and I want you to know, I really cherish our new friendship.

Dily, Dily, *Dily*, oh how I love you! Thank you for making me cry with laughter, indulging in all the gossip with me and for being a kickass friend. You are so, so talented and amazing and beautiful! I'm endlessly thankful for you, babe.

To my comma loving friend, Jade. You keep writing those essays with only commas. We'll be the comma army, party of 2! Thank you for all your kind words and support. I am so grateful for your friendship. Keep killing' it, girl.

Cat, you beautiful, beautiful woman! You are a goddess and I am in awe of you. Thank you for being so kind and warm and so incredibly talented that you need nothing but the barest description from me for cover designs! I'm so blessed to be working with you.

To my street team! Inga, Shawna, Jess, Rebecca, Erin, Alannah, Sue, Sam, Emily, Kiyahnah, Erin, Becky and Layla. You are all fucking awesome. Thanks for bearing with me as I do everything last minute. For your sense of humour and genuinely laid back nature when it comes to my last minute emails and erratic rambling posts. I am so very, very grateful for all your hard work. And also, thanks for reminding me I should have sent you posts and graphics when I forget!

And finally to you, the reader. I couldn't do any of this without you. I am eternally grateful to you for being on this journey with me.

ALSO BY K.L. TAYLOR-LANE

SWALLOWS AND PSYCHOS

PURGATORY

BOOK 1

PENANCE

BOOK 2

PERSECUTION

BOOK 3

Printed in Great Britain
by Amazon

19567487R00269